SOUTH

Frank Owen is the pseudonym for two authors – Diane Awerbuck and Alex Latimer. Diane Awerbuck's debut novel GARDENING AT NIGHT won the 2004 Commonwealth Writers Prize and Diane was shortlisted for the Caine Prize in 2014. She has long been regarded as one of South Africa's most talented writers. Alex Latimer is an award-winning writer and illustrator whose books have been translated into several languages.

SOUTH

Frank Owen

CORVUS

First published in Great Britain in 2016 by
Corvus Books, an imprint of Atlantic Books Ltd.

This paperback edition published in Great Britain in 2017 by Corvus.

3 5 7 9 8 6 4 2

A CIP catalogue record for this book
is available from the British Library.

Paperback ISBN: 9781782398929
Open Market Edition ISBN: 9781786491978
EBook ISBN: 9781782398912

Printed and bound by CPI Group (UK) Ltd, CR0 4YY

Corvus Books
An Imprint of Atlantic Books Ltd
Ormond House
26–27 Boswell Street
London
WC1N 3JZ

www.corvus-books.co.uk

When I was small I studied US geography,
The teacher said: 'Would you stand up
and list the states for me?'
My knees began a-knockin',
my words fell out all wrong;
Then suddenly I burst out, with this silly song:
Used to be a lot of states
fifty all-in-all
But now there's just the North and South
divided by The Wall.

FELIX CALLAHAN

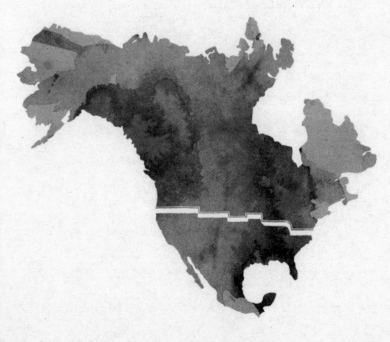

1

Felix Callahan sat on the rusted exercise bike, naked. He had hung up his dripping clothes bachelor-style and they were drying against the opposite wall. As they stiffened they dripped a line of dots onto the dirt floor below. Old men pedal slowly, but with each turn of the coiled copper wheel the light bulb above him shimmered brighter and cast a wavering halo on the ceiling, a small, insistent glow against the dark. 'Jesus bids us shine,' Felix told himself. 'Yessir, He does.'

Over his head was the shack proper, laid out like many a single man's lodgings – part bar, part mausoleum – but here in the room below was where Felix did his best work. The light played over the piles of books on the floor, the bronze instruments on the makeshift desks, and the ancient Califone tape player settled on a cardboard fruit box. When Felix finally climbed down, his withered thighs shaking, he'd charged the swollen eighteen-volt car battery enough for forty minutes of power, maybe an hour. It would have to do.

He limped over to fetch a cracked glass from a crate. Felix liked things nice. He set the tumbler on the table and filled it halfway with a brown liquor that looked like cough mixture and tasted worse. It made his eyes water but – goddamn! – it sure woke you up.

He turned, his skinny shanks flexing, and opened a drawer. The rusted Llama Danton was under a stack of maps, some printed, most hand-drawn. He nodded a greeting to the gun and laid it carefully on the table next to the bottle. He sat in the better of the chairs, and behind him the tape player waited like a patient on a drip, connected to the battery with wire interrupted by nodes of brittle duct tape.

Felix needed to get his head straight. Two days ago he'd been out looking for chickadee eggs when a woman stumbled past him, calling for her dog, Pavlov. Felix had stayed hidden in the fescue and watched her go. She'd caught something bad. Brain viruses started with dementia and only went one way. He was willing to bet there was no dog. Maybe there never had been. But *she* thought there was, and that was what counted.

When he was sure the woman had gone, Felix came out, rubbing the small of his creaking back. He could handle most of the viruses. There was something comfortingly medieval about the boils and rashes, and they ended pretty quick, anyway. It was the speed at which the sicknesses ate their hosts that freaked him out. Renard had engineered that, Felix thought. He was the kind of asshole who would want results. Old-time viruses had taken a couple of days to incubate, but the ones that had started blowing in after The War were different. And Renard had had time to observe disease, Felix supposed. All that time up north, watching and learning as the president gave him his head – and all the laboratory equipment he needed. That was the kind of man that made Felix afraid: one who hadn't been bad at the outset, but found that he liked the power – the kind that would poison someone, take notes as they died, and call it science. Like Pavlov, now that he thought about it.

But the kind of crazy that came with lonely was what spooked Felix, because you couldn't fight that. Dog Lady had once had a family, hadn't she? A place people knew her name, somewhere to bunk, a husband, maybe, or a wife – Felix wasn't inclined to judge, and even the fur traders had a right to live. The War had wiped out all of those pernickety permutations. And, really, what was there to hang onto now, if you were the only one left? Survival was fine, but Felix thought that a man needed a purpose. And a purpose went hand in hand with community. 'Love and service,' he said softly. Take that away, and the mind went with it. How did you hold on to your sanity? It wasn't enough that he had set up the weather boxes, though that sure as fuck filled his days. The longing had gnawed at him for a long time, and soon after that he'd wired the car battery to the exercise bike.

He'd laid his story down on tape, everything he figured worth knowing, in two thirty-minute segments. One for each side, like the North and South. And when someone like Dog Lady wandered past and rattled his cage, he'd sit down and listen to the tape. He promised himself that if the voice on the tape began to sound like someone else, or began to talk about things he didn't recall, he'd pick up the pistol and eat it. And he would not think too hard before he did it.

The speaker in the tape player was gone, taken long before Felix had picked it up near Hayden, stashed in a tin box in the rotting ruins of a holiday cabin, but he had found a pair of headphones in an abandoned music store days later – pink, with a pussycat on each side. *'Cool cat, looking for a kitty,'* Felix sang to himself whenever he saw them. Now he fitted the headphones over his ears, running the cable over his shoulder like a tail. He took a long drink from his tumbler and leant back in his chair so he could press play on the old machine. It whirred, and his recorded voice was deep and distant, stretched out a little further each time he played the tape. He rested a hand on the gun, breathed deep and closed his eyes.

'Felix,' his past self warned, 'I hope you've still got the balls to have that gun on the table.' He nodded and smiled.

'Okay. Here we go. My name is Felix Callahan, but you know that, don't you? I was born in Norman, Oklahoma, back when it was still a place.' Felix had done the math. He'd kept track of his birthdays as best he could, adding another year to his tally each fall when the buckeyes turned orange. He figured there wasn't a lot left to celebrate, so they were important – a reason to save up rations, a night to get drunk. He poured himself another drink and raised the glass in the gloom: 'Had more than my three score and ten, so amen to that. Seventy-nine shitty birthdays – give or take a few of those times I was laid so low I didn't see the seasons changing.' He downed the drink and went back to listening to his younger voice and the mystery of his old life.

'I had older brothers, once upon a time, and a mother and a father, the way it ought to be. I was the youngest by far. Not remembering it much probably means it was pretty smooth. There was milkshake vomit in footwells – that I remember – and broken arms from trampolines, and crackers in turds. The usual.

'The War was where it all went wrong. Hitler's war, though that's not saying much, is it? I mean the Second World War. I remember the feeling at the end there, of the narrow escape we had all had, the West. When I heard about how my older brothers had stormed ashore and saved the Allied asses – that there was the first unpicked stitch that turned into the unraveling of civilization. Our corner of the quilt, anyhow. My brothers re-enacted those war scenes when they came home, like it was a game, gunfire coming from the hills: *gack-gack-gack*. Afterwards, when the show was done, there was always a silence when you were supposed to remember the soldiers who had died. It made me feel like Clark Kent, when he takes off his glasses, you know? America was invincible if young men would die before letting it fall apart. That's what I believed. We all did.

'But while everyone was slapping backs and shaking hands, the real threat was creeping up on us – and no one took any notice. I heard about it first years later on the radio. It was playing through the window of a corner shop in downtown Manhattan, that tinny newscaster's voice, the smell of deep-fried yeast and sugar. I stopped to listen since I'd not heard news for some time. That, along with the Yankee scores, was the first I ever heard of the proposal: a Unified America. Another guy had stopped there too and both of us shook our heads and smiled.

'"Same money works here as it does in Montana and Utah and the Dakotas. That's as unified as it gets," the man said. I nodded and bought a donut and a soda like I was trying to prove the point.

'What was I doing all the way up there? I'm glad you asked, Future Felix. You're a nice guy. I ended up opening an appliance store in Greenwich Village when I was twenty. I mainly sold TVs – installed them myself, too. There were only so many times I could hear my brothers go on about the war. They could make each other laugh or cry by saying things like, "Remember Frosty Joe?" or, "Abbiamo surrender!" Me, I was an outsider: too busy dirtying my diapers to fight the Germans when it all began, and by the time I was eighteen the whole damn thing was done and the carpet had been rolled up and packed away for next time.

'I had to get out of Norman. New York was the only place I knew anything about. I thought I knew it because we used to listen to Lights Out on the radio every Wednesday. Man, I loved having the bejeezus scared out of me back then! One story stuck with me – about the ghosts of the animals from the Natural History Museum living in the sewers beneath the Empire State Building. That was where I was heading – to stand on the sidewalk and peer in through the manhole covers, just for kicks – when I stopped for the soda and the donut and heard about Unified America for the first time.

'Soon after that came the legislated slum clearance of Greenwich Village. The Northerners wanted parks and new buildings: rent was cheap for those brave enough to pioneer. Or dumb enough, I hear you. I bought three television sets from a store in Jersey and ferried them, one by one, to Felix's Television Emporium, clutching each set like a newborn on my lap as the Hoboken Ferry bobbed across the Hudson. Got a cat, a tuxedo, and called him Dallas because he was a cowboy. He was good for business: made people come in when they saw this fat-ass tomcat curled up in the window. Reeled them in. Whenever I sold a TV, I could buy two more. Then I made enough to afford a car and save my back from the newer sets, those motherfuckers with their twenty-pound glass screens. Twelve years I was there, and that included a failed marriage. I remember that part real good, let me tell you. But you don't need to know all that. I still had Dallas. We sidewalk specials got to stick together.

'I didn't pay much mind to politics until the day that a UA member was voted into the US senate. As soon as he was in, he called for a national vote on the topic of unification. I laughed at the idea. It became the new How's-this-weather? "How're you gonna vote?" I'd ask as I approached a customer, and they'd smile and say something like, "Same money works here as it does in Utah. Can't see how much more unified we need to be." Then, when the customer came over to pay, I'd finish the joke by taking their money and looking at it closely, turning it over in my hands a few times and saying, "This ain't Iowa money, is it?" We sure yukked it up.

'The joking stopped a few years later when there were enough Unified America supporters in the senate to force a vote. Over the December of . . . jeez . . . nineteen-something . . . sixty-five? Seventy-five? Shit. It all looks the same to us geriatrics. Anyhow, one December came when every American was forced to return to the state of his or her birth. Kinda like Bethlehem in the wayback, know what I mean? The population of New York halved overnight. I closed shop and took the cash from the register and waited for a taxi to take me to the airport. I'd packed my things that morning. Not much: a couple of changes of clothes, a toothbrush, a copy of *The Martian Chonicles* I meant to reread. I'd need to be back in the city pretty soon if I wanted to make up for the loss of the best business weeks of the year. The Jamaican lady in my building, Mrs Bishop, promised to feed Dallas.

'JFK Airport hadn't ever seen so many people, all of them muttering about the crush and the reason for it, the waste of our time and our money. I didn't know one person who'd voted for Unification. The moaning reinforced the feeling that we'd all be back here in a fortnight, bitching about the same things, being crushed under the same armpits and shoveled through the same doors – only in the opposite direction.

'When the plane took off, I didn't even look out at the city, I was that sure I'd be back. Of course, I never was. Poor Dallas—'

Felix snatched the headphones off his head in mid-sentence,

as though he'd been stung by a hornet. He stood and pressed stop on the tape, listening. In the sudden silence he heard the shack above him creak, expanding its joints in the midday sun. Whenever he was down below he heard the ghosts walking overhead. He couldn't count the number of times he'd climbed up to peep out and found nothing. He was getting that creepy-crawly feeling again now, but he could talk himself out of it. Today the tapes had made him paranoid, the unquiet eye of a gathering storm. Some days they were a comfort; some days they were a torture. Felix wasn't sure what was worse – knowing that everyone you loved was gone, or knowing that they were still circling in some less than friendly form. He shivered. He needed to lay down. This was the time he missed Dallas the most – the furry warmth in the darkness, solid and familiar, even though the cat had been surrendered to history. Somewhere his small bones were littered, from the teeth in his clean skull to the bones of his tail.

Felix went over to his bunk and stretched himself out. Imagine if he was out there now, stumbling into the storm that was coming, calling, 'Dallas! Dallas! Where are you, boy?' He'd shit his pants if anything came out of the trees to answer his call.

2

The two brothers fled through the mesquite and along the valley ridge. Some way behind them came the Callahans, stocked with rifles and rage and vengeance.

Garrett thought that he ought to be used to it by now, it being a week since Bethlehem Callahan had given up her thin ghost, but he wasn't. Some part of his mind was back there with Bethie, watching, hidden, as she lay dying, and maybe it always would be. He pictured her egg-yellow soul coughed up out of her chest and into the wind, where it would join the rest of the dead as they swooped over the living left behind on the Colorado plateau.

Dyce watched his brother side-on but knew better than to say anything. At least they were making good time, not running, exactly, but moving fast, following the course of the Yampa River and zig-zagging over the places where they would leave heavy tracks. The morning had been fair and, anyhow, they could take a couple of rain showers and keep going as long as the chafing wasn't too rough. The jeans they'd traded in Glenwood Camp had been a bad idea and the boys had swapped them some days back. Now they hiked in cargo pants like an advert from the adventure catalogue they'd used for fuel – one where the dudes were outdoors because they chose to be, not because they were being chased across the country by lunatics.

It was only the wind that slowed the boys down, because then they had to find shelter until it died. No one was crazy enough to be outside when there was a chance of new viruses blowing in – crazy, or suicidal.

The stopping didn't hurt their escape much: if they were hunkering down someplace then the Callahans were doing the same. Stopped like a paused TV, Dyce thought, reruns of the Road Runner and Coyote in a rictus till the dogs stopped their barking outside and Garrett pressed play again.

Dyce had learnt to feel the wind's slow rising in his sinuses, a primitive thickening between the eyes as the air pressure changed and the cells responded, as if he were regressing: now man, then amphibian, reduced at last to bacteria, ready to start the cycle all over.

He was grateful that no one traveled at night. That was one quick way to meet your maker, and it could be something simple, too, something laughable and deadly at the same time – a missed turning, a wayward root, a blind fumbling for a place to shelter from a sudden gust, a rabid field mouse striped with panic.

The boys checked each other a couple of times a day without knowing they did it. Their ears had become attuned to the cough that turned wet, the sneeze that propelled a virus six feet through the air to the next carrier. So far, so good. Dyce laughed at himself. Being pursued like cowboys in an old-time Western, and all he could think was that he wasn't sick yet. *God darn, boy! You git goin' and don' stop till you hit the Klondike!* Garrett looked at him funny, and Dyce sobered up.

"Member that time Dad took us to that cave up Salida way?"

Garrett nodded, saving his breath. It was hard to forget. Turned out to be the last road trip they'd all take together before he died, before even the dregs of gas ran dry and folks left their cars abandoned on the roadside – the American Dream scoured for cloth and stuffing and engine oil and radiator water that turned out to be bitter with standing. Any color, Henry Ford had said. Any color as long as it's black.

The rock face had looked close enough until they were all out in the dust, treading the soft shale. Dyce had on his Batman pajama top, Garrett remembered that, a size too small already, and that their father offered to carry their backpacks even though he was sick by then. Proper sick, pale as paper. They scoured the cliff face, searching for the orifice their father had sworn he'd seen through the Lark's busted windshield. When they all got up there it had disappeared.

'We were up there for, like, days.'

'Months.'

It had been half an hour, max, but Dyce wouldn't ever forget the feeling of clawing for purchase on the smooth, impersonal stone, praying for a crack to open up and let him in; the relief when it finally did. He bet that sex didn't come close, though Garrett said different.

That scramble among the rocks had stood them in good stead. Now they fled through the rocky landscape, sticking to the trees. *Cowboys and Indians*, thought Dyce. *And the Indians always lost.* He remembered – how had he forgotten? – that Garrett and his friends used to tie him to a bristlecone pine and poke him with whippy little sticks until he cried. He had never told. Eventually they had stopped whaling on Dyce. There was a little retarded boy called Teddy next door, and Garrett had discovered that he was mute. One time they left him trussed up for the whole afternoon. His mother hadn't come to find him, or seen the rope burns: she was just happy that normal kids wanted to play with him. *It wasn't me*, Dyce told himself. *I was just watching.*

'Garrett.'

'What?'

'Wind's rising.'

'You sure?'

'Can't you feel it?'

Garrett shook his head, the faint scars of his old acne making shadows on his cheekbones. 'You're the sensitive one, *virgin*.'

Dyce let it go. He ran his hand through his hair. He would need a haircut again soon. Garrett just let his grow: he was the only guy Dyce knew who didn't look dumb with a ponytail.

'You know we need to start looking. Be dark soon either way.'

Sometimes the looking was quick – a shack, an abandoned mine shaft, some convenient opening in the side of the earth that welcomed them in, as if it had been waiting. Other times they spent an hour or more searching for a likely spot, some-where they could bed down before full dark. Once or twice they hadn't been able to get there, and those nights weren't worth the stretching out: the jeebies from dusk till dawn, praying the wind stayed away. *Except it's not a nightmare*, Dyce told himself. *This is just how it is.*

The boys stopped and dropped their packs, the buckles jin-gling like spurs. They listened for a minute, for steps approaching, the sound of a rock loosened by a misplaced hand or a scram-bling foot. One of the advantages of sticking to the ridge was that you were always looking down on strangers approaching. Weird how you got used to the vigilance. *We be some baaad-ass outlaws*, thought Dyce.

They stretched and Garrett's backbone clicked. He wasn't used to lugging twenty pounds around the whole day. They'd gotten a bit too comfortable in Glenwood.

Garrett gave Dyce a little push. 'You go.'

'Man!' Dyce tried to stop his voice rising in a whine. Garrett was too old to be pushing him around that hard: it hurt. 'It's your turn!'

'Yeah, but it's your thing.' It was the closest Garrett would get to a compliment, Dyce knew. He sighed. Another concession. Somewhere in his head there was a list.

'Look after my bag.'

'*Duh.*'

Dyce wasn't two paces off the track when the leaves and grasses began to twitch, as though they too were lengthening, cracking their spines. The wind had come quicker than he'd figured, which he knew meant it was going to blow hard, an all-nighter. He tied his cloth mask around his face, just in case, and went back to fetch his bag. Garrett didn't say anything but Dyce read his eyes peering out from above the mask, hard with fright: *You better find something DOUBLE quick. I'm watching you, little brother. Impress me.*

He beckoned. There had to be a rock face below them.

The boys dropped off the side of the ridge, sliding where they could, clawing at silver beard stalks. The lip of rock above gave some shelter, a few more precious seconds to search, the difference between a full night's sleep and twelve hours of suffering.

3

Beside a pair of young spruces, it was the only thing on the ridge, and at first Vida thought it was a scalp, its reddish strands blowing gently back: mermaid's hair, white girl's hair, hair like a horse's tail.

It was perched on the top of a long pole. Further down there were sets of instruments that looked like cups on a carousel, slowing and then speeding up as the wind sighed and puffed in tired gusts. It was picking up speed more steadily even as she watched. Fuck. Too far to get back to her ma and the house now.

How much time? She swallowed against the parchment of her throat and squinted into the pale light. No one to block her way. There was never anyone out in the hills anymore. Crazy Lady this morning had been an exception. She'd followed Vida for ages but had fallen away a couple of hours back, still spitting gobs of phlegm onto the track and cursing her ghost dog for his desertion. She had been a big old sign, hadn't she? Vida had to take more care: there were fewer people, but they were desperate.

Hell, so am I.

So far she had kept to the tree-line, out of sight. There was more wind on the plateau but it didn't seem to collect the way it did in the valleys, ferrying the viruses onwards. Vida quickly breathed into her palm and sniffed, but there was no sign of sickness. She'd save her surgical mask for when she really needed it. That she had escaped so far was a true-by-Jesus miracle, isn't that what her mama would've said in the early days? She heard Ruth's voice: *Man proposes; God disposes.* Vida cracked her neck and shifted her sweaty backpack. *Move on, girl*, she told herself. One quick look. This time the voice that came through was the slippered mammy from the *Tom and Jerry* cartoons. *Mm-mm-mm! Time's a-wastin'*.

She limped out from the trees down onto the bald track.

The box had once been painted white, its sides louvred against the wet. It was about her height and not a hive, after all. That was a real shame: honey was just about the only thing that helped a weeping wound, and Lord knew she'd seen enough of those in the last few weeks.

Vida peered through the peeling slats but the inside was dark and secret. It ticked faintly, like a mechanical heart. *Or a bomb*, Vida thought, and backed away again. *Fuck, that was dumb. Could've been a booby trap. Don't you learn?*

But there could be something useful inside, her rag-picking conscience insisted. *Come on, Veedles. Open it up and take a look. How bad can it be?* Vida scrubbed at her eyes with her knuckles and was newly disgusted at her hands, the scratches and scrapes, their ashy shade. She wasn't ever going to get used to rubbing animal fat into her skin. She didn't give a shit that it was something her ancestors had done: this was one law of her mama's that she wouldn't be following. A girl had standards: older fat stank, and the fresh stuff had better uses.

Vida looked at the torn nail of her thumb and saw it again in the sand outside their house, the clapboards shifting and creaking as she worked, as if the place would loose itself from the soil and move into some deserted town on its own. Vida imagined her mama inside, cocooned in her blankets, breathing shallow and feeling each blow of the spade as if it would separate her ribs from her sickly spine. The grave had to be deep enough that the coyotes couldn't get at what was in it, but the earth knew the lie for what it was, and resisted.

Vida stared at the weather box, weighing up the risks of opening it. *Just do it, Pandora.*

She circled the container and its wooden marker pole, skew against the sky, looking for clues. Now *there*, at the very top, was something she recognized: not a scalp but a stuffed bird perched on top, beak into the wind. A rooster in his past life, Vida thought. He looked nothing like that now, as if someone was working from memory when they made him, and they hadn't been paying attention the first time. The thing reminded Vida of the story her ma told about Medio Pollito, the half-chick who was cosseted in his coop. When he left home to search for his other half, he was torched for his arrogance: *burnt to a cinder*, Ruth always said, and Vida suddenly wanted her world back, with its talking animals and ordinary people, where good was rewarded and evil punished. She wanted to believe in the magic of numbers and the safety of community and *Black don't crack*, but right now it was just her and the box, watched over by the zombie cockerel in the fading light.

Girl, get over yourself – it's not voodoo; it's a weather vane.

Vida edged forward and poked at one of the slats. The plank rattled, loose as a tooth in a glass jaw. She wiggled it out of its brackets and inspected the interior of the box. It looked like the tiny hospital rooms her ma used to work in during The War, the way she'd described them, anyways: glass and steel and their accurate, useless measurements of time passing. At least the air was fresh back then. Here was a maximum–minimum thermometer – even Vida could see that – but also some other devices. A barometer, she guessed, although she had never worked out why people needed something to tell them what the weather was doing when they were right in the middle of it. And that? A little brass sphere like an alchemist's globe. A hydrometer, maybe. Lately she had come to appreciate water in all its forms. Dragging a stew pot across the countryside and then heaving the thing home twice a week made you appreciate a drink, especially since the borehole ran dry.

Could she use these instruments? The mercury? Maybe siphon off some alcohol? How heavy would they be to lug around? Vida had learnt the hard way to keep her pack weight down. She envisioned herself ripping the thermometer and hydrometer from their nails. Probably not worth the effort, especially in the hard wind coming.

The real question was: would someone be coming to check on the weather box? Before The War, containers like this were inspected every twenty-four hours, but now weather prediction wasn't just a hobby for an eccentric, or part of a government program. Vida remembered the bald TV man who had stood in front of a synoptic chart, tapping at it with his baton. *Teeth*, he had joked, and pointed to a cold front coming in, its blue back arched like the Loch Ness Monster. *Teeth and gums*. Vida wondered if he was still alive now all these years later. Back then the weather was an inconvenience; at worst a chance to stay home from school. But the wind had turned out to be more important than they had thought, and not only because it carried the spirits of the dead with it, the way her ma's stories said it did.

The wind had turned out to be very fucking important indeed.

And here it came. Vida watched the little leaves shaking. Shit. There was no way to make it back in time, the wind was rising fast and her limbs were Jello from the climb. Old lady's legs. Vida searched her bag for the surgical mask, and then put it away again. Not yet. They got saturated too quick. *Save it*, she told herself. *Use the blue bandanna and save the good one. And MOVE! Look for a place to wait until the worst of the wind is over. You know what to do.*

Vida scanned the rock she had covered already that day. A crack: that was all she needed. Some small and kindly sheltering space.

It didn't take long.

She crept into the cave as far back as she could, hugged her knees and waited.

4

Up ahead the rock split and shadowed and Dyce shifted like a dog to inspect it. No game trails; no bones or fur. It smelt okay – not great, but who was keeping score? Not like they were packing a can of Lysol. The wind was whipping the air around his face, anyway. Dyce reached an arm into the cracked darkness and waved it in the merciful space inside. It would have to do. He dropped his bag and squeezed in sideways. When Garrett arrived, he followed the sound of his brother's buckle straps, and they slithered like bullsnakes into the dark.

They sat cross-legged in the gloom, breathing into their sleeves, waiting like runners to get their breath back. They tried to measure the lungfuls so as not to disturb the air. *Keep the outside out and the inside in*, sang Dyce's brain. Easy to say, but the veil was thin. He lowered his arm and breathed, nice and shallow to start with: acclimatizing, expanding to fill the space.

The cave held the stale human smell of leakage and occupation. In the old days that had made for warmth and companions; now it meant contagion and quarantine. They strained for telltale noises – shuffling, swallowing, breathing – but the wind outside made it all but impossible. Dyce gave up.

'Fire?'

Garrett shrugged, his universal response. A small angry flame flickered in Dyce's chest and he damped it down. *It's just us*, he told himself. *The two of us. We have to make nice.* He could hear Garrett swallowing hard against the rawness of his throat. That was where every phage struck, even if it came through the eye or the ear or, worse, the privates, like those vampire catfish that wriggled up this one guy's dick when he swam in the Amazon. Anyhow, a virus always attacked the throat first: it loved the mucous membranes, and it felt like a rusty nail moving down the gullet.

No fucking fire, then. They were used to these dark hibernations: sometimes they lasted a day or two. Dyce remembered how, early on, they used to curl into balls and cover their faces like mummies, unable to talk – or unwilling. You ran out of thoughts, Dyce decided, a place between sleep and death. It was as bad as solitary confinement. People lost their minds.

And, like prisoners, the boys had found ways to keep themselves busy in the dark, single-minded as moles, sick of each other. Dyce felt around in his bag, his heart giving a quick clench when his fingers missed it, but it was there alright, his eternal stick of wood and the knife that went with it – an Opinel his dad had given him, worn down now, the slot in the handle too big by double for the blade that folded into it. Dyce made mermaids. He always had. If he did enough carvings in the dark of hibernation, he would eventually make something perfect and recognizable and whole. Someday, with the right time and effort, he would make an instrument. What Dyce missed most was rock 'n' roll.

It hadn't happened yet. Dyce knew that when the wind died and they emerged in the sunlight, Garrett would name the misshapen thing he had carved and turn it bad. 'Horse,' said Garrett, and Dyce's siren with her fish tail and blank face became a hoofed and galloping animal, extinct. 'What is that? A fucking phage?' and there she turned in Dyce's hand, venomous, sharp-toothed, inevitable. 'The Michelin Man?' and the abandoned dead rose before him, their joints thickened. The carvings that turned out okay were the ones he had done the quickest, from the fewest strokes: with enough practice you internalized the muscle memory. If only he could stop himself showing them to Garrett every single time.

Dyce blamed the swan.

When he'd first started carving he'd sat out in the yard and tried to make something from the ivory piano key he'd found in the gutted pre-school. He hadn't intended for it to be a swan. It started out as a mermaid, but Garrett had seen its torso and figured it was a bird, the tail its wings. It was the only thing he'd ever asked of his little brother, and Dyce, dumb-struck by approval, had obliged. Garrett hung onto it for a couple of years, polishing it on his pants-leg in the dark till it was smooth, almost wet to the touch. He gave it to Bethlehem even before he'd caught scent that she was pregnant. Dyce had asked Garrett as they high-tailed out of Glenvale whether he'd taken the swan. '*Jesus, Dyce!*' was all Garrett had said. Had the Callahans ripped it from her throat when they laid her in the ground? Dyce could see them telling each other it was too pretty to go down in the darkness.

Fuck them *all*.

He ran his fingers over the stick's ivory bark, a good piece of birch. He wasn't up for whittling today: lately everything made him feel tired, and he was having a hard time seeing the point of the running.

'Garrett.'

A gusty sigh in the darkness. Garrett was opening his bag, Dyce could hear. Looking for his tools, maybe. Or the salt tablets. Sometimes they helped.

'Do you really, really know where we're going?'

'I told you. The coast.'

'But why?'

'You know why.'

And Dyce did. He just didn't believe it. Garrett repeated things because he thought that reinforcing them would make them come true. Sometimes they did. Like calling their cousin Larry 'Lard-Ass' until he ate his own weight in unhappiness. But they weren't kids anymore. This was different.

This mattered.

'There's a reason we're passing fewer and fewer settlements the closer we get to the sea.' The moisture in the sea air made it double deadly, wind or no wind. Humidity kept those tiny killers alive. The first waves of viruses had driven people steadily southwards: folks saw the southern coast as the best place to set up camp – furthest from the source of the plagues, close to the bounty of the ocean.

How wrong they were.

'Yeah. Can't figure a way of getting to the sea without going near the coast. Let me know when you crack that one.'

'Plus we don't have a boat.'

'No shit, Sherlock.'

'I'm not so hot at swimming, Garrett.' *Mainly because you nearly drowned me one summer, you asshole*, he thought. Garrett had held him casually under the brown water of Tumblesom Lake until Dyce had thought his head would burst, like the old Scout song about Running Bear and Little White Dove, pulled down by the raging river and ending up in the Happy Hunting Ground. Dyce hadn't been able to get rid of that song, even as he felt his lungs emptying themselves. That ballad had been etched into the grooves of their dad's most enduring LP. When all the others were lost or broken or scratched to hell, there was always ol' Running Bear drowning in a river.

I did pass out, he told himself. *I passed out and a mermaid saved me.* One of the older girls, Dillon's sister, had dragged him onto the jetty, her undersized costume pulling tight against her breasts. The water was unfriendly ever after. Dyce had cheated death and he knew not to take another chance.

'You're going to have to get good at it.'

Dyce fell back quiet. He heard Garrett laying out his kit on the cold floor of the cave: the rusty iron needle; the thread made of long grass or maybe gut; the fresh-skinned pelt of their last meal. *Waste not, want not*, Garrett liked to say, but Dyce thought that he just enjoyed killing things.

He'd seen the striped woodrat before and after it had served its purpose; though half a mouse hardly gave back the calories spent on the catching and cooking and chewing, it did offer a tiny, delicate skin. Dyce had often watched Garrett sewing in the daylight: his brother knew what he was doing. He had challenged himself to work at the same craft without being able to see his hands. In the dark he would have to be more careful, Dyce thought. No more injuries than they absolutely had to have. There was no anti-tetanus shot.

Dyce imagined each step. Garrett would fold the woodrat skin so that it was inside out. He would sew tiny, blind loops in a neat row from the neck, along its stomach, right to the asshole. Then he would sew up the slits that ran from the belly sutures outward to the feet, all the while stroking with his greasy thumbs for lumps and errors.

Next, Garrett would rub the woodrat between his palms to soften the fibers of its skin until it was warm and smooth. He would pull the creature in on itself, like righting a used sock, so that the fur was on the outside. If he'd had the skull, he would have inserted it so that it would sit in its proper place in the head – eye socket matched to eye hole. It really was that simple.

But this rodent was too small for the boys to spare its skull. They had eaten every bit of it, bones and all, and kept it down, too. Dyce had counted himself grateful for his dad's survival lessons. They'd hated them, but when the electricity finally stopped for good, they were a distraction from the blank TV. With the woodrat's skull already cooked soft, chewed and swallowed down, Garrett would have to search around his feet for a pointed stone and feed it into the face of his creature at the chin. Eventually, if he did it right and didn't break the fragile skin, the stone's point would reach the woodrat's nose and *voilà*! Mickey would have a face again.

Dyce heard the scraping and scooping that meant that Garrett was gathering handfuls of sand and funneling them into the limp sack of the body. You had to fill it tightly from the neck down, make sure that the granules reached the insides of the legs.

The final stitches were always the hardest, and Garrett would take his time on these, sewing from the chin to the gullet. When he was done, he held the rodent upside down over his open hand, waiting for a trickle of sand, then feel for the guilty holes.

When he had more light, Garrett would select from his bag a pair of dried juniper berries and position them inside the eye holes. The woodrat needed one for the nose too: the soft, fleshy nub never survived the skinning. Dyce hated the finished animals. They always looked pregnant with death, droopy-headed, seed eyes blank – staring at him from The Other Side. What was the point of them, either? Garrett's crazy totems.

Dyce saw him sometimes when he was done with one of his

creatures, combing it with his fingers to neaten the fur. It was then that he could see his brother loving someone like Beth Callahan. Had she laid her head softly in his lap? There would be no shotgun wedding, even when everyone could tell Garrett had knocked her up. Used to be you'd plan your life in years. Now it was months and weeks when no one had any right to think they'd see the next blessed, windless summer. Getting pregnant was always going to end that girl, anyway. She was already half-dead when Garrett fell in love with her. There hadn't been much of her to begin with, and then the hunger and the sicknesses had taken their share.

But the heart and the dick don't talk to the brain, do they? Garrett's heart brought her its flowers and all the frogs he could trap down at the stream and roast over the fire, offerings like chocolates in a box. And his dick wanted somewhere warm and wet, and Bethie was pretty if you imagined meat on her bones. The Callahans, with their badges and their boots, were never going to take kindly to the idea of losing their girl-child. One way or another it was going to end with both of them deep in the dirt. And now that she was gone, the rest of the Callahans were going to make sure Garrett followed poor Bethie just as quick as they could make him.

But they couldn't make Garrett sorry. They couldn't take that away from him. Dyce listened and knew that the work was steadying his older brother and his broken heart. He set the creature aside, and the boys laid themselves down.

Dyce reckoned about an hour had passed when the phage arrived. And they'd been so careful! He heard Garrett swallow and felt the scrape as if it was in his own throat.

First the scrapes, then the sweats – the body fighting the virus by red-lining all systems.

The boys had seen a lot of people infected with a bunch of different phages, some so mild that they passed within a day. Others worse, much worse. Dyce shuddered. He couldn't help himself.

Jay Loram had caught something while they were camping near the Colorado River. It killed off his nerves. He couldn't feel if he needed a pee or if his hand was resting on a hot frying pan, or if his neck was burnt to blisters from a day of walking in the sun. Dyce had seen him bite down on bird shot and shatter two teeth. Jay had spat them out in his hand, bloody and jagged without even a grimace. If you didn't know about the virus and you came upon his body, you'd think he'd been tortured to death. His legs had been cut and bruised; three toes were missing – their stumps festering. A bone in one finger was sticking up sideways and his mouth was so rotted that there was no color in there, just a black hole, and it stank like a dead dog's guts. That's what got him in the end, Dyce thought hysterically. *Brush and floss, little nuggets! 'Cause there are no more trips to the dentist! Yeehaa!*

But trips to other places: those abounded. Mrs Fordice had come home from the wood one evening with a temperature so high that people said they could feel her pass by from across the road. She hadn't recognized her own daughter, wasn't sure where she was or why she'd been out in the trees in the first place. Mr Fordice had dragged a drinking trough out of the stables and into the courtyard and they put the old lady in there for the night, changing the warm water for cold every fifteen minutes. In the morning she was dead, her body mottled orange and purple and red like a poisonous snake.

The external illnesses were pretty bad: they ruptured and melted the skin, made people lose hair or grow scabs.

But the brain viruses were the purer evil.

Dyce had known Niccola Drew before she died. They had been at each other's parties as kids. She had gone early on to work as a cleaner for one of the doctors up near the border and caught something from an organ tray. After her throat, it went right on upstairs to her brain; Do Not Pass Begin. She had started getting her left and right confused – women, right? – and put it down to lack of sleep.

But then she had started to have memories of things that she knew had never happened – fucking terrifying things, she told Dyce. She knew, rationally, obviously, that her father hadn't murdered her. But she had kept seeing him standing over her with the bent tennis racquet.

One night she had left her bed, boiled the kettle and scalded the skin off his face while he slept. At least she had the sense to run away, Dyce thought as he rolled over, trying to find a spot in the dirt that his body had already made warm. They had found her hanging by her neck from a tree. There was some kind of heroism in that, wasn't there? Taking yourself out of the herd before you did any more damage? *Garrett definitely thinks so, although I'm not seeing him doing the same,* Dyce thought. *Nope. That fucker is hanging in there, like his life is so awesome it's worth saving.*

As if he had heard the thought, Garrett moaned, the sound of someone with their demons right behind them. *Or the Callahan marshals,* thought Dyce. *Which is about the same thing.* He tried to see his brother in the darkness. Nothing.

He crept closer, trying not to touch Garrett accidentally with his bare skin. You never knew how these things were transmitted, and contact was not smart.

Garrett was drenched and muttering. Dyce thought of Nic Drew and her dead daddy with the skin boiled right off his bones, and he wished he had his whittling knife to hand. What he would do with it, he didn't rightly know.

Now his brother had subsided. It sounded as if he was drifting in and out of consciousness. You just had to let them sweat, Dyce knew. The fever was one good way to get rid of a sickness: the burning fried the germs and purged the system.

And if the fever meant that they were already dying, you couldn't stop it.

Garrett lay there beside his woodrat, their bodies heavy and limp.

Dyce scooted a little ways off and then stretched out his fingers so that he could keep touching Garrett through his shirt. That way he might manage to get a couple of hours of shut-eye. Not enough. Never enough. That was what freedom was, thought Dyce as he closed his eyes again. Freedom from vigilance. Rest.

The boys' snores rose softly.

In the darkness at the rear of the cave, Vida sat up and straightened her legs. She had been hugging her knees for so long that it felt as if they'd turned into a tail.

5

The wind had stopped and the cave mouth was bright white with morning sun. It hurt to look out. The rays didn't reach far: the back of the cave stayed blackly quiet and dank, smelling now of their own bodies, mingled with the older odor of creatures who'd sheltered here before. *Stone soup*, thought Garrett. *Everyone lends their flavor.*

He massaged his neck for raised glands. The virus seemed to have burnt itself out overnight. The salt tablets really did work. He'd dissolved two on the back of his tongue, determined not to gag, and it was worth it now. Rare good news.

He reached over to Dyce, grabbed a leg and shook it.

'I've made flapjacks!'

He never tired of the joke, Dyce waking up thinking the world was how it was before – and then the disappointment of no flapjacks, not just for breakfast, but ever again.

But the leg under his palm was thin and strange. Garrett pulled his hand away. Dyce had changed in the darkness, whittled himself into one of his own carved totems. The replacement leg was skinny, and it was very, very stiff, as if its owner had frozen in place. *Oh, Jesus*, thought Garrett. *It's a body! He died in the night!*

But the fabric was rougher than Dyce's cargo pants – denim, maybe.

Garrett shuddered. It was worse than when that crab spider had run up his leg, all the way up his shin, past the knee, up and up till it was hemmed in at the belt line.

He reached out again in the darkness and this time he found Dyce properly. He shook him and then pulled, half-dragging his sleeping brother towards the cave mouth.

'Jesus, fuck, Garrett!'

'Shut up!'

He pulled his brother's sleep-heavy body over the lip of the cave, and vaulted his own ungainly self out after. Dyce lay twisting on the gravel, rubbing his eyes, Garrett looking around for a weapon and wasn't this always the way? Dyce dreaming, and Garrett on guard. He picked up a twisted stick, burnt black at the end. Better than nothing.

Behind them in the cave there came a dragging, and Garrett was suddenly sure that out of it would emerge some creature, a moth-balled dragon snuffling irritation at the disturbance of its treasure, slow to anger and impossible to appease.

The legs in the faded jeans appeared first, then ten splayed fingers, like someone playing a piano. They searched for purchase on the outer wall of the cave and anchored themselves. The boys watched, unable to run, as if they were stuffed with sand.

A face hauled itself into view, masked cowboy-style with a printed blue handkerchief.

Then the woman crouched in the dirt, a fighting stance, but held up her empty hands.

'Fuck Renard,' she said, her voice muffled.

Dyce swapped a look with his brother. Garrett recognized the phrase, the mantra of the resistance – the not-so-secret password pledging allegiance to the South. But the revolt had come and gone years back, the war of another generation. The way things were now was the way they had been since the boys were just kids. The old phrases came back to him as he stared at the grimy woman: *Aegroto dum anima est, spes est.* The only Latin their dad had gotten a handle on, that's what he had carved into the back of the bathroom door. He thought it was funny: while they suffered through the cramps and the diarrhea, they could consider the famous words. *While there's life, there's hope.* And of course Garrett hated it; hated that he had to read it every day, sometimes twice, sometimes nearly fifty times. What the fuck did some Roman prick know about it? Try a new virus on every wind. How about that, Cicero? Try churning out Hallmark cards when everyone you know is dead and you're shitting your soul out of your ass. Fucker.

The woman reached round the back of her head and began untying her mask. The ashes from the cave had streaked her cheeks like camouflage. There was a patch of white flakes on her braids that made her look like a skunk. *No,* thought Garrett. *A woodrat.* She looked thirty-something. *Too old for me,* thought Garrett. *But not bad shape.*

He held the blunt tip of the stick towards her, uncertain.

'Hey, now. No harm done,' she said. 'In fact, you owe me. I could have—' She drew a long brown finger across her neck. 'Found this cave before you last evening. I didn't think it was, ah, smart to show myself right away.'

Garrett prodded the air, his cheeks red under the little scars. He was twenty-four but his voice still sometimes jumped, and he hated it. 'Where's your partner? Who're you travelling with?'

'You can lower the big stick, sunshine. No partner. Least, I used to have, till last week. My ma. Our house is just along this ridge.'

Dyce, ever the conversationalist: 'Where's she now?'

The woman looked down. 'Snake-bite. Buried her a couple of days back.'

'What kind of snake?' Garrett, testing.

'Rattler.'

'You sick?'

'Nothing bad. Little cough, but it seems to have blown over.'

'So why're you out here?' asked Dyce, getting to his feet. He brushed the gravel from his hair.

'Need to get to the next town now, don't I? Can't be staying in the death house. Life goes on.'

The boys were silent, wondering how much harder it must be to travel on your own, hiding from everyone. Another rhyme everyone knew off by heart: *If you're alone, don't come home. Two or more and you're in the door.* Loners were trouble: escapees or crazies or carriers so sick they had been expelled from the southern towns. Sometimes, if they were organized, they gathered in ghostly camps, like lepers.

'Where's your stuff?'

She was definitely twitchy. 'Back home. I was just checking out the best route to Fieldstone. Day-pack's back there in the Taj Mahal.' She jerked her thumb at the cave. 'I didn't exactly have time to pack up.'

Again, the boys and their look.

'Looks like you need some travelers to be vouching for you,' said Garrett.

'Looks like.'

'We can vouch.'

Vida's eyebrows shot up. *Oh-oh, here it comes,* she thought. *Now we parley in the saloon.*

'Just need two things,' Garrett said. He looked over to Dyce. 'Three things, actually.'

He's enjoying this, Vida thought. *He really is.*

Garrett held up his index finger. 'First, I need to see your ma's grave. Can't be vouching for some runaway thief, or killer, or contagious *outcast*. Need to see that your story holds up.'

'Done.'

'Next, I need a weapon. Some grayhounds after this rabbit. You got a gun?'

'Only an old pistol at the house. No bullets, mind. It's yours if you'll take it. What else?'

'A clean pair of panties for my brother.'

Vida's mouth stretched wide in a smile. It felt strange, the muscles creaking with disuse.

Dyce kicked a clod of dirt at Garrett. 'Yeah. Let's stand around chatting up strange women a little longer, dickwad. I'm beginning to see eye to eye with the Callahans.'

Garrett's face fell. 'Shit, yeah. Let's move.'

'Woah, there,' said Vida. 'You got Callahans after you?'

'We got about half a day on them, I'm thinking.'

'That changes the picture a little.'

'It's a take-it-or-leave-it type situation.'

Vida watched them maneuver back into the cave, pushing each other, scrabbling for their bags. God, they were like kindergartners.

Still, there wasn't a whole lot of deciding.

The three began the trek back to her place in silence, walking Indian-style, fast and single-file, Garrett leading because he had the most to lose.

They kept the pace up where they could, slowing over rocky sections and when the buckthorn thickened up. It was the

end of tick season, but there were still the last red hangers-on
clinging to the tops of the grasses. Dyce figured he knew how
they felt, empty, despised, desperate for nourishment. Never the
other way around, never on the attack. Still, he didn't like them
enough to pick up any blood-sucking hitchhikers.

Garrett stopped at the crest of an outcrop, and the other two
hung back in the fescue. He looked back along the track for
the Callahans. If he didn't know them better he'd have been
optimistic about escape. But they were out there, close behind,
his smell in their nostrils, making them quiver. Not seeing them
was worse. *Nightmarish*, people used to say, and it was true: they
were being chased to their deaths. They could never run fast
enough.

Vida set her pack down and grappled with a flask of water.
She wiped the rusted neck and offered it to Dyce, who shook his
head. Not yet. He didn't want to have to piss along the track and
leave their scent out in the open. That was just plain stupid.

He held out his hand. 'Allerdyce. And he's Garrett.'

Vida nodded, not touching him just yet. She caught his
eyes, ice-blue like a husky dog's, their flesh rimmed with sweat-
speckled dirt. *Diamonds in the rough*, she thought, the song
starting in her head. She blinked. 'Vida. What you do to get
yourselves hunted?'

'Not *yourselves*.' Dyce nodded at his brother. Garrett still
stood above them, scanning the horizon. '*Hisself*. Callahans got
no problem with *me*.'

'What'd he do?'

'Got a Callahan killed.'

'Ay.' Vida shook her head. A death sentence. 'One of the
twins? Or the other boys?'

'Bethlehem.'

'*Jesus H. Christ!* He killed the Callahan girl?'

Garrett was watching her now, his face cold. As if he didn't know how bad it was! The only natural-born daughter in more than a decade. And the baby she was carrying – My *baby*, Garrett told himself. *Mine, mine, mine* – also a little girl. It must have been. A miracle baby, made up of the scraps of the two of them into something better, made to rocket forward into the future when her parents were gone, their histories and wishes and hopes laid down safely in her bones.

He'd watched from the long grass as the older women delivered Bethie of her terrible burden. Garrett saw her body twisting up against the hands that held her down, an animal shrieking in the trap. He knew he ought to run, but he needed to see the baby – even if it was still-born, the way everyone knew it would be, coming this early. After the long hours they had wrenched a silent, bloody thing from between Beth's thighs, the bag bluish around its face. The tiny body had lain in the dust like an old-time squirrel squashed on the highway while the women clustered around the mother, her eyes rolled back in her head. The sudden hard silence pressed against Garrett's eardrums, so that he thought the plates in his head would shift. There had been so much blood!

Now Dyce shrugged.

'Don't you care?'

'It doesn't matter. Done is done.'

'And where you gonna go to escape the *marshals*? They're everywhere! It's their *job!*'

'Garrett wants to find a boat. Head out over the sea.'

'For *what?*'

'You ever hear those stories about the places the sicknesses can't reach?'

'Yeah. Don't forget Bugs Bunny. And the Tooth Fairy. And heaven.'

'Well, Garrett believes.'

'Do you?'

Before Dyce could answer, Garrett hopped down onto the dirt.

'What you girls talking about?'

'Nothing.'

'And where's this house with the gun?'

'Almost there, right, Vida?'

'Sure. Almost there.'

6

The house was ancient wood, more falling apart than hanging together. The shingles were cracked. They'd fallen like teeth and left black holes that reminded Dyce of Jay Loram's shattered mouth. The windows were boarded up, the glass long gone save for the pair of sliding doors that led onto the porch. There were still shards in the rims of the frames, sharp as gleaming fangs in the morning sun. The blocked-out upstairs windows looked down. *The eyes of the place*, thought Dyce. *And they're watching us.*

One of the first lessons their father had taught them was that if something didn't feel right, you walked away. *Always. Don't wait for the thing you sensed to come get you. Just clear out. Leave it and move on.*

Ha! There wouldn't be anywhere to go if Dyce obeyed the voice in his head. Every minute of every day didn't feel right. Where would he clear out *to*?

He hadn't felt this strongly about a place in a while, not since they'd discovered those bodies in the Fairview Orphanage. He knew by the time they were on the path up to the front door. Vida's place felt bad. *Alive* bad. Dyce wanted to say something, but he knew better. He'd never hear the end of it.

He glanced over at Vida but her face was blank.

'We make this quick,' said Garrett. 'Can't waste time. We see the grave, you get us the gun and we're gone.'

'Aye-aye, cap'n.'

Vida led them around the side of the house first, through the shadow of the upstairs story, especially cold on their shoulders. The grass and dirt were still damp where the sun didn't get, greasy underfoot as the ground tilted up and away from them.

And there on the hillside beside the house was a mound of dirt covered over with stones. At the head of the grave was a cross – two sticks tied with string, a kid's work.

A kid, or someone in a hurry to get gone.

A bunch of long-dead globemallows was weighed down by a rock, and Dyce imagined the weight of that stone, of the sand and gravel and moisture, and even those delicate flowers, all resting on the body below it. A crushing weight. The weight of dying.

He nudged Garrett with his shoulder.

'Happy?'

For Dyce, the sight of the grave was proof enough, but Garrett went closer. He rested a boot on the mound and inspected the dirt between the rocks.

Don't do that, Dyce wanted to say. *That's disrespect. She's gonna rise up and throttle the life out of you with her dead hands.*

'How long you say she's been dead?'

'A week, give or take.'

'Snake got her?'

'Yeah, I told you. Rattler out from under the porch back there. Killed it myself.'

Garrett leant in and tweezered a pale-green shoot from the dirt with his fingers. He held it up to the light then laid it in his palm and examined it.

'Okay,' he said, eventually. 'Looks like a week's growth, given the weather. No coyotes come digging?'

'First few days they came but I was watching. Tried to snare one as a lesson to the rest but it got free. They stopped coming the night before last. Figure they know Ma's for the bugs now.' Even coyotes had standards, Dyce wanted to say. He saw that Vida's face was bright with sweat. But they all were, weren't they? He wiped his forehead. *Get on with it.*

But Garrett's eyes were glassy as he stared down at the grave, the labor of love it so clearly was. In his mind he was somewhere else, doing the things he'd known were coming, things he'd never got to do. He was digging Beth's grave, rolling her in and laying her out at the bottom of the hole, face up with her stick-thin arms folded across her chest. Covering her over with leaves before backfilling the soil, all the while keeping the dirt off her face. He was collecting rocks and layering them over the top, armoring her body against the night scavengers. He was making a cross out of wood, just like this one – not because it stood for any belief, but because it's what right-thinking people did. It would be a marker and a sign and for once he would be doing what was right by Beth. Last, the flowers his girl had always liked: fireweeds and fairy trumpets, columbines and penstemons, yarrows and mouse ears.

'Garrett.'

'How's that gun coming along?' he asked.

Vida led them back to the porch, showing them which planks were rotted through and where to step if you wanted to keep your leg. She grabbed the sliding door with two hands, one high and one low, and eased it open. Fine paint chips rained down till the gap was just wide enough to squeeze through. She stepped first into the darkness and Garrett followed.

The house was musty and damp, like paper wet through with urine, the smoke of old fires. Dyce came last, fighting his urge to stand guard outside. Garrett wouldn't buy it, he knew.

The boys stood on the frayed rug waiting for their eyes to adjust. Dyce noticed Garrett had his hand on his hip, cupped ready over his knife. Maybe he felt it too. Maybe it was just how he stood now that the Callahans were chasing him.

Vida was gone into the house. They could hear her opening doors and shuffling around upstairs. The creaking of her weight ran right through the structure, making it mutter from its dark corners.

Vida knew that the boys would take some time to find their bearings, which bought her a minute to check on Ma. She filled a glass from the pot of stream water in the kitchen and took it up to the loft, where the old lady lay nestled under her layers of blankets.

'Ma,' she whispered. She heard the woman turn over. She was conscious. Hallelujah! 'Ma, I've got some travelers.'

'You going to try for Fieldstone?' The voice in the dimness was quavering.

'I'll get meds and I'll come back as soon as I can. I'm leaving water for you. Feel for it on the table.'

Coughing. Vida was glad the red-blind eyes were hidden.

'Did they see my grave?'

'They thought it was real pretty, Ma.' She adjusted the blankets. She knew better than to open them.

'I'll pray for you.'

'To who, Ma?'

'Anyone who'll listen.'

The Jesus days were long gone, but some things are habit – praying and cursing, both. Vida took her mother's empty glass from the table and made it back down the stairs.

Her travel bag was in the passage where she had left it, undisturbed. Vida felt for the hard edges of the swollen remedy book. It was there, hidden deep under the dried locusts and the dented canteen, her torn lumberjack shirt. The brown envelope pasted in the back flap was still intact. Her ma's old seeds always traveled with them. Some she'd brought over from South Africa like a dowry when she'd moved to America; the rest she'd collected on the slow route from far North to deep South, her own Trail of Tears. Everywhere she went Ruth sowed a garden first thing – not grass or flowers the way other people did, but a medicine garden. Not only for the teas and poultices she cooked up, thought Vida, but because of the immigrant's disease: homesickness. Now Vida stopped and ran her finger over the tiny seeds through the pocket of the back page. They had settled into the paper, pressed into pimples under the weight of the book, dormant until they were called into service. It had been Ruth's, and now it was hers: the history of her family in biology and Braille. The book was the only thing they would never be able to replace.

Vida went on to the guest room with less care now. She found the gun hidden in the piano, lying on the rusted wires of the thing's insides, its busted tendons and collapsed veins.

When she came down, Dyce was inspecting a picture on the wall and Garrett was searching the sideboard. There was nothing in it, Vida knew. Whatever could burn had been burnt already; whatever could be of use was being used. Didn't they know that?

'You got water here?' asked Dyce when he saw the glass in Vida's hand. He approached her, forgetting his reservations about the house, and took it before she could protest. He was walking through to the kitchen and calling back, 'Is it this, in this pot?'

She wanted to shout, 'Don't drink from that glass!' She wanted to think of some clever way of pausing the moment, stopping Dyce in his tracks. But every thought she had ended with the boys finding out about her ma, almost dead upstairs. Even if they could see past the lying, they'd never travel with someone exposed to sickness.

Vida just stood, and Garrett came over and took the gun from her. An old break-top Webley. He felt its weight and looked down the barrel, then cracked it open and eyed Vida through the chamber.

'What's got you so spooked?'

7

They'd cleaned Bethie up some. Wiped the dirt streaks that had run down from her hairline and collected in the creases beside her eyes, and scrubbed the scabs from her legs. Her dull cotton blouse, smeared with blood on the hem and patterned with specks of yellow phlegm, was soaking in a boiling billycan. They'd dressed her instead in a floral shirt and stuffed it with grass to hide her sunken ribs and her meatless breasts and also, thank God, that hollow gut. The swan pendant had gone to one of them too, taken and tucked wordlessly into a pocket.

An aunt had worked dirt into a paste and rubbed it into her paper cheeks to give back the glow she'd lost all those months back, long before the baby and the sickness. *Colorado*, she'd thought over and over again while she'd painted the red mud onto Beth's skin with a finger. Her hair, thin and brittle, had been braided and dotted with tiny white flowers, and when the women were done and had laid her out, arms folded, in the room at the back of the church, she looked more alive than she ever had. Certainly since anyone could remember.

It was no secret that Beth had hated the way she'd been treated in life, as more than human. The only girl-child born to a lineage of men: what an honor! Once the Callahan clan had recovered from the shock, they took her birth to be a blessing:

a miracle, something to be protected and nurtured – and looked at from a distance.

To compensate, Beth had dressed in jeans and kept her hair scruffy and insisted on doing her share around the Glenvale settlement. Garrett, when he came along, was the logical end point of her rebellion. He treated her like an ordinary woman, special only to him and valuable for who she was, not what. And sure, the boy was head-over-heels but, Lord knew, they fought a lot. Maybe that's what Beth had liked about it, thought the aunt. The imperfections, the unpredictability, the irritations were all laid over something real, something between affection and lust.

Now, lifeless, the Callahans claimed Beth back. With her arms folded, her hair braided into a halo, her skin painted cherub-pink, she was an angel again – and that made Garrett the Devil.

'Keep her cool,' the aunt said, fanning her. A trio of boy cousins joined in, waving their hands around her body, cooling her skin and keeping the flies from settling on the moist slits of her eyes. With Beth attended to, the woman left the room and informed her husband that the funeral could begin.

'Can we hold her together just a bit longer?' Hugh Callahan asked, staring off into the haze on the horizon. There were still Callahans arriving from distant settlements, walking in through the wooden gates of Glenvale with their hats held to their chests but their face masks on. There was only so much ceremony a man could take.

'Closed casket, sure, but if you want it open . . .' She scrunched up her nose.

Hugh went to greet the newest arrivals.

'Goddamnit!' It was the first thing Paul Callahan said through his moist face mask. 'I got one hand holding my hat on my chest here, but I got my quicker hand free.'

"Preciate that, Paul, but Gus and his eldest are going to find Garrett. Right now we're here for the family. When we're all wrapped up and that hole is done being a hole, your quick hand can do as it pleases.'

'Course. But goddamnit!' He pulled his mask down now and spoke quietly. 'You know if Tye is coming?'

'He's why I'm delaying this thing.' Hugh pointed across the lake to a stand of dead pines. At the very top sat a feathery shape. They knew the bird would have its legs tasseled, and Tye would be carrying the hood. The Callahans had always had hunting birds – not a lot, but one or two for every generation, and a man to go hunting with it. Someone sharp-eyed and keen for meat.

'That's his harrier. Been there since last night. S'pose the old man's not as quick as he once was, 'specially now without that old horse of his. He was never more than a couple of hours behind that bird.'

The grave had been dug beneath the old birch tree, the one you saw as you walked down the steps of the church. Hugh went to inspect it for the hundredth time.

It was deep, the bottom so black it seemed the hole reached down indefinitely. Speckled in the strata of dirt and rocks were the bright-white circles of severed tree roots, ancient holes through which to glimpse the lights of heaven.

Oh, little town of Bethlehem! How still we see thee lie.
Above thy deep and dreamless sleep the silent stars go by.

Hugh had been singing that in his head all day and it seemed as if there was some significance to it beyond the obvious. Maybe it was just something to subdue his brain and drive out the images of his boot pressing down on Garrett's neck. A rhyme to keep his mind hallowed.

He hated every minute of this waiting and congregating, speaking the very words of constraint to his cousins and uncles that Beth's father had spoken to him: words that Gus had blatantly ignored, his bulk as stubborn as his temper. Gus would not pretend that he liked Bethlehem. She'd been disrespectful of everything she'd been given since the day she was born, but he sure as shit wasn't going to sit by and let a Callahan get killed, Bethlehem or anyone else. He'd packed his rifle and rations for the chase, left as soon as he heard that Garrett was on the run. When Hugh went to see him off, he'd repeated, *Stay and let's bury Beth. We're here for the family. When the hole's filled we can find Garrett.* But he'd said them without passion, for the sake of doing what seemed right. The words were faithful but the message in them was very different: *Go, and let us bury Garrett. Go and do it for the family. When the hole's filled he'll be long gone.*

The three boys fanning Beth's body had been replaced by six others with a paddle of bark in each hand, and by then the funeral lunch was served and done. In the old times there was a side of ham, but those days were long gone, and they knew it. Now the women were washing the plates and pots on the lake shore, scrubbing at the grease with handfuls of sand. They saw the harrier take flight from her tree and watched as she wheeled above them and came to rest on the arm of a man. Tye Callahan had not been to Glenvale in forever.

'I hope that you've not delayed the funeral for me,' he said as Hugh greeted him.

Why send the bird if you didn't want us to wait?

Instead Hugh answered that they had indeed waited, that they'd wanted as many Callahans as possible to attend.

'Well, let's get it going then. I got other business I need to get done. New place called The Mouth sounds like trouble. Heard about it?'

'Nope.'

'You'd be wise to keep a better eye on things down here,' Tye said. He carried two packs but did not set either down.

No one mentioned the smell as Beth was brought out of the church, down the steps and across to the birch tree. Children were pinched by parents for pulling faces at the stench, and many in the crowd adjusted their face cloths to fit tighter.

Beth's father emerged from his house, weak and pale from grief. They led him over and he stood at the head of the grave and watched as the body was lowered into the dark.

He spoke, faltering, as the shovelfuls of sand covered her over, about her life and the gift she was, what she loved to do on sunny days and how she'd never been a burden, sewing things for her little cousins when the wind confined them to their houses, doing her share of fetching water and fire wood. He also spoke of the courage it took for her to overcome the illness she'd caught when she was nine, an illness that had taken three grown men to their graves.

But it was really only he among the Callahans who grieved the loss of Bethlehem. As he spoke there was among the congregation a restlessness, a shuffling of feet stilled only by the fingering of cold steel triggers standing ready in their holsters. Bethlehem had been a totem for the Callahan name, not a person. The totem had been tampered with, desecrated and spoilt, and that dispossession called for revenge.

Beth's father had barely finished speaking when Tye made his way to the head of the grave. His harrier swayed but never lost her footing, the scales on her feet as dry as the puckered skin on his hands.

'Enough of this,' he said, his hands shaking. 'We've all come here from a long way off for a common purpose. A girl is dead: but worse than that, a *Callahan* is dead. Drop your flowers on her grave and let's go put this right.'

He adjusted his packs and walked out the gates of Glenvale. It took a minute before anyone dared follow, but when they did they left together, polite at first until they were some way off and then waving their rifles in the air and hollering.

Even the men with shovels had gone. Hugh and Beth's dad were left beside the unfinished grave. The two of them took up the implements and replaced the remaining soil, spade by sorrowful spade, patting it down. And then they ringed it with stones and hammered a rough cross into the earth.

When it was done, they looked out across the empty grass, trampled by the vanishing crowd – and they saw one man returning.

Paul Callahan walked back into Glenvale proper, past the church, until he stood beside the grave once more.

'I didn't ask,' he said, out of breath. 'Bethie's baby. Did it live?'

8

Vida couldn't help looking sideways at Dyce as they walked, scanning his face for signs of sickness. When he caught her looking, she made excuses.

'Thought I saw a jackrabbit.'

Maybe the virus had died on the rim of the cup. It could've done. It was cold in the attic. Maybe Dyce had somehow managed to avoid infection. Could he have sipped from the clean side?

It was just when Vida had convinced herself that Dyce was in the clear that she saw him grimace and clutch at his stomach. She said nothing.

'Smell that?' said Garrett. 'Something's burnt.'

Vida lifted her face and took in the air. Yes, it smelt like pine ash: the acrid aftertaste of it meant that it was not fresh. Vaporized resin from a blaze usually stung the nose, but this was aromatic and delicate.

Over the next rise, they saw what it was.

Fieldstone Camp was gone.

A black smudge ran down the mountainside. At the bottom, the camp gates were a mess of splinters, like charred and broken bones.

'Looks like you won't need us to vouch for you,' said Garrett.

'No, looks like I won't.'

'I'm keeping the gun.'

'Yeah. Fine.'

'What you going to do?' asked Dyce. The sweats had begun, but he was fighting to keep the pain from showing. 'We could take you on to the next camp. Nothing I know of between here and the coast, though.'

'Yeah. This is the last one. *Was* the last one. You go on. Not like you have time to waste.'

'And you?'

'I'll see what I can find here and then head inland. Maybe find another settlement.'

'If you change your mind, we'll be heading along this ridge.'

'Jesus, Dyce! Hey, everyone! We're heading along this ridge. But *shhh*. Don't let the Callahans know!'

Garrett turned and walked on. Dyce nodded his reluctant head at Vida and turned to follow his brother.

Within a minute, they were gone, swallowed up in the thickets of mesquite.

The stub of the camp was huddled against the mountain for protection. The rest of it sprawled up the slope of the ravine that cut into the rock. A stream poured down the center, splitting the settlement down the middle. Where the water ran deep or wide, the people had built little wooden bridges. Vida followed the line of the stream with her eyes, squinted up the slope until it disappeared under the cover of low trees. High at the lip of the cliff the stream reappeared as a waterfall, the water hard against the ears in the hush. In a hundred years there would be no sign that humans had ever lived here.

Only one structure still stood in the ruins, a ramshackle barn of thick logs. 'Little house on the prairie,' Vida breathed. How pleased they must have been to raise the new roof on that one, the sap rising to sting the builders' nostrils, everything possible, green to the touch.

By the time she got deeper into the camp she was resigned to the bodies. A pair lay side by side outside their burnt shack, two mounds of soot, like the place that fell under the volcano. *Vesuvius*, Vida's mother said in her head. *Vesuvius. Never forget. It could happen to you, baby girl.* In a splintered pine tree sat a row of turkey vultures, squabbling among themselves but waiting for her to pass so that they could glide back down and peck at the crispy flesh. 'Family, hold back,' Vida told them.

Further up the slope was another corpse, curled up beside the river as if the woman had made for the water when the fire came. Vida bent to examine the scuffed earth around her scorched skirts. Bear prints. *A scavenger*, she told herself, *just like me. No shame in it.*

If anything of use had survived the fire it would have to be inside the barn, right? Vida followed the bank of the stream upwards, stepping over the pale-green shoots of bullrushes that spiked out of the ground. She could see no life in the river, no frogs or newts plopping terrified into the water. Here a dead heron lay twisted around a rock: the water tugged relentlessly at its head and feet so that they waved, animated. Vida picked up a stick and lifted its body up and over the stone. She watched it tumble downstream, losing feathers as it went. Not worth the risk of eating a dead bird. Hardly any meat, anyways. She moved to drop the stick, then hesitated. No harm in being prepared.

The stairs that had once led up to the barn door were gone. Vida hooked her boot on the plinth and pulled herself onto her stomach. She had expected darkness inside like a cow's stomach, but the roof tiles had fallen away in patches: jagged light streamed through the holes. She stood up, the shattered tiles crunching under her feet.

It looked as if the interior had been untouched by the blaze. There was a counter at the far end, a couple of stools. Vida couldn't see all the way along, but there were other rooms coming off the main space, curtained like the whores' bedrooms in an old-time saloon. Vida felt the homesickness rising in her and choked it back down. Not so long ago people had come here to feel that they still belonged to one another: to pass along their warmth and light and conversation – *all the things that make us human*, she thought.

Behind the counter sagged a shelf of half-empty bottles and a range of dead insects. Vida flicked idly at one upturned carapace. Spiders and roaches mostly, roof-dwellers smoked out by the fire. Looked as if the bear had been in here too: there were prints in the dust, and gashes in the wood on the counter corner.

She held up her stick and poked it over the counter, half expecting the bear to be asleep on the floor, sated with whatever awful rations it had found in the ruined camp, turned to poisoning or early hibernation.

But the space was clear. The bear was smart enough to have returned to its unscorched home territory, back to the slopes, nose to the wind.

Vida scrambled over the bar. She began inspecting the unmarked bottles, uncorking each in turn and sniffing them. *Home-brews, Goldilocks*, her nose told her, watering. *And some a whole lot better than others.* The first had a fruity smell but it lacked the acetone punch of a good disinfectant. The second was stronger, but mold was growing up the bottle's insides.

She had just opened the third bottle when the man's voice came from behind her – gravelly, unused, left for dead.

'I'll have a splash of that there white lightning, if it's going.'

Vida dropped the bottle and turned, her stick like a sword. The bottle bounced at her boots but didn't smash.

The thin man sat on a stool as though the bar was still serving and he was in need of one for the road. His hair was dark and long; he'd tied his beard just below his chin with a piece of string like a pirate, so that from here it seemed neat and clean. Vida bet that he stank up close. They all did. But she noted that his eyes and nose and ears were dry, and he seemed pretty calm. No infection, then.

But still. It paid to be cautious.

'Am I going to get some service here, or should I take my business elsewhere?' He was twisting a small piece of cloth in his hands. A handkerchief?

She played along. 'It's been a quiet week behind the bar, mister.'

He nodded. 'That it has.' Twist, twist. There was something wrong with his fingers.

'Where is everybody?'

'Haven't you heard?'

'Heard what?'

'Summer camp. They all packed and left for a seaside break.'

'Assholes. I can't believe they didn't tell me.'

'You have to *be* a friend to *have* a friend, camper, 'member that.' He set the cloth down beside him and pointed at Vida. She recoiled. The index finger was missing from his left hand. In its place was a smooth pinkish nub. He wiggled it at her. 'How's that drink coming along?'

Vida rested her stick against the counter and bent to search for glasses. There was a stack of clay cups there. She blew into them – a dead beetle, its glossy abdomen dulled – and then set out two. She retrieved the fallen bottle, Stringbeard's slitted eyes on her all the while, and filled both the beakers.

He lifted his cup. 'Cheers to the queers. Applause to the whores. May prostitutes flourish and fuck be a household word.'

Vida cocked an eyebrow but drank hers down. She'd had worse. It was strong and sour, like bad cider or mead gone musty, wrong and full of pollen. What was it her mama used to drink? Snakebite. She swallowed hard.

Stringbeard hadn't flinched. He dabbed at his face with the cloth that he set back down again. It was none too clean, Vida saw: there were rust-colored streaks on one side. *Don't know that I'd be putting that rag near my mouth, no, sir.*

He refilled his own cup. Vida let him, keeping hers out of his reach.

'I saw you come down the pass.'

Vida nodded.

'I hope you weren't coming to visit family.'

'No. Just passing through. See who's around. Maybe stock up on supplies.'

'Food?'

'I'll take whatever's useful.'

He nodded. 'I feel that way myself. These are hard times for everybody, little sister. Hard times.' He picked up the handkerchief in his subtracted hand and stroked his face with it. The lace at the edge of the cloth was ragged with friction. *He's not wiping. He's grooming himself*, Vida thought with a kind of horror. *That's why his beard looks so neat. It's all the stroking. That's his blankie.*

'Do you live here?'

'I am indeed a resident.' He was slurring. 'Lived in Fieldstone since it started.'

'What happened here?'

'Town got infected: some kind of crazy brain virus. Made them torch the place.'

'And you're not, uh, infected?'

'Oh, some. Who isn't?'

He dabbed at his nostrils again. *Fuck*, Vida thought. *He IS sick. How did you get that so wrong, Veedles?* She moved her hand along the side of the counter towards her walking stick.

He was sweating freely now. Maybe the booze had flicked a switch somewhere. 'If you wait long enough, you get the better of this virus. The blackouts stop. The rest too. It all stops.'

'Is there anyone else here?'

He laughed, then looked sly. 'Sure. Lots of people. They won't help you, though, kiddo. They're sleeping. And you don't want to be waking them up.'

'How did the virus get in? Settlements are usually so careful.'

He drank, silent.

She tried again. 'Was it sabotage or something?'

He slammed the cup down. The hooch sloshed over his ruined hand.

'Who the fuck told you about that?'

Vida jumped. He really was crazy.

Stringbeard pressed the heels of his hands into his eye sockets. 'I mean, what have you heard about the guy who sabotaged Fieldstone?'

Vida pulled the stick closer, keeping it hidden. 'Nothing. Nothing at all.'

'It wasn't *me*, if that's what you're thinking.'

He poured the last of the bottle into his cup, along with the pips and rinds of some pulpy fruit, yellow as pus.

'It was *them*. *They* locked me out. I built half this village. Who do you think chopped the wood for these beams?' He pointed up, but Vida kept her eyes on him. He shook his head, the tendons like pulleys on his neck. 'You can't say that locking me out was fair. My children were inside. My wife.'

'But you were sick, though, right? You caught something on the wind? That why they locked you out?'

'We're *all* sick! All of us. You can't tell me nothing about sick! Or about sacrifice!' He held up his indignant left hand. 'I lost a finger cutting the wood that made Fieldstone. *They owed me!* What do you make of *that*?'

'So you, what, burnt the place?'

Stringbeard subsided, the fight going out of him. 'Ha. No. That's not on me. I didn't do any of the burning. That started from inside. I just tried to bring the town round to my way of thinking.'

'How?'

'Infecting the stream. Up top. Like cholera. It only takes one. It seemed to do the job.' Incredibly, he was smiling at her, the corners of his eyes drooping. *You and me*, his face said, *we know how it goes.*

'So why aren't you . . . dead, if you don't mind my asking?'

Stringbeard shrugged. 'All I know is that I've been given a gift. I sure did catch something nasty on that wind. Stayed out too long hunting and couldn't find shelter in time. Virus affected my brain, made me unreasonable.

'So when I come back they see me cussing and fuming and they won't let me in through the gates – the gates I fucking built! Hours pass this way, and I say my prayers and stare at the night sky and make peace with my end, though, if I'm honest, I'm not going quietly: *Let me in, you fuckers! I'll kill you all!* That kind of thing.' He shook his head.

'Now I'm outside the gates, dead sick already and along comes another wind and, blame the rage, I don't just hide under a rock. I stand up outside the gates while everyone else is locked away, and I breathe this new pestilence deep into my lungs. I breathe it in like a, like a, knife in the guts, and I gulp it down to twist the blade – to end it all. The honorable thing, right? I know I'm going to die – two viruses means double dead.'

Vida nodded.

'I curl up right at the foot of the gates so that when they find me there in the morning they'll have to drag my body away. Someone I know will have to come out and take me by the stiff wrists and pretend not to recognize my face as they do it. *Fuck* them.

'But instead of the eternal night, I wake up, froze only half to death – and I'm sitting there outside the gates, wet right through with dew and sweat, and I'm thinking how true it is that two wrongs can make a right. They can.

'Two viruses were in me, and they'd found a balance, and they kept me alive. Just call me Lazarus.

'I took that revelation to heart, little sister, and I repaid Fieldstone's wrong with a wrong of my own. Dragged my shivering carcass up the slope to the waterfall and I leaked a little mucus into the water. 'Cause we're all in this together, right? You should have seen it! Long strands of the stuff setting off downstream, like boats. Then the fire. Now we're here.'

After Stringbeard's recitation he regarded Vida closely, scanned her up and down, as though he could see through her clothes to the unmarked flesh below. To distract him, Vida let go of her walking stick and found another bottle on the shelf.

She poured the thick brown liqueur like malt into their cups. They sipped; it tasted of banana peels and salt and the dirt under her fingernails. Stringbeard was wiping his face again; his eyes were wet, blinking against the creamy yellow threads that had gathered at the lower lids.

'So what now?'

'I'm going to rebuild it,' he said. He twisted a corner of the fabric into a cone and shoved it into his ear, working the cloth around until it hit the sweet spot.

'Fieldstone?'

'Yup. It'll be smaller. And I'll move it up the slope a bit.' He examined the muck he had extracted from the ear canal.

Oh, Jesus. If he eats it, I'm going to retch, Vida thought.

'Well, I wish you all the best.'

He flicked the cloth, cocked his head. 'You could stay.'

'It sounds nice, but I can't.'

'I'd like you to stay.'

His hands were beginning to shake again, and she reached out secretly for the stick.

'I'd like to stay, very much.'

'Then stay.'

'My mother is sick. She's—'

Vida had not finished speaking when he launched himself over the bar. Stringbeard's crazy weight fell on top of her and held her down, her hands pinned to the floorboards.

'Shh-shh-shh,' he was saying, his hot breath puffing down into her face. Vida kept struggling, kneeing his ribs and kicking her boot heels against the butchery meat of his back and sides.

He ignored the strikes.

The string of mucous had come loose from the corner of his eye. It dangled low over her face, the fungus of his beard prickling her neck.

Stringbeard blinked, deliberate, and the strand fell slickly onto her cheek, the corner of it touching her lips. So quickly, and it was done. 'I'm keeping an eye on you, baby,' he panted, and then he let go of her hands.

Vida bucked to throw him off. She scrubbed her sleeve across her face. He watched her like a lover, then stood up and walked across the room to the doorway.

'My invitation stands,' he said.

He hopped down onto the burnt earth beyond.

Vida grabbed a bottle from the shelf, pulled the stopper from its neck and poured the booze into her mouth, gargling against pestilence. She spat it out on the floor as soon as the saliva rushed to mingle with it, diluting the alcohol. The roof of her mouth blistered on the fifth gulp, but Vida kept going. She only stopped when she got to the end of the bottle.

9

Vida waited a minute or so but Stringbeard had disappeared. Probably gone to piss out the gallon of booze he had drunk, she thought. She needed to go herself.

Vida threw her stick over the counter and followed it, her knees and elbows taking most of her weight. *I'll pay for that tomorrow.* She was remarkably unscathed, considering the last few months of her existence. From the outside there was almost no way to tell that she and everyone she knew were working their way through the End Times, edging towards some reckoning. The survivors weren't always the ones you thought.

Vida wanted to run, get as far away from this place and that man as she could, but there was a reason she was here at all. Meds, meds, meds. Where were they? No one made camp without a stash for emergencies. Her boots clacked dully over the boards of the barn, sending up little puffs of sawdust as she went, so that at any moment Vida expected a fiddle and banjo to start up behind her, a frilled chorus of good-time girls to burst out of a room backstage, poised for leg-waving and giggles. *If only this was a musical,* she thought. Wouldn't that be a dream worth waking up from?

At the first doorway she pulled the pale curtain back, but the room seemed to be for storage. There were sheets draped over chairs, the shapes underneath like upturned woven baskets, or a piano again, something that required human intervention to make it sing. If she wasn't careful, Vida told herself, she was going to come over all sentimental. *Save it, sister*.

The next room was empty, and it began to register with her that searching for a bathroom was pretty pointless, considering the sorts of acts she had been performing outside for a while now.

'A girl can dream, can't she?' Vida breathed to herself as she went on. 'Does a bear shit in the woods? Yup, yup, yup. And so do I. Desperate times, friends and neighbors. Desperate fucking times.'

The third room, of course, was a bedroom. A dormitory, maybe. At least it looked that way to Vida from where she stood in the doorway, hesitating at the boundary.

In the gloom she saw that someone had, very carefully, laid out every pair of shoes they could find so that they made a square at the edges of the room, like a fence. They were arranged in twins, all facing inwards towards the myriad single beds and the big bed in the center – high heels, boots, runners and pumps, some like the strappy ones Ruth had tried to make her wear once, long ago. Mary Janes, she had called them, the old name of a forgotten child like a talisman. All the school kids in South Africa still had to wear them, her mother had said, and laughed.

She bent to look more closely at the display, and the smell rose to meet her: sweat and foot dirt, but also something like bacon gone rancid, the old grease congealed no matter how hard you tried to get rid of it. She thought of their backyard barbecue, the grid blackened with all the burnt offerings of the years.

Vida stood up quickly and swung her bag around to search for her handkerchief mask. She still forgot, sometimes. Unbelievable. The cloth was little help for the stink, but some part of her felt safer behind it.

Vida scanned the beds again and this time she saw that there were small shapes lying in them, their coverlets pulled neatly up.

You don't want to see this, her mind told her. *It's not going to be anything but terrible.*

Still she approached the beds. Their faded covers turned out to be old quilts – the kind that rich ladies back in the day had hung on brass rods from their walls: to be looked at, not used. Vida breathed through her mouth and stared.

The small faces that were turned up to hers were mostly bald – their hair burnt clean off, but the skin resisting. It still stretched in places across the glossy bone, the tendons yearning tight towards absolution. The jaws were strung open, and Vida found herself leaning in to look at the dentition, and the real horror of what she was seeing struck her solidly in the chest.

The heads only held milk teeth.

Vida sat down, and then realized how close she was to the dead kids and their agonized smiles. She scrambled away on her hindquarters and shoved the shoes out of the way when they stopped her escape. Her brain ran on. *The Tooth Mouse is coming! The Tooth Mouse is coming!* How could he stay away from this undefended bonanza?

She let the chorus cycle. Sometimes you had to go with it until your clean self came back.

Her breathing slowed as she worked it out.

This is Stringbeard's family. He saved them, didn't he? He took them home and put them to bed, so that they would be safe and sound.

If I had the nerve to get all the way to the big bed in the middle there'd be Missus Stringbeard in all her glory.

But I'd be finding Sleeping Beauty minus her panties. 'Cause that's what he's carrying around with him. Even big boys need their blankies.

Indeedy. This was Stringbeard's Lazarus family.

And he was sure as shit going to come back.

Vida hauled herself to her feet again. She was shaky: maybe the hooch, maybe the shock, or maybe the other. She'd never really been sick, proper sick – but then again no one had ever dripped mucus directly into her mouth. Maybe this was the beginning of Stringbeard's rage working its way to her brain: these shaking hands, this hollow dread. Vida tested herself, tried to think straight, tried to remember things about her life and about her ma's. She tried to line them all up in a row, as if doing so would prove something. Dad and The War and the horse and the house, the color of the sitting room curtains and the chip in the enamel toilet, the Sunday waffles and the gray Tuesday meatloaf and then no waffles and no meatloaf and no Dad. No anything.

How can you tell if you're going mad? They always said that the insanity test was a simple one. If you thought you were going crazy, you were probably sane. But folks like Stringbeard, who saw no wrong in what they were doing: those guys were long lost. Gone dogs.

Vida hitched her pack and backed out of the morgue room. Carefully she made her way back to the bar. Was there anything here she could use? Something antiseptic? She took the smallest bottle from the shelf. Some of that juice had burnt. She poked her tongue gingerly at the insides of her cheeks for the raw patches, but it was alright. Vida slid the bottle into her pack. The mouth healed real quick, didn't it? The cells in the eyes and in the mouth worked twice as hard as the rest of the body.

That was what you found when you rubbed your eyes in the morning: that was sleepy dust sprinkled there by some kindly genetic sprite. No matter what you saw the day before, the next morning was your chance to start again.

Except if you were part of the Lazarus family.

Oh, get over it, she told herself. *Enough! They aren't the first dead and they won't be the last. Now get the hell out of here unless you want to end up the same.*

The field outside was quiet. Vida stepped down from the doorway. She crouched and ran in stretches, as if the burnt grass would shield her from the predator she was sure would follow.

But there was only silence. She wasn't sure what was worse.

She had to find the boys again, no matter how much Dyce had deteriorated. Find them and stay with them this time. It was better to stick together. She'd go on with them toward the coast, maybe find a deserted and crumbling pre-war city and hope to find Ma's medicine there. What did she call it? Some African word. *Muti.*

And besides, she owed Dyce some nursing duty. It was the least she could do, having some experience of the sickness as it ate its way through her mama's flesh, sending her incontinent, then blind, then floppy as a corpse – all her life's achievements melting into a steady stream of effluent as she lay in her tormenting blankets the same as Lady Lazarus: the joy and the learning and the courage come to nothing at last. It was the least Vida could do, considering that it was her fault Dyce was sick at all.

Then she wondered whether her ma was even still alive, whether leaving her alone in the house had been a terrible mistake. What if she'd died already?

She should go back.

Yes, go back and be with her.

But what use was there in going back just to sit by her bedside and watch her liquefy? Vida had set out for medicine and she'd return with medicine, even if she had to hike back through the night and risk the wind. *Come back with the goods or don't come back at all.*

Vida passed over the remains of the Fieldstone gate and looked back up at the dirty stream, sullied by ash. Stringbeard didn't seem to be following her, thank God. Probably playing house with his ghost family. Vida snorted with a terrible laughter like vomit, and put her hand over her mouth to stop its exit.

It wasn't difficult, in the end, to find Dyce and Garrett's tracks – they were punctuated now with rancid black shits.

Dyce was deteriorating fast.

With a trail this obvious, so were Garrett's odds of escaping the Callahans.

10

Felix felt the cuffs of his wet shirt again, then looked over at the pencil-scratched chart he'd pinned to the wall with a shingle tack. The wind would pick up soon. He weighed the time between his clothes being dry enough to wear and the enforced hibernation the coming breeze would bring. An hour, maybe. He'd give his pants half that time to dry a little more: the other half he'd need for a slow walk to the stream outside to fetch more water – slowly, legs wide apart to keep his pants from chafing his thin skin. Like a cowboy. Felix snorted.

For now though, there was still power in the battery, and rather than let the ancient cells leak their energy into the atmosphere, he'd make the most of them. Felix sat back down at the table with the gun and his drink. He settled the head-phones over the shells of his ears and pressed play. The story was the same as it always was.

'We voted at the New Freemason Lodge on North Porter. That building had no windows: can you believe it, Future Felix? Smelt like paint and wet concrete. We took one car from home, me and my brothers all squashed in the back. The car wasn't built for that many grown men, but it made sense to go together. Dad let Mom drive, and he played tour guide, point-ing out everything that had changed in the town since I'd been away. And I'd been away a while – twenty years, I reckon. I was thirty-nine years old. As hard as my dad tried to say otherwise, I didn't see that much had changed.

'At the lodge they made us wait outside in a line in the wind. They let us in one by one. We all put our crosses next to NON-UNIFICATION. And that was that. It was over. We went for breakfast – pancakes at The Road House while Dad went on about the architecture of the lodge and my brothers tried to pick up the waitress, like they were twenty instead of closing in on fifty. Mom stared at the menu for ages and then ordered what she always did – hard scrambled eggs on white. They didn't get out much.

'The results were supposed to come in on the weekend, but it came and went and no one heard any word. Another week passed. My return ticket to New York expired. The thing was, I couldn't stand sleeping in my old room. It had not been touched, except for one thing: the dog had been using my bed. Mom had washed the sheets but there were black hairs everywhere, the smell of Dixie's piss in the foam mattress.

'Of course I tried to call New York, ask my landlord to check on the shop, but there was no answer. I tried Mrs Bishop too. Both lines were dead, like there was a blackout. There had been a couple of those that summer. Makes a city panic when that happens. People get crazy: rapes, all kinds of stealing. I tried them again every hour, but I think I knew there was something real bad going on. I could hear my money being burnt, my TVs carried off by looters.

'Eleven days after the vote, I tried Mrs Bishop again, for the thousandth time, and got a pre-recorded message saying that the Northern states had all voted for Unification: it was all set to happen. That was all there was. Our votes hadn't meant jack-shit. It was like they were always going to do it.

'I had never thought that war was romantic. That's for little kids with their action men and their pop guns. It was different for my brothers. They opened their safes and searched the attic and the cellar, stacking up the weapons they'd hoarded over the years. It's amazing what people can accumulate.

'At dinner Dad ranted. It was always about the South and its history and culture and struggle. He used to say it real quiet, "Those fuckers up north", and Mom let him get away with that language, because it was true. *"Those fuckers up north just want to get their hands on what we got, but we'll show them."*

'It was true, I guess. They did want what we had the oil, for sure – but most of what they wanted was our say in how America conducted itself. For some time there'd been this idea that America could do much more for the world and for itself without the bullshit of dealing with all fifty states. You know that story? The man married to forty-nine wives who's trying to build a garden shed? After everyone has their say, it takes thirty years before the shed is built – and the kicker is it's not even a shed in the end. It's an outdoor shower with gold taps and no running water. Northern states seemed to buy into the idea: it was sold to them pretty hard. But the South was never going to go for it – maybe we just kinda liked the idea of an outdoor shower with gold taps instead of another fucking shed. Bear in mind that back then there were more garden sheds on the continent than people.

'And we all had our theories about what the North was going to do with all that power, anyway. Colonize Russia. Declare war on China. Fuck up Mexico once and for all. Finish the job they'd started on Africa.

'And how's this? To fight the North, the South needed to do exactly what we voted against: we had to unify. Some of the more radical radio stations broadcast a plan, set out by a collection of governors and town mayors. It was really happening.

'We drove north in convoy, a stream of buses filled with men of all ages, armed and ready. I was in a yellow school bus with my brothers and my dad. Gabe gave me a handgun, and Levi tried to make me handle a shotgun. I rode with the guns across my lap. I thought they would burn if I touched them, but when I did they were cold. Some of the others were trying to get up the spirit to sing songs, to take our minds off where we were going, and what we were going to do. But when I looked outside it was the same – dark and drab and dry – except that there were already fewer vehicles on the roads. People were beginning to understand that fuel was a problem.

'We traveled for forty-eight hours, day and night, clean out of Oklahoma and into Kansas. In those eleven days of silence, the northern states had set up a frontline that ran from coast to coast – through California, Nevada, Utah, Colorado, Kansas, Missouri, Illinois, Kentucky and Virginia. If you think that's quick, remember Berlin. The chain-link goes up first, and then they start tearing up the streets. The concrete comes later, but by then it's too late. All you really need is some men with guns and a taste for killing, and the fear does the rest.

'On the morning of the third day, the school bus stopped. And there it was. In the distance, running across the road, was the barbed wire and the concrete blocks. Behind them were police cars and men kneeling to rest their rifles on the barriers, aiming them right at us. Two weeks earlier, I'd been selling Emersons and Magnavoxes and Zeniths to these very people. I stepped off that bus and found a trench to bunk down in, and I knew that I would never see New York again. Goodbye, Empire State Building and the A-train. Goodbye, pretzels and muggings and Son of Sam. Goodbye, Dallas, you furry ever-loving fuck.

'I suppose you can judge the length of a war by how long it takes for the first shot to be fired. We were Americans. How could we kill one another? No one pulled a trigger for a full two years: it was all posturing and positioning and failed negotiations. That's when I heard Renard's name for the first time, this doctor who was treating the president for whatever the fuck.

'After that, I don't remember much. People died, in The War and because of it. Dad survived a heart attack while we were marching west to bolster the line near Phillipsburg and was sent back to Mom. They were old people. They would die soon, and I think The War had a lot to do with that, even though they weren't in the fighting hand to hand. In a war, everyone is fighting.

'The Southern frontline had had no real training. It had started out straight and turned jagged pretty quick. We made good ground in Kansas, but the line sagged across Nevada and Utah. Word was that in Kentucky we were doing well too.

'Thank God for Texas. It was slow to join, but six years in we found our forces doubled and our strength tripled. I never knew there were so many guns in the United States: Gatlings, RPGs, assault rifles. We stabilized Nevada and Utah overnight, but we had to make sacrifices. It didn't help that the men who ran the refineries were the ones who went to fight on the frontline. First rations, then no fuel at all. No cars on the road but the military.

'Then Canada joined the North, and the frontline was in no man's land while more talks went on. I saw my fortieth come and go. Gabe got shot in the leg but wouldn't go home. Levi joined the saboteurs: he used to come back from across the frontline with stories of exploding bridges and food trucks driven over cliffs and cables cut, sending whole towns into darkness. It's amazing how quickly a place turns into a ghost town when the lights go out.

'Over the next years, the fighting dragged on. I don't know how the South hung on. I guess the stories of the Civil War kept people going – but look how that turned out. And then The War was closing in on twenty years, and the North was hurting. The boys up there had not expected anywhere near such a violent retaliation, and here we were, handing them their asses. We began to push further north, breaking lines that had been entrenched since the very beginning. The soldiers we killed on the way were easy meat: pale and undernourished, ghost fighters.

'We were driving the last of the Northern soldiers from some Nebraskan town when the first wind came. We had no idea what was happening to us. The soldiers we were pushing north stopped as the wind began to blow, and they turned to look at us. I searched for some kind of trap – explosives on the buildings or a car bomb, but we were okay.

'It was the smell that gave it away – a sulfurous whiff that caught at the mucous membranes and made you choke. I thought of mustard gas and Agent Orange and the colorless shit that the Russkies used to knock off journalists, and I fucking knew it was something like that. I felt the scrape in my own gullet and watched as the guys around me turned paler, then greenish, then began to bleed from their orifices, like rats poisoned in a factory.

'Renard.

'They must have let the president's crazy doctor loose in the laboratory. This was full-scale germ warfare.

'When we figured what it was, we turned and ran as best we could. Men were dropping alongside me as we went, coughing up clumps of their lungs, vomiting blood. I couldn't stop to help them. The Northern soldiers were scared shitless too. They had the vaccine, I found out afterwards, but no one was sure how well it was going to work.

'I found a Jeep, one that had belonged to a commander. I figured he was dead. I took it and then I drove south as fast as I could. I had to hold the wheel with one hand and steady my wrist with the other, I had the shakes so bad. I still don't know if it was the virus or the terror.

'When I came to the first uninfected soldiers, I managed to stop the Jeep, and I told them through the sweats to get to shelter.

'I can't say why I survived that first wind. Some people just did. Something in the genes that makes some of us immune. Or lucky. One in a hundred was the number they put to it, and I was that one. The North had won The War, and Renard had destroyed his own country to do it.'

The tape buzzed and then stuck, and the play button popped up with a click. Felix took off the damp headphones and then he downed the rest of his drink. Just thinking about that first attack made his throat itch.

He sighed and stood and felt his clothes for damp again and took them off the line anyway. He'd need to hang them up when he got back. He made a mental note to find a spare pair of trousers and a shirt somewhere – even if they were torn or worn thin as ghosts.

Once he was dressed in his moist clothes, he hunted in the gloom for the bucket. He found it beside his desk and picked it up with a groan, the hinges of his knees aching with each move-ment, his hand already burning where the wire handle would etch a red line into the palm on the return journey. Maybe if he made enough trips he could change the lines of fortune lettered there.

With one hand he climbed up the ladder and through the trapdoor. The room he heaved himself into was a single man's space – another table, a chair, a couple of shelves. He closed the trapdoor and settled the grass mat neatly back over it. You couldn't be too careful. He kept going, out onto the step, where he stopped, blinking against the bright morning sun.

The air was moving, gentle and warm, but it wouldn't stay that way for long. The grey hairs on his arms were trying to stand up as the pressure changed. Felix looked out over the stand of nut trees and the stream, and felt that he was doing okay, considering.

'Wind's coming soon, old man. Better get that water before you're holed up.'

He stepped off, into the dirt. There was an old cowboy song he often cued up to keep his mind from wandering down dark passageways, and he sang it now.

11

Dyce had kept his illness from Garrett for as long as he could. Now he squatted behind a curl-leaf bush and shook as the shit poured out of him like blood. God! He knew exactly how Garrett would react – as though the death-dealing virus in his brother's veins was a personal inconvenience; as though Dyce had invited the illness through a weakness of character. Any help he got would be fuelled by disdain. Worse than the disease: it would be torture.

Garrett could hear the violent turning of his brother's stomach from where he stood.

'Damn it, Dyce!'

When Dyce emerged, his skin was a grayish yellow. He stumbled back across the gravel to Garrett.

'What the fuck's wrong with your eyes?'

'Can't see so well.'

'No shit. Looks like they're *bleeding*.'

Dyce was trying not to rub at the prickling. *The log*, he kept thinking. *The log in your own eye.*

'Let's just go.'

Garrett set off in front, shaking his head, and Dyce followed, doing his best to keep up with the red blur of his brother that snaked over the sand at his feet. Every now and then there was only the shadow: there were no insects or boot steps or cussing.

And the darkness, creeping in from the corners of his vision.

The shadow. The shadow. Follow the fucking shadow, the way you always do!

But then it was gone and Dyce's world was given to blood-red and all the way over to black.

❦

He woke because Garrett was dragging him, holding under his arms and pulling him over the dirt to the shade of a ponderosa pine. There was gravel in his mouth from the way he'd landed on his face. His teeth crunched when he clenched his jaw, experimental. *Jay Loram*, thought Dyce. *Jay Loram, slow down. Save a space for me.*

'You ought to leave. Just go. Callahans don't give a shit about me.'

'I'll leave you when I leave you. I don't need an invitation.'

'First shelter we find, leave me there.'

'You think I won't leave you? When the time comes, I'm gone. You can stop with that just-leave-me shit. I'm not buying.'

Garrett went off a little ways. He scrambled up a rock and looked back along the ridge. In the distance he could still see the black speck of Fieldstone, its charcoal rubbing, its erasure.

But no Callahan marshals just yet.

You close, you fuckers? You just biding your time?

Garrett took Vida's gun from his pocket and rested it on the rock beside him. He reached down deep into his bag and pulled out a pair of loose bullets. He'd done a swap with a woman in Glenvale – dead goose he'd found under a tree traded for two bullets and a prairie bonnet he'd given to Beth as a joke.

The bullets were too small for the chambers. Garrett tried closing the gun. At least it held them tight, kept them from rattling. There was no telling what would happen when he pulled the trigger, but it made him feel better to have a loaded gun on his hip.

He kept scanning the brush. From far away the shack was camouflaged by a stand of flowering almond trees, but Garrett spotted it anyway, half hidden in the shadow of the crumbling dam that spanned the dry river gorge. Pre-War, for sure.

And it was out of the wind.

He looked back at Dyce where he lay under the bush. He wasn't going anywhere soon.

'You wait here, little brother. Pilgrim's going to inspect that shack.'

Dyce moaned in his fever dream.

As Garrett moved through the trees, their pale blossoms brushed against his face, and he thought, *It's spring. God damn it! It's spring and we're still here!* There was some victory in that.

The surrounds were clear of the prickly weeds that grew on open ground. Out front there was also a hitching post, though the horse it had once tethered was long dead.

Garrett thought back to the last live horse he could remember seeing, maybe four years back on the outskirts of Bitterspring. Miserable old mustang mare long past her riding years, and yet there, pressing down on her ancient spine was an enormous woman – too fat to walk more than a barn-length on her own.

And that was not the last they saw of the pair. No, sir. A month later, he and Dyce had come across them in the open desert, the mare unburdened at last, collapsed in on herself and decomposing – and her owner too, just out in the middle of nowhere. Garrett wanted to think that it was the horse's idea to walk and walk until the gates of heaven opened. Heaven, or the other place.

He sent his hand over the smooth planed wood, unable to stop himself. Garrett had always liked the way horse poles had looked, circles grazed down to the dirt like well-tended graves. As it became clearer that all the horses would die, the foliage returned. The old poles were hidden, the bones carried off by coyotes.

They couldn't say what wiped out the horses: virus, probably – a side effect of something intended for humans, or else deliberately sent by Renard to kneecap travel. Containment. Getting anywhere was real slow going. He and Dyce would've been at the coast over a week ago on horseback. Fuck Renard for that too.

It was as if the entire geography of the continent had changed overnight. With horses you could have ridden the banks of the Yampa clean out of Colorado if you wanted. Not anymore. The universe had shrunk all the way down to the size of a tennis ball. Hiking two days in any direction was about as far as anyone got before the wind came or their rations ran out.

And further than that you needed some strong motivation. Suicide or dementia, most often.

Or Callahans.

Garrett wished he'd taken a horse and ridden up to see the border wall when you still could. He and Dyce had wanted to see it just to know it was real. Paint a dick on it. But there'd been no real reason to go – no reason to risk their lives and the horses' too, just for sightseeing. That was old-world thinking, from a time when cars criss-crossed the landscape at a hundred miles an hour, their bellies full of cheap gas, their drivers headed wherever the notion took them. Now The Wall was out of reach, same way the coast seemed to be. It was just an impossibly long way to go on foot. If they were to make it, they'd have to walk clean off the map to get there, further than anyone had been since the horses reared up and fell over. But when Dyce asked, as he often did, Garrett packed away the fears and reservations, because that was what adults did. *What's a bit of walking, anyway? Good for the heart and double good for the soul. Just one foot in front of the other till we hit the beach.*

At least they were even: the Callahans had nothing to help them along, either. The men were older, mostly. Older and slower, but with more to grieve. Garrett imagined the popping of their knees as they hunkered around night fires, their faces grimy and concentrated, identical.

Now that he was up close, Garrett saw that the shack was small: a lone wooden step and a hardwood door. Someone was looking after it, though. The door was patched around its edges with rags and string to keep the wind out. There were spots of new mud covering the unseen cracks.

Garrett reached for the handle and stopped. Somewhere there was distant singing, like an angel's chorus or a radio station, but then the sound resolved itself into a man's voice, ancient, crackly as a scratched record.

He stepped back from the door and looked around for a hiding place, then slid behind a cottonwood stump.

The voice, nearer:

Get six jolly cowboys to carry my coffin,
Get six pretty maidens to bear up my pall.
Put bunches of roses all over my coffin,
Roses to deaden the sods as they fall.

Then swing your rope slowly and rattle your spurs lowly,
And give a wild whoop as you carry me along.

And in the grave throw me and roll the sod o'er me,
For I'm a young cowboy and I know I've done wrong.

The man limped from the thicket of blossoming almonds. He was carrying a pail that sloshed and spilled with each slow step. Garrett watched his approach. The man stopped on the step and turned back and scanned the clearing as though he felt the eyes on him. His clothes seemed dark and damp, full dry only at the sun-warmed shoulders. He wore no mask. For an old fellow that was usually one giant step closer to winding up dead – but he didn't seem concerned.

He took a notebook and a pencil stub from his back pocket, and wrote something down. He took one last deep breath, turned and opened the door, and was gone like the White Rabbit.

Garrett stepped out, unsure why he'd hidden. It had seemed in the moment like the safe thing to do. He had no back-up, no watchful Dyce expecting him to meet obstacles head-on. He stood in the man's dusty footprints and looked back along his path, trying to see where he'd come from, and instead he saw the breeze whisking its way over the distant hilltop, the grasses blown flat as though a giant comb was being pulled through them. The spruces bowed and shook. Fuck. That was Dyce's job – to watch for the wind, for the rising signs. Garrett had grown lazy, too used to the watchdog. He looked up the hill again, to where he'd left his brother.

He'd never get up there and down again before the full force of the wind hit. Dyce would die in it, and that was a stupid way to go. Garrett squinted against the light.

Along the ridge there was coming a dark shape, swift and agile, two-footed.

It was heading straight for his brother's body. Garrett wanted to shout but could not, caught between two fearful unknowns.

But there was no real decision to be made. He took off at a run through the stand of trees between them, willing his arms to pump the air into his flattened, ungrateful lungs.

Now the person was bending over Dyce.

Too late! Too late! Too late!

Garrett tripped over a tree root and went sprawling. He slapped at the hard earth.

The person turned to look at him in surprise from where she was pulling Dyce up.

'*Vida!*'

'The shack!'

She was going to try to fling Dyce over her back like a fireman. *Like Wonder Woman*, thought Garrett. He wanted to laugh. He got to his feet and went to help her as she struggled to load Dyce onto her own frame. And she had done it too. She had turned her back on him and was stumbling down the slope towards the shack. Every now and again Dyce's boots dragged and bumped on the ground and she had to shift his bony weight. *Not Wonder Woman. A wasp pulling at a wolf spider.*

Garrett caught up with her and held her arm and said, 'Let me get him.' She began to argue, but Garrett had two decades of brotherly authority behind him, and she saw that it was no use. She allowed him to drag Dyce over and sling him across his own shoulder.

'Get the door!'

They could hear the wind now like rushing water. It hit the valley floor and stirred up a wall of dust, the hand of God sweeping the sinful aside like the old-time song.

Vida twisted the handle and slammed her shoulder into the door. It opened and Garrett blundered forward and fell into the interior, spilling his brother onto the floor. Vida caught a last glimpse of the dust storm, angry undead fingers of dirt grabbing for them. She got the door closed as the grit hit, peppering the wood like buckshot.

12

Garrett flinched in anticipation of a blade or a rifle in the ribs, the welcome he expected from the old man.

But there was nothing: just the blackness and the whistle of the wind shoving at the walls and trying the door. *Little pig! Little pig!*

Garrett reached and felt around for Dyce's body and untied his ripe face mask to let him breathe.

'Sorry for the intrusion,' Garrett spoke into the darkness, just in case. He made his voice gruff and threatening. There'd be the *tch* of a match on flint at any moment, and a candle to light up the space, and wouldn't that be a relief?

But it didn't come. No reply, neither. Just a faint tinkling, every now and again, coming from outside. It unnerved Garrett. *Where are you, old man?*

'Who you talking to?' It was Vida, struggling to catch her breath.

'An old man. Saw him come in here.'

'You sure?'

'Oh, yeah. *Sorry*. Must have gone into the other shack. So many fucking *shacks* around.'

Vida felt the front pocket of her pack for a book of matches. Two left. She'd gotten so good at using her flint for fires that she'd not used these last matches in over a year. She knew what the cardboard said:

Eagle Motel – Your Home on the Road!

She felt for a match and struck it. It fizzed and died, too damp or too old or both. The next one sparked and held briefly. *Come on, little critter.*

It flickered and grew and Vida held it out at arm's length.

In the middle were two chairs and their little square table, one dead candle presiding. She muttered, 'Thank God,' and went to light the candle. Then she stood and sucked her burnt fingers.

Behind them sagged an empty chipboard cupboard sporting water damage, swollen with black streaks of rot growing from the ground up. A ragged grass mat lay snug on the floor, but the focus of the room was the colored etching on the wall, the glass fallen out of the frame – a house in an apple orchard with two horses grazing out front in their green heaven, one piebald, the other a dusty pink with a blond mane and tail that made Garrett think of Bethie. His heart shrank into itself. God, he hoped she was somewhere half as decent as the horses!

They turned back to Dyce where he lay sprawled on the ground, waxy as the candle, throwing a limp shadow as if his spirit self was hovering just above him, making up its mind. Near his mouth was a spatter of stringy bile like a cartoon speech bubble, jagged-edged, untouchable.

Vida folded her arms. 'I don't see no old man.'

Garrett didn't answer. He got busy searching behind the cupboard for a door, feeling the walls for a seam, some sign of an exit. Would she never shut up?

'You know, my mama always believed in ghosts. Her religion came and went, but she never wavered when it came to the ghosts. When her ladies came to her, about to drop their babies, she said they were in so much pain that they could see clear to

The Other Side. Your mind does strange things when it's under stress. I can see now that you're worried about your brother.'

Garrett grimaced and kept up his moody pacing around the table. 'I'm not given to hallucinations.' *You fucking idiot*, he nearly added. *Great. A psychic. Just what I need.*

Vida pressed on. 'That candle's going to give us a half hour's light, friend. Then we better be ready for hibernation. Spend it looking if you want. I'm going to see what can be done about him on the floor over there.'

Vida took both her bag and Dyce's, and began unpacking them on the table, laying the items out in neat rows like a tarot reading. Garrett itched to stop her. It was a trespass. Rifling through someone else's pack was unforgivable, even though he knew Dyce so well he could list in his head everything that was in that bag. Garrett pressed his lips together but said nothing. There they were:

The smooth stone
The Opinel
Birchwood sticks
Two carved mermaids
A flint and striker
A ball of fat nestled in leaves, salted but rancid
Shards of dried turkey meat
One honeycomb – sucked clean
A battered tin of herbs
Salt tablets
An army surplus canteen

Vida opened her bag next. Garrett edged closer to see what might come out.

A recipe book, stained and bulging
Five dried locusts, minus a couple of legs
A flint and striker, the same kind everyone carried
A bottle of hooch
A water canteen
A lumberjack shirt
Two surgical masks with elasticated ear straps, once white
Lumps of charcoal
A knife, its handle bandaged with strips of leather

With everything laid out, Vida opened her mother's remedy book. It was an alchemist's notebook, a weather chart, diagrammed and doodled with plants and rocks and animals that were connected by arrows that also pointed to pots and fires and beakers: the recipes of a lifetime written and then overwritten, self-corrected and no space spared, a map of the human mind.

She paged through it and nodded to herself. Pressed the pages open and laid a piece of birchwood on top to keep the pages spread for easy reading. She took a pinch of the fat and flattened it on the table, then crushed a nugget of charcoal into the center. Out of her tin she took horehound leaves tied with cotton in a bunch. She powdered some between her palms and added them, along with a heavy dose of dried yarrow, and only a pinch of sagebrush seeds. Then she curled the edges of the fat up and rolled it into a ball.

'Missing a whole stack of ingredients, but get him to take this along with as much water as he'll drink.'

Garrett looked at her.

'I know what I'm doing, white bread. My mama was a midwife.'

'Yeah, and I once knew a guy who knew a guy whose uncle was a doctor.'

Vida glared. Garrett shrugged it off. Other things to think about. He went over to Dyce and propped his brother up in a corner.

'Allerdyce! Hey, little brother! Come on, come on. Open those creepy eyes. Prodigal lady made you some medicine.'

Dyce moaned. When his mouth opened again, Garrett worked the tablet past his teeth and onto his tongue. He held the canteen up to Dyce's mouth. He drank and coughed and then slumped back against the wall.

With the candle fast puddling on the table, Vida packed the bags right and set herself up in a corner. Garrett did the same, taking the opposite, like a boxer. The candle sizzled and went out. In the gloom Garrett could hear Vida crunching down on something – a dried locust? He'd hardly eaten all day but he wasn't hungry. Hadn't been since Beth passed over. The Death Diet. He took a plug of bear fat from his own pack and let it melt in his mouth, then washed it down with water.

After a long silence Vida spoke up. 'Wind's a blessing for a change.'

Garrett adjusted his pack under his head. 'You and me got a different understanding of that word, then.'

'Callahans were going to catch up with you, Dyce being so sick. Bought you some time.'

'Hallelujah.'

There was another stretch of silence between them. Vida was restless.

'What's across the sea?'

Garrett groaned, as though he was being disturbed from a deep sleep.

'You know, I don't know. Maybe nothing, maybe something. Could be worse there, could be better.'

'But what picture is in your mind when you think about it?'

'You wanna know?'

'I asked, didn't I?'

'Okay.' Vida could hear him sit up. 'It's me and Dyce. We're in a nightclub, like a kind of whorehouse, dark with tobacco smoke in the air . . .'

'Oh, God. Forget it.'

'. . . and there's a woman standing in front of me, buck naked . . .'

'Jeez. Spare me.'

'. . . and her skin is perfect – no scars or welts or rashes or redness or blisters. Just the skin the good Lord gave her on her birthday. And I'm just looking.'

There was another pause.

'Is that it?'

'Yeah.'

'No joining of your giblets?'

Garrett laughed. 'That's a different dream.'

She turned away from him, into the corner, and they drowsed to the tinkling outside. It was coming faster now, a tiny hand somewhere nearby shaking the nuts from the trees, maybe, like those silver balls her mama's pregnant ladies oftentimes wore over their unborns, a songline for the little hand to hold when it crept through the flesh.

💀

Vida had thought she would sleep no matter what, but the little bell was annoying, jangling at the edge of her mind like an alarm, some niggling reminder of a chore she had yet to do.

Outside it was afternoon, but they had to sleep whenever they could. There was a tiredness that settled on you when you were moving around: it never seemed to disappear entirely.

Vida sat up now in the low hum of her sleep deprivation, and the muscles in her calves cramped in protest. She had tried to sleep curled up, gripping her legs for something solid and familiar. That wasn't smart: they had gone numb right away, and now they felt as if they belonged to someone else. She kept thinking of the Lazarus babies, how their legs probably felt the same, like that game she had played long ago: Dead Man's Finger.

When Vida tried to close her eyes she was surrounded by the children in their sooty mounds. She felt the tendrils of Stringbeard's beard, tickling her face in the dark, like a good-night kiss from a drunken daddy.

How had she ever slept, before? She had forgotten how.

At last she did.

She was back in the bar. The bear was there this time, slumped in the doorway, blocking her exit. The animal snores rose unbroken as Vida stepped over the fur, blackly matted with oil. The creature smelt of the death it brought with it; the rancid marrow and broken bones of the food chain.

The snorting stopped. In the silence the bear's eyes flicked open and tracked her.

She backed away slowly. *It's still sleepy time, Bruin. Nothing to see here.* She turned. Behind her, of course, on his barstool, was Stringbeard. He had fused with it, some hybrid of man and fitting. He watched her with his wet, red eyes and sipped, sipped. Vida expected him to lick his lips.

She kept backing away. She didn't want to go through the curtain again: she knew what would be there, didn't she?

The dream was merciless. Vida pulled aside the blackened hessian sacks, her heart bitter with the hard knowledge of sorrow.

But the tiny beds were empty. The big bed, too.

The Lazarus woman was standing at the window, looking out, surrounded by her children – pink and healthy, one and all. They had put their shoes on, sockless. One by one, they smiled at Vida and she saw their teeth, pink-rimmed at the gums, sharp and white at the tips. Coyote kids.

The woman beckoned. *Why don't they ever talk in dreams?* Vida wondered, but she came closer so that she could also look out of the window. She had to wade through the children, and they stroked her legs as she moved among them.

Vida looked out. On a distant hill she could see the wind blowing, moving toward them at speed, agitating the leaves as it came. The children began to hold out their hands to it, as if they could take the air in their arms. This wind had substance. It swirled in coils of transparent fibers, the sinews of ghostly bodies the angry yellow-gray of tornadoes. Vida heard the wisps whistling and sighing as they approached, an army of the diseased dead. The hungry ghosts would envelop all of them – the Lazarus family and Vida herself, screaming as they smothered the living.

Vida turned to run, but the woman grabbed her wrist and pointed again at the scene outside.

Stringbeard and the black bear were striding out across the grass to meet the wind's battalions.

The two stood side by side, crouching low against the solid body of the earth. When the phantoms were upon them, they sprang, man and beast, trailing mucus and mangled fur. They kicked and clawed and bit the air as it shrouded them, and they disappeared under its onslaught.

Vida woke in the false darkness and felt for the clammy hand of the Lazarus lady. It wasn't there.

Of course it wasn't.

She exhaled in relief. Where was her water? She reached into her pack for her canteen and sat all the way up, hot and bothered.

There was something about that dream. When her stepdaddy had died, she and Ruth had taken to recounting their dreams as they ate their scanty breakfast: you could do that when there were only the two of you. Vida still missed Evert terribly – him and his horses. The last of the black cowboys, he always said: the great-grandson of old Nat Love, the famous Bronze Buckaroo. Whether it was true or not, he had loved her and her mama pure and strong, and everyone had known it. Most of the time Vida thought it was over, the mourning, but then there were days that brought back the lightning bolt of misery and loss. Grief made you sharper, didn't it? Made you appreciate what you had left – the things you still had to lose. With Evert gone the two women were left to make sense of the events of their days and nights, and so they talked first thing. The rest of the day would be about the ladies who came to see Mama, crying and clawing their abdomens, moaning that their time had surely come. Vida had long learnt that when a woman in labor was brought to their house, Ruth was a midwife before she was her mother.

Mama thought dreams were like trances: the meaning was always hidden in plain sight. Your mind was trying to tell you something you already knew, and you had to shut up and listen. The dream had something to do with what Stringbeard had told her. What was it? Vida shut her eyes tightly, as if that would make her remember. She pictured Evert with his lasso, the rope whirling over his head as a new horse bolted.

Two wrongs sometimes make a right.

Vida sat up, trying to clear the sleep from her mind without shaking the dream out altogether.

That was it. Two wrongs; two viruses.

The bear and the leaking man.

Why was she so sure they belonged together? Each one left alone in that barn would have massacred the children, and chewed through the wife. As a unit, though, they had done something else entirely – faced an outward attack instead of turning on the obvious victims.

They had offered protection.

Vida clunked herself on the knee with her canteen. That was it!

Stringbeard's double infection had been random. But what if she could find two viruses that would negate each other's symptoms? Pair them up so that they turned harmless? Or transformed themselves into something else?

Could there be a virus out there that would fix Ma?

Vida sipped at her canteen in cautious celebration.

Even the lunatic side effects didn't seem so bad from here. It was a crazy idea, but with it came the treasure-box glimmer of hope. And what other choice did they really have? Her search for medicines, for salts and oils and herbs, was just delaying the inevitable – giving Ma's body time to fight the infection, buy an extra day, a week, a month. What was the sense of drawing it out if all there was was this suffering? You and your spectral children, the descendants of misery and malady, staring through some eternal window.

It could work. It MUST work. It must.

Vida lay awake, her plans swirling, nagging and ghostly. Finally, she slept again.

This time she dreamt of Ruth and Evert and Dyce and Garrett and a girl she didn't know, vital and healthy, playing ball out behind the wooden house.

13

Garrett woke to a scratching noise coming from near the table. *Rats going through Dyce's bag, I'll bet. Gorging themselves sick on bear fat.* He sat up slowly. *Eat up, little Hansels, little Gretels. I'll take rat stew over bear fat eight days a week.*

Now Garrett stood up quietly, straining his eyes in the blackness.

Below the table he saw a dull slit of light. A trap door?

And more: a pair of eyes.

Quietly, quietly, the two humans regarded each other.

There had been a trapdoor spider that lived under the old cottonwood back at their house, where the earth was always damp and compacted between the serpentine roots. His home was a perfect little circle in the dirt: if you weren't looking you wouldn't know it was there. Dad, being away most days, working all week and training for the reserves on the weekend, wasn't there to say, *Don't you dare shoot your catapult at those pigeons,* or, *What do you plan on doing with the squirrel once you catch it? Or, Leave that little spider be.*

But there were still rules. Garrett's code of honor.

'If the pin breaks, it's game over, okay? He wins. And we only fight him once a day. After that he's tired and it's not fair.'

For weeks, the spider had its daily battle, Dyce always asking when it'd be his turn, Garrett never willing to share.

He'd choose a pin from their gran's old sewing kit. He'd drag the tip of it along the ground, like the footsteps of a wounded beetle. He'd come walking from a yard away, for the full effect, and his pin-insect would scuttle closer, and then closer, Garrett mouthing shark music all the while, Dyce watching, still as bones. Then, if he'd played his part well, the circle door would spring open and the spider would lunge at the pin and there'd be a moment when the spider realized its mistake.

And here was the real skill in the game: to get the pin wedged in the hole before the spider closed it. Only then would the real battle begin. The spider would tug and tug. And if the pin held, which it seldom did, the lid would open slowly, slowly, and the boys would see the desperate black legs gripping the lid.

Once it was up, and victory unthinkable, the spider would let go and retreat into his burrow, and Garrett would flip the lid down to cover the hole.

After a fight he and Dyce would go out collecting bugs for the spider. The boys would stun them with a flick to the head and then leave the offerings at his doorway. Respect. Sacrifice. Later, Dyce would call it what it was: conditioning.

The day it all ended was also the day it began. He'd nagged his way into a turn, and Garrett, bored of the contest, had finally conceded. Dyce copied his brother's long amble closer and closer to the door, stopping occasionally to inspect a leaf. Then the moving away again, the scuttling.

He managed to lure the spider out first time, but in the race for the door he misjudged the distance and spiked it through its abdomen. The creature didn't try to secure the lid: it limped down to the bottom of its hole, bleeding ichor. The insects they left outside were untouched.

The boys came back the next day with a cross made of lolly sticks, and whacked it into the dirt with a stone.

Now, peeking out from his secret bunker, was no spider.

The old man.

Garrett stepped closer, rolling his heel on the floor to dampen the sound. The old guy didn't move. One more step.

Garrett tumbled forward and jammed his fingers under the lid.

He heaved the trapdoor open. The old man fell back in fright from his perch. He sprawled, naked and groaning, at the bottom of the wooden steps. There were shards of glass around him on the dirt floor; he held his hand against the leaking gash on his head and cursed.

When the old guy fell quiet there came again the sound Garrett had heard since they'd first taken shelter in the shack, a constant and distant ringing. *Tinker-fucking-bell.* Worse when the wind picked up. Wind chimes? In another time it would have driven him nuts.

Garrett realized that he could see the brightness of the fresh blood. The old guy's room was lit, not with candles or a fire, but electricity running through a bulb that hung from the ceiling. It had been years since Garrett had seen a glowing filament, and its presence unsettled him – an ancient magic that he'd never understood.

The room was long and narrow all the way along. Pinned to the board siding that kept the soil at bay there were maps of the continent, moth-eaten and creased, criss-crossed with weird geometries. At the far end a curtain divided the room, making a private space beyond. Along one wall, hanging on a string, were the old man's clothes, drip-drying bachelor-style. A corroded zinc tub of dirty water sat below them, big enough for a load of washing or a cramped bath, a digger's camp. *Oh, my darling Clementine*, thought Garrett. Near the tub was the old guy's desk, piled to the low ceiling with books, one weighted open to a special page with a rusted weathervane, like a skull and crossbones. Beside the desk was a modified exercise bike, wired up to a beat-to-shit car battery. Exposed wires ran up the wall: the source of power for the dim bulb. Garrett knew he looked like a rube but he couldn't stop turning and turning as he took it all in.

'Wow.' Vida's voice behind him was still muzzy with sleep.

Garrett tested the steps with a boot and then began to make the descent into the glow below.

'Let me go first,' she said, and pushed past Garrett. She knelt next to the man and held his head tenderly in her hands, like a back-room artifact in a museum.

'Going to need to sew that up.'

The man groaned in protest. He didn't try to cover himself, and Vida didn't bother looking at the old socks of his genitals. He was beyond shame.

'I have a needle. It's clean.' She didn't say, *It's a fish hook*. He didn't need to be worrying himself about that. 'I'm sure we can steal some cotton from a hem somewhere.'

The man tried to get to his feet, and he made it on the second effort. He shouldered Vida aside in the small space and went over to a bureau. He began to search through the drawers, the blood from his head wound dripping bright and steady, streaking his thin cheeks like war paint. Behind him Vida lifted her chin and rolled forward onto the toes of her boots to get a look at what medicines might be there.

From a drawer filled with scraps of cloth and a jumble of multicolored wool, the man extracted a sewing needle and some thread.

'You sure you can sew?'

'Yeah, I can get the job done. But I'm not near as good as this cowboy.' Vida thumbed at Garrett.

'Can't be sure I want him fixed yet. Best you take point while I make up my mind,' Garrett replied. He reminded Vida of the kids at the dinosaur display in her stepdaddy's museum.

The old man sat down on a wooden stool under the old bulb that hung from a rafter.

'Wash your hands good,' said the old man. 'And tell him to stay away from my books.'

'I can tell him same as you can. I'm not his mother.'

The old man kept one yellow eye on Garrett as Vida went back to get the alcohol she had taken from the Lazarus place.

Like a big old buzzard, she thought, threading the needle: the scarred folds of ageing skin, liver-spotted and yellowing; the bald head rimmed by tufts of gray hair; the unashamed naked-ness of the man and his drooping scrotum.

'We're sorry for the intrusion,' she said, making conversation. 'Would never just barge in like we did, but the wind caught us in the open. One of our, our, party is sick.'

Garrett laughed to himself. Before it was just him and Dyce. Add one crazy woman and suddenly there was a party. *Yeehaa! Gimme some of that sugar and tar-tray-zine!*

The maps on the walls were familiar. Garrett examined them so he didn't have to think about the sharp inhalations the old man was making as Vida sewed his head back together. He'd learnt what America looked like as a kid: they'd all had to mem-orize the rhymes, the cheats to jog the memory of the activities in each place. *The straighter its edges, the less interesting the inside.* He'd learnt that from his dad. A lesson he figured was true of anything – a state or a person.

But across these maps were long arms, storm fronts, Garrett knew that much – extending right across from coast to coast. Garrett studied them for a while and then went back to see Vida finish off the stitching. It wasn't a bad job: a bit lumpy, maybe. She was dabbing at the skin, mopping at the bloody tributaries so that he wouldn't have a heart attack if he ever did catch a glimpse of his broken self passing some unmerciful shiny surface.

'How does it look?' the old man asked. The color was coming back into his face. *Not a fainter, thank fuck.*

'It looks like your modeling career is over.'

He snorted, then sobered, remembered to be offended.

'Thanks for the stitches. But I wouldn't have needed them if you hadn't come in uninvited. What gives you the right to barge into my place? My *private* space?'

Vida busied herself with rolling up the thread.

'Didn't figure someone like you would really care,' replied Garrett. 'I saw you out in the open without a mask. Seemed to us that maybe you were ready for the good Lord.'

'How many old folk you see around these days?' The old man was getting up, making his shaky way over to a scratched desk.

'Can't say many.'

'There're reasons I've lived as long as I have. One being the sanctity and secrecy of this hole.'

'What are the other reasons?'

'You really want to know?'

'Sure. Pretty keen on making it past forty myself. I'm not too proud to take advice from an old naked guy. Might get me where I'm going in one piece.'

'And where would that be, now? If you don't mind my asking?

I figure we're practically family already. Never was particularly fond of my own.'

'Me and my little brother are heading to the coast, then we'll steal a boat, head off past the breakers. I sure am getting tired of this-all.'

The old man threw him a shrewd look.

'Yeah, and I'm going to ride a rainbow to the pearly gates. Only folk I know who've tried what you're planning had no other options. You're either a man of great faith or you're being hunted. Which is it?'

'Bit of both. The faith's been growing since I've been on the run.'

'Sounds like you'll be dead in a week, one way or another. There's no advice I can give that'd make any difference. But wipe those tears away, son. We'll all see you on the other side soon enough.'

'What does that mean?'

The old man took a book from the table, opened it and held it up. It was filled with notes and charts and dates, with wavy lines and temperatures.

'I've been charting the weather for, oh, about a decade now. I know when the winds are coming and when it's safe to be out.'

'Oh, shit,' said Vida, as something clicked. 'Was that *your* weather box out past Fieldstone?'

'The Stevenson screens, like beehives on legs? They're *all* my weather boxes. If you fucking touched one . . .'

'Didn't get a chance to. Wind picked up.'

'People got no respect these days. Spend my life repairing my boxes and replacing my instruments – trying to make those totems creepy as shit to scare off the scavengers.'

Vida was quiet. She paid close attention to the maps. Some had areas of tiny penciled lumps drawn on them, like treasure troves.

'You look inside?' the Weatherman asked. 'Was it all still there?'

'Reckon so.'

'So you know when the wind's going to blow?' asked Garrett. 'That's gold. Better than gold, 'cause it's useful. You should tell people. I don't know . . . *do* something with it. You're a, a, god with that information!'

Vida looked sidelong at him.

The old guy sighed. 'There's no point.'

'Maybe not for you, old man, but for other folk.'

'Just don't see the purpose. See these maps on the wall there? Once in a while – every hundred years or so – there comes a big storm, blows right across the continent. It's coming soon, going to wipe us all out, stir up them viruses that've been laying low, turn the air to poison, flood the plains, wash the mountains flat. All of that biblical shit. Whatever you care about – gone. We are long overdue for the apocalypse, Sonny Jim.'

'Thanks, Noah. You are building a boat, right?'

'Young man.' The old guy leant in towards Garrett, the stitches lacing his head up tight as a shoe, like they were keeping his brains in, but only just. 'This ain't no joking matter.'

Vida stepped in. 'So when's this thing due?'

'Been due for a few years now, live Yellowstone. Could be here next year, or the year after. Could be brewing on the horizon as we speak. Hard to say. But Renard fucked with everything when he set them sicknesses upon us.' He shook his head.

It looks like a football, Vida thought in amazement. *An old-school pigskin blown tight with someone's breath.* She thought of all the faded pictures she'd seen: young men staring out at her from another time, miming hardness, their hair slicked back and their arms crossed over their chests. All gone now.

Garrett walked over to look at the maps again.

'The arms – they aren't cold fronts, right?'

'Yup. Previous storms. The real big ones. So bad they didn't even bother giving them ladies' names. One from 1900, which was a great way to sing in the new century, and another one a hundred years before, same thing. Took out a lot of people – but they didn't have the viruses all together back then. If it was one at a time, or even one of a kind, you have a chance, with the right antidotes, and quarantine. But disaster medicine only goes so far in the End Times. This time round we're fucked. Germa-fucking-geddon.'

Garrett noticed a tiny brass bell hanging from a red wool string that ran up and through a hole in the floorboards above. He tapped it with a finger and it tinkled, the source of the fairy chime that was the soundtrack to his frustration.

'What's this?'

'It goes up outside. Tied to a branch so I know when the wind's blowing bad.'

Garrett felt his face heat up, the blood rushing around his eardrums.

'How long's it been quiet?'

The Weatherman didn't need to answer.

In the stillness of the room they all heard the voice coming from outside.

'Garrett! Garrett Jackson! You in there?'

14

Vida moved first. She climbed two of the steps and reached for the trap door. She pulled it closed just as the shack door opened. She and Garrett and the Weatherman stood silently, listening as Gus and Walden Callahan blundered around the room above them. Their voices, clear as day.

'He in there, Pa?'

'Shhh. Just fucking *shhh*.'

A board, squeaking under a boot.

'Ah, Jesus.'

'What, Pa?'

'It's his brother. And he looks about the same as Bethie does.'

'Allerdyce?'

'How many brothers you think Garrett's got?'

'Just the one.'

'Yeah.' A sigh. 'So it's Allerdyce.'

More footsteps: Walden entering the room.

'Ah, *jeez*.'

'We been tracking them sticky black shits since Fieldstone, Walden. Someone's insides dissolved. You expecting lavender?'

'But where's Garrett?'

A long silence. The questions Walden asked Gus chafed, wearing him down slow and stinging like hell.

The idea had been to bring Walden along, harden the kid up on the trail, but with each step Gus had regretted it. He'd have caught up with Garrett this morning already if he'd set out alone. For long stretches he'd let Walden walk out front, and he'd watched him walk – lifting a boot and swinging it, letting it land wherever it fell. How was this a Callahan? They did things a certain way – walked with purpose, for one. You lift a boot and plant it where you want it. People see you coming and they know. Even Beth was more Callahan than lame-ass Walden, with his soft hands and his puppy-dog eyes.

And, goddamn, a Callahan filled his clothes! Back in the old days they were built like Gus: meaty, mountainous, impassable. A couple of times Gus had looked up at his eldest – waddling along over rocks like a sea bird caught up in a fishing line – and he'd thought about pulling his gun out and shooting him right in the back. *Aim for the spine, 'cause a mite left or right and you'll miss the kid outright*, he told himself. He'd thought it through, could say it was Garrett. There was no shame in it. What did that make him? The world's worst father? For damn sure. But, first and foremost, a Callahan. What else was there, when your kids could be wiped out by a snotty nose? Family was something you made as you went along.

'You think he'll be back, Pa?'

'His pack's here. His brother's here. He's sure as shit coming back. So close the door and make sure your gun is loaded and drawn. And don't shoot me in the dark. You nail me, Walden, and you better hope it's between the eyes.'

The three below heard Walden close the door.

'How long do you think 'til he's back?'

Again, no answer. Gus saving his breath for the coming showdown.

How old was he, anyway? Vida wondered. She and the Weatherman stared up at the floorboards. Without knowing it, they'd risen on their tippy-toes, straining.

Garrett motioned them together with his hand and they huddled.

'Weatherman. There another exit?'

'Yeah. Old water pipe.' He jerked his grizzled chin. 'Behind the curtain. Only ever tried it once so as I'd know I could fit. Don't reckon you'd make it.'

'I'm slicker than I look.'

'Huh.'

'She would, though, right?'

'Easy, tiger. I can volunteer my own services,' said Vida.

'Relax. You can both go up the pipe. No reason to get your panties in a bunch.'

Vida could see the cogs turning in Garrett's head, like one of the Weatherman's instruments.

'I'll need some cover. Element of surprise and all that.'

She nodded.

'One of you has got to go up and out, and then come round the front. Going to need some heavy footsteps, maybe some whistling – make them think I'm coming back. Meanwhile, I'll be sneaking up from below.'

Like a demon, Vida thought. 'I'll do it,' she said.

'And you, old man?'

The Weatherman glanced at his books and shook his head. The blood was dry, Vida noticed, and crackling in brownish flecks. He would heal just fine.

'I'm staying.'

Garrett went to the curtain and drew it back. The pipe was definitely big enough, some part of the original dam. It still trickled water.

'You'll be fine,' the Weatherman said. He was checking instruments, tapping at mercury behind glass. 'Wind's down, at least. You'll just have to be real quiet.'

'I'll tell the marching band to stand down.' Garrett's mouth pulled sideways. 'Hey. A bad joke's better than none at all. Am I right?'

He gave her a real smile now, and they nodded at each other. *See you on the other side.*

She mouthed, *Good luck,* then scrambled in and began to wriggle her way into the slippery darkness, the slime lodging under her fingernails. But it was a good green, Vida thought. Not of infection, but of life: everywhere tiny ecosystems battled the odds, their small cycles preserved.

She went on. There was hardly any space. *Like being born again,* Vida told herself, and thought of the stories Ruth had told her about her midwifery trials: the long nights of struggle and blood, the feeling that your body contained something larger than itself, and that the universe was working through you. *It's the ones who resist who tear the worst,* her mama always said. *You've just got to give yourself over and trust.*

Trust who? Vida always asked. *God?*

No, said Ruth. *Yourself. When the time comes, you'll know what to do.*

But, really, what else could she have said? Vida thought that you couldn't tell a woman in childbirth that she had no say in what was happening. *Best-case scenario: your insides are rearranged. Worst-case: you die. Whatever happens, your life will never be the same.* It sure motivated a person.

Vida wondered if childbirth made it easier to bear the sickness and the suffering later on. Your own, maybe. But not your children's. She felt kind of sorry for Bethie's father, but Mrs

Callahan must be a hundred times worse: a daughter and a grandbaby gone in one go.

Vida wedged her elbows against the concrete sides of the pipe and pushed with her feet, inching forward and upward, all the while trying to be quiet. The same movements, over and over, and no way to tell her progress. She could hear nothing behind her, and after minutes of climbing there was still no light, and no sign of any end. Vida felt the rising of panic. There'd be no way to climb out again backwards, and her wrists and elbows and toes were bruised, she could tell. There was no choice, and so she kept going, up and up, picturing a ladder going on into the clouds, holding fast to every imagined rung.

The smell of the pipe was changing – straw, maybe, something that reminded her of barnyards or stables. Vida's head knocked painfully against something solid: it crumbled a little against her fists when she hammered at it. Dried mud and grass, she hoped, the Weatherman's camouflaged lid.

She lifted an arm and punched against the plug, pictured Stringbeard's face.

Another blow and Vida broke through. Fingers of daylight tickled her face.

She worked one arm up and out, over the lip of the pipe. She pulled her body up until her other arm came free. Then she sat on the rim and raised her legs as quietly as she could. Some trees, but she saw no humans in the landscape, so Vida flopped backwards, panting. *One minute*, she told herself. *I deserve it.*

For a minute she lay beneath a dogwood next to the pipe, streaks of algae covering her clothes like mucus, and she stared up through the leaves at the sky. *How many times in my life have I done this?* Despite herself, Vida was comforted. The afternoon was quiet, the clouds high and the sun in its last quarter.

The light on her skin felt healing; the leaves she lay on were warming to her body. Crickets actually chirped, hidden away in the foliage. A chickadee darted from branch to branch searching for them, maddened with hunger and possibility.

I could just get up and walk home, she thought. *Take a wide berth around Fieldstone and be back with Ma sometime in the night.* Garrett and the old man and even Dyce would be a memory, a dreaming sidestep from the path of her real life.

But then her breath returned, and Vida stood up, her biceps and knees stiff with effort. *I'll keep that thought*, she told herself. *Keep it for when I really need it. I always have the option of quitting.*

She worked her way out of the trees and past the cottonwood stump. Cursing her own loyalty, she began the walk to the door, making her steps slow and heavy-footed, scuffing her feet in the dirt.

Garrett heard the shrill, tuneless whistle, faint and distant. Then a whisper from above them.

'He's coming, Pa.'

Garrett had left his gun upstairs, but he had two knives – one his own and the other he'd taken from the Weatherman's table, the sharpened arrow of a weather vane.

Garrett crept up the stairs and crouched down beneath the trapdoor, ready.

Today I'm the spider.

He lifted the lid a crack and then, hearing no movement, he opened it wide, letting the weak light into the room, thin as vapor. Still the Callahans didn't move, too focused on the door and the whistling to notice the lightening of the dead black around them. Garrett could see their outlines on either side of the door, the bison and the sapling. He glanced over to Dyce's corner and caught the glint of his eyes like a cat in a car's head-lights. He was awake.

Finally! My hard work toughening you up's paid off.

Garrett prayed his brother was sensible enough not to give the game away.

Dyce groaned, theatrical, as Garrett lifted himself from the hole in the floor. He kept on moaning from the gut, deep animal sounds that disguised the tap of his brother's boots on the wood, and disgusted the Callahans. Walden shushed him.

Gus shushed Walden.

Vida was close now. She'd finally found a tune: 'Jingle Bells'.

Garrett waited for the last moment, till the footsteps were right outside the door and he knew the hairs on the Callahans' necks would be bristling like hunting dogs'.

Garrett lunged at the bigger of the shadows. He sank the spoke of the weathervane into the man's neck and felt the warm spurt of blood on his hand. There was a gurgling scream, the sound of a man waking to find that his nightmare had come true, and then Walden was shouting, 'What's happening, Pa? Where are you?' To his credit, he started forward. Dyce was rolling around, panicked, struggling to hear where Garrett was placed.

Gus's body collapsed, the feet drumming like a hanged man's heels, and Garrett swiped at Walden with his fist, sure that the son would be too terrified to fire his piece. The punch met Walden's jaw and there was a crunch – teeth? Bone? – and Walden staggered backward. He had raised his gun in the dark, half-falling over Dyce as he went. The boy on the ground took a hold of Walden's leg and tried to hang on. Walden kicked him off and fired again, the gun kicking back against his hand even after all his years of practice.

Dyce, deafened, scrambled over to Garrett's bag, felt for the Webley, and held it up, the red blindness keeping him from finding a target in the stillness.

'Garrett?'

The shack was quiet.

Except for the gurgling.

A hand took hold of Dyce's bicep and then made its way, spider-like, all the way down his arm. It pulled the gun from his fingers.

'Garrett?' he asked again, hopeful.

He knew it wasn't his brother.

Walden turned the gun on Dyce in the dimness, saving his own bullets, and pulled the trigger.

The undersized bullet jammed in the chamber and exploded: it blew the top clean off the gun, and took all the fingers on Walden's right hand as it went. In the flash of the blast Dyce thought he saw a man through the veil of red: Garrett standing behind them with a knife. Walden shrieked, and kept shrieking, his calls for help, for his mama, for anyone to *please-Lord-Jesus-help-me!* a soprano against the roaring that was coming from Garrett. *Oh, Christ! He was hurt too!*

Dyce blacked out.

When Vida tried to open the shack door, it was lodged tight up against a body. In the low daylight seeping through she saw the thick, hairy arm, and the released blood.

She leant on the door and pushed. With one foot inside, she managed to roll the man away. Gus Callahan was still alive, one hand clamped down on his neck, keeping his ghost from escaping through the gash. She ignored him. Let the asshole suffer.

Beyond Gus was Walden, lying in the pooling blood, his gun hand and arm a mess of bone and toasted flesh. And the smell!

Bacon, Vida thought. *I'll never be able to eat it again.* She covered her nose and mouth and kept looking.

Garrett was on his knees, his shirt dark and wet, one hand cradling Dyce's face.

'Garrett,' she called, trying to make her voice soft, the way you would for a horse.

He toppled backwards off his heels and Vida rushed forward to catch him. He was drenched in blood. It took her a moment to realize that it wasn't Dyce's. *My God! My God! My God! Look at the hole in his chest!* Vida felt her brain wheeling for escape.

She grabbed Garrett under the arms and pulled him towards the door, over Walden and over Gus because it was easier not to go around. She laid him down in the dirt outside the shack, the horse pole at his head like a gravestone. There was no point.

She sat cross-legged and held his head in her lap. The scars from his old acne looked as if they had smoothed out a little. They must have bothered him back then. If he had lived till he was sixty, they might have disappeared altogether.

'Fuckers,' rasped Garrett. He bubbled as he tried to speak.

Vida laughed and shook her head. The tears fell on Garrett's face.

'How is everyone?'

'Dyce seems okay. As okay as he was before. And I saw the Weatherman's pruny butt cheeks running off into the trees.'

Garrett smiled.

'No one should have to see that.'

'Callahans are not in great shape, but you knew that. Big guy's bleeding out and the weedy one's stabbed to shit.'

'Then it all worked out okay.'

'Yeah.'

Garrett closed his eyes, and Vida shook his shoulder gently. The blood welled out of the hole again, unstoppable. Garrett moaned.

'Sorry, buddy. But you got to keep those baby blues open.'

His tongue came out, licked at the corner of his mouth. 'Tired.'

'Then I got something to show you. But you're gonna have to imagine the cigarette smoke, and some honky tonk.'

Vida stood up in the fading afternoon light in the bare dust outside the Weatherman's shack and began to undress, her eyes dark on the dying man.

She took off her filthy shirt first, then her boots and her socks and her jeans.

'Does this mean I'm not going to make it to the other side?'

'Shut up for once, Garrett. Don't ruin it.'

She stepped at last out of her underwear and stood naked before him.

There was not a scar or pockmark or welt upon her. Vida was whole and perfect, smooth as a clay vase.

Garrett strained to keep his eyes open, mesmerized and disbelieving, the revelation she'd saved up for the very end.

'You've never been sick!'

'Yup. This is what it looks like.'

15

Garrett fell silent. Vida stood still in the gathering dark, dumb with divulgement. She'd learnt not to tell her secret to anyone, to keep herself covered up, to act as though beneath her shirt and jeans she was just as twisted and scarred as the next. The secret of her health metastasized with each year that passed.

An unscarred five-year-old? *How lucky!*

Ten and no blemishes? *The Lord is watching this one.*

Disease-free at twenty? *She is a wonder and a sign.*

But thirty-four years old with not a mark? *Cut off her hair to make a potion. Boil her fingernail parings into a broth.* She is protected and she must pass it on.

Vida looked around for her discarded clothing. Maybe that was what had prevented her and Ruth from joining a settlement, she thought. Having to explain the inexplicable. Maybe it had worked out for the best. Vida had always had a hard time liking settlement folk: they came contagious with judgment and fear. Those things seemed to step arm-in-arm with the real bad sicknesses. *Spared both by being spared the one*, Vida told herself.

The sharing had felt right, for her and for Garrett both. The slipping away of your spirit had to be a terrifying thing, like the shock of birth, with its transition into the cold, dry world. He was gone.

Vida shivered, and not only with the evening air. The first stars were out, determined, prickly as pins. The foliage behind her kept rustling, and Vida made an effort to scramble back into her shirt, shiny with dirt and poor as it was. If she was going to be a coyote's dinner, it would have to undo her buttons. 'Opposable thumbs, motherfucker,' she said under her breath.

When the Weatherman stepped into the clearing, she was panting, on the last button. He looked at her, his scabbed head to one side. He held two books and nothing else.

'Go on. Say something,' Vida told him. 'I dare you.'

He pinched his fingers together and motioned to zip his lip. 'There ain't much high ground for a man wearing his birthday suit.' He regarded Garrett's half-closed lids and sighed. 'He gone?'

Vida nodded, and found her bottom lip trembling. *Don't you do it*, she told herself. *Dead is dead and at least he didn't suffer. Later. Later you can cry like a baby.*

She squinted down at her front and began re-buttoning where she'd mismatched the holes.

'You didn't stick around? What about the rest of your books?'

The Weatherman flapped an arm at her. 'Gunshots have a way of setting a man's priorities straight.'

He didn't seem cold, despite his nakedness. Now he walked over to Garrett and squatted beside him, his scrotum hanging low in the dirt.

Good thing he died midway through the nudie show, thought Vida.

'Ah, shit,' said the Weatherman. While he was offering his Western prayer, Vida looked back at the shack in the distance. No sign of any activity now, but part of her continued survival was never giving up the habit of watchfulness. Maybe women were more used to doing it.

As she checked the entrance to the building, the shadows in it shifted. Vida saw a figure leaning in the doorway: a golem, one meaty hand to the neck where she knew he'd been stabbed.

'Fuck!'

The Weatherman stopped his rumination and turned around. 'Gus?'

Gus staggered out into the grass.

He must be bleeding badly to move as slow as he was, Vida thought.

Should she go back into the shack and find one of the discarded guns? She could shoot Gus in the back without a flicker: no fair's-fair, high-noon showdown here. It would even up Garrett's sacrifice, bring the final tally to a neat and favorable score: two–one to the survivors.

The Weatherman moved to help him, but long before he reached the man, Gus's free arm shooed him away like a cobweb. The two watched him warily. They could save him the torment, lay him down beside his useless son. Big Gus was a suffering animal, a buffalo wheezing through a torn throat, hobbling out into the night to find some place to die.

The Weatherman tried again to take Gus's arm, but he would accept no help. The back of his open hand caught the old guy and knocked him down. He stayed there in his defeat, panting. He and Vida watched Gus Callahan walk to meet the approaching dark.

'Vida?'

'What?'

He pointed at Vida, at the body of Garrett, as if it had just dawned on him. 'You never said it was Callahans.'

'Was that important?'

The Weatherman pounded the ground where he lay, like a little kid in a tantrum. '*Goddamnit, woman! You never said it was Callahans!*' The shouting was the sudden eruption of an afternoon's worth of attack and surprise, of escaping with his life.

Vida pursed her lips. 'Didn't know it'd make a difference.'

The Weatherman scrambled to his feet, as though he'd been stung by a scorpion.

'*It makes a difference.*'

He began jogging back to the shack, and got inside and down the steps to his laboratory. Vida expected him to slam the door on her, but she followed. She went through the doorway as the Weatherman returned with his lantern. They looked around.

'Jesus.'

Walden was a mess of gashes. He'd been run through a dozen times in the chest, and four or five times right in the face. Dyce lay beside him, his pants leg soaked through with blood, solid as a crayon. Vida came closer. Dyce's chest was rising and falling, hitching shallow breaths, like a dog under anesthetic.

'Oh, God. He's been lying here the whole time.' *It was a kind of baptism*, Vida thought. All that blood. She would never get used to it. And if Walden was carrying some sickness, they were all fucked.

The old man tightened his lips. 'Move him, then.'

Vida took Dyce's feet and the Weatherman grabbed him under the arms. 'To the mat there. Let's go.' They tugged, panting. The Weatherman was grunting with effort. For a sick boy, Dyce was sure heavy.

'You know, I'm no fan of the marshals. But it don't make them any less family.'

Vida dropped Dyce's feet. His boots thunked unhappily on the floorboards.

'*You're a Callahan?*'

The old man stood up with his hands on his hips. *Dear God! When would he get some clothes on?*

'By birth and by name.'

'Shit.'

'Come on now. Pick this boy up and finish the job.'

They wrestled Dyce's limp body onto the dusty carpet, away from the blood, and Vida listened again for his breath, careful not to inhale.

'So now what?'

'Now there's going to be more of them coming. They're going to want, want, *payment* for these lives. And I'm going to tell them word for word what happened here: I got no reason to protect you and this kid. But for the sake of keeping everyone's blood in their veins, I'm not going to tell them what I'm going to tell you now.

'You listening? Walk off now, into the dark. And when I can't see you no more, change course and go some other way, 'cause I'm going to sing like Tweety Bird.'

'But what about Dyce?'

'Take the kid if you think he's going to make it. No sense burdening yourself with another corpse. We seen enough of that today. Just put some distance between yourselves and this place, and pray that rain falls to cover your tracks and the night-time critters don't get a scent on you.'

'Thanks,' muttered Vida. 'You're a real fairy godmother.'

She grabbed her pack along with both the boys'. She got busy laying out their contents on the table. She'd only be able to take one bag: she had to cull.

Garrett had had nothing of real value, save for the needles and the dried turkey meat. At the bottom of his pack there was a stuffed squirrel, the tufts on its ears like aerials in the lantern's light. She turned it over. It was beautiful in its craftsmanship, the stitching invisible, sewed to look alive. The squirrel didn't smell none, so Vida packed it. Something for Dyce to keep.

He moaned. Vida went to him and tipped some water from her canteen into his mouth. He choked and she sat him up like a baby, patting his chest clear.

'How are you feeling, little brother?'

Dyce groaned, the sound deep and rising from his guts, up through the chest, over his swollen tongue – leaking out into the air like the cough of a sweet potato left too long on coals.

'Got to keep going. Callahans still coming. More of them than there are of us.'

Vida stood up. She reached down and pulled Dyce to his feet. He hung limp, and then he managed to stand on his own two feet, gingerly, as if he had pins and needles.

'If it gets too bad, I can try and carry you. Fireman's lift.' Vida grinned, and then remembered that he couldn't see her.

He leant on her and they went out slowly into the night.

Behind them the Weatherman followed, keeping to the bushes around his shack, then to the kindly almond trees in the stand. The leaves rustled in the shadows. When he saw that they were okay, he stopped, and then watched them disappear from sight.

Vida looked back as they went. When she judged that the light of the shack was distant enough, she changed their course.

'Come on, big guy. We're heading for the last place they'll expect.'

16

Felix pulled Garrett's body inside. Then he closed the shack door and pushed the table, sliding its legs through the pooling blood until it was shoved under the door handle. He tried not to look at the blood. It made him dizzy. He saw Rorschach pictures – horses galloping through water; spirits caught and twisting in the branches of a cottonwood. The table wouldn't stop intruders – stall them at best – but the barricade made him feel as if he was doing something useful.

He said, 'Sorry, boys,' and stepped carefully over the stiffening bodies of Garrett and Walden. Then he opened the lid of the trapdoor that had slammed shut in the scuffle, and climbed back down into the darkness. He'd move the bodies in the morning light. Right now he was twitchy as a gopher. Felix stood at the bottom of the ladder and put his hand over his heart. Still pounding. There'd be no point in lying down to sleep. The battery had died and he had to fumble in the blackness for the bottle of booze – it was around here somewhere – and oh, the burn and blessing of the liquor as it seared a new pathway down his gullet!

But he needed a little light on the outside too. That battery was always dead when he needed it. '*Fuck* Renard,' he muttered. 'Fuck him for the goddamn 'lectricity, too.' Felix heaved himself onto the split foam of the bike's saddle and started to pedal slowly. It was always hard-going at first. You had to limber up. But it was getting more difficult. He didn't know how many more revolutions his knees could take. 'Spent my whole life on them,' he said out loud, and took another short one from the bottle. He coughed, but the light was growing as he pedaled, like he was the god of the dawn or something, the wheels of his chariot dragging the morning across the sky. Felix laughed at himself, and slapped at his bony yellow chest with his free hand.

The light also brought clarity. Now he could see blood leaking through the floorboards and plinking onto the second last step of his staircase. He'd stood in it on his way down and had padded smears of red around the room: the dotted line on a pirate's treasure map. 'I,' Felix told the stains, 'have run out of fucks to give.' He would deal with the whole catastrophe tomorrow. Right now he needed a lullaby.

He climbed off the machine and dressed. His clothes were dry enough: Some days he didn't mind the damp in the material. It was the odor of tiny, living things: company. When he was fully clothed he sat at the table and sipped from the bottle, went at it real purposeful this time until the battery ran flat again and the light went out.

But it was too creepy to sit there in the dark with the dead all around him. Spooked, he clambered back on the saddle and spun the bike wheel as fast as he could. The bulb brightened until the little room was light as day, and then he lost his nerve. What if the filament burnt out? Then he'd be fucked. He thought back to when he was a little kid – two or three, maybe, when he still liked to be held and cosseted, before the menfolk got hold of him – and how his mama would rock him and talk to him, the meaning of her words nowhere near as important as the hum of her chest against his ear. He wanted it back. He wanted it all back. But the closest he could manage was the tape and the machine and his own sagging voice. When he judged it safe again, he sat once more at the table, leant back in his chair and flipped the tape over. Felix listened to side B of the recording, this time without the gun to hand, while his heart found its old familiar rhythm.

'That first virus at the frontline wasn't engineered for longevity. That came later, when Renard woke up to the fact that he could tailor the sicknesses any way he liked. And he liked them to cause the most harm they could, to make us suffer, as it turned out. They kept on giving, like a scorched-earth policy. Yessir, he had a taste for revenge. But that first one was an experiment. It affected the frontline and some miles beyond, and then kind of dissipated in a pretty clear line of dead Southern soldiers. Confined as it was, that virus still turned the South into a land of women and children.

'I don't recall where I stopped the Jeep or how that day ended, but when I woke I was lying in a patch of vomited army rations, and I cursed myself for the waste that was, but the fever I'd come down with had broken. In the days after that I rejoined the soldiers in a nowhere town. What *was* its name, now? Hoxie? But then they were all nowhere towns after Renard had his way with them.

'But I found both my brothers in that small group of survivors. That was real funny, wasn't it? Then it dawned on us that it might not be coincidence. We found that about half of the men who survived shared our surname – cousins of cousins' children, connections that ran back some way. The rest had Callahan blood in their heritage if we looked close enough, and those that didn't couldn't say for sure where they'd came from, and we figured that meant the same thing. Things happen, and those things ain't always legal.

'The North knew better than to try to claim all the land from Arizona to North Carolina. It was the Wild West out there, still full of Non-Union types who had lost The War but not their resolve. The smug Northern soldiers who camped in our towns brought word of concession talks. They wanted a delegation that would represent each Southern state. The group that they put together over the next months was ridiculous: weak-minded, ceremonial men who'd hidden away instead of defending their homes – cowards who were willing to concede anything you asked. I am proud to say that it was my idea to send a task force along with the delegation. To ensure their safety, don't you know? Somehow it was granted.

'They chose Des Moines for its centrality. Ten of us were loaded into a bouncy little cargo plane. What do you call that? A quorum? Ten-strong: enough to feel like we had some authority, enough to make a difference.

'The town looked like hell when we got there, all weeds and blistered paint. In the war years it had about fallen to pieces and I saw how much stronger the South had been, back before the virus came. Even poxy little Hoxie had not been left to ruin: the women and children had got to painting and sweeping while the men were away. If it had been a battle to the end, our women and children would've come out swinging. We did not give up.

'The ten of us in the escort group were housed near the State Capitol building. We spent our days watching the proceedings under the golden dome. We were presented with a one-way, non-negotiable set of demands – and even if we'd had stronger men representing us, there'd have been nothing they could do against the threat of more viruses. Stop me if you've heard this before, and I'll tell you that at least when Abe Lincoln did it, there was a kind, fair man in charge of proceedings. With Renard we didn't stand a chance. We figured he wasn't the head of the beast, but he was the brains of it, for sure. At night we kept plotting what we'd come along to accomplish in the first place – the assassination of Renard. With him gone we might have had a shot at going back to war. If that happened, we might have a chance of winning after all, fair and square. A do-over. Wouldn't that have been fine?

'Don't get me wrong. It wasn't a spur-of-the-moment thing. From his time as a saboteur my brother Levi had learnt how to wire a bomb. Getting the pieces for one would be easier than getting our hands on a gun. We began to document Renard's routine by the minute, planning when and where to plant it to get the most advantage out of the explosion. By the time the surveillance was done, we knew when Renard needed a shit even before he did.

'It was round about here that we first started saying FUCK RENARD. Started as a joke, kind of, and then got gravity and stuck around. A slogan, you call it. "Eff Ar", guys would say to one another, and crack up. But it was really an affirmation of our resolve. Man, we meant to plug him good! Atomize the fucker. A taste of his medicine, and see how he liked *them* poisoned apples. And the one who said it most was this dude named McKenzie, as we sat in the kitchen and drank hot sugared water because we had been so pleased to see coffee that it hadn't lasted the weekend. Bit of a weirdo, but then The War did that to some people. Brought out the worst in them, magnified it, and gave it somewhere to play so that it could do the most damage. Anyway, McKenzie liked birds. Always going on about how in the olden days, if you were fancy-ass, you had a hawk for hunting. All kinds of different birds, actually, depending on your rank. Wanted us to call him Hawk-Eye. Heh, heh. It never took. You got to earn your nickname, else it doesn't stick.

'The bomb took longer to make than we hoped. We had to make it good, because we only had one try. Each ingredient had to be requested from the Northerners who were our wardens. This week, a can of deodorant. A bottle of Coke. Hair gel. Two weeks later, a toaster. Next month, an extension cable for the tricky toaster.

'We all met in our kitchen the night it was done, our ten-man resistance – and we laid out the plan on the table, the bomb sitting there in the middle like a Christmas pudding. It was not an elegant thing, but it was small and that was all that mattered. McKenzie had volunteered to position the bomb in the cistern of the toilet that only Renard used. The trigger would be linked to the flush handle. Levi talked him through the procedure of installing it, over and over until we were all sick of hearing about ball-floats and stopcocks. We nearly crapped in our pants because right then one of the wardens came in, said Renard's wife had heard we were out of coffee and so here was some more. We sure did appreciate that. She seemed like a nice lady. The warden didn't say nothing about the plan on the table. We were all sitting forward with our elbows jammed over it.

'On the day of the blast we did the same stuff we usually did, so that we didn't raise suspicion. As soon as we heard the explosion, we'd need to get the hell out of there. Our official diplomats had not been let in on the plan. We were sure that they'd be killed for it, and that was the way it had to be. Sacrifices had to be made. War was war. Many more would die in the service of their states.

'We were expecting the explosion at 11 a.m., or just after – we'd all wandered close to exits, ready to run. But time just ticked on. At 11:32 a.m. I went down a spindly white staircase to the first floor, but the hallways were empty. I checked the bathroom where McKenzie was supposed to set the bomb. It wasn't in the cistern. We'd surely been found out. *Fuck*.

'And then the bang came – from next door. The ladies'. The shock of it threw me to the floor. I was covered in grout dust and shards of white tile and, man, those things can slice you like a guillotine. I had the sense to get up and run. The wall that separated the two bathrooms had a hole blown in it, like a cartoon safe, and there were suddenly sirens everywhere, and I heard the security men coming. What a fuck-up.

'It was only later, when I was alone and on the run, that I heard that Renard's wife had been the one killed. I was in a diner, trying to get a last good steak-and-fries dinner down me before I had to go back to the other side. I banged on the table with my fists and swore so loud that the waitress came by and asked to leave. I did, and I went without paying, too – which was a good thing since I had no money. Killing Renard was one thing, but taking out an innocent like his wife was something else. We had given him a reason to persecute us. The concession talks were ruined. It was the end of the South and all it stood for: freedom and independence. I remember praying for the Rapture out there on the pavement in front of Hank's or Frank's or whatever it was called, but the good Lord was looking the other way.

'I did not know for sure what happened to Gabe and Levi, but I had to assume they were dead. I assumed the whole quorum had been wiped out. So much for our brief. But there was some good news too, in amongst the bad – a glimmer, anyway. The

North had no way to track me. I hitchhiked west, hoping to cross back over the border into Kansas and work my way back to Norman. Check up on my folks, gather myself and decide what to do next.

'I kept going west, trusting my own shitty sense of direction and distance, trying to factor in the speeds of trucks I'd slept on so's I could tell how many more days to keep going. I never felt I was far enough. Maybe it had something to do with being on the run, the feeling that someone was going to catch up with me, but by the time I turned south I'd overshot Kansas by about eight hundred miles. I found myself in Colorado without the energy or the inclination to fix my mistake. I hunkered down and waited for Renard to retaliate.

'And, boy, did he ever! It came real swift. First they rebuilt The Wall so that it was truly impenetrable, like a fortress in a fairytale. The North wanted it to last for ever. I knew what it was costing them to construct it. And while that was going up, the new viruses started coming.

'But these ones floated. They rode the wind like those seed-pods that need travel to pollinate. The sicknesses came right the way across the Southern states. And people were caught short, the same way they must have been in 1918 when the Spanish 'flu took them out. Now it wasn't just the soldiers in the frontline: Americans everywhere in the South died by the millions. In a couple of days the land stank with the rotting, as if something had changed at its deepest level, like the Devil had been uncovered and was working his way up from hell.

'I started tracking the weather then, writing notes in my journal, trying to stay one step ahead. And that's also when McKenzie found me. Don't ask me how. Against my judgment, I took him in. Veterans got to stick together, right? He seemed like a changed man. Contrite. Said he'd fucked up majorly, said he needed to put it right. I bought it. He'd been collecting front-line survivors – Callahans, mostly – and been putting together some kind of law enforcement, so the South could restore order, how he put it. What he proposed made sense: it was a troubled time. All the usual supports had fallen away, and people were turning on each other. And I don't just mean the usual – looting, rape and pillage, and all that happy crappy. I mean *cannibalism* in some places, ordinary folks getting *murdered* for what they had. And not just killed – tortured before they died. It was a bad time, and I got roped in. I am ashamed to say it.

'McKenzie took it into his head that he would be leader of the fiercesome Callahans. He actually dropped his surname and took ours. Tye McKenzie became Tye Callahan. My mistake was to trust him again, to think that by changing his name and putting on a sad face, he'd changed. He hadn't. He fucking hadn't. He was still Wrong Toilet McKenzie.'

Felix let the tape run on, into the sound of his old self fumbling for the stop button and then the hiss of blank tape turning. He got up from the table and stepped cautiously on the sticky floor to his bed. He lay on his bottom sheet and stared up at the wood boards above. He thought, as he often did, how different the world would be if old Hawk-Eye McKenzie had found the right toilet.

17

The Callahans were hungry. They'd left Glenvale fuelled by anger and inspired by the old clan leader's call to arms, but those emotions had ebbed as the night grew darker and colder. They were hardly prepared for a long journey, and some had turned back when they saw the sun setting with no sign of Garrett. 'Better to go on home and fetch supplies than to freeze to death out here,' they'd told each other. Tye had watched them go, his harrier perched on his forearm. He had said nothing, but marked each traitor man. He would deal with them later.

The remaining Callahans, foolhardy or determined, had chosen to camp below the ridge for its shelter. There the trees were thick around them, big junipers ringing the outside, tight-knit shrubs and weeds closer in against the wind. They lay curled around the campfires, five or six men to each, turning now and again like sausages on a rotisserie, sizzling with discomfort and resentment. At first the flames had seemed to give them courage, and they had only ridiculed the deserters, calling them cowards and wet blankets.

But now, lying in the gathering dark, spooning with the coals, then turning and thawing out their backs and buttocks while their noses and cheeks and knees turned rictus-stiff, they imagined those who'd returned and wished they could trade places.

Tye let them talk, listening to the bitterness. He knew that it served no purpose unless a man could harness that ill-feeling. Like tonguing a mouth blister, the warrior Callahans imagined the others back in the softer life of Glenvale – hot water for a bath, and a plate of dried catfish stew, saved for a special occasion. And then balm for the soul, too, just as important: a warm wife and a cup of poor-man's bourbon. Tye kept one eye on each man and boy as he mentally placed them in the family hierarchy. *Orientation*, he told himself. *Got to see which way the land lies.*

Night was the worst time to be out in the open, but they had no choice. Pet dogs had turned their backs on domesticity years ago, ever since food became scarce. Now they roamed like wolves, scarred and skinny and scared of nothing, hunting in desperate packs to bring down rabbits and deer and bigger animals too. The men were used to the occasional howls; wolves or dogs, it didn't matter anymore. Bears and mountain lions also came out, along with snakes and owls and coyotes – the inedible carnivores. Most of them were healthy enough on the outside: the viruses didn't seem to be cutting down the animal population none, the way they did with the humans. But every now and again you came across a creature infected by an illness that made it fearless or fierce or just plain contagious. There were stories of starving men who had trapped a wolf or a lion and then found its flesh infected by another fevered critter it had swallowed down. The effects didn't show on most meat-eaters, but the well was poisoned, sure enough. Like dying of thirst on a raft in the middle of an ocean. Payback, Tye guessed, for all that other business back in the day. Ebola. HIV. Bird fucking flu. He stroked the harrier's head and she rested against him, her body slight beneath her feathers.

Kurt, one of Bethie's towheaded little cousins, came up now from his place at the cooking fire. He held up a bowl to Tye, who laughed. The boy had managed to snare a jackrabbit as well as a tortoise somewhere along the way. He must have seared them on the coals and distributed their meat to some of the older Callahans, because they were chewing, and the grumbling had died down. Tye saw that Kurt was using the tortoise's upturned shell as the bowl. A pair of charred, gristly ears poked up out of it.

Slow and steady don't win the race no more. But neither does fast and nimble.

Tye nodded at the boy and took some of the meat for himself. Then he chose a femur for his bird. She snatched it and began crunching it in her beak. For a moment the others were silent, reminded of her wildness. The harrier ignored the men, cracking the bone clean through to get at the marrow, her tongue the gray-pink of an alien.

The howls came again, and the men reached automatically for the weapons that lay always close to hand. So it was that Gus Callahan had sixteen rifles aimed at him as he stumbled out of the dark toward the fires. One red hand was clamped to his neck and he was croaking as he breathed, gargling like a clogged cistern.

'Lower those goddamn guns. It's Gus,' said Tye in disgust.

One by one the rifle barrels dropped. The others sank back with the relief that it was a man, not a rabid cougar, or worse – a ghost maybe, from one of the colonies where the sick gathered to rot and die.

Gus was staggering closer, crazy for companionship. He couldn't walk straight.

'Let him down. He's hurt.'

The Callahans all got a good, long look at his face in the firelight. A metal spike was poking out between his fingers at his neck, like an Indian arrow or Halloween mask. But it was no act. Gus's shirt was black with blood; against it he was pale as a ghost, his essentials leaking from him out onto the ground, as if they were determined to find a river and make their way down to the sea.

'Christ! What happened to you?'

Tye shouldered the men into action. 'You. Get some blankets. You and you. Start boiling some water here.'

The men began gathering blankets in their arms and looking around for their billy-cans. Tye saw the cousin boy's stiff face and hardened his heart. They had to learn.

'I want him on hot rocks in five minutes, and when I say I want warm water, I mean boiling. Hot enough to skin him if we need to.' He jabbed his knife at the boy. 'Sharpen this and hold it in the flame 'til I tell you I need it. You. Go get my bag and look for yarrow leaves. And a bandage. And a needle and thread. And if there is anyone here saving his moonshine for a better occasion, he'd better think again.'

Gus's arrival was a disaster but also a distraction. Soon the whole camp was up and digging holes, collecting rocks, passing Tye what he needed to patch up the big man. Finally, they were doing something together.

Tye talked as they worked to lay the hot stones in a shallow trench. He made the Callahans cover them over with sand and a blanket, and Gus was helped down onto it.

'Like a Dutch oven, boys. That's right.'

He knelt to get a better look at Gus's neck in the light of the fire. The ragged flesh around the arrow was purple.

'What the fuck *is* that, anyway?'

Gus held up a flat hand and gurgled. He strained to sit up and the blood from his ruined mouth dribbled over his lips.

'Give him some water.'

Gus shook his head and gestured for Tye to come closer, to lean in and listen. Through the mess of his throat came a word, wet with vengeance and thin as cotton.

'Weatherman.'

'What the hell? Where's Walden, Gus? Where's your boy got to?'

He licked his cracked lips, a man in a desert, crawling towards some distant mirage.

'Dead.' A single tear popped out from below Gus's eyelid and plinked out, like a boy in a cartoon. Somehow that one teardrop was worse than anything else. Tye wiped its traces away. No tears on a Callahan. It was too late for that.

'Was it Garrett?'

Gus tried to sit up, and fell back against Tye instead.

'He's dead, too.'

There were whoops from some of the surrounding men.

'Shut the fuck up.'

Gus was still straining to get his message across.

'Got to get them for me.'

'Who, Gus?'

'The fucking brother. And the girl.'

Gus slumped backward, unconscious. Tye took his chance and grabbed the metal shaft. He yanked it out and it gave, slurping against the wound. Gus jerked but didn't come round. Tye gave the weathervane arrow to one of the men, who looked at it in his hands and then set it carefully down like an instrument. He wiped his hands on his jeans.

'Everything! Now!'

The men looked at each other, but again the boy cousin came forward and handed Tye his knife. Its nicked blade gleamed red from its purification in the flames.

'I said everything!'

Then Tye worked fast: slitting the sides of the wound and squeezing out all he could so that the blood eventually ran bright and thin. The flesh sizzled and burnt as the nerves and the vessels were sealed by the blade.

'As long as it's mostly cauterized.' Tye was talking to himself. The others looked on, useless, apart from the little cousin who knelt like a pageboy at the throne of a pharaoh.

Tye sluiced out the wound with boiling water. He didn't look at Gus's face. It didn't matter if he came round: Tye wouldn't stop his surgery. The others would just have to hold him down.

Gus stayed under in the merciful black.

Fifteen minutes later, Tye was sewing the wound closed.

He sat back on his heels and waited, but there was no fresh blood seeping from the stitches. Then he pressed the yarrow leaves against the gash and bandaged it tight.

'Got to keep him warm. If he's not dead by morning, he'll make it.'

Tye turned to where the others had dropped the arrow. He picked it up and inspected it, turning it over in the firelight, rust on rust.

Only one man still had use for things like this.

'Felix.'

18

Vida didn't exactly know where the ghost colony was. From what she'd gathered from the Weatherman's wall maps, it was somewhere north-west, not too far. It was shown as a shaded area ringed with crosses and filled in with those penciled lumps. *Not treasure troves*, she thought. *Graves.*

There was some climbing to do, a narrow river to cross – but that was okay. They had been through worse. It was the last place the Callahans would reckon she was headed, and once she got past that invisible line of crosses and moved into the land of the lazaretto, the Callahans would give up the chase.

Wouldn't they?

No sane person went to a ghost colony, unless they were sick. Or were looking to get sick.

But outrunning the Callahans was only the second reason she'd paid such close attention to the Weatherman's maps. A bonus.

She would find the nearest ghost colony, a petri dish of viruses collected off every wind in the last few months, and she would try to find a compatible virus for her ma. And for Dyce too, of course, because that was her fault. She would carry him to safety if it killed her. Even empty of liquids and solids, he weighed more than that big old zinc tub of water she'd had to drag back to the house once a week. She would suffer to do it, and that was payback.

That's just crazy, some part of her said, and Vida wondered whether Stringbeard's infection had had its effect. *I would know, wouldn't I? I'd be able to feel it in my bones.* It was a ludicrous plan, she knew, but it was all she had right now.

And they had to get a move on. Her eyes grew accustomed to the starlight and the rising quarter-moon shrunk and reflected everywhere. That poem her ma had loved, like it was some vision of heaven: *Silver fruit upon silver trees.* Vida had never liked it, the idea of bleaching out the daylight colors from everything important. Macabre. Black folks ought to know better. Anyway, nowadays she looked at the moon to see if there was a ring around it. The halo meant bad weather, and that was that. She snorted at herself. *Keep walking, Veedles. Got things to do and people to see.*

When the moon had shifted, Vida began to make out the terrain around her. She could navigate around a boulder or a bush instead of crashing into it as she had been doing – choose a new course, like a stream running down a slope, guided by gravity.

But with her night vision came another distraction. There were shadows all around her that seemed to move as she did, mimicking their pilgrimage. It took all of her will to keep her head down, to blind her eyes to her creaturely imagination, to keep her hands holding onto Dyce, rather than letting go in favor of the flint in her bag.

Once she was out of sight of the shack, she laid Dyce down in the dirt and felt his forehead. Still hot. He looked at her dully. Moving him had been a bad decision. Vida undid his belt, unbuttoned his cargo pants and worked them off over his welted legs. The material was wet through with urine and Walden's blood, and streaked white with the contour lines of dried salt around the hems. Vida placed the pants on his chest and threaded the legs under his arms.

She propped him up, the two of them back to back. She reached round for the cloth handles, which she pulled over her shoulders. It made it easier to carry him, but it would be slow progress, she knew. Alrighty, then. This would be another part of her penance.

Vida crouched forward and pulled tight on the pants to keep Dyce snug against her back. Then she straightened up as best she could and moved into the darkness. Vida walked and thought of her stepdad's baseball mantra as he whistled the old tennis ball past her nose, out on the grass.

Attack the ball, Evert kept telling her.

Vida had never really grasped his meaning – or the ball. She had always shied away from the thing as if it were an enormous, angry bee. It wasn't until later – after Evert had died and she and Ruth were alone again, heading south and having to defend themselves from swindlers and bandits and the crazy ones with brain worms – that she finally understood.

There was no more baseball.

There was only survival.

What Evert had tried to teach her was this: when something's trying to knock you on your ass, sitting on your heels is a big old welcome sign. Go meet a threat if you want to survive it. Shake its hand. Look it in the eye.

Vida liked to think that that's what she'd been doing ever since: honoring him, the kind, ineffectual man who'd stepped in and made a daughter out of her. That's what she was doing now with this sick kid on her back, wading through the dark, thick as water, as blind as him or her ma, each step also a drag and a heave. But it was progress. Sometimes that was the best you could do.

The narrow river she'd seen on the map appeared to her first as a distant, wet hum. It grew louder until she felt the smooth, round stones of the bank underfoot, making her ankles roll. She did not hesitate at its edge: there was nothing to gain from waiting or looking for a more suitable crossing.

Though the winter ice had melted, the water took longer to accept the new season. The cold made her suck the air in through her teeth with every step, the water rising from her shins, to her knees, then her hips. She felt Dyce start awake at its touch, his breath puffing out, a drowned sailor startling at the siren who had taken him below.

'Easy, Allerdyce,' Vida said, just as she'd done for Garrett. 'Stay with me back there. Better give your brother some time alone with his woman. Might not want to see what he and Beth are doing outside them pearly gates.'

Dyce fell still and Vida felt something warm run down the small of her back, scorching hot in contrast to the bloodless chill of the river. She was instantly glad they were in the water, both for his pride and for her chances of getting his disease. Vida waited for the smell, but it didn't come. She kept wading, her thighs pushing through the water like blades. Times like these she felt superhuman.

The opposite riverbank was also stony, and beyond that, the land began to climb. Vida pressed on, her legs burning with each sloping step. The stars above faded behind the silhouettes of trees; she smelt the fresh acid of pine. Underfoot the needles were soft and slippery. Sometimes she slid backwards, dropping Dyce so that he rolled gently up against the trunk of a tree and she had to re-truss him and step more carefully. There was a forest soundtrack now too – howls and growls and scuttling. The trees made tall dancing shadows, every one of them a black bear raised up on his hind legs, or a mountain lion mid-lunge.

Vida had been caught out in the dark a few times in her life, misjudging the time it would take to get home, or misremembering where a shelter had been – but those times she'd only been out an hour after sundown, long before the night hunters began prowling. The deep night was something else: soon it would mount to a carnival of screeching and scratching.

Once there was a soft padding beside her, something large and stealthy walking along in step with her. The end, when it came, would contain no time for her to make sparks from her flint. Not being able to see was the worst part. At least if you saw your end-time coming, you had a chance to prepare yourself. How bad had it been for Dyce, who could still not see three feet before him? Little brother Allerdyce, who didn't know yet that Garrett was dead?

When her fears overcame her, Vida lowered Dyce to the ground. She felt around for a stick and, just as her stepdad had taught her, she swung the bat in the dark. It connected with a pine trunk and the brittle wood of her bat shattered. Rotten shards rained on her. She gathered Dyce again and pulled him on, the haunting gone, or more distant than before.

Vida limped on, and prayed for morning light.

When it did come, she sat exhausted, too tired to arrange Dyce more comfortably where he lay and slept off his sickness, and she saw she was not twenty paces from the crest of the climb. *There are times when we are closer than we think*, she told herself. *Halle-fucking-lujah*. Above her, along the ridge, was the tall pole – a pants-leg windsock hanging limp. Vida let herself cry then.

She wiped her face and scanned the hill below her in the growing dawn. She'd come a long way. The dam wall was a speck of black, the river a trickle. That was where the Callahans would come from, when they did. She looked in her bag for the dried turkey meat, not caring that it was stringy and old: it was a change from the bitter crunch of locusts.

As she chewed, she examined the pole again. There were no instruments attached to this one. The last outpost. The ghost colony could not be far now – just beyond the ring of the old man's weather stations. She gave herself over to lying in the warmth for a few precious minutes. The first rays of sun seemed to stroke her skin, maternal.

Vida leant over and inspected Dyce's face. His skin was gray. She had not been vigilant in checking him in the night. He could have died. She might well have dragged a corpse over a mountain.

Vida steeled herself and felt his cheek. It was warm. She held his head and tried to get him to drink some water again, but this time it dribbled out of his mouth and into the dirt. She kept watch over Dyce with one eye as the forest through which she'd battled transformed in stages from cool shadow to the vivid, hot green of anxious life.

Vida sat up again and focused on the dam below. *Come on, you fuckers. I'm waiting for you.*

And there, like ants, she saw them coming, a swarm descending on the Weatherman's shack.

Better get going, Veedles. Them Callahans never been dawdlers.

She stood to gather her burdens and looked hard at the marks behind her in the dirt.

She could not tell what they were, at first. She stepped past Dyce and loped down a few paces, close to the ground. There they were: the prints of her own leather-soled boots, and behind them the two parallel gouges of Dyce's heels like train tracks.

But alongside and sometimes crossing over were another set.

Not bear or lion or coyote or dog.

Barefoot and human.

Terror energized her.

She sprinted for Dyce and lifted him again onto her back, half-slapping, half-dragging.

'Wake up! Wake up! *Wake up!*'

19

Tye Callahan woke before sunrise. He pulled his arm from beneath his blanket and reached for his harrier. She arched her neck at the interruption, but was where he had expected her to be – perched above him on the log.

He removed her leather cap, and she flew up into the pre-dawn dark towards the dimming stars. He watched her go as he always did. Up there she would feel the air thinning, stop flapping and spread her wings to circle in a wide arc, the Callahan camp with its ember markers the axle on which she turned. Then she would spiral outward, testing her feathers for changes in pressure, for any distant and gathering wind.

With no sign of it, she folded her wings and plummeted back to Tye for her reward. Today it was a quarter of dried perch spine and a paper-thin dorsal fin, edged with transparent flesh. She ripped into her breakfast, harness jingling, as Tye woke his men.

'Ten minutes and we're moving,' he called into the black.

He went to check on Gus. The huge man was still breathing: shallow, though. Looking at him, Tye doubted his own prophecy about his being well if he survived the night. Gus needed to drink and to eat, and who knew how much sustenance he'd manage to slip past that gash before infection settled in?

Tye picked out the two men most eager to return to Glenvale, those who had grumbled most about spending the night in the open, and tasked them with stretchering Gus back.

'You wanted to turn back. Now's your chance,' he said. Initially he'd imagined a stiffer punishment, but carrying Gus back would do just fine. It wouldn't be easy considering the terrain they'd covered. To round it off, Tye added another motivation.

'If he's dead before he reaches Glenvale . . .' He trailed off, letting the thought hang. The two gaunt Callahan faces had been staring at him, and now they dropped. There was every chance Gus would die anyway: he didn't look as if he'd hang onto his ghost till sundown.

Tye grinned. 'Now take off your shirts.'

'Hey, now. What do you want them for?'

'You boys got to make a stretcher, don't you?'

They scurried. The two men began searching the nearby foliage for long poles for the litter, harrying each other to work faster. They stripped a couple of saplings, and then Tye made them thread the poles through the sleeves of both shirts. The two looked at their work in dismay, not daring to object for fear of being made to stay when their freedom was so close at hand. The shirts would have to be sacrificed. They thought, but did not say, that if the big man really did get too heavy, they could resign themselves to Tye's punishment – dump Gus in the woods and skedaddle. The coyotes would finish the job. The critters would think it was Christmas come early.

They heaved Gus onto the stretcher, and he stayed on, like Tutankhamen heaved upright in his sarcophagus by treasure hunters. And then off they went, the two stretcher-bearers at the head, each hauling at one pole, the end of the travois scraping in the dirt as it went. They would leave a trail a mile wide, but who was checking? Tye watched them go and thought that they made such terrible woodsmen that they deserved to die. But they probably wouldn't – not unless stupidity was contagious.

He rolled his blanket and tied it tight at the top of his pack. The others were industrious, strapping the char-bottomed billy-cans onto packs, kicking dirt over the dying coals, rolling and folding and stretching, a chorus of spines clicking and joints popping. *White men on the move*, thought Tye in disgust. You could tell it over in the next county. Shee-yit. Renard could probably hear it wherever he was, holed up in his compound over the border.

☠

They reached the Weatherman's shack just after dawn, damp in a haze around the nut tree glade that clung to the earth and rose waist-high, the kind you saw in olden-day cemeteries. It was like wading through watered-down milk.

Felix Callahan had been busy. After he had seen Vida off, he had dragged Garrett's body back inside the shack until he had the energy to decide what to do with him – and Walden too. There was no point in giving the dead boy up to the night dogs. They'd be back the next night and the next if he did, the long, low moans of not-quite-wolves rediscovering their heritage, baying to be fed. Then the snarling and the fighting over the flesh would start as they turned on each other, crazed with greed and bloodlust. A man deserved to sleep in peace and quiet.

Now the Weatherman stood on the step, ready to meet his maker, his old handgun stuck in the back of his belt. He hadn't worn it in years. It was good to be in clean clothes – freshly rinsed and almost dry. He waited for the messengers of his fate to materialize out of the carpet of fog. He hadn't slept much, either. Blood still leaked between the floorboards and he'd had to keep a bucket below, an old copper spittoon, to catch the drips. *Ping, ping, ping.*

The bodies above him were unsettling, for sure, but more so was the prospect of what would transpire in the morning. He had lain awake wondering whether Tye was still alive, and whether the rumors of his wind-trained bird were true. Felix felt a stab of envy at the idea. If he was alive, Tye would surely be the man leading the charge to find Garrett – and now Dyce and Vida too. Felix would be standing face to face with a rival he hadn't spoken to in more than twelve years. The last words – *Run, you fucker!* – rang in his ears as clear as the day he heard them. Then the crack and whine of the bullet that lodged in the back of his leg; the terrified scream of Marigold as she bolted, her hooves tattooing the fright endlessly into his chest.

Being a Callahan was a hard life, and not everyone was cut out for it. In the early days the clan had been built on honor, populated with self-appointed saviors and sheriffs: punishing the transgressors, weeding out those gone crazy – and those who were crazy from the start.

When the diseases didn't show any sign of slowing, just kept floating in on every wind so that things turned desperate, it got so that the Callahans would ride into town and the guilty would flee. Most of them died out in the open, caught by the wind or the wild creatures. The ones who stayed took a bullet for their sins.

But the responsibility had never sat well with Felix. That kind of power turned constitutional, like an infection. It rotted a man from the inside out.

It had ended one late afternoon when Tye sat down with Felix around a campfire, frying up quail eggs in a rusted skillet – never enough for the both of them – and told him he'd had a visit from a man from up north.

'What do you mean "north"? Huntington?'

'Further north.'

'There ain't nothing north beside the border.'

They were quiet while Felix did the math.

'North of the border?'

Tye added a spoon of fat to the fry-up.

'You shot him, right? 'Fore he opened his mouth.'

'Thought to do, but I didn't. He had some interesting things to say. A proposal.'

'Then you shot him?'

'You want to hear what he said?'

'Nope.'

'The North needs eyes down South, Felix. They asked us to be their eyes. Way I figure it is that they ask us or they ask someone else. Least if we're doing it we get a say.'

'A say? Fuck *a say*. It's the fucking North! Renard's *soldiers*? No damn Callahan is going to be party to that shit. Have you lost your fucking mind?'

Tye watched as the eggs crisped around their edges, browning, their yolks turning pale.

'Gonna need you to do some considering, Felix.'

Felix stood up, drew his gun and aimed. Tye let go of the frying pan. It fell into the coals and hissed.

'I've gone and done all the considering I'm going to. You're talking to me like you made a deal already.'

'You going to shoot me? Good old Felix Callahan, thinking with his rusty iron dick.'

Felix held the barrel against Tye's head in a show of bravery he did not feel.

'Felix. Cousin. Either we're part of this or we're ruled by it. We don't have no option.'

'Godammit, McKenzie,' he said, and turned away.

'It's Hawk-Eye.'

Felix snorted. He went over to Marigold, real casual, hitched a boot in a stirrup, and hauled himself into the saddle. He knew that if he hurried or showed his nerves, Tye would be scrambling for his gun. Felix jabbed his horse in the ribs and she was away. Then the shot, purposely aimed to cripple him, not end his life. He didn't limp just because he was old. There was history, there. Payback, a long time coming.

Now Felix felt the weight of that same handgun stuffed down the back of his pants, loaded up with his last two bullets. He didn't move as the Callahans gathered in an arc around the doorway of his shack. And Tye. Come to finish the job.

Tye stepped forward, the rumored bird on his shoulder.

'Felix. Still alive?'

'Long time, Cousin. How's the traitor's life treating you?'

Tye pretended to hold back a laugh. 'We bumped into Gus last night.'

'Oh?'

'Said he came by here last evening. Had a bit of an, an, *altercation*.'

'Yeah. He tell you Walden got himself killed? Along with Bethie's boyfriend, that Garrett.'

'We're after some loose ends, then. Any idea where they may be?'

Felix pointed out past the almonds.

'Saw them head out that way, but it was dark by then. Hard to tell for sure.'

Tye motioned to Paul.

'Go check inside.'

Paul Callahan did as he was told, stepping past the unresisting Felix. As he went he knocked the Weatherman hard against the shoulder, just to show he could.

'Be my guest,' Felix said softly.

He knew Paul would find Walden and Garrett lying side by side on the floorboards, dead as rusty doornails. He wasn't going to move them none. They listened as Paul searched downstairs and found no one else. He reappeared, wiping his face.

'Like he says.'

'Then we're wasting our time here.' Tye's voice was rough, all pretense at social engagement dropped. 'Find their tracks and let's get moving.'

He looked hard at Felix, down all the long years of consanguinity. Felix ran a hand around his belt and grabbed hold of the handle of his gun, just in case. For a minute the two old men considered each other, two sides of the same familial coin.

Tye turned and walked away but stopped and turned back, slow and determined.

'You heard of this place, The Mouth?'

'The what?'

'Never mind.'

The Weatherman watched him walk off toward the trees, his raggedy men following. He did not let go of the gun until he was out of sight.

20

Whoever had followed them in the dark of the forest was gone by dawn, ectoplasm evaporated in the daylight air. The tracks simply stopped, vanished from the loamy skin of the mountain. Under Dyce's damp arm Vida shivered to think about the strange man – and it was always a man, wasn't it? – ambling beside them, listening to her grunts of effort, never once making a sound himself. Was it Stringbeard, drawn like a housefly to the odor of her exertion? Was he the shape she'd swung at? What had he been waiting for this time?

Nope. It wasn't the Lazarus daddy. He'd been lithe, but his movements weren't calibrated properly, and that made him loud. He was jerky as a puppet, and the strings were pulled from the inside instead of out. He could not move undetected the way their shadow had slunk beside them.

This was something else altogether. Vida didn't know if there was some relief in that.

She stopped again and waited for Dyce to finish his retching and come back. They had acquired some queasy dance steps of their own. She would shuffle first and he would stagger in time. *Yee-haw! Swing yo pardners by the hand!*

'Sorry.' He was trying to wipe his mouth. She held up his shirttail to help.

'*Stop.* "Sorry" gave up about two days ago. Let's just agree you're sorry and let the whole thing go. When you stop being sorry, you can say so.'

Dyce tried to smile at her, and Vida caught a whiff of the acid reversal of his insides. Didn't smell bad-sick, though. It was weird the way that some people did. They always had, to Vida. The woman at the till would open her mouth to say good morning and it was beyond halitosis, some ketonic upheaval that happened when the body began digesting itself – and that before the real diseases were written plain on the faces and bodies of everyone she met. She wondered if Dyce had ulcers yet.

They realigned and went on, passing by the Weatherman's last lonesome windsock. At the end of their slow ascent they rested on the rocky spine of the crest. Vida glanced back to check on the Callahans' progress. She blinked. They were gone from beside the shack. She scanned the surrounding area and then gradually widened her search. Fuck! They were almost at the river. She recalled her night of dragging. It seemed like at least an hour before she'd reached the bank. These men had covered that ground in minutes!

And worse. How had she not realized it? Vida looked with dismay at the shape in the foreground, the red and blue canvas a bold human sign in the grass: her pack. She had dropped it in her panic.

She squinted down the slope. The pack looked to be lying upside down, its contents spilled in the dirt like a fat kid's stocking at Christmas time: her shirt, the tin of herbs, her canteen – and, oh Lord, Ma's remedy book.

Fuck.

Was there any way she could get back there for it? Lay Dyce on the wet grass and just scurry?

She couldn't. There wasn't time. Every step forward she took with Dyce on her shoulder, the Callahans ran ten. Every step back would be twenty. As she calculated their chances, the last of the pursuers crossed the river and disappeared out of view into the forest below.

'FUCK.'

'What?' Dyce's voice was weak, but at least he was with her and showing an interest. He had not stopped shivering, his bare legs goosebumped.

'Left my pack. *I left my fucking pack.*'

'Well, shoot. How am I gonna do my lipstick now?'

Vida shook her head. The book wasn't just Ma's – it *was* Ma. Her life in pages, her heritage brought over from Africa in the envelope of seeds. Right here, right now, at the top of this mountain, Vida had to make a choice.

'You're lucky you're not your brother.'

I'd leave Garrett in a heartbeat.

'Shut *up*,' she told herself.

'Huh?'

They turned, leaving the pack like a fallen soldier, a sadness deep in Vida, not just for the book but what it meant – everything she'd collected in her lonely life. She and that pack had been through hard times together: blood, sweat and tears – lots of those – soaked into its fibers like it was a living thing. Could only ever have taken it so far, she thought in consolation, imagining her soul pulling helplessly on the straps with invisible fingers, her withered body dead beside it. Can't take it with you.

Vida looked down over the crest into a valley, shallow and scrubby with bushes and rimmed with stands of birch.

'Where's the line?'

'The line?'

Vida had been expecting some physical delineation in the earth, like the places that are either side of a meridian – a couple of crosses, or branches laid end to end, at least. A fence. A *sign*, she thought. *I just really need a sign. I'm so tired of doing everything on my own. Ancestor guys? Now would be a good time to show yourselves.*

Okay. That was a joke.

Okay, it wasn't. It was a prayer.

Her hopes seemed silly now. Why would a ghost colony go to the effort of marking its borders? They had better things to do than town planning. They sure as fuck didn't care where they started and where they stopped. Only outsiders did.

She helped Dyce up again and they hung on one another. *At least I know how it feels to be old even if I don't get there*, Vida thought. She arranged her feet side-on and tried to slide them on the fallen leaves, side to side, skiers slaloming between the scarred trunks of the white birches. The cripples shuffled by the bones of a deer, disconnected and pale, stuck in clumps of hair that looked human. She caught a flash of her own bones in that pile, bleached by sun, picked clean by larvae and the little black under-rock beetles and microscopic creatures, all hungry, all merciless.

They straightened up as the ground leveled out. Dyce was walking better now, was more aware of where he was. He kept lifting his face up to the sun, as if he was charging some internal battery.

'Where's Garrett?'

'He's coming. Don't you worry. Got to keep moving if you want to see him. Keep walking. So you help me out here, Allerdyce. There was only so much energy in that bag of locusts.'

He made a face. *Baby*, Vida thought. *This is nothing. If you only knew what you might still have to do!*

Vida had caught the grasshoppers about a month back. A swarm came through the way they did, a casual plague. Each passing season the swarm seemed a little smaller, come looking for the fields of corn that used to be out these parts. As a child she'd seen them in all their glory, a thunderstorm of ravenous insects flying light. They moved as one, with a numbing hum and the whine of rubbing chitin. The main force of the storm hit out near the horizon, so that only the stragglers came past the house – sitting on the screen doors or getting caught up in the washing. The mohair fibers of her stepdad's blue sweater caught on their serrations like Velcro. Her mother spent days pulling them off in their constituent parts, like a biology lesson: head, thorax, abdomen. And then their tiny feet, stuck like burrs.

When Vida saw the lonely cloud of locusts coming this time, she had grabbed a pillow from the sofa and run, pulling the stuffing out as she went, dropping it like snow and hoping the critters would choose to settle nearby. They had, on the other side of the hill behind the house. It was slim pickings compared to the bounty that she recalled, but she still managed to half-fill the bag – plucking them from the grass stalks until the sack was kicking.

And this was treasure!

I don't care, she thought. *I don't. I'll do whatever I have to. Don't got time for niceties or shame.* She shook her head and then looked back at the ridge they'd crossed over, waiting for the silhouettes of two dozen hats to appear against the morning sun – two dozen hats shielding two dozen heads filled up with hot Callahan hate. There was a big bird in the sky, wheeling overhead as if Dyce and Vida were already dead and turned to carrion.

And there they came, jostling for the lead, jogging over the rocks, swarming like locusts. Didn't they ever get tired? Maybe vengeance moved you faster. She could see now that they had pulled their masks up over their faces. It must be hot inside there, with the panting and the fear of contagion from the colony; their own hot breath bringing the risk of death with it. Suicide.

Vida made out an arm, pointing. They'd seen her.

'Come on, Dyce.'

They limped together, as fast as they could. When she dared to look back again, most of them were hidden in the birch trees like some hideous party game. But up on the ridge four Callahans stood with their hands on their hips, watching her and not trying to hide it. The hidden halves of their faces made them seem only half-human, like the Klansmen her mama had told her about.

Vida pushed on. She could hear the Callahans now, the thud of their boots, the crack of sticks underfoot – and Tye's bullying and threats to the cowards who'd given up the chase. Five more men stopped at the edge of the trees, puffing. The rest continued, unrelenting.

And then, thank God, Vida's boot struck a rock in the dirt before her, and she quit. There was a whole row of rocks, a line after all.

Vida crossed over, careful not to disturb the arrangement, more precious than a funeral cairn.

How much further do I need to go to be safe?

The Callahans were close now, but thinning. They knew that they had lost this round. Who knew what might be circling in the aura of the place, what might be in the air? One old man had made it to the line of rocks and there he stopped, debating with himself. Was that the carrion bird on his arm? Vida watched as he drew his gun with his free hand.

A shot rang out, so loud it made her wince.

She pulled Dyce behind a low rock and lay flat on her back, panting and staring up at the sky, too late to see the blur of the passing bullet.

'Jesus! Fuck!'

'It was a warning shot, that's all,' she said. 'He just wants to scare us.'

'Well, it worked.'

Vida reached for Dyce's hand and held it.

There were footsteps.

He wouldn't.

Would he?

Vida peered around the rock, keeping her face low, hidden in the grass. Tye Callahan was coming, bird on his arm, rifle raised. Walking straight for their rock.

'I've come a long way for this.' From behind the mask his voice was loud but dull, an old blade worn down with brutal use. Tye Callahan didn't yell.

Vida squeezed her eyes shut.

But the voice had stopped.

In the silence Vida heard the bird's wings as it struggled into the air, and then the rifle thudding to the hard-packed boundary ground. Why didn't he pick it up?

She opened her eyes.

Massed behind her was an army of raggedy soldiers, half-dead on their feet. They held guns and sticks and knives. Some could barely stand; others shivered despite the sun. They all had weeping skin, raw with blisters and rashes and warts. Vida let her eyes travel down to the missing fingers and the hands cramped into claws.

'You going to leave the way you came, mister?' said a dark man without hair. 'Or you coming upstairs with us?'

For the first time in his life, Tye Callahan turned and ran.

'Well, I guess that answers that.' The bald man stretched out his hand. One shoulder was a little higher than the other. 'Welcome to Horse Head, ma'am.'

21

Tye Callahan kept running. As he went, he pulled his shirt off and tied it over his face mask for double protection. The men were leaving quicker than they'd come, beating a path through the birches and up over the lip of the ridge, rolling and sliding and tumbling their way back to the safety of the pine forest.

Vida slumped back. *I'm strong*, she told herself. *If Stringbeard couldn't kill me, nothing will.*

The soldiers were waiting for her to gather herself. She sat up and looked more closely at the decaying battalion. They regarded one another in the rising heat. This was a detachment of the almost-dead, already reduced to their essentials, flesh peeling back from the determined bones below. The Callahans had been less afraid of the guns than the rotting hands that held them. The soldiers could have come brandishing willow stalks and earthworms and still found themselves left with Dyce and Vida, the hunting party gone like patchy fog across the Colorado plains.

The crooked soldier held out Vida's pack. His head was shaved – or the hair fallen out of its own accord. He looked as if he might have had a Comanche somewhere in his family.

'Yours, I believe.'

'Thank you. I thought it was gone for good.' She felt for the recipe book and the old envelope pasted into the back.

Everything was still there. The Callahans had been too intent on chasing them down to ransack their belongings.

The man spoke, his voice strong though his back was bent to the will of his disease.

'All are welcome.' He gave them a small smile. 'None stay too long.'

One of the women went on, as if it was rehearsed. 'These are our hills and we watch them well.'

Vida nodded. Of course they did. They had something to protect. She inspected each grim and faithful face, steady with purpose. There was no leader among them.

'Now,' said the bent man, 'should we show our visitors some colonial hospitality?'

A few confederates came forward and helped Dyce to his feet. He had not spoken since the chase. *Thank God he can't see who's holding him up*, thought Vida. The group turned and muddled back to the settlement.

It sat on the leeward side of the hill, as all the new towns did, but it was otherwise foreign to Vida. There were no walls or fences around it, no gates to keep the unwanted out of the fort. The shelters were collected in groups, constructed in the old style with poles and planks and grasses, set in teepees here and there, or over holes cut into the slope and lined with tufts of straw. Vida felt a tug that seemed like time travel. *My God*, she thought. *People have been making houses like these for thousands of years*. There was some comfort in that, some expertise. With a jolt she realized that it was the first time since the sicknesses had come in earnest that she felt as if people knew what they were doing, that they had the sense and the hope to plan for the life to come, that they were going to meet it with their eyes open and their hands joined. *Fuck Renard*. As they went on, people greeted the soldiers, unsurprised to see them. There was no right way to enter, no permission or proof of wellness required, no need for a fellow traveler to vouch for your status and sanity.

And then, of course, below the settlement was the familiar shadow, the shadow township of the dead: the mounds of dirt as the Weatherman had drawn them, the graves dug by the dying for those gone on ahead, and for themselves. Vida began counting. Some had crosses set over the heads, others not, but they were all looked after – cleared of weeds and converted into small gardens of clover and stonecrop and shooting stars. And dandelions and yarrow, of course, always and everywhere. Vida's fake grave for Ruth seemed careless in comparison, not a respectful memorial but a hole to hide a body, nothing more. No ancestral spirit would be satisfied with that.

The bald man was leading them through the middle of the town. Up close, the shelters themselves seemed to be less well made than the graves – temporary places of safety for nomadic people; those moving between this world and the next.

The confederates showed Dyce to a shelter where he could lie in the fullness of the morning sun. Vida knew what it meant that there was an empty shelter waiting for them, sleeping mat and all: it didn't take a brain surgeon to figure it out. She looked down toward the graves and gave a nod of thanks to the departed who'd left it behind. Vida watched carefully as a woman with a wheezing cough came to Dyce with a medicine: yarrow stems pulped into a warm brew, it smelt like. She helped Dyce sip at the froth until it was cool, and then he downed it. The woman took the bowl away, and then came back with a coverlet for his legs. Vida inspected the weave: long grass, tight enough to warm, loose enough to breathe, and the smell! Mown fields, back when there was season and order, the scent of childhood and sweet, dry summer, and her stepdad calling, 'Veedles! Here it comes! Catch the ball!'

The bald man had moved inside a pale tent, to nurse someone else, Vida thought. It seemed fairly organized. What was the word her ma used? Egalitarian. They just took care of each other.

He poked his head out. 'Come on in here.'

'You sure? It's safe?'

He nodded and retreated, making space. She lifted the flap and went inside. He was wiping the mouth of a frail woman but made sure to shield his hands from the spittle. Even Vida could tell the patient was a coughing fit away from crossing over to the deadlands.

He sat back again, his skew spine making him rock a little. He kept one eye on the dying woman but gave Vida his attention.

'What you got? Can't tell from the outside.'

'Why do you want to know?'

'What is it? Brainworm?'

'No.' Vida smiled. 'Maybe, actually. But I'm not really here for all that.'

'All what?'

'Dying, I guess.'

The woman moaned, and he shushed her and rubbed her chest, high up, like a child. She managed to open her eyes. She was concentrating on Vida, who shifted.

He went on. 'This woman *is* dying. Don't be afraid to look at her.' Vida did. 'But the rest of us – we're all living. This settlement works. Just tell me. You have nothing to lose.'

Vida felt ashamed, and her shame made her tell him nearly everything: about Stringbeard, about the double infection and the cure she dreamt. She told him about Dyce and she told him about Ma, who was a week further along and that much nearer to death.

As Vida spoke, the man leant forward and looked her deep in the eyes, searching her pupils for dilation, for the flecks of red that might tell on the brain virus.

'Heard about Fieldstone, but not that fellow. Got a good few recruits from there. But in all my days I only ever seen double viruses *kill* a person. We still got to be cautious here. No sipping from the same cups and such.'

Vida felt another pang of guilt and wondered whether he had made the connection about Dyce and the water, and how she'd been too selfish to make him stop.

'But I'm not ruling it out, mind. These are strange times.'

Vida nodded. *Don't ruin it. Don't get hysterical. And don't laugh. There's a chance he might listen.*

He went on. 'So what are you saying?'

'I'm saying that this place' – Vida gestured at the cloth sides of the tent and the whole textured settlement beyond it – 'is perfectly placed for us to find out how it works. *If* it works.'

'You mean testing people? Making them sick? That sort of thing?' He was already shaking his head.

'Think about it before you say no. Just *think* about it. Please. These people came here to die. This could give them another chance.'

'Not sure that kind of testing is fair.' Vida looked away, her heart a rock thrown in a river. He hadn't finished. 'But I suppose I got no jurisdiction to disallow it.'

'Let's talk hypothetical, then.'

'Hypothetical settles my nerves some.' He wet the cloth and wiped the woman's cheeks and neck, careful, Vida noticed, not to touch her skin.

'Anyone you think might be a candidate for Dyce?'

'Dyce your traveling partner?'

Vida nodded.

'What's he got?'

'That red blindness, plus a bad fever. And the shits.'

'Don't they all?' The man fell quiet, and then made up his mind. 'You might not have noticed, but one of our men followed you last night.'

'I sure as shit noticed! Thought he was a big cat. Tried to brain him with a branch.'

'Whoa.'

'What about him?'

'He's got day blindness. The other kind. Virus got him one evening – caught out in the open when the wind changed. Over the night he starts seeing things clear as day. Critters in the bushes, leaves in all their detail, owls and bats above. Course he feels like shit, but it's worth it. Told me the stars above are like a highway straight to heaven paved with jewels. Then the sun rises and Sam – that's his name – Sam's in agony. Like barbed wire right into the corneas. He pulls his mask up over his eyes and manages to find his way here. We wrap him up, feed and water him like he's a baby deer and all that. Then, as soon as the sun's gone, he's up and he's okay again. Like a vampire.'

'Can I see him?'

'You still talking hypothetical?'

'No.'

'Before I do that, you want to tell me your name?'

'Vida Washington. And you are?' *Running Horse, I'll bet.*

'Peter Stuyvesant.'

She snorted.

'I know, I know. You aren't the first, and you won't be the last. Just call me Pete.'

22

Tye Callahan stopped running as soon as he figured the air was safe. Running came second only to crying in the Callahan code of honor. He stood, panting, as his harrier came to roost on his shoulder, faithful to the last. His scattershot group was congregating, man by man, near the thin river below the pines. They looked like they were slapping midges off their bodies, all feeling for raised glands in their necks, or swallowing hard, waiting for the first signs of the scrape. What a sorry bunch of assholes!

'Quit it, you sissies! If it's gonna show up you'll know by sundown, and being afraid of your own shadows ain't going to stop it coming.'

Most of them let their hands fall, but every now and again, as Tye berated them, he saw a hand creeping across a chest, or a palm slapping at the back of a sunburnt neck.

'Who was it who stopped on the ridge? Who gave up?'

Tye knew already. He'd taken careful stock of each man's courage.

'Don't make me fucking shoot you in the back on the trek home. Show me you have at least a teaspoon of guts. You call yourselves marshals!'

Three men stepped forward, unable to meet Tye's eyes. Paul Callahan hung back, at the end of the line of sorry men. Tye glared at the three who had presented themselves, and they took their hats off to hold over their chests as though they were singing the national anthem – or shielding themselves from a bullet, putting one more layer between themselves and the wrath of the old leader.

Tye pulled his gun from his belt and cocked it.

'Course I'm not going to shoot you.' His dry lips drew back. It was worse when Tye smiled. 'We're Callahans. We're a team, right?'

The three men smiled hopefully and nodded.

'Course you fellas had the guts to stay the night, and that stands for something now, doesn't it?'

The men agreed, terrified, clutching their hats, scrunching the leather in their white fists.

'So here's the deal I'm going to make with you, out of the kindness of my heart and because we are brethren.'

The men shuffled, swallowed.

'When you all get back to Glenvale, you're going to find the first couple of Callahans who turned back last evening – the first three who got home to their wives for a nice wet fuck and a bottle of moonshine – and you're going to shoot them for me.'

'Well, now, Tye,' the oldest of the men began. 'We're good men here, all of us. Even those fellas who left. But they got their reasons. Now I'm not suggesting they get off scot-free, no way . . .'

'Too many good men, that's my damn problem. How's about I shoot some now, save you the trouble?' Tye raised his gun and the men around him began shifting out of the line of fire. If they moved too fast, he might strike, the way adders did.

'One of these two things will happen. Either way, someone pays for their cowardly ways. Your choice.'

The three marshals nodded, pale with fright but thinking that they might survive the discipline session after all. Tye could see the thoughts wheeling in their heads: *We don't have to kill anyone. He doesn't have to know*.

Then Tye swung his crooked arm round and fired his gun. The bullet hit Paul Callahan in the chest. He fell forward to his knees, disbelieving, and Tye's bird fluttered away to sit on a nearby branch.

'There were *four* stopped on the hill, Paul. I saw you,' said Tye, slow and calm.

He turned to the line of men. 'Now you all listen good. *I see everything*. We clear?'

The men nodded, stunned into agreement.

'When he quits that twitching, you bury him – and I don't want a fucking marker on the grave. This man's disappearing. I want no sign he ever existed. *No one's* gonna be paying no respects.'

The posse was quiet, unmoving as Paul lay wheezing in the dust.

Pathetic, Tye thought to himself. *They all just let me do it. Standing there, watching one of their own dying in the dirt and no one lifted a fucking finger. Shameful.*

It didn't take Paul Callahan long to die. He breathed his last and still no one moved, afraid of another explosion from their leader.

'Bury him!' bellowed Tye. The men began scurrying to get his body into the hard-packed earth.

Tye left them to shifting stones and looking for sticks to loosen the ground. It would take time, but there was no rush. He knew where the Jackson boy and that woman were. He wasn't likely to forget. Once Tye Callahan had marked you down in his mind, there was no getting away.

He crossed the shallow river by the stepping stones and walked some way off into the shrubs. He found a clearing and searched out the smoothest rock for a seat. He needed to get comfortable: he had a message to send.

From his bag he produced the tiny cylinder with its straps. His harrier was used to the harness: the capsule was light. He called the bird down from her branch with a whistle and she came to him.

'Neither snow nor rain nor heat nor gloom of night, girl. You up for a delivery? You remember how to do it?'

She cocked her head and pecked lightly at his sleeve.

'Easy! That's my writing hand.'

He reached into his bag and brought out a dried perch fillet for her. It sure stank, but she loved the fish. As she ate, he stroked the soft speckled feathers on her back.

Then he found his notepad and a pencil stub. He pressed on the rock, crouching beside it, and wrote as small as he could. He knew Renard, and so he chose his words carefully, trying as best he could to trim the rage from his prose. With the right tone, Tye could win back the trust his men sorely lacked, not just for his leadership, but for the Callahan name as it stood.

Attention: Renard – A Message from Tye Callahan

Greetings from the South,

I hope in the years I've kept a watch on things below the border that you haven't once questioned my loyalty. I have burnt bridges and found myself firmly on your side.

I write to you here to tell you that I have grown to see eye to eye with your way. I have found that this Southern breed is hardly worth the air they breathe, and I include my own no-good family when I say that. The reason I raise my enduring loyalty will become clear as you read on.

I am currently very far south, beyond Glenvale and the remnants of Fieldstone even, further than I myself have been since my horse died. I am right on the edge of the settlements, and I had thought that there were none further.

I see now that I have been wrong in my estimation. There are rumors from my men, as well as others I have had to question in the line of my duty. There is a settlement not far from here that survives to defy you, Renard. They say it is immune to the viruses, and that it does not expel any sick as the other places do. An enterprising man who needs a base in the South might take the opportunity to look into this settlement. They call it The Mouth.

If I myself had a man on the ground inside The Mouth, I would not be writing a letter based so heavily on hearsay, but those Callahans who have tried to infiltrate the place say it is run by someone else altogether: a man who does not acknowledge you. It is a worrisome problem to someone of your worth.

I have seen firsthand the sort of rebellious locals in these deep Southern lands, and though I had hoped to visit The Mouth myself in order to give an account, I have come to feel that doing so will serve no purpose beyond delaying your intervention. My sources are trustworthy and this matter needs to be dealt with swiftly. It may deserve the same treatment as Snow Peak received.

And here is where my loyalty raises its head. Send scouts – in my mind that would be wise – and I will be glad to lead them so that we might have a full report of the settlement's strengths and weaknesses.

*And if, perhaps, you later raise an army to demolish The
Mouth, might you consider a small detour for your forces? I
have recently had trouble from a ghost colony called Horse
Head, situated not far from Fieldstone. Without vaccines I
cannot set foot across the boundary – otherwise I would not
be bothering you with this trifle. This place has given refuge to
two murderers who felled one of my best men. My revenge on
them is tied to my leadership of this clan that has served you
so well over the years.*

I hope it will continue to serve you for years yet to come.

Faithfully yours,

Tye Hawk-Eye Callahan

Tye rolled the letter up and slotted it into the canister. When
his bird was done eating, he strapped it onto her so that it sat
along her spine like a quiver of arrows. She stretched her wings,
settling her feathers against the foreign shape of the tube on her
back. Then she swooped into the sky, heading north.

When Tye was back with his men, he called the young
Callahan over.

'Kurt, is it?'

The boy nodded.

'Go get my other bag and follow me.'

When the boy picked the pack up it jangled, metallic and
heavy.

'What's in here?' he asked.

'Mind your manners. Just a little something for the ghost
colony. Nothing fancy.'

23

Vida checked on Dyce first. He was asleep, curled up on the dirt with the grass blanket over him. She had no idea where his cargo pants had gone. She'd used them to carry him until just before the ridge. Maybe she'd forgotten them beside her pack. A couple of days without much sleep and her brain felt glassy, smooth in places, splintering in others, the thoughts disconnected, memories falling through gaps. Vida assessed herself for illness as she always did, but she figured she didn't feel much more worn out than she should. Could a virus make her feel any worse? Her ligaments grated, her head pounded, her breathing had been reduced to shallow puffs. She envied Dyce his sleep and considered lifting a corner of the grassy quilt and climbing in beside him. She was surprised at how tempted she was by the idea, his flesh as familiar as her own.

Instead she started up the slope to find Sam, trying to set everyone she saw in their place in the system. It was like a hive: there was an energy in Horse Head Camp, people getting on with chores where they could. Some, like Dyce, slept – too sick to be of much use – but those that were able wove grass into mats or washed clothes or dragged themselves down to the graves and sat in the sun, weeding. Vida and Ruth had spent a few months in settlements on their trek south, and none of them had had this kind of purpose. In settlements, and out in the open too, you were always eyeballing strangers and friends and family – especially family – for a sweaty forehead or the chills, a rash, any sign that disease was coming for you and yours. And of course everywhere you went, whether it was to deliver a glass of water to your ma in bed or journey further to join a town, you got the same eye in return – judging, assessing, suspicious. Everyone was a carrier until they had proven that they weren't.

Not here, though. Vida felt light.

She asked at several shelters for Sam, and at each one they pointed her up. High on the slope was a structure different from the rest only in that it was closed. The others mostly had their curtains and makeshift doorways wide open to the sun because it burnt away the bugs. Darkness bred secrecy and rot.

Under the outer shell of foliage Vida noted the layers of thick plastic and then the sheets of solid bark layered together like the clinkering on a Viking longship, designed to block out the light. The War had made everyone an engineer. She knocked on a strut of wood, cautiously, aware she was a nuisance.

'Sam?'

'Who is that?' Inside the shelter she heard someone yawn. Damn. She'd woken him up.

'Name's Vida. I'm told you escorted me up the mountain last night.'

'Ah, yes. Miz Bear Snack herself. You're lucky. There's been a rogue bear around – sick, I think. Comes sniffing round the graves at night. I've been out watching, tracking. But I found you.' She could hear him stretching, the air coming out of his lungs, slow and pleasurable, as if he was smoking. 'And you almost clocked me one with that branch for my troubles. It was a real interesting night. For a change.'

'Glad I could be of service.'

A pale arm stuck itself out through a gap, translucent as a gecko on a childhood night-light. Vida shook the hand, hoping she was doing the right thing. It was warm with sleep, heavier than it looked.

'Pleased to meet you,' came the voice. 'How's Potatoes?'

'What?'

'The dead weight you were dragging like a sack. How's he holding up?'

'Potatoes is okay. Seen better days.'

Shit. Vida winced at her choice of words.

'What can I do you for?'

She crouched and then sat. 'I've got some, uh, peculiar questions I'd like to ask.'

'Favorite kind. Shoot.' Another yawn, like a bear coming out of hibernation.

'Your sickness. You don't by some chance suffer from chills? Maybe, ah, constipation?'

The yawn turned into a cough. Vida heard him slapping his chest. 'You often get to meet the boyfriend's parents?'

'Sorry. But I can explain.'

So she did, the whole story all over again from the beginning – and ending with her plan to combine two viruses.

And what she needed right now: a specimen of Sam's saliva.

When she was done there was a silence. Vida wondered if it took your body a long time to adapt to having your days reversed, like that travelers' disease in the wayback. Jetlag. Or maybe it was like working the night shift, the way her mama used to when she first started out as a nurse, always trying to catch up to the daytime folks, never quite getting enough. Sleep debt, Ruth called it.

'I'm happy to spew in a cup for you, but it sounds like it's Potatoes you'll need to convince. Or you just going to slip it into his water?'

'Not exactly. No point in convincing him if I don't have the magic potion first.'

Vida heard Sam rustling around inside his shelter, then a cough and a splat.

His hand appeared again through the hole, this time holding a tin mug, wet inside with off-white, bubbly phlegm.

'This is my bodily fluid, given for Potatoes,' Sam intoned. Then he dropped the priest bit and went on in his normal voice. 'Let me know how it goes.'

Vida took the mug, pincering it gingerly between two fingers.

'Thanks. Really. Thank you.' She said it although she wasn't sure just yet if she meant it. She wouldn't even know the donor if she saw him in the daylight. And, sure, she could look harder, search higher and lower for more candidates that were better suited – or just other options, period. But the limited time meant limited choices, and there was nothing she could do about that. All the reasons not to try it suddenly reared up, burning in her chest now that she was holding a cupful of the plague. It made Vida shudder to think that she would go down the slope like Moses off the mountain, stepping neat between lean-tos so that she could offer Dyce a sip from the poisoned chalice. It would make him Ma's taster, cringing at the knee of the despot.

She didn't think she could do it.

Because things had changed, hadn't they? It was silly, but she felt safer knowing Dyce was with her. *Trust you to pick the only guy passed out on the dance floor!* Dyce had been an invalid for ninety per cent of the time she'd known him – and still it was true: she *did* feel safer. If he drank from the mug and died because of it, he wouldn't just be some hick gone from the earth, the way she'd figured him that night in the cave. There was a brightness to Dyce. If he were to die, all those shining strands would snap and it would just be Vida and Ma again. Them two, in the dark. And then maybe Ma on the way out too, and then where would Vida be? Outcast and alone, carrying the blessing, carrying the curse. She couldn't do it.

When she reached Dyce, Vida was crying. His pants had been found by some kind and attentive soul, washed and then hung over a twinberry bush to dry. Vida hardly recognized them clean. They looked so *normal*: khaki rinsed clean of the red and brown of his insides. His, and some others' too. The ones who hadn't made it. *I will remember their names*, Vida told herself. *I will not let them be forgotten.*

She wiped her face and sat beside Dyce, unsure of whether he was awake behind his closed lids.

'I hope you're listening,' she said, 'because I got some things to tell you.'

Vida kept her sore eyes on the bright-flowering grave mounds and she told him everything: about that first day at the house; her ma upstairs in the attic; the dirty glass he'd caught her red-blind illness from; the cheating log-filled grave out back; about Stringbeard and her double virus theory and how sorry, sorry, sorry she was now; how she didn't really know what else to do but bring this mug to him with the spit sample that would either end his life or save it. She told him everything except the one thing that she couldn't: that Garrett was dead and left behind, and he would never reach the sea.

Vida set the mug down beside them and buried her face in her folded arms. She wept, and wiped the streaks of the new tears on her sleeves.

When she dared to look at him, she found Dyce propped up on one elbow. He was holding the mug so that it shook, his bloodshot eyes open. He looked at her.

He *looked* at her.

'"Sorry" died a couple days back,' he said, and then he tipped the drink into his mouth.

24

The cooking fires from the camp woke Dyce in the late afternoon. He shifted his bare legs, a little tender from the full day of sun. Vida was asleep there on the dirt beside him, curled up as though she'd fallen from where she sat, just keeled over, punch-drunk in the fight with exhaustion.

He moved around to get a better look. Her legs were twisted, her chin propped on a folded palm, her cheek pocked by the grit. Dyce thought of the pictures in the *Life* magazines his dad used to get: the suicide girl who had landed so neatly, her skirt demurely down, her hands clamped at her sides, death-defying. It never happened like that in real life. Dyce had learnt that over and over in the last few months. But Vida looked nothing like that sallow girl. She lay, a full woman, rosy and close, full of life. For the first time in weeks, Dyce felt himself get hard. He moved to cover his crotch with his hands. Wouldn't that be just great? Sleeping Beauty wakes with the prince's dick waving in her face.

He blinked. His eyelids still felt scratchy and hot, but his vision was clearer, and that was a fact. Vida was the first whole thing he'd seen since Garrett had faded away in front of him on the bad-luck path. There was a dim veil over everything he saw, but the shapes and shadows made sense in a set of kindergarten

color wheels. *Blue was purple*, Dyce thought. *Yellow was orange.*
Green was brown.

He felt better too, post-surgical, as if the sickness had gutted
him like a rainbow trout – sliced him open and discarded the
useless internal organs – but at least he didn't keep trying to
pass out, and he could keep a thought in his head that wasn't,
Oh God, here it comes again. A couple of times back there he
had expected to feel the hot slither of intestines hitting the wiry
ground under his ass.

Okay, that memory does it, he told himself. His erection
subsided.

And if he could see, actually *see* Vida beside him, then
when she woke up she could tell him where Garrett was gone.
It seemed like days now since he'd heard anyone say, *I've made
waffles!* It filled Dyce with a dread that he realized was loneli-
ness. He had never been without his brother before, his comfort
and his torment. The real legacy of the diseases was that they
snipped the bonds of friends and family: you were left unteth-
ered to float across the earth.

He reached over and shook Vida. She tried in her sleep to
spring up and he started to laugh.

She slapped his shoulder. 'Why you laughing? You crazy? You
don't wake a person like that!' She smoothed her braids over
and over, as if she could press the dream world back inside her
skull so it didn't spill over and infect this one.

'I'm sorry.' He tried to stop. 'You just looked like, like, this
pig we tried to catch.'

She left off smoothing her hair, but her hands were still
shaking. 'A *pig*? Are you kidding me?'

'A feral pig.'

'This better be good.'

'Garrett thought it was asleep. Couldn't believe the thing was just lying there. Had to prod it with his shotgun to make sure it wasn't already dead.' From some sickness that would spread to them, Dyce meant. Garrett had had no expectation that the hog would spring awake the way it did.

'Ended up the buckshot hardly grazed it. It just took off, squealing.'

'Dumbasses.' Vida smiled. Her double-virus plan looked to be working, and the relief was cool on her skin.

It didn't last.

Dyce waited a beat. There was no good time and no good answer. 'So where is he? Garrett?'

Vida's smile faded, and the hot flush of guilt returned. She didn't say anything, still spooked by Dyce's bloodshot eyes, trying to distinguish the real world from the dreaming one. There were red-blind eyes there too.

'He's gone, right?'

'There was nothing I could do,' said Vida. It was lame, she knew. She watched Dyce carefully, keeping her eyes above his waist. This was when he was going to freak out. People had different breaking points, but if you were going to lose your shit, now would be the time.

He was trying to pull himself to his feet while shielding his groin. Before Vida could explain, Dyce cut in.

'Nothing *anyone* could do. Nobody going to stop him from reaching the coast. But fuck! I expected a goodbye, at least. Even if he was just giving us the finger, you know?'

Vida nodded, numb with guilt. She'd long wrestled with what she'd tell Dyce about his brother. The truth – that he was gunned down by Walden Callahan – was likely to serve no good. None of that hero shit applied now. Dyce would blame himself.

And, worse than that, he'd blame Vida. He was right to do so. Without Ma's sickness laying Dyce low, he could have fought at Garrett's side. Two on two would've been more than fair, with only Weedy Walden to back Gus up. Dyce would leave her if she told. Yeah, she was sure of it. Let him think Garrett had survived the skirmish and skipped to the coast. Dyce would need company. And, besides, it hadn't even turned into the big lie she was prepared to tell. He had done all the work himself.

'You were out cold. And he did say goodbye. Even left you something.' Vida reached for her bag and took out the squirrel, heavy as a boxing glove. She held it up for Dyce, but he just looked at it.

'*Ears McCreedy?*'

'What you talking about?'

Dyce was smiling the kind of smile that hurt.

'I fucking hated that we had to kill that squirrel. Used to eat the bird seed in our garden. When the tuna cans were done, Dad snared it. Then stuffed it; showed us how. Garrett only kept it 'cause I hated it so much. Now Ears McCreedy is all I get? Figures.' He shook his head.

'What a guy,' said Vida.

'Garrett's probably laughing it up right now.'

'You going to take it or just wait for my arm to drop off?'

Dyce held the squirrel and stroked it a few times. It was a neat job. Taxidermy was easier when you had the right tools. Now he dropped it beside his pack.

'Rats with bushy tails, he called them.'

'That's a lot of effort for a pretty terrible joke.'

'That's my bro. Can't believe he actually left, though. I mean, we spoke about him going on, or me staying behind – but I didn't figure either of us would ever do it.'

'No option, really, after he killed those two Callahans. Pretty certain the rest would be coming and no way he was outrunning those guys with a dead weight.'

Dyce looked at her.

'Sorry, but you were. And he seemed pretty torn up about leaving you, just so you know. Made me swear to save you from the coyotes. Don't make me regret it.'

'Fuck. I remember bits. Just wish I could remember him leaving. I feel like I could have *said* something.' Dyce sighed, but deep down there was some sort of release – relief, maybe. He had dreaded the ocean, dreaded toppling their boat in the waves and having to swim, miles from shore with no hope of another mermaid rescue. 'You reckon he'll make it all the way?'

Vida nodded. 'Callahans took up on our scent, followed us here. Garrett's long gone now.'

Dyce rubbed his temples, then felt all the planes of his face as if they were new to him. *Maybe they were*, thought Vida. He had lost about a quarter of his body weight. A fat Dyce was unthinkable.

'How you feeling?'

'Okay, I guess. Better. Getting my appetite back, I think. Never thought that being hungry would make me happy.'

'I'll see what I can scare up for you before I go. Maybe get you some pants.'

'Whoa! Where you going? We just got here.'

'Got to get to my ma as soon as, remember? It looks like the potion worked on you, guinea pig. Now it's her turn. Gotta be quick.'

'You going now? The light's already fading.'

'Yeah, not much I can do about that. One miracle is enough for today, and I don't have the Old Testament strength to pray the sun to a standstill.'

Vida took the tin mug from the ground and walked off up the slope. Dyce waited. When she came back, it was with a handful of thistle roots and a tiny rack of charred ribs from Sam's camp-fire. *Change of guard*, she thought. *Now it's night shift.* Sam would take her back to her ma's place as quick as they could go, dodging the small traps of the forest while the Callahans snored.

She handed Dyce the food. 'Not squirrel, and that's all I can say. Best I could do.'

Dyce found his mouth watering. How long had it been? 'Magnifique. My compliments to the chef.'

She sat and watched as he wolfed the supper down, the little bones crunching between his teeth. He grimaced as he caught a splinter now and again in the soft meat of his cheeks. Then she went to pack her bag. Dyce stood and walked gingerly over to his cargos. They were almost dry, stiff on the sunny side. He took them back to the shelter and spent some time threading his thin legs into them. *Oh, don't*, Vida thought. *I kinda liked you the way you were.*

Afterwards they saw the pink glow dissolve behind the ridge. As the air turned chilly they sat closer, the good warmth of their sides seeping through their clothes, ectoplasmic.

I should feel sorry for your skinny ass, thought Vida. *Except I don't. This feels like something else entirely but it's just because we've been so long in each other's space, is all.*

When the black of true night had set in, Vida stood at last and shouldered her pack. Dyce turned to watch her go. He felt that he could remember every detail of her leaving.

It was only when she was merged with the mess of shelters that he realized he'd been watching her in pitch darkness, his eyes seeing in the starlight, clear as day, Sam's nocturnal vision passed invisibly along.

25

Vida was asleep on her feet, stumbling along. Sam had tied her wrist to his waist with a band of cloth, as if she was a toddler on reins. *I may as well be*, thought Vida. She was more than useless. High clouds blocked the moonlight and created a dense black through which they moved quietly, left alone by the night creatures that were their companions, as well as the Callahans. Vida kept expecting to come to a clearing where the men would be arranged in a tight circle, their sleeping forms guarded by the old man, the one Dyce called Tye Callahan. The harrier would be beside him, man and bird yellow-eyed and watchful with hate.

Sam had been pushing her hard, and she was grateful, even when her legs were not. When Vida tugged on the tether, he stopped and let her sit, and they put their small packs on the ground to rest. But it was never any longer than a minute and then they were up and moving again – down, down, down. It was better to keep going. The route back to the house was turning out to be not as far as Vida had thought. She'd cut back a long way on her journey to the ghost colony.

They crossed the river at a shallow point, hardly higher than Vida's ankles, and began the climb up the other side in the direction of her home. *When this was all over*, she promised herself, *I am going to have a mustard bath. A real hot one.* She didn't care how many kettles she had to set over the fire to get the water hot enough. It would be worth it. A bath, and a trim for her nails, fingers and toes. She was tired of being dirty. It wasn't always the kind you could see.

Sam himself had stopped twice to vomit, and each time it was a reminder to Vida that the man was really sick. His willingness to help her had not been offered out of boredom. She wanted to ask if he was okay, but they'd spoken about being quiet, about attracting as little attention as possible.

Sam *must* know that the double virus had worked on Dyce, but he was unwilling to test it himself. Vida didn't know why. Maybe he wanted to wait and see the side effects. Maybe – and this made sense to the reptilian part of Vida's brain – he didn't want to risk losing his night vision.

Sam had stopped. He yanked on the cloth and pulled her close to him, and she bumped into his pack.

'That your house?' he whispered.

Even if she hadn't been able to see anything, the smell would have told her where they were. The scent of the night-blooming herbs in the medicine garden wafted to Vida and made her throat close with longing. She wanted her mother back – soft and aproned, spooning the rooibos leaves into the teapot, her back against the window, safe from everything outside. In Vida's dreams there was always an electric light bulb directly over her mother's head, like a halo.

Now she squinted into the dark, expecting to see nothing – but there were little streams of light spiking through the holes in the downstairs window boarding.

'*Shit.*' Vida felt the familiar, hot rush of adrenalin. Another fight coming.

'What?'

'Someone's in there, and it's not my ma.'

There were folk camping in her lounge.

Of course there were. There'd been no sign of anyone home. Usually the smoke from the chimney or the washing hanging on the verandah would be enough to put off the wrong kind of travelers. There was no point in risking getting too close to lone strangers. Better to just pass on by. But an empty house: that was an invitation.

'Stay here,' Vida whispered. She unknotted the cloth loop and moved forward, keeping her eyes trained on the windows. There was no sound coming from the upstairs room where she had left Ruth, wrapped blind in her blankets. None downstairs either, where the squatters would most likely be camping out, counting their blessings and drinking her wine.

At the side of the house she stood on a broken cinder block and peered inside the room. A muffled man lay on the floor in front of the fireplace, while two others sat dozing beside him in armchairs, rifles at their feet.

And they were wearing her shirts, the soft fabric stretched tight against the trespass of skin.

Vida stepped down from the block and moved to the next window for a better view. The man on the floor, she could see now, had one of her ma's hospital bandages wrapped tight around his neck, bright-red blotches seeping to the surface like the outlines of lost continents.

Gus Callahan.

Fuck.

The man was made of iron. She watched his chest rising and falling, the breath sending the sweat to his hairline. One of the men got up and dropped another piece of wood on the fire – Vida's wood! The wood she'd spent days collecting! They were blazing through it, luxuriating in the stolen woodpile. She wouldn't be surprised if they torched the place when they went, just because they could. *Sums up everything you need to know about a Callahan*, Vida thought, sourly.

She tiptoed back to Sam.

'Three men. Two with rifles, one injured.'

'What's the plan?' In the light from the house Sam looked pale and sweaty.

'Are you sure you want to get involved?'

He shrugged. 'Kept you safe this far, didn't I?'

Vida eyed him. 'Okay. I need to get my ma down here so we can get her back to camp.'

'Where is she?'

'Upstairs. I'll try get in and out through the kitchen.'

'No offence, but can you carry her by yourself?'

'I think so. But I'll need a distraction outside beyond the sliding doors.'

'What sort of distraction?'

'Shouting in the dark? Angry home-owner with a rifle? That kind of thing?'

'Okay.' He tucked in his shirt. 'I think I can do that.'

'And I'm going to need you to spit in that cup again.'

He rooted it out from his small bag. She wanted to turn away. *What if it didn't work this time? What if it was an accident, a fluke, and Dyce was dying even now?*

She heard the rasp of Sam gathering the phlegm from his throat. He hawked it into the mug and handed it to her. The tin mug felt heavy, like a grail, weighted with its own importance. It made Vida sick to imagine the lump of dense, gray mucus it carried.

'Thank you.' The warm spot made by the phlegm was making

her want to drop the mug. 'I'm going to get Ma now. Try not to get shot.'

'Yeah. That's pretty much my life philosophy.'

The two of them tiptoed to either end of the house, and then Vida ducked down beside the kitchen door and waited for Sam to get going.

And then it came.

'Who's that in my house? I got a gun here! I'm not kidding! You all better get yourselves cleared out of here!' Sam had turned hick in his performance, Vida noticed, channeling pure hillbilly outrage.

She heard the startled cussing of the two Callahans, and then some stamping around on the floorboards as they went for their guns. Vida twisted the kitchen door handle and moved inside. The old smell of home, damp and inviting, enfolded her and she breathed it deep. *Keep moving, baby*, she told herself. *Otherwise this will be your last whiff of it.*

'Finders keepers, Daddy!' one Callahan shouted. 'We not going nowhere!'

'I ain't playing around!' Sam was bellowing, really putting his heart into it, fired by indignation and melodrama.

Vida moved into the passage. She could see Gus lying dead still on the carpet, feet towards her, a cushion propping up his huge damaged head. Even if he did see her, what was he going to do about it? She went on her way, stepping quietly up the stairs – heel-toe, heel-toe – remembering where each one squeaked. It gave her time, and it was as she ascended the attic stairs that she understood that she might be too late.

She might have come all this way just to pay her respects.

Vida stopped. *Please*, she thought. *I don't even know what I'm praying for. Just, please.*

Downstairs, Sam was embracing his role. 'The Lord above knows whose house this is! *He* ain't gonna find it hard to judge the souls I'm about to send Him!'

Vida waited for her eyes to make the most of the dim light in the room, and tried to make sense of what she saw. Under the window the bundle of blankets was flattened.

Ruth was gone!

Vida ran to the bed and reached down to feel inside the covers, sure that the body had been removed like a leper. Would the Callahans have had the respect to bury her in the garden among her plants? Maybe the false grave had found its use after all.

In the dark Vida's hand settled around a wrist. She'd forgotten how frail her ma had become in her sickness. And since Vida had been away the woman had become a skeleton, the flesh shiny where it stretched over her bones.

But it was still warm, wasn't it? If she was dead, it hadn't been for very long. Vida kept her fingers there, feeling for a pulse, but there was no sign of the flicker she expected and her own thudding heartbeat was getting in the way. She moved her hand to her mother's throat, feeling for life.

There. Was that a pulse?

'Ma,' she whispered. She felt like a little girl who had woken from a nightmare, seeking comfort in her mother's bed.

There was no reply.

Vida felt for her ma's face. She found the mouth and parted her lips, and then she poured the lump of phlegm out of the cup and into her mother's mouth. The glob caught on the front teeth and sat there.

Oh, God! Oh, God! Oh, God! It's going to fall on the floor and then I'll never find it!

She used two fingers to shove the quivering mess into the woman's mouth as far as she could, and then she wiped her hands over and over on the sheet, long after they were dry.

Don't choke, Ma, please! Just swallow your muti like a good girl and don't throw it back up!

Vida listened for commotion downstairs but the stand-off was still going on. Good old Sam.

She waited for her ma to make a sound, but the woman was motionless. Vida wiped the old face with a corner of a sheet and decided how best to carry her. She would have to keep Ruth's head tipped the right way so that the phlegm had a chance to stay down. But compared to dragging Dyce, her ma was hardly a challenge. Her pack, with the sand-filled squirrel, weighed about the same.

'You're lighter than Ears McCreedy, Ma,' Vida told her, and lifted the unconscious woman. 'It's payback time for those nine months you carried me, right?'

She made her slow way to the top of the stairs and listened again.

The Callahans, furious, shrill as fishwives: 'We're not moving till morning! Best you go find someplace else for the night before we blow you a new asshole!'

Sam, mean and loud: 'I brought nothing into this world, but I'm taking you dickwads out! Say your prayers!'

Vida had made it to the bottom of the stairs when she heard the crack of a gunshot. Ruth jerked in her fever dream – hallelujah! – but didn't wake.

'You're okay,' Vida told her, her heart hammering. 'You hang in there, Ma.'

She turned and peered into the lounge. The two embattled Callahans were crouched, rifles pointing out into the dark – but the gunshot had woken Gus.

When he saw Vida he struggled to sit up, clutching at his torn and bloody throat with one hand. The other was clenched. He clawed at her despite the intervening distance. Then he opened his mouth and Vida panicked and crashed out through the kitchen door into the night, heaving her mother's limp body with her.

When she looked back she saw that her dread had been for nothing. The two gunmen had not even turned around. Gus Callahan would never be able to warn them: he was mute, the damage to his throat sealing his voicebox.

Vida waved.

She turned back to Ruth and kept going, stumbling for the few moments before Sam came to join her and take the lead back through the forest, taking turns with her to hold her mother upright on the path. He was high with excitement, and for them both the return trip to the ghost colony seemed effortless. If she had had the breath, Vida would have sung for joy. Her ma was alive, Sam had saved them, and Dyce was waiting for her – but what lifted her spirits most was the look on Gus Callahan's face as he watched her escape: the helplessness, the soundless scream, the absolute defeat.

26

In the day or so that followed, Ruth and Dyce seemed to heal at about the same pace, two voyagers in the new country of the camp. Vida kept careful track of the changes. Their eyes didn't lose the redness right away – they still looked like vampires caught at dawn – but in the excruciating sunlight Vida could make out their pupils, big as olives, ringed only with a band of the colored iris: blue for Dyce; brown for Ma. The vomiting had stopped and Ma joined Dyce in eating again, their jaws working, their bodies savage. It would be a few days before Ma would start talking properly, Vida reckoned, as she spooned the stewed dandelions into the two of them. They were like babies, having to learn everything from the start. When Ruth dozed off, her mouth would hang open like a wind-blown door on a loose hinge, her tongue lolling. She looked dead. Vida would gather her bones together, stuff the dry tip of her tongue back behind her teeth and roll her over to face the grass wall of the lean-to so that she didn't scare the few kids who had made it to the camp. They had enough to deal with.

She didn't go to any of the funerals for the same reason, though it was some comfort to know that the rituals were still being observed. Somewhere there were always a few brave souls keeping the lights shining against the dark. *It must be some use*, Vida thought. One day it would be over, the sicknesses all burnt out, and the people who were left behind would have to start over. It would be easier to do that if your conscience was clear.

People kept finding reasons to limp past their shelter, making detours on their way to tend the graves. Vida knew what they wanted: signs of improvement, signs of hope. The word had already begun to spread, and why wouldn't it? Folks were asking around, searching for compatible symptoms, their opposite number in the camp whose unlucky virus might make them into a new sum, a fresh set of possibilities. She had seen the fresh outcasts from surrounding settlements welcomed here like celebrities, mobbed with questions, set upon by old ladies with their hands on their hips who stood over the bewildered guests. All the ordinary rules of interaction had been suspended, as if everyone had been struck with Alzheimer's, traveling in time back to some half-remembered childhood playground.

'Does your back hurt when you pee? 'Cause that's only time my back doesn't hurt.'

'That there a boil on your foot? Looks like a boil. See here? I got boils on my scalp.'

It had taken Vida four days to sleep off her exhaustion, as if the more she slept the more she craved. The next day was another kind of trance. She spent it making traps, a dozen of them. Her fingers worked almost without her thinking about them: *muscle memory*, her stepdaddy would have said to her. *Your body knows what it's doing, even when your brain feels like it's empty. Keep your mind wide open while you work, and see what you invite inside.*

Vida remembered it well, the excitement of finding a dead rat in a trap of her own making, the raw pioneer pride in the wires. And the look of approval in her mother's eyes too, when she brought the kills back home – a watered-down version of the look that she reserved for her pregnant women: that deep-set admiration of motherhood. It made Vida hot with resentment whenever she thought on it: she wasn't going to be tying herself down with rug rats, that was for sure. She liked to walk unencumbered too much. And anyone could get pregnant. Anyone at all.

In the old days Vida had upwards of thirty traps set up around the house – outside in the fields, but inside too, as the rats grew bolder with deprivation. Vida lay in bed at night and thought she heard them advancing on the house in a ring, orchestrated, their eyes glittering in the small glow thrown by the fire left in the stove, their whiskers trembling with excitement and suicide. The rats had come closer as the months dragged on, and what was to stop them, really, once they realized that they far outnumbered the two humans left inside? In her mama's house was treasure: white flour, sugar, fat – the last staples of the old regime, when there was still the possibility of birthday cake.

That day she had tested nearly all the traps and found nothing until the last. She had lifted the rock, grabbed the limp rat and run back to the house with her trophy. At the outside table Ma smiled and clapped her hands together – quickly, twice, the way she had taught Vida to say thank you when she was little – and then took it from her and laid it out, as if the raggedy gray rat was a beloved pet on a vet's table.

'Get me some of those little sticks, baby,' she told Vida. 'And a rag.'

She had pushed the rat's unprotesting eyelids open with one of the sticks and looked right in. Then she pointed its snout up at the sun, and levered its mouth open so she could see down deep along the pink gullet. Vida saw the ridges on the roof of its mouth, the incisors like a staple remover. Ruth had once told her that rats needed to keep gnawing, to grind down their everlasting teeth and keep them from skewering their own lips. It had seemed wrong to Vida, to have that kind of anxiety built right into the species. Well, there was no more gnawing for this guy. He lay on his back on the table, his testicles big as marbles and just as useless to him now. Vida's ma covered her hand with the rag and felt the rat's abdomen, kneading it like dough. Then she stopped and took Vida's hand, directing her fingers to a spot under its neck. There were two lumps under the cloth.

'Raised glands.' She looked down and shook her head, and Vida wanted to cry. 'Can't risk it. Sorry, baby.'

Vida had taken the sick rat and buried it deep in the heat of the compost heap. That way, in time, it would not go to waste – something else Ruth had passed on to her the same way that the calcium in the rat's bones, the minerals in its flesh, the proteins in its fur would feed their small crop of carrots and beets.

But even her successes hadn't bought her Mama's love in its purest form: that was reserved for the strangers who limped to her door, weeping and crying out that they were dying when what they were doing was giving birth. Vida had returned from a day out setting deadfalls, her fingernails blue to their moons from being crushed by rocks too delicately set – but with a haul of three prairie dogs to compensate. When she reached the porch she sang out, 'Davy! Davy Crockett! King of the Wild Frontier!' Vida was looking forward to the evening. Mama would make a proper meal and devote the tiny skins to the patchwork in progress, and she could soak her sore hands.

But when she stepped inside, Ruth was in no mood for coddling or praise. She sat, knees together, in the raggedy armchair, paying no mind to the spots of blood on the carpet.

'Mama? What happened? You hurt?'

Ruth was glassy. 'Young girl. Fifteen, maybe. I helped her.'

'She gone?'

Mama nodded. 'Said her sisters were waiting for her. But they didn't want to come inside.'

Vida wanted to move on. Her muscles ached, and Mama was being creepy. Birthing always eclipsed any other achievement, and Vida was sick of it. She held up the booty.

'I got prairie dogs. Three of them.'

Mama nodded. 'Her name was Ester. She spelled it out for me, when she could breathe. You know what she said?'

Vida sighed and dropped her arm. 'I don't, Mama. What did she say?'

'Said, "Ester is the Queen of the Underworld". I told her I never knew that.'

'Why would you give your child a name like that? It's bad luck.'

Ruth shook her head. She sat in that armchair a long time before she got up and moved around the kitchen. Vida got out the vinegar and scrubbed at the bloody spots in the carpet.

In the camp now, Vida regarded her new traps and decided to go out with them. The appetites on Dyce and her ma were far outpacing any stocks the camp could provide. It wasn't rationing, exactly, but when everyone was ill, the little food they grew or found had to be as nourishing as they could make it. She felt guilty with every mouthful of her own, worrying about the next, sicker, person who might need it more. But Vida's patients had proved that they were on the mend. She could go out into the surrounding scrubland and feel that her conscience was clear.

Back when you could still get supplies, Ma had once traded a half-full gas canister for a dozen tubes of expired peanut butter. They would use up a tube until it was done – squeeze it from the bottom, roll it up tight to press the last speck from the cold nozzle. That's what Ruth was now, thought Vida, an empty tube, paper thin, rolled and massaged and trodden on until she had given up all she could. She needed to be refilled.

'Gonna catch me some peanuts,' she muttered to herself.

The man who was following her could see Vida's lips moving when she turned to the side every now and again, but he was not close enough to hear what she was saying. Pete had followed her out into the scrubland where she was laying the traps and assembling a couple of deadfalls for unwary prairie dogs. He had thought that his stoop and dragging foot would attract her attention, but they were some way from the camp now and he had realized that revealing himself would be more and more awkward.

He hunched down further and tried to quiet the dragging sound of his slow foot – stepping over the obvious sticks, avoiding the driest grass. When she finally stopped and took off her pack, he crouched low. To show himself now would prove he'd been stalking her, but if he waited half an hour he could stumble out and act just as surprised as she was. *Oh, I didn't know you were going this way too! What a coincidence!* And so he watched her through the grass like a big-game hunter.

She sat first for a while to gain her strength: any exertion burnt scarce calories, and Vida had made sure that she was getting hers mostly from the early spring roots and pin cherries. Catching a couple of rats or shrews would be welcome. Ma, especially, had eaten her fill of dandelions, and they were all craving meat – dense, hot protein to rebuild their wasted muscles.

The sun was up and the wind down, the ground dry from lack of rain. It was, if you were sensitive to them, criss-crossed with the pathways of tiny travelers – ideal for traps. In the early days back home, Vida could set ten or fifteen traps and come back the next morning for eight or nine critters. But the camp was different. Too many people, not enough resources. You couldn't leave a trap overnight; a strangling chipmunk or a squealing mouse caught under a deadfall would be snapped up by a wild dog.

Pete watched as Vida collected sticks and searched for the right kind of heavy rock. She lay flat on the dirt for minutes to set up each trap. Alone, she seemed to move differently, heavy and distracted. When she was done setting up a couple of the traps, she leant against a boulder and threw stones at a rotting tree stump. Pete was glad to see it.

There was a rustling in the grass behind him, and Pete turned as quickly as he could, his back wrenching. The porcupine bustled towards him, as if the grass had grown legs and was rising up against them.

Pete leapt up from his hiding place, his knees popping, and ran towards Vida's boulder.

'Hey!' she began, but then she saw the rustling porcupine, determined to attack. Vida picked up one of her heavy stones and threw it as hard as she could. Her stepfather would have been proud of her, she thought. *I hope you're up there watching, Evert.* Pete was trying to scramble up the boulder.

The porcupine stopped, trembling like a pensioner caught in traffic. Its head was gashed open. *Don't let it suffer, Vida,* came her mama's voice, and she went as close as she could.

The porcupine had given up trying to lacerate its enemies. It lay down, spines clattering, like a show pony doing sums in the dirt. Vida kept hammering at its head with the rock, fueled with a kind of cold rage. When she stopped she realized that she was salivating.

'Remind me not to piss you off,' Pete said.

Vida turned the porcupine over with her boot, careful not to get caught on the quills. Then she took it by the feet and brought it over to Pete. It was lighter than she expected.

She laid it in the open ground to inspect it. 'Leader of the army that scared off the Callahans, hey? You can come on down.'

'I didn't know what it was,' Pete defended himself.

Vida found a twig and prized open the creature's bloodied eyelid. Inside, the whites were clean, the iris strong and brown.

'What you doing out here, anyway? Spying on me?'

'No, no. There's a rogue black bear around. Comes at night to dig through our graves. I'm just doing a sweep for paw prints.'

Pete noticed Vida's raised eyebrows and he dropped the pretense. 'Actually, I wanted to talk to you. Away from the rest.'

Vida narrowed her eyes. She had had these talks before, with young bucks in other settlements. Vida had always blamed it on the way she looked. In places where everyone else was sick, her blazing health and energy made her shine like a torch. *Oh, for a lazy eye!*

She worked the twig into the porcupine's mouth and pulled it open. Behind the yellow teeth the tongue was pink. She leant in and sniffed. It was okay: raw, like butchery meat, and musty, like pine.

'People at the camp, they're starting to experiment like you did.'

Thank God it wasn't the I've-loved-you-since-I-met-you speech. *Oh, really?* came Ruth's voice in her head. *What would*

you do if it WAS that speech, honey child? Flutter your lashes and
say, 'Oh, thank you, kind sir! But my heart belongs to another!'

Vida banished the voice and frowned, turning the porcupine
over to check its glands. 'What do you mean?'

'Rumor is that yesterday's funerals were both folks who'd
tried your theory and got it wrong.'

'Shit.' Vida set the creature down and stood up fast.

'Course that's their choice, right? That's the risk. Not as
though they had more than a couple of weeks to live, anyways.'
Pete shrugged, his crooked shoulder set higher than the other.
'But I been thinking we need a system. Can't be hit-and-miss
like this. There's got to be some way of making the process
more, more, *scientific*.'

'And?'

'And, I figured, since it was your idea, since you got it right,
maybe you'd take the lead – like you suggested, set up some sort
of clinic.'

'*Me?* No. That wasn't what I was suggesting. But you ought
to ask my ma. She used to be a nurse up north. When it comes
to sickness and such, she's the one person you want to know.'

'How many people you know?'

'Maybe five. Including you.'

They laughed.

'I'll make you a deal,' Vida said.

'What?'

'Carry this guy back to camp, and I'll run the idea past her.'

27

The porcupine meat definitely helped, in all kinds of ways. Dyce struggled up and insisted on skinning it, despite the effort it cost him. Vida stood back and let him do it, though it gave him the shakes so bad she was afraid he would hack a finger off with his knife. She told herself that it was a good sign that he was tired of lying around. The quills off the porcupine they stuck into the soil so that any skin flecks would rot safely. They could give you blood poisoning if you weren't careful.

Afterwards, Vida gave them out around the camp; they were useful for sewing or skewering or digging out splinters. She was not so generous with the soup, but people would understand, wouldn't they? There was not a lot to spare after Dyce and Ma and Vida had picked it apart, and Vida set the remains, mostly skin and bones, over the fire to boil down into a broth as they sat in a triangle around the flames.

Vida talked most, speaking into the gaps, as much for Ma and Dyce as for herself. If you told it enough, the story turned true – the Callahans chasing them, the hunting bird, Stringbeard and the Lazarus family, how Garrett had made for the coast. She watched Dyce as she talked, and wanted to stroke his hair. She wondered if he saw his brother in the bow of a stolen boat, one hand on his hip, the other shading his eyes from the glare of the sun as it flashed on the dolphins leading the way to his promised land. It was an ice-water shock to her every time she remembered where he really was: buried, hopefully, out behind the Weatherman's shack. Or worse – picked apart by roving coyotes, his femurs cracked and thrown into the corners of the continent.

Ruth listened close, looking hard at the two of them as if their bond was something visible, a thick rubber band. Sometimes she circled a hand to tell Vida to back up a little and explain again, especially about the murdering Callahans. Often her eyes were wet, but it was hard for Vida to tell if they were tears of pity or pride, or if the burst blood vessels had learnt to heal quicker under the film of moisture. Either way, she was grateful for the cure.

When the stories dried up, they bedded down for the night, and it was a relief to lay down when the sun went, not worrying about the revenge of the Callahans or the pursuit of wild creatures, unless you counted Ears McCreedy, who went everywhere that Dyce did. Vida and Dyce had taken to sleeping alongside one other. The spring weather was fair, and their little shelter was hardly big enough for two; three was impossible. Dyce had spent one day collecting wood and grass to extend it, a tiny alteration to their home that Vida called the granny flat. Ma took the hint and curled up there, leaving Vida and Dyce to enjoy the comforts of the main house. *This is how it happens*, Vida told herself. You work your whole life – you teach them everything you know – and then you hand it all over to your kids: the house and how to live in it. She was tired in a way she hadn't ever been – the fatigue that comes when the body is exhausted and the mind is overworked.

At first the intimacy had just been the touching of sides to keep warm, but as Dyce grew stronger, so did his interest, and

Vida was glad to waken in the night and find someone's bold arm draped over her. The end of the world made some things easier, but relationships weren't one of them.

In the morning they went about their work as if the connection hadn't happened, and it seemed easier to ignore it, the same way that she didn't ask him about how he sometimes twitched and called out in his dreams. She knew that, behind his eyelids, he was seeing Garrett.

In the daylight, Vida tried not to give it too much thought as she worked herself into a state of tiredness that would give her sleep. But in the afternoon, when she was helping to cover over the grave of one of the recently deceased, she found herself scraping the soil back with a flattened stick and looking forward to the night. Not to the sleep itself with its softness and obliteration, but to the time when she and Dyce could touch, and she would feel his hot, sweet breath on the back of her neck.

That night she lay pressed against his spine in its furred flannel and reasoned with herself.

He's still a stranger.

He's too young and green.

This is just lust. The natural survivor urge, is all. The clockwork of our bodies.

And the kicker, if the other reasons hadn't been convincing: *he's going to leave you for sure when he finds out you lied. You killed his brother twice.*

Before, it had always been Ruth and Vida to the bitter end, amen, but now things were hazy. She planned to ask Ma about what Pete had suggested – she really did – about her leading the plan to combine viruses. She was only waiting for her ma's energy to return so that they could discuss it.

Wasn't she?

Vida sighed and turned over. Dyce stirred and she craned her neck to check on him. The goddamned squirrel was posed near the pillow, his shiny black eyes fixed on her face. 'Relax, Ears,' Vida told him.

But what if Pete's plan worked? What if Ruth took on her old nursing role again and chose to stay in the ghost colony? She would want to do her bit, Vida knew. That wouldn't work for Vida, would it? She was pretty sure she didn't want to live here. The place was for sick people. They were getting better under their own steam, sure, but Vida wasn't one of them. She already felt claustrophobic: everyone knew her name and greeted her by it. What if her ma stayed and Dyce wanted to move on? What would she do then? *Stay, stay. Stay with Ma! That's the way it's always been. Always will be. Right?*

Vida sighed. She would never get to sleep this way, worrying about everything coming to get her in the days ahead. She was here, now, and the smell of Dyce was making her crazy. *I'm tired*, she thought. *I'm tired, and it's wearing me down. It'll be easier in the morning.*

She reached one hand down between her legs, where she found she was already wet, and electric. She rubbed at herself – one minute, two – and then came the shudder in the darkness, the single good and true thing in the last forty-eight hours.

Dyce lay on his side, listening to Vida's breath speed up, the little pants for air as she tried to keep herself quiet, and then the sighing as she subsided. It was all he could do not to turn over.

28

It took Felix two days to bury the boys.

Garrett was first up. He'd kind of liked the kid. Reminded Felix of himself all those years back in New York. All mouth and nothing out of reach. Walden he'd not spoken to before he'd turned the way he was now, icy and slack-jawed. Felix could judge him only by his sun-shy skin and the hair still parted cleanly, even though the boy had struggled in his death throes. Garrett's grave was deeper, the stones piled up in a cairn. Walden had a couple of spadesful of dirt thrown over his chest.

'Sorry, boys. I know I'm playing favorites. Looks like someone got killed by a rockfall right next to a grave,' Felix told them when it was all done and he stood regarding his work. 'But that's just the way it is. The fucks are running real low right now. Real low.' He reckoned they would understand. Walden would, anyhow. Even in death he had the look of the underdog.

Felix hobbled back inside, made it back down the stairs to his room so he could lay his carcass down. He didn't feel much better than the two boys back there in the dirt. Some of it was the guilt. He'd not been out to check on the weather boxes for – what was it now? One, two, three, four, five, six days? – and that was bad. Staying a step ahead of the wind relied on data, on the familiar circuit he walked as often as could, like a nurse doing hospital rounds. Once a day would be ideal, of course, but a man could end up chasing his own raggedy tail. He'd been meaning to go the day that Vida and Garrett and Dyce stormed in, just as soon as the wind died down. But that day had run away in a blur, hadn't it? His head hurt when he thought about it. Felix ran his questing fingers over the rough stitching in his scalp. The day after that was what? Tye's visit. Then he had begun the digging of Garrett's grave – and underestimated how much the manual labor would sap his strength. He'd slept late the next morning and only got round to Walden's grave near noon, and it showed.

He couldn't wait another day. He'd have to get going even though it was already late. Felix tried to get up again but his legs were shaking and his body would not obey the order to stand. He slapped at one thigh.

'Come on, old man! You're not dead yet.'

He managed to get up. What did he need? His bag was packed with the usual: some jerky to chew on, get the blood going again; water – always water; and then his notebook. He thought a while and then added his Llama Danton. Felix didn't usually take the gun with him on his rounds: it was bad juju. That kind of thinking made a man twitchy, and twitchy was an invitation. But knowing that Tye Callahan was in his neighborhood unsettled him some. 'Better safe, eh?' he told the gun. He sat back down on the lip of his cot. That was all he could manage. It would have to be tomorrow.

☠

Felix set out early the next morning, but he was frustrated straight away. He didn't have enough information to make the wind calculations as accurate as he wanted. He had his face mask tied loose around his neck, ready for when he needed, and now he tugged at the material to loosen it. He hadn't used the thing for over a year; it was more habit than anything else. Once a ladies' scarf, now it was a pale and ragged paisley worn to the warp and weft. Maybe one of them hippie chicks had worn it at Woodstock for a bikini. His thigh and back muscles were complaining as he climbed the incline, but they warmed up slowly when his body realized he wasn't going to get back to bed any time soon.

'Come on, you old fart. Just got to stick close to the ridge,' he told himself. 'Get a couple more readings.'

The absence of information made him uneasy, but there was also something weirdly exhilarating about being stranded this way. What was the song? The one about not having to be a weatherman to know which way the wind was blowing? Close enough. *Weatherman, do your thing.* Felix kept his eyes on the distant hills. You could have all the fancy instruments you liked – and he did, the way that men had collected cars in the old days – but the most important thing when you were telling the future was this: know your territory. He said it again, to remind himself. The obvious things were the ones you forgot. Thought you were smart, when what you were was cocky. Look at Walden. Garrett too. Young and tough, and under a bunch of rocks.

The next box looked as if it was all in order. Felix opened the front and took the readings from the gadgets: thermometer, hydrometer, barometer. The maximum wind speed had been marked on the gauge on the anemometer. Now he reset it and wrote it down, mumbling the numbers to himself so that they didn't slip his mind. He secured the door with wire again and patted the lid, as though the contraption was an old dog – the homebody breeds from before, when they were still friendly. Felix took a slug of water from the canteen, but didn't sit. He ached from the digging and a long rest would only make it worse. He dreaded to think what the next morning would bring him.

Felix kept to his old path that wound up the side of the mountain. He had a view of the valley and his little shack – now the two fresh graves beside it – and of the river and the nut trees and the opposite peak. He'd never gone beyond there. That territory was ghost colony and those poor fuckers could have it.

He walked on towards the ruined settlement of Glenvale. He'd smelt it burn. In hiding, he'd watched as the straggling survivors found their way across the river and all the way up to the refuge beyond the crest. Now Glenvale was gone – most of it, anyhow – but the ghost colony persevered. The ones that started small had less to lose.

Felix wasn't paying close enough attention when the next weather box came into view. It was still there, which was good news. It was only as he stepped into the clearing around the box that he saw the man's legs protruding from the open side.

'Hey!'

The legs jerked once in surprise, and then the man pulled himself out from underneath. He struggled up and looked at Felix, blinking too fast against the sunlight. He had a scraggly beard that he had tied with string like a Christmas present, and he was stroking it now, cat-quick. *Why did they do that?* Felix wondered. It reminded him of Walden's hair, slicked back and parted. *For what? The prom?*

Felix freed his arm from the pack strap and slid the bag around to his chest so that the gun was invisible but in reach.

'You know whose property you're tampering with there?'

The man shuffled, as if he couldn't decide which leg should take his unsteady weight. Drugs, Felix would have said, if this was thirty years ago. But he saw it now for what it was: one of them brain viruses. *Fuck*. You never knew which way those fuckers were going to jump.

'Yours?' The man was making an effort to parley.

'You bet your ass it is. Now, what you taken?'

Stringbeard opened his hand. It shook a little. On the mapped palm lay six rusty nails.

'Alright. You're going to put those down, right there. Then you're going to back away. And *then* you're going back to wherever you come from. And you better stay clear of these boxes, or I'm coming guns blazing next time. And I mean that.'

The man rubbed at his eyes, as if he couldn't quite believe what he was hearing. 'Take it easy, old timer. This is a misunderstanding. I'm an honest man. Just out looking for whatever might help me rebuild my place. Needed me some nails and the hardware store is closed.'

'What place?'

He threw a hand in the direction of the long-distance carnage. 'Fieldstone.'

'Thought Fieldstone was gutted.'

'Like a trout.' He grinned, skew, and the beard shifted down an inch. 'But I'm making it new again. Making it nice for me and my family.' He wiped his forehead.

'You all okay there? No one sick?'

'Nope. We were the lucky ones – and I'll tell you what else: we recruit. You ain't exactly in your prime, but then, who is? We could do with the extra set of hands. How about it?'

'It's a two-part answer: "No, thanks" and also, "Fuck off".'

'Look, I reckon if we could sit down and talk, I could change your mind.'

Felix squinted at the man. The sweat was standing out on his head again, and the eyes were crusty, for sure.

Stringbeard was starting to inch closer and that made Felix fumble in his bag for the gun. When he pointed it they both saw his trembling, but there was no other way for this to go: he knew the brainworm when he saw it.

'You back the fuck up or I shoot you.'

Stringbeard didn't flinch. 'Wind's picking up,' he said mildly.

The asshole was right. The cups on the anemometer were turning slowly. Felix checked up along the ridge and saw the spruce branches jostling. There wasn't much time.

'I got shelter,' Stringbeard was saying. 'No harm, no foul. When this is all over you can come on back and help me rebuild. My wife will be glad of the company. She don't get out much. Now come on over here and we can shake on it.'

Felix shook his head and checked back at the ridge. The spruce was being shaken more violently, like an old man in a coughing fit. The wind was coming fast.

Stringbeard took his chance and leapt at Felix, a vicious dog who attacks when a man's attention is elsewhere.

Felix fired, hardly knowing what to pray for.

The bullet hit Stringbeard in the chest, right through the soft flesh of his lungs and heart, and out again at the other side.

Felix turned and ran back along the path, the wind a ghost dog biting at him, pulling at his clothes for purchase. As he loped he pulled the face mask up over his mouth. He took two paces and then he stopped.

The cloth was wet on his lips.

He yanked it off and held it up. The pale fabric was spattered red with the wind-swept blood of the man lying dead behind him in the clearing.

29

The next morning, Vida woke with Dyce's sleep-warm arms around her. Ruth was up already, sitting and poking at the smudged gray embers of the fire. Vida wriggled free from Dyce's hold and went to join her, and the two of them idly threw kindling on the undecided flames so that the leftover porcupine soup would serve them another meal.

'Hello, baby,' said Ma. Her mother's speech was labored and a little slurred, but it was her own true voice, not just the hunger, and Vida had missed it. She smiled. Though her ma had been there for a couple of days, listening and then looking through those wet, red eyes, she had only really just arrived. Maybe disease was a kind of near-death experience. You faced yourself and tried to talk your demons down.

'How you feeling, Ma?'

'Tired. Sore. Better.' Ruth smiled back.

'Nothing porcupine soup couldn't fix, then.'

They regarded the pot. Vida tested the liquid, but it was still night-cool.

Ruth nudged her daughter gently with her elbow. 'And you too, you know, not just the soup. Thank you.'

'Just call me Porcupine Girl. I could get a suit.'

'And I could sew you a cape. Some sequins on the quills.'

'It would be hard to run, though.'

Ruth snorted, then winced and clutched her stomach. 'Don't make me laugh.'

Their weak laughter dried up. Vida laid her head on her mother's shoulder. Ruth smelt alright again too, her own sweaty cloak of illness untied from her throat. She stroked Vida's head.

'Your braids are getting real fuzzy,' she said. 'I can redo them for you sometime.'

'It takes too long, Mama.'

'How *are* you?'

Vida shrugged, adolescent. 'Doing good.' She knew Ruth wasn't asking that, exactly. She looked quickly at Dyce, then back at her mother. 'I been better.'

'You like that boy?'

Vida burrowed her chin into the collar of her shirt, embarrassed, unsure.

'Vida. I been blind, not *stupid*.'

Vida poked at the reluctant fire. The bottom of the soup pot was only lukewarm, but she dished the food up anyway, for something to do.

'Ma, I got something to run by you.'

'I'm listening.'

'Pete – some people – asked if I'd stay in here in the camp, set up some way to know who has what sickness. Work out how to combine them the way I did for you and Dyce. I told him I was just lucky, and that you were the real medicine lady. I told him they should ask you.'

Her mother sipped at the soup and pulled a face. 'Is this them asking?'

'I guess.'

'And what you think of that?'

Another shallow shrug. 'I don't know. It might work.'

'What's your Plan B, then? Back to the house?'

'I don't think I can, Ma.' The full force of what she was saying suddenly hit Vida. She set her own soup down. That part of her life was well and truly gone, the old ties to childhood severed by disease and the dying men who came after them.

'Why not? The house still standing? The garden left, at least?'

'Callahans gonna come after me and Allerdyce, Ma. They not ever going to give up. You should have seen that Tye and his bird. Don't know what options that exactly leaves us.'

Ma looked at the cup in her hands, her lips pressed together. Vida knew that look: love and disapproval in equal measure.

'Would you stay here, Ma? For now? Try to help out? They need a proper nurse, someone who knows the plants real well.'

'I don't know. I suppose I'd like to stay. Helping's what I know best and they've been very kind. Then again, I'm getting on. Suppose that's a reason for and a reason against. Need to do some thinking, I guess.'

'We'll go for a walk around after breakfast if you can manage. Show you the place.'

Vida poured the last of the broth into a billy-can and rested it back on the duller coals.

☠

When Dyce woke, Vida and her ma were two tiny figures walking slowly among the graves. He knew what each would be thinking: how neat each plot was kept, how carefully tended. Maybe it took death to make people realize they were human.

Dyce moved closer to the fire. There was a warm mug waiting there for him. He smiled when he saw the garnish floating on the surface: a bright-yellow yarrow flower.

He hadn't seen the woman heading down the slope to the graveyard until she was almost upon him. She looked weak, and there were white patches of scalp showing through her blond hair, but she was intent, a leprous milkmaid carrying a scratched-up bucket.

'Morning! Hey, there! Excuse me?'

'Morning.' She stopped.

Dyce didn't recognize her: a newbie. Up close he saw she had welts criss-crossing her arms and neck. He tried not to stare at the bald patches on her head.

'Can I ask you a question?'

She nodded, wary.

'Where you come from?'

She cocked her damaged head. Was she mute?

'Your settlement. Which settlement were you at? I mean, before you came here?'

'Eel Ridge.'

'You see anyone on your way? A guy? About so high? Dark hair? Maybe walking like he was hurting?'

She shook her head. *Jesus! She looks like whatever she survived nearly killed her*, thought Dyce. *Like she belongs in a mental asylum.*

'Okay. Thanks.' He tried to think of other things to ask her before she took off on her slow, blank journey to find water.

'Long shot, I know, but you heard of any, uh, settlements between here and the coast?'

She laughed, a little choking sound low in her thin throat. 'Where you wanna go? We're at the edge of the world here, you know that?'

'Well, now. That's not strictly true.'

She set her empty bucket down, then changed her mind and picked it up again.

'I did hear talk of one. But I never been there, myself.'

'What's it called?'

'The Mouth. Weird name, huh?'

'You know if anyone arrived here from The Mouth in the last week? I just want to ask if they've seen my brother. I could do with some news.'

The woman leaned in closer, confiding, and Dyce had to force himself not to retreat.

'The Mouth, they say, don't expel their sick folks.'

'For real?'

'I heard that's 'cause they *got* no sick folks.'

Dyce looked carefully at her. She went on.

'Sounds too good to be true, right? But people want to believe these things.'

'I know I do.' Dyce pretended cheeriness. 'Tell me there's a man selling ice cream sundaes and I'm first in line!'

The woman gave him another one of her looks and left Dyce to sip at his breakfast. The marrow fat sat congealed on the surface, rich and rancid.

'The Mouth,' he said, trying the name out as he chewed on the yarrow flower.

30

Felix crouched on the leeward slope, coughing. The phlegm that he hawked up lay streaked with red when it landed in the dirt. His cloth mask was long gone, blown away and caught on the bones of a chokecherry bush, a blood-spattered flag of surrender.

The same wind kept blasting him with grit and the invisible poison it hurled along. Felix knew he was in more trouble than he could handle. This was it: cold Mister Death was coming, and not a horse in sight, neither. So much for the apocalypse. The end, when it came, was always going to be an anti-climax.

He laughed and then coughed. He took the Llama Danton off his belt and checked the bullets in the magazine. He'd done it that morning already, but he needed to make sure they'd all moved up one the way they were supposed to. The first time would have to pay for the rest: he wasn't sure he'd be able to pull the trigger twice.

The bullets sat neat and ready, tarnished but not so bad they were unusable. The rusted spring had worked, hadn't it? It would fire. The gun still smelt the way it had years back: the tang of powder, the bite of hot metal against the soft webbing of your palm. These were the objects worth saving, the ones made in the forge of men's dread and understanding, the things that gave you options.

He practiced, holding the gun to his temple, and looked out across the valley. Not a bad view to have etched on your corneas till the beetles came. Or the dogs, more like. Whatever had already happened – and whatever else lay ahead – the pines still cascaded down the opposite slope and the river was a bright line of mercury in the sunlight. The almond trees he had worked for still danced as the wind pushed at them. They resisted. He had put down the same dogged roots. The shack was the only home he had.

But for fuck's sake. A virus was a whole other world: a kingdom of disease. Even if it wasn't the kind that made straight for your brain, a man's gut made him do strange things. Most of all, the sickness made him a sitting duck. Felix lowered the gun and swallowed hard to test his throat. It was definitely coming, but there was time. His body had always let him down – night cramps, headaches, shin splints and torn tendons – but its large-scale disintegration wasn't right. He would sit at his table as he'd always thought he would, close his eyes and end it there, before somebody else did it for him in a way he couldn't imagine.

Felix set off down the slope, making for home, staggering and unsteady against the rude shoving of the wind. He fell twice, and both times he grazed and cut his arms on the loose shale: downhill was worse than up. Wasn't that always the way?

At his shack door he stopped and turned round, making a circle as he took in his last view of the world. Then he'd had enough. He hobbled inside and shut the door on it.

He found the bottle of liquor on the sideboard in the dim coolness and took two big swigs that burnt his throat. Even taking into account his eyes having to adjust, the place was too dark: he would have to power her up one last time. He climbed up onto the bike and turned the cogs until the light grew strong enough to see his possessions.

'That's right,' he said. 'Sun shines out of my ass. Yes, it *does*!'

But it wasn't funny. He had to spend his last few minutes in his right mind. Felix pedaled and as he went he looked closely at each book and map and instrument as if it were a museum exhibit. Things sure got gravity, didn't they? Time went by and they meant something to you but nobody else. He got off the bike and patted the sweaty seat. Then he picked up his brass sextant, heavy and precise, alchemical. '*I am the master of my fate*,' he intoned. '*I am the captain of my soul.*'

He set it down and moved on to the tape player. How many times had he listened to the recitation of his history?

'Once more can't hurt, now, can it?'

The player whirred acquiescence, and then the sound of his own name made him shiver. 'Felix,' said his past self, the smartass, 'I hope you've still got the balls to have that gun on the table.'

The gun.

Where had he put it? He had been outside. Then in here. On the bike, right? Felix squinted into the shadowed corners. What had he done with it? He let the tape play on as he searched for the weapon.

Not in the bag or on the sideboard where he'd fetched something. What had he gone to get? The bottle.

He went upstairs and checked. Nothing. Then he went out front of the shack and stood shading his watering, panicky eyes against the empty landscape.

He was halfway up the slope again before the rage kicked in.

'Jesus! *How could you lose it, you old fart?*'

But then the thought came swirling that he'd lodged it too loosely on his belt on purpose. Maybe his sick brain had already poisoned the rest of his system, hollowing him out like a gourd.

All told, he must have searched the hillside for an hour, desperate for the gleam of metal.

He gave up and went back to the shack. He sat down against the tethering pole.

'Okay. I give up. Where's the closest gun, then, you asshole?'

The answer was simple.

The ghost colony. Had to be.

He struggled up again. He'd pack a bag real quick – just something to eat. He wouldn't be staying long when he got there, would he? He had a pressing engagement with dementia. He made his way back inside the shack.

The day turned and against it Felix Callahan went walking, the lyrics of a hundred childhood songs falling at his heels.

'The cat was Dallas,' he kept mouthing to himself. 'The cat. His name was Dallas.'

At the river he stopped to check the canvas bag for food. He reached in, feeling for jerky or nuts. There were none.

He looked inside and then tipped the whole bag upside down. He'd packed its pockets with dirt and dried grass.

31

The Mouth.

Even the name was fearsome. Maybe it was the soup, but his own mouth was dry. Dyce looked at Ears McCreedy in the pack where he had been set to keep him away from the fire. The idea of losing the little squirrel turned something like a vise in Dyce's chest. Strange, after all the times he'd told Garrett to ditch the thing.

'You got to eat a whole extra meal a week just to carry that sand bag around. It's a waste of calories.'

'Keeps me trim, now, don't it, Fatty?' Garrett had lifted his shirt, shown off the scarred skin stretched over his ribs, the horrific punch line to his joke.

Dyce stared Ears down. The pupils were black plastic eyes for a teddy bear that his dad had found in a sewing kit. There was something wrong about the perfection of the work on the squirrel's face. Garrett's handiwork always had an obvious flaw – the stitches prominent, or too much skin folded in on itself, which made the creature gaunt, the tail shriveled, dry as jerky. And Garrett knew they were bad. He didn't do it because he liked the way they looked. Ears seemed real: that was all.

It kept Dyce thinking about Garrett, about how he could be alive and well and somewhere else, on his way to freedom in another country across the water. The trek south to the ocean was another thousand miles. Even without the Callahans on Garrett's tail, getting there would be nigh-on impossible. The closer he got to the coast, the more the wet sea air would foster the viruses. The still air itself would turn to poison. And the onshore winds with their heat and humidity would make it worse. On his own Garrett would miss the signs of the rising wind, no question. Dyce was sure he would find himself out in the open, without the right kind of shelter. All his life he'd relied too heavily on his little brother to clean up, to apologize, to take responsibility. For Dyce that had meant that whatever big talk Garrett had delivered about going on alone, he'd never meant a word of it. They'd been inseparable because they needed to be – the bravado and the smarts in equal measure. Garrett needed him. Right?

Garrett needed him, and this ghost colony didn't. Not the way it needed Ruth.

How long would it take him and Vida to catch Garrett up? He and she were both healthy, getting stronger by the day – and they had each other for protection.

And not just protection. Dyce remembered Vida's desperation in the night, the smell of her body between them, the way she had got up first and left in a hurry.

Oh, man. He remembered.

And would it be so wrong, anyway? The two of them? She wasn't that much older, was she? Maybe a ten-year gap between them. People did it all the time – and that wasn't even when the world was ending.

'Come on, Ears. Give me some of that squirrel wisdom, buddy. What do you say?'

Ears was no fucking help at all.

Vida and Ruth walked up slowly between the shelters. As they went, she made an automatic note of the wind, blowing north. She was constantly vigilant, more so after the Weatherman's dire prediction, waiting for the thunderous orange sky that would precede the deluge. If he was right, every hundred years was the end of the world. The super-storm when it came always wiped out the things people called civilization, the way the Great Galveston Hurricane of 1900 did, and a hundred years before that with The Big Rain, and again a hundred years prior to *that*, before people were naming their weather – when the severity of the thing could only be counted by the number of bodies that floated past, human and animal. *We run to the places that are the least help to us*, Vida told herself.

But Horse Head was peaceful. The wisps of smoke rose from the friendly fires, straight and slow, until they hit the stream of air above, forced up and away by the mountain ridge. *I hope they're grateful*, Vida thought. These folks got their own personal groundhog standing by.

She hadn't really paid close attention to the people, not since she'd had her own problems to take care of, but she saw again as she walked that the groups of residents were not regular families at all. Not traditional ones. There were no mothers or fathers with their children here, neat four-square units built for buying cars. These were new-world families, built from the remnant outcasts. There were men and women taking care of each other, sure, but they had formed themselves into groups that took care of the kids, the scared and lonely ones who'd been shut out of their home camps and made to walk away.

And we are part of them, Vida thought. *We've done it too. You can't just look after your own.*

Vida and Ma walked slowly among the people at the graves, greeting the sick who were tending to the dead. A man wandered over with his basket of roasted sweet potatoes. Vida handled a hot one for her mama and divided it. They would share it, as they shared everything, its skin crisp and sweet. They watched the man hand the rest out to all who would take them, until his basket was empty. Hoarding was for the living.

Vida looked at Ruth and saw she was tired. 'Let's sit here and have a picnic, Ma.'

She wiped one hand and then helped Ruth to sit on a stump at the edge of the camp in the shade of a pine. Ma puffed her cheeks and looked at her half of the sweet potato.

'Vida, baby. I'm going to stay here.'

'Okay. Should I come by and get you later?'

'No, I mean that I'm going to stay here, in the camp, and help. And I think you should go.'

'What?' Vida felt the tears pushing up from her chest, a tap that had been turned on.

'You're right,' Ruth said. 'I think I can help. I need to do *something*. And it's time you did your own thing, anyway.'

Vida wanted to say all kinds of things to change her mother's mind, but the tears were getting in the way. She gave in to them and put her arms around Ruth, who let her cry against her chest. Ruth talked and her voice made her sternum vibrate against her daughter's cheek. Vida tried to calm herself but she ended up thinking of all the nights her ma had stayed up with her when she was scared or sick or just lonely. How did you ever let go of your mother? It made her cry harder, a storm of tears that had been a long time gathering. Ruth kept going, her potato cooling in her hand. It was better to say it all, get it out right away and not let it fester.

'Of course, you can stay if you want. That's your choice. But I'm going stay and help. I had a lot of time alone with my thoughts those nights in the house, Vida, and I did not like what I saw. There are a lot of things I have to put right – demons that followed me all the way from up north that I need to parley with. You know some of the story but you're not ready to know all of it, and one day I'll tell you. But, right now, you just need to trust that there are things I need to make right, and I think I can do it here.'

'Then I'll stay too.'

'I can't see Dyce wanting to stay here, baby. He's too young. He's going to go looking for his brother, and you need to decide whether you going to follow him. You want my advice? When he goes, I think you should go along. Not 'cause I think you should marry the boy and have his kids – Jesus, no! – but because he's going someplace. And I'm done going places. I'm saying this because I love you. You've always been a part of my story, but now it's time to start your own.'

'We're not *books*, Ma.' Vida sniffed.

'You of all people should know how important books are, Vida. You keeping the recipes safe?'

'I am, Mama. Don't worry.' Vida didn't mention the spilled bag, the remedy book lying beside it in the morning sun, damp from the grass – and that she'd chosen already between Dyce and the book.

Between Dyce and Ma.

But maybe it wasn't Dyce she'd chosen. Maybe he was just an option that wasn't Ma – a choice different to the only one she'd ever had.

'But I won't go. He can go. I don't care. I won't.' The words out of her mouth sounded hollow even to her own ears.

'Don't decide yet. I'm going to stay, and that's all we need to say for now. Now wipe your eyes.' Ma, her message delivered, tore into her sweet potato, wolfing down the orange flesh. Vida held onto hers but couldn't bring herself to bite into it.

'I think I will sit here for a bit, baby girl,' said Ma, after the last mouthful. 'Come and find me later.'

Vida was dismissed. She stood to go, and when she was some way off she turned to watch her ma sitting with her head in her hands. *At least she's sad about it*, thought Vida. When Ruth saw Vida watching her, she wiped her face and forced a smile and a wave. It turned into another gesture, and Vida saw Dyce coming up the hill. He looked healthy and quick, purposeful, swaggering. *Give a man a pair of dry pants and he thinks he owns the world*, thought Vida. Ma was right that he wouldn't stay. And Vida knew, just watching him walk to her, smiling and dirty, that she would go with him. He was a gateway, a big old fucking door to some other way of living. She wiped her eyes on her sleeve. Maybe it was the hushed air, making her weepy. Her cells knew that the weather was changing, and the rain would be here soon. Not yet, but soon.

'Where's your ma?'

'Resting for a bit.'

'So, I got some news.'

Vida had not thought her heart could sink lower than it already had.

'I heard about this place. Settlement they call The Mouth.'

32

Dyce spent the rest of the morning going around the camp, asking people what they knew about The Mouth – its exact location, in particular – while Vida sulked and checked the weather. So far he had not found anyone who had been there themselves, but the third- and fourth-hand accounts made it sound like heaven.

And heaven was due south, in the cleft of a valley. It made sense, Dyce thought. Protection from the wind. The name, one man said, came from the fact that it used to be a copper mine. He wheezed as he talked, whole sentences in sharp breaths, but Dyce could make it all out pretty clearly. The Mouth was where the series of tunnels began. There were probably dozens of little shafts and air vents and caves, an extra blessing if the wind ever did find its way down the slopes. But what did you do if there wasn't space for everyone? Dyce wondered if you left the worst-off outside – the feeble and the old – to take their chances. Let nature take its course, and all that. He had always hated that saying. Nature wasn't fair, and it wasn't always right, either.

But the best part about The Mouth, if Dyce's calculations were correct, was that it was beyond the edge of the world – beyond the reach of the Callahan clan, and on the way to the coast. Whatever order the Callahans brought was likely not welcome there, so Garrett at least stood a chance of survival.

The Mouth probably ran itself too, the way Horse Head did. The little pockets of resistance maintained their own structures, but their freedom was hard-won.

When Dyce told Vida about it he'd expected more of a reaction, but she was subdued. She folded her arms and looked at the ground and kept saying, 'But how do you know for sure, Allerdyce?'

It irked him. 'You got anything of your own to add to the pot?'

Her mouth tightened and they stood in silence, looking out to the horizon. Beyond it the clouds were gathering, menacing and mute, readying themselves for attack.

The scream, when it came, pierced the lowering sky between them, and they watched as a woman came running down the slope towards the camp. She kept shouting and waving, high-pitched and desperate, like a long-dead siren come back to life. Dyce and Vida couldn't make out what she was saying: as her feet thumped on the ground the air was punched out of her. She would be with them soon enough – and you never knew if it was a brain disease that was doing the talking.

When she reached their shelter the woman stopped, her hands holding her sides as she caught her breath. But before she could talk she bent over and retched like a dog. Dyce and Vida jumped back as the strings of bile dangled down towards the earth. The woman wiped her mouth on her sleeve and then spat out her words like vomit, panting in between.

'Allerdyce! It's Sam. Oh, God! It's Sam! Other side of the peak!'

Dyce felt his heart ratcheting up, the urgency passed on like a fever.

'Where, exactly?'

She straightened and pointed, her thin arm shaking. 'Straight over the ridge.' Dyce followed the line of the limb, the blackened fingernail. She looked as if she'd been digging in the dirt.

He set off, and Vida followed. He had not tried running since he'd been sick, doing only as much as he felt he reasonably could while his body did its best to catch up with his expectations. But now that he was actually doing it, he felt good – nimble. He pumped his legs and Vida, surprised by the burst of speed, had trouble keeping up. At the crest Dyce zig-zagged over the rocks and down, feeling the way the air changed as he went. Here it was fresh, rising from the muddy valley, green and pine-scented and energizing.

Every couple of meters he called out. 'Sam! Sam! If you can hear me, yell!'

A couple of hundred yards down, beyond the stone border of the colony, Dyce heard the moans. They adjusted their course, stopping and listening for the sounds every few seconds to get their bearings. Then Dyce heard Pete calling out.

'This way! Over here!'

Dyce pushed through the foliage and found himself in a clearing. Pete stood to one side, his brown face pale with horror. On the ground was a body with its ankle held in the claws of a bear trap. The man's face was hidden under Pete's jacket, but Sam's voice was still his own. The skin that Dyce and Vida could see had once been so pale it was blue, like a drowning victim, the veins mapping the surface. But the hours in the sun had burnt and blistered the skin, and each time Sam twisted away from the trap he rubbed himself raw. Under the jacket he kept moaning.

Dyce came closer and saw his leg, the bone snapped by the spring of the trap. Flies circled the sticky mess.

Oh, Jeez. I can see the marrow!

Pete touched his arm and Dyce shook him off. 'Sorry,' Pete said. 'You've been exposed to whatever he has, right?'

Dyce nodded.

Pete went on. 'I can't touch him without getting infected. But you—'

'Get me a branch, then. Quick.'

Pete dodged off, glad to have something to do, and Dyce bent to inspect the trap. Rusty and sharp-toothed, laid recently, fingermarks in the dirt where someone had scooped leaves to cover it over.

And a feather: long-shafted, banded gray and brown.

Dyce picked it up.

Tye fucking Callahan.

He handed it to Vida. They looked at each other and then she set the feather aside. 'You gonna try to get that man out of there?'

Dyce sat on the down-slope and found a grip for his fingers on the jaw of the thing. Then he tried to wedge a boot heel into the gap. Sam screamed in pain.

'Easy, easy, easy,' Dyce spoke, as much to himself as to Sam. He looked at Vida and gestured at Sam. Vida knelt and spoke to him – stroking his arm through his shirt like he was an animal she had to gentle: careful, always careful. He'd suffered bad here, she could see, his hands bloody from trying to free himself, the palms and fingers cut in his fight to be free before the punishing dawn.

'Pete! For fuck's sake! Where's that branch?'

'Coming!'

He appeared, out of breath, with a chunk of damp wood in his hand.

'Okay. On three I'm going to open it. Then I want that wedged in here, right?'

Pete nodded and aimed at the jaws like a knight with his lance ready to pierce a dragon.

'One . . .'

Vida gripped Sam's arm.

'Two . . .'

Sam brought the wood closer, right to the lips of the beast.

'Three!'

Dyce dug his heel in and pulled. The ancient spring groaned and popped, readjusting itself, and the teeth opened slowly. Sam shrieked. Vida looked over at Dyce. His face was red with the strain, his neck a web of sinews and muscles, his lips pulled back against his teeth.

When the trap was open just wide enough, Pete jammed the wood in. Dyce let go, his hands wet with blood – his own and Sam's co-mingled.

The wood held.

Dyce took hold of the trap and worked it off Sam's leg, past the splinter of bone and over his bare foot. The calf was shredded. In the wound Dyce could see specks of rust and dirt, the welcome mat laid out for infection.

'Got to get him back to my ma,' said Vida. 'Can you lift him?'

Dyce winced. 'Give me a second.' His back was in spasm from the exertion. He leant back against the pain. He would pay for that the next morning.

'Wish we could help.'

'I'm fine.'

He stretched his neck from side to side and then crouched down carefully beside Sam. He had blacked out. Good. Dyce slid his hands around the man and laid him over his shoulder like a baby. Sam was light, skin and brittle bones.

Pete shepherded Dyce back to camp, showing him the best route and pulling branches aside to let them through. Vida left them and went to find Ruth. She knew the drill by heart: nest the knife in hot coals, boil the water, collect the yarrow and honey.

Ruth was used to the carnage. Vida watched as she set her mouth and then asked, 'Trap?'

They nodded.

'You,' Ruth shooed Dyce out of the way, 'go and do something useful.' She turned to Vida. 'Same as always. Hand me that hot water.'

She set about cleaning the wound on the unconscious Sam. This was the beginning of her clinic, step one in garnering trust and giving purpose. A couple of people were gathered, watching as Ruth set the bones back into shape as best she could, but Sam would always walk with a limp. Ruth went on to scrape and cauterize the wound.

Dyce called Vida aside, still bloody – his hands red up to his elbows like gloves, his boots and the cuffs of his pants too.

'That trap was fresh.'

'What do you mean?'

'It's not some old forgotten bear trap. That was set a few days back, max.'

'Callahans?'

'Yup.'

'Fuckers.'

'Not sure if you're thinking of staying on here but, if you are, I reckon this changes things some. We can't let these folks suffer for protecting us: can't let that happen. We leave now for The Mouth and pray it exists. It'll give us a good few hours before sunset.'

Vida wanted to argue, or at least challenge Dyce's authority in making decisions for the both of them, but he was right. She couldn't stay. There was relief in that, the decision made for her, the guilt of abandoning her mother evaporating into the clouds bulking overhead.

'I'll get my things.'

33

Vida found her mother down beyond the graves. She was shirt-less, washing the blood from her hands and face in a bucket filled from the camp's most reliable water supply – a greenish pond. Vida watched as Ruth scrubbed at her nails with a stick. Vida knew she would have chewed it into a brush, the same way they had cleaned their teeth back home. Ruth's shirt was hanging over a stand of reeds, streaked with rust-colored stains. When she saw Vida coming, the pack on her daughter's back seemed to settle its weight between her own shoulders.

Ruth stood up, dripping, her chest wet in its slip.

'Mama. We haven't said goodbye to the others.'

Ruth nodded and dried her hands on her skirt. Even to herself she smelt like chlorophyll and sunlight, a growing thing. She didn't trust herself to speak.

Vida went on. 'Didn't want them arguing against us going. Thing is, we need to. It's not about whether we want it or not, after what happened to Sam. That was deliberate, Mama. The Callahans are bad, pure and simple.'

Ruth sighed. 'I know.'

Vida jigged the pack on her back. Dyce was waiting, with his own new pack. 'Tell the others we left a little something to show our appreciation.'

'I'm not that little.'

They both smiled but couldn't laugh.

'I'm going to come back, Ma, sometime soon, to see you.'

'I'll be waiting, baby doll.'

Ruth's face was wet. She pulled Vida close and hugged her tight, breathing her daughter's smell, familiar as biscuits. 'Don't forget to do your hair.'

Dyce came down now too, and the women drew apart. He said his goodbyes to Ruth and held her cold hands. Then he walked down the slope. When he got to the line of stones marking the perimeter, he stopped and waited for Vida. Dyce held out his hand. They stepped over together, back out into the wild world.

They wound their way down the mountain, moving quickly and sticking to the rocky sections in order to avoid having to push through the brush.

'You know, a bear trap's got to be just about as valuable a thing as you'll find right now.'

'It cost him to leave it,' Vida agreed.

Dyce was right. A metal trap set each night could snare a deer or a porcupine or a jack rabbit: that Tye had left it behind was a statement of intent, a clear and present threat. Vida knew that they wouldn't shake him that easily. He was enraged that they had escaped him, furious that the detachment of the diseased had driven him away, maddened that he was just about the last of the real Callahans. It was a good thing they were moving along, and from now on they would have to be extra careful.

'Sleep with one eye open,' Dyce muttered.

'We always do,' Vida said. *If you only knew the half of it.*

The two of them walked on, ears pricked and eyes on the distant trees. As soon as the gentle movements turned into swaying, they would have to find shelter again: the old story. It was a kind of relief for Dyce, who had always been the one walking with his head up, scanning the rim of the horizon while Garrett plodded along, face to the ground, oblivious to the small deaths that stalked them everywhere.

The wind kept steady over the next two hours – strong enough to ruffle their clothes and make the little hairs on their arms stand up, but not hard enough to make them scuttle for safety and lose precious traveling time. It was a fine line, less science than art. As they went, Vida felt her heart beating in its abiding rhythm. She was ready, she told herself, for whatever was coming next.

'You ever think about horses?' asked Dyce. He was; he always was. He was thinking about them right now while his shins were scraped to shit on the thorns, even through his cargos.

'Jesus. All the time. We're going to a place that no one we know has ever seen, and you know what? It's probably fifteen fucking *miles* away. I've got to stop thinking of distance like we still have horses. Drives me nuts. With horses we could be to The Mouth and back in time for breakfast, instead of this shit.' Vida gestured at the ground around them and Dyce knew what she meant – the proximity to the sharp end of nature, the obstacles and nuisances a car or a horse once smoothed over. 'The whole world might as well be sixty miles square, for fuck's sake. I guess that's what makes Garrett's coast trip so, so—'

'Stupid?'

'I was going for "romantic".'

'Definitely stupid. Though, since it's Garrett's dream, that kind of goes without saying.'

Dyce smiled at her, and she saw the love and frustration. She felt the same way about Mama.

Over the next rise they saw the first signs of human set-tlement in the area. The track changed from its wild growth; more bare spots turned up, and eventually they found at their feet an asphalt road, cracked all along its edges, grasses growing through it like a skeleton. In the distance there were the con-crete uprights and faded orange roofs of an old town – long abandoned, they guessed.

The towns were the first places that people had quit. The concentration of sick, especially in the early days, meant that contracting two or three viruses was more likely than not. Back then no one had understood where they were coming from, or what they would do, and people went out to meet their deaths from the mumps and the common cold. No one Vida knew had been as lucky as Dyce and Ma. It had been a massacre.

The highways had posed the same problem because they were the obvious arteries along which the sick and the well both travelled – and so they too had been abandoned and left for the animals and the self-seeding herbage to reclaim.

Now Vida dropped her pack and lay down on the double yellow center line. The asphalt was hot on her back, but she'd missed roads – all the places they could take you that were worth going. They had been important, hadn't they? The connections across the whole continent. As a child she'd often imagined that – the road outside their house as a continuous thread that reached out like a handshake, as branched with possibilities as the tree of life. She had always thought that there would be mil-lions of people at the other end. Now the roads, without cars to drive on them, had grown longer, pointing to every horizon you could never reach on foot, stretched thin and connected only with each other. Some, if you followed them, simply vanished underfoot – crumbled and weathered as you watched. Others had been swallowed by foliage. Still others had been dug up, the black goo extracted and used as wind-proofing for houses that her ma said were like the shanty towns back home.

Dyce laid his pack beside Vida and sat down.

'You know, Garrett used to dare me to lie in the road like that. Trick was to time it between cars, lay down and count – one Mississippi, two Mississippi – real slow, until you heard the rumble and absolutely had to get up, had to get to the curb.'

'He ever do it himself?'

'Once that I remember, 'cause it was hard to forget. He was eight. Can you believe it? Laid himself down and just waited, hands behind his head like he was making a real big show of it, you know? Casual. The cars saw him and had to stop since he's sprawled out half in each lane. Then this man and this woman start shouting to him to get the hell up and quit being so stupid, and Garrett just lies there. He got to four hundred and thirty-three Mississippi, four hundred and thirty-four Mississippi until the man literally drags him to the curb by his collar.'

'He sure knew how to win dumbass competitions.'

'World champ.'

Dyce opened his bag and found his share of the locusts. He crunched one in his mouth and swallowed its spines along with a swig of water. He made a face. 'You know what I would really like?'

Vida blinked sleepily. 'What?'

'If I never had to eat another one of these fucking insects again in my life.'

Vida snorted. Dyce waited, and then he said, 'You know I'm hoping we don't find Garrett, right?'

She lay quiet, shading her eyes from the sun with her arm.

'I figure if we find him, it'll just be his body, you know? He's had a week's head start. If he's been lucky then he's long gone. I just want to hear that someone saw him come by.'

'There's a lot of open spaces, Dyce, 'specially down this way. If he was half smart then he'd keep his head down, try not get himself noticed.'

'Yeah. Still. He's kind of hard to miss.' They were silent, picturing Garrett's wide shoulders, the scars on his ruddy cheeks.

Vida rolled to her side and looked at Dyce.

'When last did you spend a night in a pre-war town? Come on, cowboy. My treat.'

34

The other thing about towns that it took people a long time to realize was that they were petri dishes – no one's fault, just because of how they were made. The metal and the glass and the plastic and painted walls created an easy living for the viruses that blew in, Vida had come to learn. The risk was higher when things were wet and warm, but what the viruses loved best of all was a cold metal surface, out in the open. Go figure. Right now it was neither warm nor wet. She had factored that all in, and thought that Dyce had too. They were getting real good about protecting themselves against disease; they'd sure as hell had enough hours of practice.

'We'll stay on the edge of town, right? We need to be able to see the leaves.'

'Yeah. Not long till dark, anyways. Okay, soldier. If the wind comes now, where are we holing up?' Dyce asked, testing.

Vida led the way past a row of shops, their glass fronts shattered, anything useful long ago stripped and stolen. She stopped at an open manhole and looked down into the bowels of the town's storm water system. Vida shook her head. Too murky, too damp – and a whole lot of bacteria waiting to jump. They went on.

'We'll get to The Mouth tomorrow, I think,' said Dyce. 'Shouldn't be much further.'

'Mm.'

'We need a story. They'll ask.'

'I'm a nurse and you're a—?'

'Carpenter.'

'Nice. Like Jesus's mama and daddy.'

'And we'll have to be husband and wife – better chance they'll take us both. Dyce and Vida Jackson.'

'You mean Washington,' Vida told him. He shook his head but said nothing. 'Here we are.'

She pointed to a broad building with a neatly lettered sign on the frontage: *Narrow Gauge Locomotive Museum.* The door was still intact; the walls too, mostly. It was the best they would do. They needed to sit down and gather themselves.

'We'll stay in here, right? But before we set up camp I want to show you something.'

'What?' He cocked an eyebrow.

'A surprise. Come.'

Vida took a side street that led back into the bleached heart of the lonely town. The carcasses of cars here and there lay scattered, like white bones picked clean in the desert. *Or dinosaurs,* thought Vida, *caught in the tar pits.*

'Come *on.*'

'What about the wind?'

'We'll be quick.'

Dyce followed, but he was thinking, *This is the same way I followed Garrett.* Vida was making for the center line of the road, skirting the few rusted cars.

'Really. What you looking for?'

'Relax. You'll see. My treat, remember?'

Down a second street, lined with dead oaks, she found the place – an old cinema with the ticket booth out front, the glass splintered as if someone had tried to get in. Inside the foyer there were peeling posters, the glue holding fast. Their edges were torn and scratched away, as if a boy with a screwdriver had been at them. Between the jagged white gouges they could make out faces: old film stars, long dead. *Rats*, thought Dyce. *They like paper, don't they?*

'Looks like Nicholas Cage is on.'

'Not a fan.'

'Not even *Wild at Heart*?'

'Not even after the end of the world. If we're going to pretend we're at the movies, then we're going to be in separate theaters.'

'Okey-dokey.'

Vida stepped into the open space that had been the screening room. The seats were gone, leaving their concrete steps punched with the brackets that had held the springs and stuffing. The pocked gray walls sported the same graffiti you saw everywhere in the South: hairy penises, nicknames and arrowed hearts, and *Fuck Renard*. The roof of the place was clean gone too, along with the curtains and carpet and canvas screen. Vida took a seat on a step in the middle of the room, feeling the sky slowly purpling above. No breeze yet. Balmy, even, the way dusk sometimes felt, the single moment before the day switched over completely into the night. Dyce joined her and sat down, heavy and tired, setting his pack beside him.

'This a date?'

'What was the last film you saw at a cinema?' Vida asked.

'*Terminator*. And you?'

'Never saw one, only ever had TV.'

'What?'

'We were up near the border, I ever tell you that? It was worse up that way. My ma defected from the North while she was pregnant with me, crossed the border, and that's where we stayed.'

'I think that's the first thing you've told me, other than the usual.'

They were quiet, watching the screen as though the show would start in seconds, the numbers projected over the scribbles like a countdown for a rocket, then the cigarette adverts, and a girl on a yacht, her long blonde hair flowing back in the kindly wind.

Dyce glanced at Vida. Her hair was never going to be smooth, but he liked it that way – antennae. It got springier as the moisture levels increased in the air. He wanted to twine his fingers in the escaped curls at her temples.

'Your mom ever tell you what it was like Otherside?'

What he really wanted to say was, *Who are you? What're you like when you're not being all cowgirl? And, baby, can I trust you with my life?*

Vida shrugged. 'Not much. My mama worked in the labs, started as a midwife and rose in the ranks.'

'She ever work with Renard?'

'They all did, back then. Before it got weird.'

'Before he turned into the evil physician and wormed his way into the White House, you mean.'

'Yup.'

'Then?'

'The usual. Grew up trying to stay alive.'

'What did you do for fun?'

Vida laughed. 'Fun ain't what it used to be. Same as you, I reckon: keep alive, catch a mouse, dodge the wind.'

'I carve. One day I'll make an instrument. It's the one thing I do that I don't *have* to do. Suppose that's what I mean by fun.'

Vida thought for a second.

'Photocomics. Remember them?' Vida sighed. 'Man, I loved those things.'

'That smell, right? And the weird masks and things.'

'My mama was young when she came over from South Africa. She brought the photocomics and cartoons with her – suppose that's where I got the bug. Ever heard of *True Africa*? Or *Staffrider*? The underground stuff.'

Dyce shook his head. 'Only *Archie* and Disney, DC and the Marvel guys and all that. And then, ah, Bettie Page. Thank you, Garrett.'

'Yeah, I loved those too, but they were kind of old even then. We had our own comics in South Africa: Samson the Lionheart. Chunky Charlie. Even Mighty Man, though the evil guys there were communists. But it was the photocomics that were really big. Those were my favorite. There was this one, Mami Wata – a white lady, half snake. It came from up north, I think. West Coast. But she's all over the continent, in the stories from just about every country. And Mama brought a whole stack of the magazines with her when she came. I guess she wanted something to remind her of home. Like she was ever going to forget.'

'So why did she come to America in the first place?'

'Had to, I think. She doesn't really talk about it. But there was this guy who ran a paper – Wilson Someone. I think she was in love with him. Anyway, he got on the wrong side of the South African government. They gave him an exit visa and no return, and Mama tagged along.'

'Kicked him out? For what?'

'Pick something. For things pretty much like what we're doing now. Ebony and ivory. You and me sitting here was against the law not that long ago. Can you believe it? Mama didn't want to get her head splattered in a jail cell.'

'But that was before you were born, right?'

'Yep, long before. She was working in the labs up north for most of The War – only defected toward the end, came Southside. The magazines came with her, way they always did. Back then you could still buy them here. She met my stepdad, who worked first on a ranch and then in the museum. He was great. He actually liked us, you know? Then, when I started getting pocket money, I'd buy more photocomics. Any old ones. Then comes the first of the winds, and overnight there's no new ones in the store. Then no store. People up and leave, heading further and further south. But Evert – my stepdad – wouldn't go. Figured things were bad wherever, and home was home. So we stayed and we were just, you know, careful. Never far from the house.'

'Where is he now?'

'Wind got him, same way it gets everybody. Something that thinned his blood till it couldn't clot. He died from a nick on his pinky, opening a can of spaghetti. You could have held that cut all you wanted and it wouldn't stop. My mama tried tying nylon round it to slow the flow. When he died we took off south. We had big old hiking packs. I took a stack of magazines. Turned to burning them one by one as the nights got colder and the kindling got rained on. It killed me, Dyce.

'Then we found that house. No one there so we took it, and that's the place you saw. Now I got one left; it's all that makes sense to be carrying.'

'You got it here? Let's see it.'

Vida opened her bag and pulled out the photocomic, limp with age.

'I'd have died from hypothermia before I torched this one.'

Dyce took it. MAMI WATA, blared the cover. *She Exacts Her Awful Revenge on Sinners in the City of Gold!* A frowning white woman had appeared in a gilt mirror, her blue-black tresses snaking out from its frame. Before her, wrists up in an X of submission, cowered a black man in a fedora and boxy gray suit. *His Greed Called Her Up!*

Dyce turned the pages gently. They were so thin he could see his thumbs through the fibers. Mami Wata looked like one mean lady – half-serpent, half-woman, and no escape for the men who crossed her.

'I'll have to read it properly sometime.'

'Yeah. In the meantime, *Beware her evil powers*,' Vida intoned. She took the magazine and packed it away again carefully. 'And you?'

'And me what?'

'I spilled my guts, buddy. What about you, while we're coming clean?' Vida sat back and looked him clear in the face. Overhead the sky was darkening, the purpling bruise spreading as the night came on. 'All I know about you guys is that Garrett knocked up the wrong girl and you've been in a world of pain ever since.'

'Okay. What do you want to know?'

'I want to know everything.'

Dyce didn't know how the words would come out, but there they were. 'Our dad never went to war. Had a mental thing, just a bit slow with numbers and writing and things like that, made it that he couldn't enroll. But he wasn't dumb, you know? He saw what was coming. We got on with stuff. Listened to the radio, hearing after all those years how we were winning, or about to win The War – but it never ended. Then the original plague came, and people were talking about how weird it was that it only killed off our soldiers and not theirs. For the first time we were glad that he hadn't gone to fight. But we still figured things would be okay. Your government protects you, right? I mean, why wouldn't it?

'Then in the talks – the concession talks, round about the time the South got royally fucked – my ma got sick. And nothing from The War even. Pneumonia. Regular fucking pneumonia. Course the antibiotics had all been shipped off to the frontlines. We gave her what we could, herbs and shit. When she died, my dad took to teaching us survival skills, like Boy Scouts, I guess. I think he figured there was no counting how many days he had left either, and he wanted me and Garrett to be okay. Hunting, trapping, skinning, filleting, that kind of thing. Pretty gross. Garrett really liked that shit. Enjoyed it. I liked the riding lessons. That was about it. I was better than Garrett. Just at one thing, but it was mine, you know?

'Long story short, Dad caught a virus and died when I was eight and Garrett was ten. We go from settlement to settlement now, making our way, you know. Least we did. We're a good bet. Handy.'

'Fuck.'

'Fuck Renard, you mean.'

'I grew up hearing *Fuck Renard*, but it's just something people say. It doesn't mean anything anymore.'

'Feels good, though.' Dyce lifted his head and in the soft near-evening his feathery dark hair made Vida's stomach flip a little. He looked like a wolf. '*FUCK RENAAARD!*'

Vida waited till he had quieted down. 'My mama says it was all a mistake. Said she knew firsthand, 'cause before the Concession Party went over, they found her and came asking about the North. Not a lot of defectors around, so she was gold. They asked about Renard, mostly, but they wanted to know everything she could remember. She said it seemed a little weird. But the thing was, Concession happened in Des Moines, and Ma had never been there. Still, she tried to help. Called it reparation. Not enough, though, 'cause when the Concession Party got up there, they went and killed Renard's wife. It was a mistake. They were going for him. Pissed him right off, obviously, and now the viruses are his revenge; his punishment. No way to reason with a man like that. Nothing to lose.'

'Heard similar. Sure as shit wish they'd have done it right.'

'Yeah.'

The first stars had appeared against the daylight, defiant. Dyce stretched into the silence. 'Well, thank you for sharing your popcorn. But we better get back soon.'

They walked fast through the dim streets back to the museum, past the dead-eyed streetlights and the car husks and the littered bones that had once been dogs or cats or people. They reached the shelter as the sunglow turned maroon behind the mountains. Dyce stepped inside and Vida followed, closing the door behind them. The row of high windows along one wall filtered the last warm light into the room.

'Wow,' he said.

Sitting heavily in the main space were the remains of an old steam engine, with every removable part unbolted, or hacked off, and taken. It looked like a missile, a long metal tube, made for speed and destruction, hurtling into the dark. Behind it was a painted diorama of the old west, dusty scrubland and wide open sky – and on a stand in the foreground was a stuffed bison.

'Garrett would have liked that, huh?' said Vida.

Some desperate survivor had re-skinned the thing, slit it along its sutures from chin to asshole and peeled the pelt off. All that remained was the snot-yellow cast they'd made from the dead animal – two halves glued together and bolted to the floor. The ghost of a ghost.

Dyce stepped close and patted it, then knocked on its forehead. His knuckles rang: It was solid.

'Ever wanted to ride a bison?'

'Never.'

Dyce jumped up and swung his leg over its back, then sat up as if he was racing a horse.

'Yeehaa!' He twirled an imaginary lariat.

Vida rolled her eyes. *It's a bison, not buckskin. How young is he, anyway? Like he's asking me to put a quarter in the slot. Like I'm a mom at a mall.*

Then she caught herself. No more default; the soft shell hardening into the unthinking carapace. She was being her own mother, always berating Vida for wanting to play, wanting to enjoy herself. Because what had happened then was that Vida had stopped asking to splash in the stream or climb the oak or watch the stars in the night-dark sky. If Ma had been with them, they'd never have gone to the cinema; her credo was *waste not, want not*. If it wasn't tangibly beneficial, then it was off the list and out of the question.

Vida came over to Dyce and laid a hand on the bison.

'There room for two up there?'

He grinned and slapped its bald flank.

'Shift over,' Vida said.

She jumped up behind him and landed on her stomach. He reached a hand back to help her to sit.

'Where we going, cowboy?'

'How about the Narrow Gauge Locomotive Museum?'

'It's always been a dream of mine.'

Dyce leant forward as though the bison was at top speed, galloping through the grassland. Vida leant too, her breasts pressing against his back. They'd been close like this, slept each night in Horse Head curled into one other – but night was different, and they had told themselves it was body heat. Here they were in the last of the daylight, wide awake, close and touching, their bodies rubbing as Dyce spurred the creature on.

And they were alone too, for the first time: alone and healthy, with something to celebrate.

Vida reached her arms around his waist, felt the meat on his ribs. She wiggled closer so that her legs lined up with his, and pressed against him, heat flooding her groin.

Please, she thought. *Please let him take this the right way. If he makes me ask, I think I'll die.*

Dyce leant backwards into her chest and rested his head on her shoulder.

'This is the best I've felt in a while,' he told her.

'You feel pretty good. It's true.'

'Best I've felt in weeks.'

'Months.'

'Years. In fact, since I saw Garrett's ass getting hauled off that Tarmac.'

'I'm happy to help,' Vida told him.

'But you know, I was thinking,' he said.

'Thinking what?'

'That I could feel even better if I really tried.'

'And how would you do that?'

'Like this,' Dyce said, and guided Vida's hand to the warm bulge in his crotch.

35

Vida remembered something she'd once read about real love being shared sleep. It was true.

But it was also possible to lie awake in wonder. She supposed that they must have drifted off, because she didn't feel tired – not the bone-aching weariness that she had come to know over the last few weeks. Now she lay on her side and kept her eyes closed, but the light behind her lids told her it was morning. She had heard Dyce's breathing change: he'd been awake for a while too.

And he would be looking at her skin.

Vida let him. They would have to have the talk some time, and she may as well get it over.

He was moving his hand over her hip; Vida felt the calluses on his palm.

'You're so smooth,' he said. 'Why are girls so smooth?'

Vida rolled over and faced him. 'The teeth are on the inside.'

In the early light his body looked bullet-ridden, the scars welted, big as quarters.

She put her own hand on his chest and slid it down over the sparse fur of his belly, lower, lower, down to his penis, with its hard head and their shared smell. In another time Dyce would never have been this muscled, or this thin, but deprivation made statues out of even the meekest men. Flabby meant relaxed, and relaxed got you killed in a hundred ugly ways. Now all the white boys looked like Jesus on the cross. Vida bent her head and gave him an experimental lick. Sticky and salty, but clean and honest as tears.

Dyce shivered. Then he held her head. 'But seriously,' he said. 'Why don't you have even the tiniest scar or something?'

Her tongue stopped. She drew back. 'What do you want? Warts?'

He brought his face closer to Vida, inspected her minutely: belly, shoulders, thighs. 'But you have *nothing*. Have you even had chicken pox?'

'I don't think so.'

'You would remember.' Dyce certainly did. Him and Garrett, both. The crawling itch, the scabs and pus. And the scars – tiny hillocks that flattened over time but never truly went away. Just another thing that used to kill people until they understood how it worked – and understanding how it worked often meant taking the demon inside you in a different form. Maybe that's all that evolution really was: coming to terms with the things that could kill you; finding ways to dodge the bullet and its damage.

Vida shrugged. 'I'm real careful and also lucky, I guess. And Mama's a nurse, remember: she knows all kinds of stuff. Plus we kept ourselves to ourselves for a long time, even before the viruses.'

Dyce shook his head. 'She survived too; not that many old folk around. It's weird. I'm not buying.'

Vida sighed. 'Al-*right*. Jeez! Enough.'

Dyce settled back, his long, pale limbs haloed by the weak sun that was filtering through the windows as the sun rose.

Vida relented. 'Well, what do *you* think it is?'

'I don't know. Maybe you have a really robust immune system or something. We've been camping out for a week in a lazaretto and you don't have a cough, even. And you *carried* me, for Chrissakes! You're really strong for a girl. A woman. You hardly ever look tired. Like now – we were up half the night and you look like you just got eight hours.'

'Oh, I get tired.'

'Not the way I do.'

'All I can tell you, baby, is that black don't crack.'

'What's that supposed to mean?'

'Allerdyce. Look at me. I'm an African. I was born here but my blood belongs on the continent. My hair is different to yours. My legs are stronger. My teeth are twice as hard.'

'Bullshit. That's—'

'What? Racist?'

'No – what Hitler was doing, what the slave masters did when they were breeding humans for better traits. What's it called?'

'Eugenics. But it's not. You're not getting what I'm saying.'

It would have got worse between them if there had not been footsteps outside the front door of the museum.

Dyce pulled a face. 'Tourists?'

Vida held up a finger. 'Not funny. Shh!'

She replayed the moment she'd closed the door behind them, trying to recall the twist of a key or the *thunk* of a deadbolt – but the details had been lost to her in the tingling feeling of being alone in a room with Dyce for the first time, the dark, warm possibilities of him. She bet that even if the door did have a lock on it, she hadn't latched it – and that meant that whoever was sniffing outside now could walk right in.

Vida got up and began to dress quickly, still high enough to feel the pleasant ache between her legs. She looked down when she felt the slow trickle along her thigh.

Blood.

Was she getting her period again? Jesus! It had been years! The only upside of wartime stress: your body went into emergency mode. It turned you into a man. Had Dyce seen? She looked over at him but he was busy pulling on his clothes, his skin flashing white as birch branches before it was covered. He was still wearing Sam's blood on his pants from the day before. Her blood spots weren't that bad in comparison. She would deal with them later.

Vida tiptoed out to the foyer and went to crouch at the hinges of the door – and there came a voice in the thin morning, calling out in a rough whisper.

'Pavlov!'

The caller gave up trying to be quiet, and began shouting in earnest; hoarse and wet and desperate.

'Pavlov? *Pavlov!* Come *home*, baby dog! Mama's waiting! *Ohwhereareyou!*'

Christ. Dog Lady! Didn't she ever give up? Vida shook her head in disbelief.

'It's okay,' she called back to Dyce, keeping her voice low.

'Who is it?'

Vida kept away from the windows and made her way back to him. They sat down again and she explained how she'd first seen Dog Lady the same day she'd come upon Dyce and Garrett.

'She's lost her dog. Or she thinks she has, anyway. I never saw it myself.'

'Not just her dog, it sounds like.'

'Yup. Brainworm, for sure. I don't think she's dangerous, exactly, but I'm laying low until she passes by. One day she's going to take it into her head that I've got the dog with me or something.'

From what she could tell, Pavlov was a Jack Russell. Vida had felt sorry for the Dog Lady, let her tag along behind. But after an hour or so of listening to her calling and weeping and cursing her dog, Vida had lost patience. She had tried to lose her in a thicket, but the woman had stuck as fast to her as a thistle and then collared her, panting.

'Saw you take off like that. Did you see my dog?'

'No.'

'Did you chase him off?'

'No, like I told you, I haven't seen your dog.'

'His name's Pavlov. Escaped this morning through the chicken wire, chasing after a motor bike.'

'I know. You said.'

'You seen him?'

Jeez, lady, enough.

Vida had eventually come to understand that the woman would not leave her alone until she offered some plausible explanation. So many people didn't want the truth; they just wanted someone to say something that would make it seem better. She hated to do it, not because of some moral code, but because it just seemed disrespectful. Her mama had always said that sick people were still people.

But this is self-preservation, Lord, Vida told the sky. *It's her or me.*

'His name Pavlov? Think I saw him, yes.'

'Oh, praise Jesus! Where?'

'That way, over that rise.' Vida had pointed off back the way they'd come and the woman turned and hurried through the trees, calling out as loud as she could. That's how Vida had come to find the weather box, how she'd found herself in

unusual terrain: she had not been paying the right kind of attention. But it had brought her Dyce, hadn't it? Dyce and this
feeling of using her body properly, for something good and right.
That had to count for something.

It was a miracle that Dog Lady was still around. She must
have been searching day and night for her missing hound, but
she had the sense to eat and sleep someplace safe.

And so should the two of them. The locomotive museum
wasn't good enough if a nut like Dog Lady could find it without
even trying.

'We need to get going,' Vida said.

'No flapjacks? You call yourself a girlfriend?'

Vida smiled. She wanted to laugh – to try to, anyway – but
her throat was dry. Dyce was unnerved too, and the joke fell flat.

'You can ask for your money back at the next town.'

She made a show of bustling about, readying her small bag
for traveling.

'Do we have anything edible? Feel like we worked up an
appetite.'

'I'll see. Next time it's your turn.'

'You're worse than Garrett.'

While he tied his bootlaces, Vida went through their bags
and made up a breakfast: stonecrop, mostly, along with a hard-
boiled flycatcher egg, one each, small as a fingernail and almost
as bad as eating nothing at all.

They ate sitting on the edge of the diorama, chowing down
like two old-time cowhands who had found themselves thrown
together on the dusty plains. The litter of egg shells flaked at
their feet like confetti.

Then they gathered their things, already packed snug and
ready for the day's hike.

In the foyer, they both stopped and listened for wind outside – the droning hiss of it combing the grass, the faint tickle of sand on the wood.

Quiet.

Vida hated to say goodbye to the shelter of the museum. It was a happy place. A residual orgasmic shudder ran down her spine and arms, then all the way down to her feet so that she was earthed, electric. *Lucky the storm's not here yet*, she thought. *I am crying out for a lightning bolt.*

Dyce opened the door and they were met with the orange glow of the sun hanging over the mountains. Dog Lady was gone.

'Hang on,' said Dyce.

Vida stopped, one boot dangling off the curb before they stepped out into the street.

'What?' She did the checks automatically: the horizon for wind; then turning quick to look up and down the street for animals, for bandits, for crazies; then over at Dyce for the sweats. So many things to fear.

'Wait out here a moment.'

'Why?'

'I need a shit.'

36

They skirted the town and found no sign of the woman or her ghost dog. As they marched on south and the sun stood overhead, Dyce began to worry again that The Mouth might not exist. Everything he'd learnt about it had been hearsay – and with all the brain sickness circulating, word of mouth was hardly trustworthy. Since the viruses had arrived, the reports of sightings of mythical creatures had risen steeply.

'You ever hear about the Bogum?' he asked Vida.

'The what?'

Whenever Dyce's dad had turned on the radio, in the weeks before it died and no one was going to transmit anything, ever again, they heard about people being tricked into seeing monsters in lakes or shaggy humanoids loping freely through the countryside. *It was as if the lid had been lifted on the underworld,* thought Dyce, *and all kinds of creepy-crawlies were working their way out.*

'The Bogum. The monster. Tall as a tree and covered in gray hair. He liked to watch women bathing in streams – and we ain't talking no shampoo advert, either.'

Desperate traveling women would take their chance to get clean, leave their clothes hanging from a branch if they were smart, and then scrub themselves with handfuls of grit and herbs. If they had enough time, and no one else came along to interfere with them, Bogum would keep watching as they went on to rinse out their dirt-caked clothes. The story of every sighting ended the same way – with the woman hanging her clothes out to dry only to find the branch wasn't part of the tree at all, but the leathery brown erection of the monster.

'Garrett yukked it up every time he heard it.'

'And did you think it was funny?'

'Sure. I couldn't help it. Come on! Think about it!' Washing Line Richard was what they'd come to call him.

'Dumbass. Those stories probably killed a couple more people.'

'And how do you figure that?'

'Too scared to wash properly. More infections. More likely to die.'

'That's the good Lord weeding out the stupid,' Dyce said.

'Not the *good* Lord.'

Deadly rumors weren't bad news for everyone, though. Garrett had developed a pick-up line based on the story. He'd sidle up beside a woman and tell her that he had a terrifying secret, life-changing in magnitude. She'd ask what it was and he'd lean in close and take a hold of her arm.

'It's me.'

'What's you?'

'I'm Bogum,' he'd whisper.

The woman would laugh, and when she was done, Garrett would start up again – dead serious.

'I'm not joking. It's true. I can prove it.'

'How?'

'Come out back and I'll show you the branch in my pants.'

Half the time it worked – they'd hustle out to some private space, leaving Dyce alone, red-cheeked and in awe of his brother. The other half of the time it was worth it just for the laugh.

Dyce smiled and Vida caught it.

'What's up?'

'No, no. Nothing.'

They went along, sweating and itchy, but happy to be moving fast and unpursued. When they stopped for a break, sitting side by side on a log, Dyce offered up what he'd been thinking.

'If The Mouth doesn't exist, then I don't know. What do you want to do? Maybe we could set up house somewhere round these parts. Keep a low profile.'

'There's the sea, isn't there?' Vida asked. 'Isn't that an option?'

'Not for me. That was Garrett's baby.' He didn't add, *And I'm fucking terrified of water. Always have been.* 'We'll find The Mouth pretty soon, I'm sure.'

'Yeah.'

They got moving again, this time keeping close to a ridge line, always wary of the wind. The longer since they'd had to hibernate, the more anxious they got. They both knew from bitter personal experience that the best time – the safest – was always after a massive storm. These windless days wouldn't last forever. The summer northerlies were coming and that would mean being locked away in some tiny space for weeks. The prospect didn't seem so bad now that Dyce had Vida, and not just because of last night. There was a lot of talking they still had to do. He had never had to do that with Garrett since they'd known each other for ever. *Brotherly love*, Dyce told himself. It meant that there was no news to tell or fresh arguments to settle – just shared experiences to recount to one another over and over, and those lost their appeal soon enough.

The two dipped down into the valley, their path blocked by a crumbling cliff face that jutted out above. Before them the river looped and bent along the valley floor.

'What's the next marker we should be looking out for?' Vida asked.

'Not sure. Another ridge? Or else the one we've just walked is the one they meant.'

'And after the ridge?'

'A shallow river and one more hill.'

'Let's hope we have the same idea of shallow.'

They removed their boots and socks. Vida waded in, and the icy water slapped at her ankles and sent them numb. It would go right up to her waist, she saw. Manageable, and her clothes would get a good washing as they went. The best thing for bloodstains was cold water: every murderer knew that.

When they got to the other side, Dyce stopped to rub Sam's blood from his pants.

'Got to look presentable.' He grinned at Vida, but it was no joke. They had to talk their way into the settlement: there was no other option.

The hill beyond the river was an easy climb, grassy underfoot with the odd shade tree. The two of them crested the rise. There were moments like these when Dyce was almost glad that the world had changed the way it did, when he felt like he was part of the living universe. *Maybe I won't mind all that much if I don't track old Garrett down,* Dyce told himself. *It would be nice to carry on being my own boss.*

He turned to Vida and got hold of her hand, and he squeezed it as hard as he could. He grinned and grinned at her. *Maybe we're looking for a place instead of a person, and maybe The Mouth will be it: heaven on earth, the new world.*

They looked down at the mythical settlement.

'We're here. I can't believe it. *We're actually here.*'

And they were. From up high, they could see beyond the perimeter walls, into an old mining town come to life again all these years after the shafts had surrendered their last nuggets of copper. Tiny fires were flickering, and people moved around the market just within the fence, then went on their way up or down the main street, which was edged with reclaimed structures.

And they could also see, right down at the cleft of the place, the tunnel entrance to the mines, black as night. The Mouth.

'Comb your hair, Mister Allerdyce Jackson. That's how they judge you. We are going to get ourselves in there.'

Dyce's hands went to the tuft standing up on his crown, and he said, 'Sure thing. But what are *you* going to do?'

37

The town was mostly inside the old perimeter wall – except for the lone building that stood outside, proud and unrepentant. It had the look of holiness: the original chapel, maybe. After a place gets treasure, it gets a saloon and a church round about the same time, Dyce thought, and usually for the same reasons. Now the wooden building leant on its splintery bones, a way station, neutral territory, with a decomposing outhouse settling beside it into the dirt.

'More roof than walls,' Vida murmured.

The steeple had once pointed straight up into the sky but had grown tired, sagging under the insistent prayers of the undeserving. Vida liked the specificity of it. Heaven was not just somewhere up above their heads: it was *there*. Her eye followed the line. Just left of the sun, apparently. Good to know.

'Look at the graves,' Dyce said. There were tidy rows beside the steeple, some sunken, all uneven with the passage of time. When they got closer they would be able to read the remaining headstones: mining accidents, mostly, and then car smashes and such. But there wasn't time for the niceties now.

'Where are the new ones?'

Dyce shrugged. 'Inside?'

'But why keep them so close?'

They went quiet. It had taken a year or so into the plagues before people could be held back from touching the bodies of their dead loved ones. Abandoning the last rites had seemed worse for some than anything that could come after. It was the grief talking, Vida knew. The grief and the regret. The infection reminder made her tug at the cloth mask against her neck. It seemed like a long time since they'd had to wear them.

'Masks on,' said Vida.

'I know.' Dyce patted himself down and adjusted his shirt. Then he pulled his mask up too. They walked to the door, which lay ajar to let the warm midday air circulate inside.

There were people inside the church, for sure. They could hear the voices, hushed conversation behind the door. Vida looked over at Dyce and then knocked on the wooden frame of the entrance.

The talking stopped. They heard the footsteps coming all along the length of the church, louder and louder as they drew nearer. Vida and Dyce stood back, squinting into the dimness.

A teenage girl appeared, pale, long black hair that reached down in strings to her waist. She wore a floral dress that had lost its elastic; she had to hold it up with one hand. In the other she was cradling a small cushion. At first they thought it was a baby, but that was just the way she was holding it.

Dyce knew he and Vida were thinking the same thing: *that's a witch if ever I saw one.*

The girl looked out into the bright day, narrowing her eyes and lifting her lip in a snarl that the people behind her couldn't see. But the ones in front of her sure saw it – all the way to the gumline. Her teeth were dingy at the roots. *Dirty*, thought Vida. *But not sick, I'll warrant. There's some cold fire in this one.*

'Morning,' the girl said. 'What can I do for you folks?'

Dyce spoke through his mask. 'Looking to join The Mouth. I'm Allerdyce and this is my wife, Vida.'

'The Washingtons,' Vida added, and Dyce flinched.

The woman leant against the doorframe and eyed Dyce, and Vida suddenly understood that the girl might have let him in if he was alone. But it was hard to tell her intentions. Maybe she would be fattening him up on cookies next – cookies or worse, because they weren't going to waste good food on strangers. But she would keep coming back to feel how thick his fingers were getting as the weeks went by.

'No space at The Mouth. We're full up, and it's a popular spot. It's best you turn round and get back to where you were coming from. Sorry. So sorry.' She grinned.

Vida and Dyce didn't move.

Vida spoke. 'And who are you?'

'I'm the welcoming committee.'

'Well, you're doing a terrible job.'

'Welcoming's for when there's space. So like I said – best you get going before the wind blows through.'

Vida and Dyce weren't buying.

'Can we come inside and rest a while? We've had a long hike.'

The girl shook her head. 'We've all walked a hard road to get here, cowboy. No room is no room.'

I wonder what little critters are crawling around on that scalp, thought Vida, *apart from the stuff that's going on inside her head.*

It would have gone on, but they were interrupted. The voice seemed to come from above: *the voice of God,* Vida thought, except it shouldn't be a falsetto. They all looked up to see a fat man leaning over The Mouth's perimeter wall. He was holding himself up with effort, panting, his piggy eyes squinting against the bright light.

'Leave those folks alone, Ester! It's not your turn yet, either!'

The girl laughed, but she retreated like a guard dog called off, backing away from them slowly, dropping a small kiss on the cushion until only her dress moved in the gloom of the chapel.

'I thought vampires couldn't cross the threshold of a church,' muttered Dyce. Vida elbowed him.

The fat man was still gasping. *Eunuch*, she thought. *That's what he reminds me of*. One of those ladymen that used to take care of the sultan's harem. Except that those guys paid a terrible price for their sheltered employment. They lost their balls.

'This is your lucky day, travelers. There's three spaces in The Mouth right now,' he told them. 'You want to wait in the church with the others and I'll be out later to decide who gets the thumbs up.'

'Thank you,' Vida called, but he was gone.

'Well, Ester seems nice.'

'You noticed. Seemed to like the look of you, though.'

Dyce grunted.

'S'pose we better go in.'

Inside the chapel Vida had to wait for her eyes to adjust, but Dyce could see better inside than in daylight. She stopped at the back of the church, and he took her arm. She heard Ruth's voice in her head: *This is the only way he's ever gonna be walking you down the aisle, baby girl*.

'Thanks, Mama,' Vida muttered. 'Real helpful.'

'What are you saying?'

'Nothing.'

The place smelt like old milk. Had they been keeping animals here? Cows or goats, maybe? At the front of the church a group of people was collected – some sitting in the remaining pews, some standing at the windows, grateful to have some high ground they could look out from. Ester was sitting down. *Of course she was*, thought Vida. Beside her in a row were three other women, and at first Dyce and Vida thought they were sisters. There was an uncanny paleness about them all, and they sat uncommonly still as the two travelers approached.

Not sisters, Vida decided. But with some weary sickness that was taking them the same way, like shaving a man's head made anyone look like a criminal.

Across from the row of women was a family of three, two parents and a little boy of about five, Dyce guessed. The mother was thin as vapor, and all of them had the sweats. As they watched, she wiped the boy's forehead with a green rag. She looked up and caught Dyce and Vida watching them, and tried to smile. *You're going to have to do better than that, lady*, thought Dyce. *You look nowhere near healthy enough to get into The Mouth.* It was the look of an injured animal. When he and Garrett had seen that look on a bird or a rabbit, they ended up crushing its head with a stone, or whacking it with a stick behind the skull. There were some kinds of suffering that had to be brought to an end.

Dyce and Vida both tightened their masks, and the woman set her rag down. It was a raggedy T-shirt, Dyce saw. It looked like it had one of the Mister Men on it. He bet it would say MR HAPPY. The boy had not been able to travel without it, but now he was past caring. And he bet that when the boy gave up and died – and it was going to happen sooner rather than later – that mother would hold onto the rag even when it was making her sicker.

Dyce and Vida made their way to one of the last pews still bolted down, moving around a lone man sitting on the floor as they went. He was a white guy, middle-aged, the gray creeping into his hair almost as they watched. He was quiet but he was rocking, gently, the way someone who had loved him long ago might have done in the night, and he was weeping.

'Looks like he didn't get the memo about traveling alone,' said Vida.

'No harm in trying your luck, right?'

It seemed weird to be talking in church. They sat down, keeping their masks in place, waiting in silence as though the service would begin and a holy man would appear to tell them to turn to page sixty-four and sing verses two and three of 'Jerusalem'.

Ester was whispering to the women in her pew. Vida thought, *I am keeping an eye on you, sister.* She had looked into Ester's face and seen only calculation, a single-minded meanness that made Vida more afraid than any spoken threat. It was the same look she had seen in the narrowed eyes of Tye Callahan.

The girl had made up her mind. She handed her cushion baby to the next girl over and got up. Vida nudged Dyce. 'Look who's coming to visit with us.'

Ester sat down beside them. 'Guess I owe you an apology.'

Vida shrugged. Dyce looked away. She could hear him breathing angrily through the cloth.

'So I'm sorry about what I said outside,' Ester was saying. *God, she's just a kid!* Vida thought. 'I was just trying to look after my own. Got to take care of the folks traveling with me, you know? No hard feelings, I hope.'

'*Rock*-hard feelings,' Dyce replied.

Vida looked at him, shocked. She hadn't known mild-mannered Dyce to ever lash out; that was Garrett's job. Ester had really got to him. Now the girl looked miserable. Vida felt herself feeling a little sorry for her.

'Look, whether any of us make it into The Mouth or not, I've got something I want to show you. Something quite valuable, if you're interested.'

'So?'

'Kind of thing I'd trade for a gun if you have, or for a book, maybe – depending on the book.'

Up close her skin was dry and her breath stank, even through the mask – even in a world punctuated with diarrhea and vomit. There was something marine about it, a seaweedy tang that made Dyce think of dead sailors, of the octopus pulsing in its lair. He shifted away.

'What is it?' asked Vida, intrigued. It might be some dumb-ass crystal, or some locket that a brain virus had convinced her could cure baldness, that kind of shit.

Ester reached inside her slack dress and brought out a small glass vial. She held it out to them so that the others couldn't see. No one was paying them any attention, anyway.

The vial was filled with a yellow liquid, like pus. Vida pulled her hand back.

'Hey now! What is that?'

'Colostrum! And it's fresh!'

'What?'

Ester had their full attention.

Vida knew what it was. She just couldn't believe it.

Dyce was unsure.

'The first milk that a mother makes for a baby,' Ester said. Her face was gathering color as she spoke: it was clearly an issue close to her shriveled heart. 'It's full of antibodies. They fight infection, you know. It can give you immunity against the viruses, even! It's, it's, the water of life!'

'Ester. Where did you get that? Is it from a human?'

'My sister, Julia. The one on the left.'

Dyce and Vida looked across the pews at the pale women. Julia was the one holding the cushion. Vida could see, now that she was looking carefully, that two of them were carrying: they had grapefruit-sized lumps in their guts.

But Julia's stomach was flat, though her chest was stained with tell-tale leaks that had dried and stiffened. As they watched, a patch appeared over her left breast and spread, darkening the cloth. She jiggled the cushion and muttered something into its cloth ear.

Vida's mind kept trying to connect the dots that appeared and disappeared like the little white lights you saw when you passed out. All those babies. And this Ester.

The same girl who came to our house. The one who sent my ma to the armchair for a good long time.

Dyce was asking, 'But where's the baby? Did it die?'

Ester shook her head. 'No baby. Not anymore.'

Vida held Dyce's arm and squeezed.

'She's using them, Dyce. Like cows. She's farming their colostrum.'

38

Vida and Dyce waited outside the chapel, in the high, clean light. Vida felt as if she needed to dry out, the way her mama used to do with feather pillows – set them out in the sun so that the dust mites were sent scrambling. She was still nauseous from the thought of those women, all the born and unborn babies, like the ones her mama used to doctor. She'd cleaned up after them, the slippery grey coils they expelled like an exorcism that maybe a midwife got used to, but Vida never had. Didn't want to, neither.

But worse was the end-point of the trade, wasn't it? The people who'd already paid for their doses. Supply and demand. She pictured them knocking the colostrum back in shots through their straggling moustaches, like baleen whales.

Had it worked?

Dyce was waiting for her to speak, gauging the degree of care with which he would have to tread.

Vida shook her head. 'I figure I've seen a whole lot of end-time desperation and shenanigans, you know? But maybe we've seen nothing yet. It feels like, like, I've been in Disney Land for the last fifteen years.'

He was blunt. 'It's all real. Forget her.'

'I wish I could.'

'Vida, it's not your problem.'

So why was it affecting her this way? Her stomach cramped, there, over the left ovary. She was still rubbing it surreptitiously when the fat man from The Mouth walked past them and poked his head through the church doorway.

'It's happening, people! Gather round! Everyone outside in one long line, please!'

'Where did he come from?' Dyce asked. He couldn't see a door in the town walls – not even a hatch – and they looked solid, but Vida wasn't listening. She couldn't stop staring. She hadn't seen a fat man in a while. He wasn't old-time fat but there was padding under his chin and he wasn't wearing his belt with its tongue dangling out front like everyone else. Vida didn't know anyone who hadn't sat down with a knife and made extra buckle holes all along their belt. *If you wanted to measure the progress of history*, she thought, *you could plot it on people's waists*.

Out they came, the shuffling of the condemned, scared stiff by the chance of redemption. The family stood there, neat and smiling, but they had to hold the little guy up. Dyce could hear the low groans of their stomachs digesting themselves.

Next to them was the lone man wearing a poncho. He stared ahead, eyes blank. *You got to see a lot of death to wind up single*, thought Vida. *And it shows*.

After him came the sisters, all four in a row, fecund, rotten. Then Dyce; then Vida.

The fat man was waving his hand in front of his nose. 'Satan ate a hot shit sandwich! The smell, people! Goddamn it! Get back!'

The sick family moved back a few steps but kept shuffling forward as the man spoke, like hungry dogs under the dinner table. He pulled himself together and went on.

'Look. We got three spaces, so three greenhorns are what I'm after. And up front, I'll tell you, we're not going to take the kid.' He pointed a whole hand at the child, not just a finger. If it was supposed to make the choosing process less personal, it didn't work. The mother called out, but it was the thin wail of defeat. 'Lady, I'm sorry. But the kid's not getting in. Look at him.'

As if he'd understood, the delirious kid dropped to the dirt. His mother and father hauled him up again by his thin arms. Vida expected the father to keep cursing, for the family to give up and shuffle off to lick their wounds and reassess their situation.

They didn't. Where would they go? They might stand a chance of entrance if the kid died here. Bury him and begin again.

The fat man shrugged, his chins wobbling, and moved on.

'Next thing you need to know is that no one gets a free ticket to The Mouth. We need some proof of *loyalty*. Of *intention*. So if you're chosen, you're not getting a warm towel and a goodie bag, okay? First you got to do something for us, and it's not cleaning your stepmom's running shoes or mending the fence.' He breathed. 'Today's task is *special*. If you succeed, then you're in.

'Alright. So. Starting with Daddy over here. Tell me, what do you do? What's your special skill?'

He walked along the line and pointed to each person in turn.

'Metalworker.'

'Seamstress.'

Next, the lone man. 'Distiller.'

Ester: 'Farmer.'

'Right,' muttered Vida. '*Dairy* farmer.'

The first of the three sisters opened her mouth to speak but no words came out – just a dry gasp. Ruth had always told Vida that carrying a baby gave you a hunger that came straight from the world beyond. Pica, it was called. Women ate strange things. Pregnancy gave you cravings. The women here were all signing to show that they could work – dig holes, knit, cook.

'Carpenter,' said Dyce.

'Nurse,' said Vida.

'*Really*. A *nurse*. Always a lot of nurses and doctors around. It's funny, right? Maybe it's because this world is so full of sickness. But maybe it's because you're saying what you think I want to hear. Last doctor we let in turned out to be a doctor of literature. Fat fucking help *that* was.'

'I was apprentice to my mother. She was a nurse before The War.'

'Show me something medical.'

'Like what?'

'You tell me.'

Ah, shit.

'Sure.'

Vida left the line and walked to the other end.

Come on, Vida. Sell it. This country was built on people pretending to know what they were doing.

'These three have the same sickness, probably caught out in a wind. Diarrhea and the sweats and cramps. Early stages – contracted it a couple of days back. Daddy here is worst off. Swollen liver, judging by the way his wedding band looks like it's about to pop right off those sausages. Mom's got some weeks in her. Might make it, might not – depending on diet and medicine. The little guy . . .' Vida shrugged. *Don't show him you're afraid. Don't show him how fucking freaked out you are!*

She moved on and got to the man sweating under his poncho. 'And this guy, he's not sick at all. He just *wishes* he was dead. Don't you, mister? I could help you with that, you know,' Vida said softly. 'Larkspur, water hemlock, milkvetch, death camas – and a gallon of whatever alcohol you got, to take the edge off the seizures when your organs fail.'

Then it was Ester's turn. Vida didn't look at her, couldn't bear the dead eyes and the lizard skin.

'This girl had a mental problem long before the viruses came blowing in. Day she was born. If you ask me, she should be in prison. But since prisons are long gone, I'd recommend the same treatment as the last guy.'

Ester replied in a low hiss, inaudible to everyone except Vida. 'Gonna kill you slow, sister.'

Vida brushed her off and kept moving. *Just the sisters to go. Nearly there.*

'From the lump in her gut, I'd say this woman was three months pregnant, but judging from her skin and hair, she's likely closer to seven. Same goes for the other one, except that she's closer to due. Almost nine months. The babies, like the mothers, have rabbit starvation. Protein poisoning. You had a long, cold winter, didn't you, ladies? Treatment is fat, like brain or skin – and lots of it. Maybe it will happen.'

At last. Julia.

'This one gave birth maybe a week back. She needs rest and food, and to hold her baby. But her baby is dead, thanks to her sister.'

Ester stepped in. 'What happened to the Hippocratic Oath – do no harm and all that shit?'

'Lucky I'm not a doctor.'

'And your *husband*, while we're reading through everyone's medical histories, what's wrong with him?'

Vida walked back to Dyce and caught him by the hand, knowing that she was revealing her soft spot to Ester, but not having any choice.

'He recently caught a virus that blinded him. He's recovered his sight, but his eyes are scarred.'

'Okay, enough,' said the fat man. 'You're useful. Welcome!' He clapped his hands together, as if he'd announced her jackpot win on a game show. 'And I'm going to take your partner too. Seems like he's more living than dying. So it's just the one more space.' He looked around, showy, as if he was playing Eeny Meeny Miney Mo.

'And . . . I think . . . it's going to have to be . . . Ester.' Vida heard the sighs; she herself had given one. The fat man went on. 'I hear what was said about her being a bit of a loose cannon: that's not in dispute. But we run a tight ship here.' He looked at them, warning. 'She's got initiative and we're all for that. The rest of you that didn't make this round: you're welcome to stay on in the church and see if any of these three don't make it back, because then I'm going to have to choose others. But I do advise you to move along. Find someplace else. Those I've chosen: don't get too comfortable. You're coming with me.'

Dyce and Vida hugged. The sick family wandered off, their familial bonds looser than when they'd arrived. The lone man showed no emotion, but went back to sit in the shade thrown by the chapel walls. Ester glared at Dyce and Vida. It was a mixed blessing for her. She had saved herself but lost her lucky ticket. She beckoned the other women closer. They went into a huddle, and Dyce couldn't shake the image of them around a pot somewhere. There would be babies boiling in the water.

When they were done whispering, the sisters returned to the church, slow and dreamy, floating weightless over the earth like the wind.

'You know what this means, right?' Vida said to Dyce.

'Ester's going to send us a fruit basket?'

'Only if she's poisoned the apple first. She'll try and get rid of me – and then she'll climb you like a totem pole.'

39

'When last any of you see a live horse? Years, right?' The fat man stood in the shade of the perimeter fence, glistening like a toad. Vida, Dyce and Ester stood around him. Dyce watched the man speak, but occasionally his eyes would wander up to the wooden wall behind him, searching for a seam. It bothered him that he couldn't figure out where the entrance was.

'There's been a sighting. Men on horses. Two. Scouts from up north, we think. Don't know what they're doing this far south, but they're sure as hell aren't opening a McDonald's drive-thru.'

Far off behind him, Vida spotted three shapes shifting through the grassland, two big, one small – the doomed family heading for the sea and the warm, wet, poisonous coastal air. They were staggering to their deaths, she knew. Maybe it was better than the impossible decisions that came with survival.

'So, here's your ticket. *We want those horses*. Find the scouts, kill them, take their horses and bring them back here. Didn't seem that any of the rest would be up for this, but you three have got something. Healthy enough to get there and dumb enough to give it a try. Am I right or am I right?'

The man paused and Dyce jumped in to save himself from Ester's breath.

'Where were the men last seen?'

'East.'

'East? That it?'

'Yeah. My recommendation would be to head east, find horse tracks and follow them till you see a couple of horses.'

Dyce felt the part of himself that was Garrett urging him to say something stupid, pick a fight with the guy about to throw the lifebelt his way.

'Thanks a lot,' he said. 'Real helpful.'

'Hang on,' said Vida. 'We just arrived and you're sending us out there again?'

'That a problem?'

Vida had no case. Then she thought better of keeping quiet. If The Mouth was the paradise they'd hoped for, then their feud with the Callahans wouldn't be an issue. The opposite, even. She took her chance even though she knew having Ester hear it all was unwise.

'Had the Callahans on our tail for a few days, is all. Heading back out there is giving them another stab at us.'

'A Callahan after you? You shoulda said so up front! I *knew* I liked you guys! You know which one is after you?'

Vida almost laughed. *Which one?*

'All of them,' said Dyce softly. 'Every single motherfucking Callahan there is. From the pimple-faced bed-wetters to the old man with the bird. *All* of them.'

'Tye Callahan? Jeee-zus! What you folks done?'

'Got mixed up with killing a couple of them.' Dyce wasn't proud.

'*Got mixed up* . . . Ha! I love that. Who'd you kill?'

Vida took up the story. 'Walden, for one. Then his daddy got in the way. This was all about Bethlehem, though.'

'Fuck me.' The fat man held his index fingers on his temples as though he was massaging the information into his brain, as if it was too big to fit in all at once. 'Heard she was the only good apple on that tree.'

'That's about right. So you see, if there's another way . . .'

'There's only one way. Just 'cause I like you now doesn't mean I can change things like that.' He snapped his fingers, loud and meaty. 'Things are as they are, but I'll tell you what: make it back with those two horses – and without getting killed – and we'll lay out a celebration dinner for you. A big, fat welcome for the victorious Callahan Killers!'

'No insects on the menu, and I'm in,' said Dyce.

Ester snorted. The fat man looked over at her.

'All set?' he said.

'Oh, yes.'

'Then I'll leave you to it.'

The man walked off up the fence line. He stopped, bent down with an effort and knocked on a wooden trap door. Dyce hadn't spotted it, but then that was the point – keeping the entrance hidden, keeping the perimeter strong.

The trap door opened for him and he slipped inside under the town walls like a plump rabbit into a warren. *No, not a rabbit*, Dyce told himself. *Like a spider into its hole.*

And you're the scuttling pin.

That was a thought straight from the mind of Garrett, it felt like. Dyce looked over at Vida, taking the temperature of the situation, the same way he'd done right before they'd walked into her run-down house, the same way he'd felt when his gut was telling him what his hard head wouldn't heed. *Run!* it had said. *Stay away.* He'd ignored it and paid the price. She showed no emotion. If she was scared, she hid it well. Played her cards close, that one.

'Guess we're off, then,' said Ester. 'Don't go without me, you hear? I have to tell my sisters.' They were waiting balefully in the shade, the cushion hugged to Julia's chest. Dyce thought that they looked as if they would wait for ever. He saw Ester glance at the poncho man, who was still keeping himself to himself.

Ester came back. 'Ready?'

'You go on ahead,' Vida told her. 'I want you where I can see you.'

'Which way's east?'

Dyce jutted his chin in the direction of the sun.

'East, west, home's best,' Ester sang out. She began walking, taking her fishy smell with her. *Unwashed, that's what she is*, Vida told herself. *Dirty*. The girl was moving quickly, effortless, and Vida was reminded of their age difference.

'Come on,' Ester called. 'I won't bite!'

'No,' Vida breathed. 'You're the kind that swallows whole.'

40

Tye Callahan strode down through the pines toward the lake shore. The two horsemen stayed in their saddles and kept pace. He'd sent his bumbling men back to Glenvale, back to their home camps to keep whatever weak and watchful eye they possessed on what was happening there. Tye hadn't gone with them.

He had business.

He set up camp out of the wind, instead, and waited, just him and the harrier, sending her up daily to watch for the scouts.

Renard's reply had been short.

I do not underestimate the sacrifices you have made. I am happy to oblige your requests. Scouts are en route.

Tye had felt like whooping and laughing when he read it, the paper still cold from the altitude. But though he was alone, that emotion was something undignified. Instead he sat and grinned at his bird.

'Now we wait.'

It was towards dusk of that first day when Tye saw the movement in the treeline. He set the worn boots he was mending slowly aside. He felt no spike of fear: he knew who it would be.

Tye stretched and began to walk barefooted up the slope. When he was close he called out, 'I know it's you, Kurt. I can see your hair.'

In the blue-green shade of the spruces the tuft of blond was sticking up through the grasses like the tail of a jackrabbit. It didn't move.

'You get back to Glenvale, you hear!'

The blond hair ducked down.

Tye didn't go any closer. He'd leave the boy to go on his own, let him keep his pride. One loyal Callahan left in the clan! It wasn't anywhere near enough, but it was something. Tye knew what the kid was thinking, and there was no real choice: go back to Glenvale and carry on with women's work, or stay out in the wild country on the tail of Tye Callahan and hope to gather what scraps the great man might drop. It wasn't a stretch.

Night came, blue and then purple and black, and Tye eventually heard him go – rustling through the brush like a drunken porcupine. How the fuck had the kid managed to trap a jackrabbit?

It felt good to be out in the wilderness by himself, finally. The quiet settled his thoughts, helped to clear away the old, mottled rage – or at least refine it and compress it into something cold and hard and pure. The idea of the bear trap he had set gave him great satisfaction. It was a message. They needed to know who they were up against. A man had his pride.

It took almost a week for the bird to spot the two horsemen. She had circled lower and lower, guiding them to Tye, who sat brooding and stoking the fire under a pot of coffee. Cowboy coffee: charred husks of wheat, powdered and added to water, swallowed so hot that he couldn't taste the ash and the dirt. There was a lesson there somewhere, but he didn't want to know what it was.

The scouts had been impatient to move south, for the old man to show them to The Mouth so that they could scope it out and return as quickly as they could. The southern lands were backward and dangerous – the pot on the fire was a marker of just how bad things had got when insects and ash were the new rabbits and moonshine. And the landscape had changed on them too. If that harrier hadn't led them to her master, the two men would have wandered in circles, cursing one another. Even the wildlife was more unpredictable since they'd last ridden these spaces. A bear had attacked them in the night, driven desperate with the smell of their rations, and they'd shot it through the fabric of their tent.

They had offered Tye a place behind one of them on their precious horses, but he had spat in the dust at the animals' hooves and told them that Tye Callahan rode behind no man. They had let it go but marked him as difficult. They were watching their mouths.

He led them southward, walking swiftly, his heart in time with the quick steps of the horses. This was what he was best at: the hunt. They would camp at the lake and get to The Mouth in the morning – no point in scouting it out in the darkness. Tye showed the men to a clearing and helped them set up camp. The horses stood in the shallows drinking, happy, unaware of the treasures they had become.

He'd forgotten how powerful horses were. He remembered, instead, the last months with Tumbleweed and how she'd grown too weak to take a saddle. There had been a transformation of some kind: she had become a big dog, following Tye wherever he went. When she became too arthritic, Tye had shot her.

Hardest thing I ever had to do, he reminded himself. There was no one else to tell. He'd even considered burying her in a grave like a human, but that would have been a waste. He had said the prayers over her carcass and skinned her in stages, weeping all the while. He had cut her flesh into strips for drying, but it was like flaying his own kin.

A year later he had lost about half of her to mold and coyotes. Every last scrap of her was long gone, including the territories she had helped him navigate, the nooks and crannies of the southern lands that she had let him reach. Now he had to trust others to oversee things – and look where that had landed him! Cashing in a favor with Renard just so he could get even with a couple of upstarts. It was pathetic. But it was also what would reignite the fear people used to give the Callahans as their due.

The scouts didn't talk much, and that was the way he liked it. They set about their task of clearing the space and pitching their tents. Tye offered to brush their horses down and pick out their feet – stone bruises would see the end of the mission. He'd wanted to touch them from the moment they'd thundered up beside him, but hadn't wanted to seem sentimental. Tye unbuckled their saddles and began brushing them, the sweat lines dark from the day's work. He spoke gently into their ears and they blew through their nostrils back at him. He dimly overheard one of the scouts saying to the other that he was a crazy old coot, but a man who liked horses couldn't be all bad. His harrier had taken off, sulking.

When Tye was done, he tied the horses to adjoining trees and went to rejoin the men. They had set up the camp and made a fire. He sat with them while they prepared their dinner – a fancy stew out of a couple of tins labeled *Grass-fed Beef Stroganoff* in blue and gold writing. What else would you feed a cow besides grass? Tye was amazed again at how foreign everything from the North had become: it was another country up there. Renard must be doing well. New cutlery, new clothes, new canteens and new hats. The gear made Tye look like a drifter – homeless.

But that's exactly what I am, he thought. *And so is everyone south of the border. It's better that way. Less to lose when the end-times come upon you.*

They offered him some stew, but he didn't want to be beholden to them, with their soft bellies and their fancy boots.

'I'm going to head off and find some proper shelter before it's dark,' he offered. 'You never know with the wind down this side.'

'Good thinking,' one of the men replied.

'If we're up early we can be at The Mouth by sun-up. Best light for scouting, I reckon.'

The two men nodded and continued eating their stew. Tye walked up from the shore and into the dusty pockets of fescue, one of the scouts belching as he went. When he was some ways off, he heard them break into conversation, chatting idly – free to do so without Tye sitting patiently, waiting to be offered a plate of chow – scraps, even – like a dog.

He found a crevice in a hillside, as he had known he would, a crack in the earth made larger with the endless movement of water and wind, and he curled up into it, cold and tired and hungry from the day's walk, and pleased to be lying down. One of these days he wouldn't get up again. But he had work to do before then.

Sometime during the night the unfaithful harrier came back with blood on her beak. He shared a penitent stick of dried fish with her – his last – and fell back into a sleep as deep as the grave.

The next morning, when Tye awoke, he decided that if the scouts gave him food and real coffee, he would take the offering with both hands. He gathered his things and retraced his route back to the waterline and the camp.

He noticed first that the horses were missing. For a moment he figured the scouts had gone on to The Mouth without him, and the rage rose in his chest.

But then he came into the camp proper and he saw the two bodies, the throats slit, the life bled out and staining the ground near the empty tins of stew.

41

Vida clenched her fists. How could he not know what Ester was doing? She watched them again as the girl looked sideways at Dyce under her lashes, the weird eyes shiny as oil slicks. *What is this? Fucking high school?* Every chance Ester got, she'd slide too close past Dyce, touch his hand or graze him with her stony breasts. The thin material of the floral dress did not cover her nipples properly. Every time Vida turned her head, she caught the shadows on Ester's chest, raisins against the cloth, the rest of the breast shiny and red with infection. *Milk fever*, she thought. She had seen it enough times with her mama's ladies. It could make you crazy. The vial was hidden somewhere else. Vida tried to ignore it, seeing it for what it was – a ploy to unsettle them – but it was so blatant, so undisguised. *As if she wants me to lash out at her*, she thought. *That's it. I can't give her an excuse.* Ester's sisters, blood kin or not, were waiting for her back at the chapel until they heard word one way or the other. It was just a matter of time before Vida and Dyce met with an accident, or an infection: something nasty and unplanned. Vida made up her mind to watch the girl all the more carefully.

But there was no logic in offing either Dyce or Vida before they found the horses, right? Three heads were better than one. There was comfort in that, at least. *One wrong move, witch, and I'll break you in half with my bare hands.*

The sun was low when they came to the shores of Belmear Lake. The water was greenish-brown, the surface disturbed now and then by listless puffs of wind that snaked down through the trees. They were beginning their trek around the sandy bank when Vida caught the clinking of metal somewhere on the other side.

She stopped, then hushed the others and made sure they were settled well deep into the foliage before she investigated. Ester pressed the hot stones of her chest against Dyce's back. He edged forward. It wasn't sexy; it was creepy. She was sick. He pictured the two of them rolling together in the pigweed, and then her dry lips opening wide to kiss him, the tongue jabbing at him, the teeth layered row upon row like a lamprey.

Vida pointed across the water to a clearing on the far side. Two men in store-bought clothes sat beside a fire, talking. She could hear the mumble of their distant words, noted their good boots and their spongy stomachs. It was their first sighting of true-blue Northerners, and even from across the lake they looked like the kind of men who scrubbed under their fingernails.

And behind them – oh, praise Jesus! – were the tethered horses. Vida elbowed Dyce where he knelt.

'Bingo,' he whispered.

Behind Vida, Ester reached forward and squeezed his dick through his pants. Dyce fell sideways, caught himself, and threw her hand back at her.

Vida turned around. 'I got an idea,' she said. 'How about we attack from the water? They won't be expecting that. Crawl up the bank and, and—'

'And slit their throats.' Ester grinned. Vida didn't doubt that she would do it, and look like she was enjoying herself too.

Dyce looked desperately at Vida. It would be unwise to confess his fear of water. Vida spared him.

'I been bait once before. Dyce, it's your turn. You go round and get their attention. Ester, you and me, we'll swim across real quiet. You got a knife?'

The girl nodded. Of course she did. Probably had a whole fucking armory under that dress. Ester was a cockroach.

'I just have one question.'

'Spit it out.'

'Can you swim?'

Vida tightened her lips. Another strike against Ester. *I swear, if she ever gives me the chance, I am going to wring that skinny white neck of hers, and count it as a job well done.*

Dyce grabbed Vida's hand and pressed it before she said anything she would regret, but there were no fond goodbyes – not with that girl watching them, hungry. Then he set off scrambling, making as much noise as he could: a greenhorn who'd lost the trail. He stopped once and looked back at the two women beside the lake. Ester was staring out across the water, but Vida only had eyes for the girl. *Mama-bear eyes*, Dyce thought, and that calmed his nerves some. Vida was tough, and it helped that she was covering his back.

He went on. When he came to a stream he hopped it and scared a frog into the muddied water. 'This is your lucky day, Kermit,' Dyce told him. 'You owe me.'

The scouts were terrible at their job, oblivious to Dyce's approach despite his crashing and stamping. He'd have to resort to a fit of coughing if they didn't turn soon and spot him.

The two women waited a couple of minutes, then Vida tucked her knife into her bra strap and gestured to go in. They waded into the cool, murky water, keeping to the reeds, and they moved slowly, testing the mud under their boots. The weeds along the bottom were dangerous, and Vida made sure she wasn't trapped.

The lake deepened pretty quick, with sudden dips that took your feet out from under you when you least expected.

She looked back. Ester was bold, but she wasn't careful. Her dress slowed her, too. Vida found herself waiting for her to catch up. She strained to hear what Dyce was saying through his boy-howdy act and a fake coughing attack.

'God, just swallowed me a swarm of midges back there. Protein though, right? How you boys doin'?'

The scouts would be reaching for their rifles, and raising them at Dyce.

'You folks mind if I take a look at them? Horses! Man, real horses! I haven't seen one in these parts in years.'

'Move along.'

'I will. Just, I promised my father that next time I saw a horse, I'd give it a good old stroke down the nose. My daddy's dead, you see. Had a real thing for horses.'

'I'm going to count to three . . .'

Behind Vida, Ester yelped and went under.

In a few strokes, Vida made back the couple of feet between them – the girl was mean, but she couldn't let her drown – and felt for her struggling arms under the water. But she was too wriggly to get a grip on. *Typical*, thought Vida.

Ester's head broke the surface, and she gurgled and splashed. Vida reached out for her again and got a handful of dress. She hissed, 'Shut up, Ester! Do you want to get us all killed?'

Ester shut up. They bobbed together and Vida wiped the water out of her eyes with her free hand. She checked back on Dyce. Still good. He was holding his hands up on either side, like a pastor pacifying a mob at the city gates.

Vida tugged at her. 'Come *on*. Could you help me here? At least make a fucking effort!'

But Ester wasn't moving.

'What's going on? Is your foot stuck?'

The girl reached out both her hands and dunked Vida's head under the surface, like a basket ball. Vida drew in a mouthful of water as she went down, flailing at the thin arms that were holding her. *My God, the girl was strong!*

She could see nothing through the muddy water, and felt only the weeds tugging at her boots, dragging her to the bottom as if they had come to Ester's aid like the scaly coils of Mami Wata. Vida's lungs burnt; she pictured them flattened and useless inside her chest. She reached out again and grabbed at Ester's billowing dress. Somewhere inside it she would be reaching for her knife now, Vida knew, and there was only one chance.

Vida struggled to reach for her own blade. What a dumbass place to put it! She hadn't thought she would need it until she was on the other side. Her arm felt as if it was being wrenched out of its socket, but the handle was in her reach. She fought the darkness that kept dropping down over her eyes, and angled the knife forward, trying to judge the flesh behind the material of that fucking dress. She drove the blade into where she thought her chest was and knew the impact when it happened because the girl's body rocked forward, clenching over the knife like she was trying to keep hold of it *and ohmyGod it felt good!*

It's a mercy killing, Vida kept thinking. *It's a mercy. I'm letting the poison out.*

Ester kept jerking, and Vida surfaced, spluttering. The first lungful of air was sweet as sunrise. The blood began clouding the water around the two of them and Vida pushed the body away from her. The end of Mami Wata.

Maybe she should look for the colostrum.

Ah, fuck it. That was wasting time. Let the fish have it. The fish and the mermaids.

Vida put her knife into the loop of her waistband and set her boots against the slippery rocks at the bottom. She pushed Ester's body under the water. *Tit for tat.* The air left the girl's lungs faster than she had thought it would, but the body floated, persistent.

She reached down for a rock and lifted it. She rolled it into the dress. How many would she need? Four or five big ones? She had to move fast, so that the scouts didn't see that tent of a dress, its flowers bleached into the white sail of surrender.

Vida broke the surface quietly and floated for half a minute to catch her breath, the thought of the rocks rolling loose and sending the corpse up beneath her making her move on sooner than she was ready. She stared into the water for the ghost shape, but Ester was far enough down. They only needed a couple of minutes. *Please stay down. Oblige me just once in your sorry fucking life!*

Dyce had about reached the end of his parley; the scouts had lost their patience with this babbling stranger. He didn't seem quite right in the head, but what was one more Southerner? No loss to Renard, that was for sure. Dyce looked up beyond the men and saw Vida emerge, slithering, from the lake, and for a moment she was half woman, half snake: Her jeans were wet through, gleaming like scales as they shed water. He kept talking, the quick nonsensical patter about his dad and the horses and the one time they went to the county fair, and Vida moved up the bank, shadowy, quiet – her knife in her hand.

'One . . .'

'It's just my dad only died yesterday, can you believe it? Just come from burying him, and seeing a pair of horses right away – well, that's a sign, isn't it? Wouldn't you say?'

Dyce took a step toward the horses, his hand raised to pet them. The rifles followed.

'Two . . .'

'Either it's the Lord saying your pop's okay, son – or it's the ghost of my pop crying out 'cause he missed these horses by a day! Isn't that kind of funny, when you think about it?'

Vida lunged at the nearest scout, the knife at his stubbled throat. As she pulled back and felt the tendons go, his companion turned and let fly with a bullet that sailed over their heads into the canopy of trees. Dyce threw himself at the gunman and set his hands around his neck. He squeezed and squeezed, but afterwards they found that it wasn't the strangling that had done the scout in: Dyce had been choking him so hard he'd broken his neck.

'You know who I was thinking of?' he asked Vida, looking at his hands.

'Ester?'

They were both shaking.

It was dark by the time they'd washed in the lake and eaten something to stop the light-headedness.

'Should we bury them?'

'These are Renard's men. Let's save our strength for our own dead.'

'All's fair in love and war, right?'

'Right.'

'You know that's not true.'

'Maybe not in all wars, but it sure as shit is in this one.'

They stripped the scouts' camp, saddled the horses, and set off back to The Mouth. Dyce had long ago turned pathfinder, his eyes cool and critical in the dark. They moved without talking, not wanting to attract the attention of the night critters, but also in love with the smooth flanks of the horses underneath them.

Even so, not once did Dyce lean over to Vida and whisper, 'Where's Ester?'

Some things it was better not to know.

42

They rode back to The Mouth, high on the backs of horses like long-lost royalty. There they found that the fat man kept his promises, and that the banquet had been arranged. They had heard the music from a mile away – a note now and again from instruments Dyce had thought he'd forgotten. And at their entrance, there had been three cheers for the Callahan Killers. It couldn't hurt.

They handed the horses over, along with the scouts' rifles, and in return they were shown to their accommodation – a tiny shack, same as all the others, the basic furnishings intact. There was a change of clothes there too, laid out side by side on the bed, as though whoever had owned them before had vanished right out of them, translated through the cloth.

'His 'n' hers,' breathed Vida, and they laughed. But a change of clothes was a change of clothes, and it had been so long since it felt as if someone else was taking care of them. Dyce and Vida dressed and stood smoothing their shirts, relishing the clean, dry fabric against the skin.

When they stepped outside again, they were new people. They strode tall between the shacks, arm in arm. *Look at how civilized we are*, thought Vida, *and so dashing*.

The residents of The Mouth had set their best out on the slight slope of the main street, dragged tables and chairs from the adjoining shops, and built fires all around in oil drums so that it felt like a protest or a county fair. Vida kept expecting someone on stilts. Strips of striped cloth and tattered Christmas tinsel hung in strings that looped from budding tree to wireless telephone pole, linking the hurricane lanterns.

With great care and ceremony the sweating horses were tethered outside the saloon, the first proper use of the poles in years. As soon as Vida and Dyce had dismounted, people went one by one to inspect the animals and to coo in their ears and, when they were deemed friendly, to lift their children on two at a time, for a taste of old-time travel.

After they had greeted the horses, the same townsfolk came by to congratulate them – or more likely to touch the hands that had dealt death to the scouts and would do the same for the rest of the Callahans. As they introduced themselves, Vida saw the universal hesitation, and then people shook hands firmly, contagion ignored in favor of communion.

At the center of it all was a squeaky steel-legged table. 'I know that smell,' Vida told Dyce. 'My mama used to make those – duiwelskos.' When they got up close they saw that the table was packed a foot-deep with mushrooms. Behind it a man in an apron that read FUN GUY said that they were grown down the old mines. It was hard to get your head around, and Vida and Dyce stood gaping. Mushrooms: here they were, some raw and fresh and smelling of the earth they sprang from; some dried from last season's harvest; some cooked beyond recognition.

Dyce chose a hamburger made from solid mushroom, and bit into it.

'That's the one they call the beefsteak,' the aproned man told him as the saliva spurted into his mouth. 'They don't like being cultivated. No, sir. They grow where they like. They are *survivors*. The oldest kind, probably growing under your feet right now. I hope you like it.' Dyce nodded, his mouth too full to talk. 'Because it was a *bitch* to clean.' The man laughed, his apron tight over the drum of his stomach.

As the evening went on and the tasting went with it, Vida and Dyce found themselves dazzled and then sickened by the variety. There were mushrooms that tasted exactly like meat; others that melted before you could chew them; ones that smelt like flowers. Dyce kept thinking back to the time his dad had taken them to a local eatery for the all-you-can-eat breakfast buffet – The Last Chance Motel, set right on the blacktop. It was a birthday, maybe, something special, because it was during Concession, when money was tight. Garrett and Dyce had been aware of how much it was costing their dad.

At first it seemed like a treat, a spread of eggs and bacon and toast and Jello and custard, a midnight fairy feast from a story-book. But when their dad sat them down, he told them the deal.

'This is breakfast, lunch and supper – and then breakfast again, so eat like you mean it.'

There'd only been money for two, and so their dad had sipped on water, the grim waiter watching him keenly in case he sneaked a bite of sausage.

The boys had tried their best but Dyce had made a mistake when he tried to keep pace with big-boned Garrett. Hollow legs, his daddy always used to joke, but now it looked that way for real. After they had finished, paid the bill and were walking to their car with its precious petrol ration donated to the outing, Dyce had vomited in the parking lot. He had stayed down for a long time, nose to the sidewalk and the half-chewed mess of precious egg and oats and custard. The Jello had been green. Dyce remembered his dad's expression, a mix of hunger and fury – their money lying there on the asphalt soon to be squirted away down the drain by a man in overalls, who was even now fetching the hose and tutting, as though this happened a lot.

'Jesus! Dyce!' was all their dad had said, but later that evening, while Garrett was burping and watching TV, he'd handed Dyce a napkin-wrapped muffin that he had kept back from the buffet. Dyce was starving, so he'd taken it and eaten it all, but it had tasted bad. Like guilt maybe, or disappointment.

He turned his attention back to the mushrooms. This buffet was different. It tasted like food did in the old days, when you could cut the crust off your bread because you didn't like the texture. But there was something terrifying about the idea that all those rhizomes were creeping underground even as they ate and talked and listened to the good life going on around them.

The gut-strung guitars were still twanging, and no one asked about Ester, the alibi Vida had conjured up on the ride home gone to waste. It was taken for granted that she'd died at the hands of the scouts. Dyce didn't want details, but deep down he knew that it was no accident. There was something about Vida that was beautiful and terrifying: mermaid, Venus, Amazon. He looked at her in the firelight as she sat across from him, the fierce eyebrows, the curving lips, and felt the rush of blood below his waist – but also in his chest.

'Dyce and Vida: luck and life, isn't that right?' the fat man was saying. He clapped them both on the shoulders. They smiled and bumped cups to toast.

'Can't have one without the other,' said Vida.

'Can I sit down? I *knew* you'd come back with the horses.' He had his arm around Dyce. 'You two are some *mean* sons-of-bitches. You just promise to tell me if I'm ever on your bad side. Deal?'

They smiled.

'You'll know,' Vida promised him.

'My name's Ed, so as you know. Tomorrow I'll show you around, put you two to work. But for now' – he spread his arms like a showman – 'just enjoy this. There's not much to celebrate in this life now, is there?'

Vida and Dyce ducked their heads in agreement.

She held up her cup again, topped up with the homebrew that went down hard and then kicked like a donkey. 'To friends, present and absent.'

Dyce kept the smile pasted on his face, but it lay heavy on him. There should be an empty place at the table, the way that some folks kept a chair free for the prophet Elijah. The promised land was here, not across the sea. He wished Garrett had known about this place before they'd settled in Glenvale and gotten mixed up with the Callahans. He stood. Vida watched him carefully, the workings of his mind like a wristwatch cracked open on a jeweler's bench.

'Going to ask around. See if anyone saw Garrett.'

'I'll come with you.'

Vida pushed her chair back too. It was useless, she knew, but letting Dyce go off alone wasn't right. *Let him do something to set it right*, she told herself. He let her. He could see that Vida was a little tipsy, and so what? She had had a hard couple of days – and before that he had no idea of how bad it had been. She kept close to his side as they went from table to table like a bridal couple, and let him do the talking.

'He's tall, kind of heavy in the shoulders, blond hair, acne scars that make him look like he's boiling hot all the time. He's wearing cargo pants – like these – and he's got a checked shirt on, sleeves rolled up, probably.'

'You really think we've seen him?' said one woman, drunk and pink-skinned. She waved a hand at the walls. 'These walls are here for a reason. Heaven with a view of hell ain't heaven, baby.'

They moved round the place, and they were met with the same blank stares, the same friendliness that turned sour when people understood what they were asking.

But their stomachs were full, and the booze kept coming. It blurred the lines that Dyce was trying to connect, blotted out the distrust, softened Vida's discomfort with the waste and the lavishness of the place. When the singing began, to the thrum of a pair of guitars, the last of their reservations evaporated. They gave in to the night and the feeling.

'It's going to be okay,' Vida whispered. She stroked Dyce's hair back from his face. 'Give it a little time. We can ask again in the morning, when everybody's thinking clearer. Whaddaya say?' She was a little unsteady herself, and Dyce had to keep his hands on her waist.

The musicians had gathered a small crowd, and somewhere a couple of fiddles had materialized, and other instruments Dyce didn't know well enough to say. The man who was speaking for the musicians came forward in his pointy black boots and he said, 'Ladies and gentlemen, we are going to start slow, and you know why. But we have a lot of stamina, don't we?' The crowd laughed, appreciative. 'Yessirree! We get better as we go!'

He stepped back and signaled to the others and they began an old song that pulled the childish heartstrings of everyone who heard it. People joined in one by one, or in groups, as soon as they recognized the tune, the words springing fresh from the dusty cupboards of their minds, lost and found, grabbing hold of the red thread that once bound all humanity and led them safe through the lair of the minotaur.

> *Hush-a-by,*
> *Don't you cry*
> *Go to sleep, you little baby*
> *When you wake you shall have*
> *All the pretty little horses*
> *Dapples and grays, pintos and bays*

The singers went on, and Vida protested. 'Hey, now! You all have skipped out a verse there!' Her voice was too loud, Dyce thought, and he tried to get her to sit down, but she was too enervated by the unfairness of being passed over. She turned to Dyce, her eyes bright, 'That was my favorite verse,' she told him. 'I used to sing it again and again.'

She focused on the musicians. 'Come on! Sing it right!'

They looked at each other and seemed to decide, because they launched into the next verse.

> *Way down yonder*
> *In the meadow*
> *There's a poor little lambie*
> *The bees and the butterflies*
> *Pecking out its eyes*
> *The poor little lamb cries 'Mammy!'*

Dyce pulled Vida up to dance before she could say any more, and they turned slowly, holding each other close, the faces around them blurred into arcs of flame-lit flesh, ruddied by the drink.

Vida fell against his neck and mumbled, 'You know what?'

'What?'

'I have a confession.'

'Speak, my child.'

'I love you.'

Dyce laughed. 'Good,' he said. 'I was worried you were going to tell me something else.'

They kept circling through the dancers, Dyce keeping his eyes half-closed against the giddiness, so it was Vida who saw her in the throng – the dark hair dragging at her face, wet as weeds from the river, the hollows of her oil-slick eyes.

Vida tried to get Dyce to stand still, but he twirled her again, and she pushed him away more roughly than she meant. He stumbled back and said, 'Hey! What the hell was that for?'

Vida was staring behind him. Maybe it was the drink. Maybe the specter would have disappeared.

The girl was still there, grinning at them with her bloody gums, the cushion baby imprisoned in her arms.

Dyce saw her too now, and froze, the alcohol evaporating from his blood as it chilled. Vida felt like rubbing her eyes, but when had that ever worked?

'Oh, Jesus,' said Dyce.

'It's not Ester, is it?' Vida said.

'No. Worse.'

Standing there was Julia, the last of the colostrum sisters. She had made her way in after all.

43

Tye Callahan was used to it – doing everything himself. He packed the scouts' tent, noting the black-rimmed bullet hole in the side where they'd shot the bear. It wasn't ever going to be windproof anyway, just a bit of shelter on whichever leeward hill Tye would next find himself. There were other big things too – pots and pans – that he'd have taken if he'd had a horse. But the animals were long gone and he had to limit his scavenging to the essentials. The tent, he figured, would make a pair of trousers, a jacket, even, something to keep a man dry when he had to take a chance and sleep out in the open.

He found a Mars Bar turfed out of an upturned pack, where it had rolled under the coil of a camping mattress. Tye sat on the bank and ate it all while his bird watched, restless, rustling her harness. He had to fight the nausea as he choked down the concentrated sweetness. Some things you found were like that – meant for consumption in an easier time. His body wasn't used to the soft life anymore, and things that were meant to be treats could turn on you.

What he couldn't carry, he would take up in his arms – mugs and hats and boots and sporks and maps and canteens: enough to keep an entire household alive for much longer than the two worthless scouts had ever spent on the road. Tye spat in the dust. Useless sons of bitches. He had done a better job on foot, by himself, for all their fancy gear.

The bird wasn't settling. 'What now?' Tye asked her. She regarded him, her eyes bright with message, and Tye wished he could reach out and pet her like a dog. She would probably take his fingers off right then and there. Rat with wings, the other Callahans had called her, on account of the fleas and mites attending most any bird. Still, he had always preferred her to the people around him. With a wild creature, you knew where you stood.

The bird lifted her wings a little, as if she was airing the hidden downy feathers, and she looked away. Tye went back to his riverine contemplation, rubbing his stomach. His digestion was playing up some. The Mars Bar had soured on him and now it lay in his guts, heavy as dread.

He leant into the cramp, hoping it would go away before he had to transport the scouts' goods, and tried to take his mind off the twinges that came before the diarrhea. *Look at the water*, he told himself. *Like a picnic spot. Ain't that a pretty sight?*

Except it wasn't. The water was muddied. The weeds bobbed and clung, trapping every little thing that the currents brought up and swallowed down.

Tye forgot his stomach.

There was something big caught in those weeds. Something man-size, and it couldn't move on.

He got up and went as close as he could to the water's edge, the mud sucking at his boots.

The girl was floating face-up, her long dress rucked over the bony knees, her flesh slowly taking on water like the sponges the Callahan women used to wipe Bethie's body down. This one still looked halfway healthy, Tye thought, except for the lipped slashes in her abdomen that leered through the torn cloth. She had long ago stopped bleeding, but soon the fish would get at her, and there was something awful wrong about that. Man had to stay top of the food chain. What else was there?

He took his boots and socks off, and ignored the smell. That wouldn't offend her none now. Then he divested himself of his trousers and his shirt.

The water was cold, but Tye had been worse places – and recently too. He hooked his hands under the drowned girl's armpits. Jesus, she was heavy! 'No offence,' Tye told her.

He let go and stepped back to think a minute. Then he felt underneath her body in the water. He scraped his knuckles against a rock, lodged somewhere it shouldn't have been, bound into the cloth. There were a couple of them, weighting her like an anchor. No suicide, this one, though she looked calm enough. Someone had made sure that she was dead, through and through – killed her twice.

Tye freed the rocks from the folds of the dress, tearing it as he worked.

He got the body to the bank easily enough after that. 'You want me to help you, ain't that so?' he muttered. He pulled her onto the bank where she lay steaming a little in the sun. He half-thought to try to resuscitate her – God knows, he'd had partners even less willing before, and he would again – but it was clear she had been dead a while. Rigor mortis maybe even come and gone; he wasn't an expert.

'Alright,' Tye told her. 'But it's a shame we didn't get to know one another a little earlier. I like me the black-haired ladies.'

He inspected her. What was it, exactly, that went out when a person passed on? Some light inside them that was burning, and then wasn't. He had killed a few people in his time – men and women, both – and he had never been able to put his finger on it.

'But I'm going to keep trying,' Tye said. 'Yes, indeed. Old Hawk-Eye never been a quitter.'

He squinted down at her chest. No bra and nice titties too. But there was something else hard under there, making a bump when there should be none.

Tye slid his hand under the bodice of the dress, and when he came to the soft dead nipples he twisted them. You heard stories about muscles moving, nerves and gases powering the cold machines of corpses, but there was no response.

The vial was made of glass. He lifted it out from the soaked material. The cork stopper was still in place. Whatever it was, it had survived the death struggle, and had been precious enough for her to keep close to her heart.

Tye unstoppered the little bottle and sniffed it. Not too close, now.

Whatever was inside was yellowing, with a skin on top like custard: sweetish, going sour. His roiling stomach had subsided, but now it turned over again. Tye put his head to the side and tried to retch, but the Mars Bar was stubborn and he could only heave drily, his chest hitching like a dog's.

He went back a way and sat down again. 'Don't be a hero, asshole,' he told himself. 'You just set here a bit.'

The idea of real coffee came upon him and he dedicated himself to the finding and brewing of it. Then, when it was ready, he grew ashamed: the smell always sent him back to the Concession talks and that nice Northern lady, Renard's wife, and how she had tried to show them hospitality.

But it was better not to waste good coffee. He didn't know when he would see it again. The girl lay damp and unmoving in the sun, and Tye wondered if the dead got sunburnt. He raised his metal camping mug to her. 'Something to remember you by.'

It was later, when he had drunk his coffee black and scalding that Tye figured that the stuff in the vial might be milk. He shrugged. It was not his business. Like an ant he busied himself with moving the scouts' housekeeping equipment into the hills where he'd slept, and he found a spot that would make a good hiding place. He ended up burying it all in a crevice, under rocks and dirt, pirate-style. Then he looked around for a marker, something that would help him remember the place when he came back this way. He memorized the shape of the hill – evenly curved with two cottonwoods side by side near the summit – as well as the bald patches of slope where rocks and rain prevented the grasses from taking hold. He'd lost a couple of decent things this way, hiding them away and then forgetting exactly where. A man got real specific when his survival depended on the recovery of equipment. Hills could look the same after a while, and trees too, even to the most experienced huntsman. It was no good building a cairn or setting up a pattern of stones: that kind of beacon only attracted passersby. Tye walked back to the camp, turning occasionally to see the hill from a different angle, memorizing what it looked like from the treeline.

He took up the horses' prints and followed them. Whoever had stolen them had been smart enough to take the animals through the shallows to cover their tracks, but Tye had time. He walked the shores looking for where the hoof prints reappeared in the mud, and then headed west. It took a couple of hours, but it was pretty clear where they went.

At the crest above The Mouth, he laid low, crouching into the grass. The place seemed secure, inside a perimeter wall that ran along the cup of the valley and up as far as it could go into the hills on either side, where it met the rocky cliff face. Outside the walls was an old church. Some way off was a dark shape, a man swathed so that his arms were invisible, dangling by his neck from a tree. Even from where he hid Tye could tell he was long gone, turning slow. A poncho. That's what he was wearing.

Tye switched his attention back to The Mouth. Inside the settlement people were moving around and there, as plain as day, were the two horses tethered outside a building, eating hay.

Tye crept back, staying low, and hiked up around the set-tlement to continue his reconnaissance – all the way along the cliffs to its top edge, the V where the two valley walls met. The perimeter fence continued here, but it looked weathered: the poles were roped together with string and cloth and the support pillars, which had once been dug deep into the ground, had been exposed by rain. Tye knew how it was: you couldn't be everywhere at once, and there was always a weak spot.

Satisfied with his findings, he made his way back down to the river, and sat himself down. Out came the pencil and a precious piece of paper: Renard had better appreciate it. Tye sketched a rough map of The Mouth and its surroundings, with arrows designating the vulnerable point up top.

He made a note saying that the cliffs were too steep to trav-erse, but they were ideal for riflemen. It was not as delicately worded as the first message. It didn't need to be. Tye had begun it by describing the state of the scouts, one with his throat slashed, the other's neck broken like a doll. He thought under the circumstances that a little poetic license was apt.

Tye called the harrier to him, and rolled the map as small as it would go. She accepted the canister and the note safely inside it. Tye sent her off again, north. If all went as it should, there would be no more assessing now – just an army, come to do what it should have done a week back. His job was done.

Tye sat back and considered returning to Glenvale. He packed up all he could comfortably carry and set off. But when he'd walked that way for a few minutes, the sun flashing hot on his neck, he felt his stomach tightening into a knot again at the thought of the actual return. He turned east and slowed his pace, taking turns watching the birds in the trees and the beetles underfoot, until he was all the way back at the lake. He could do with the company.

'You know, I think I might do some more fishing,' he told Ester. 'See what else the river brings me. Reckon I earned it.' Her dead eyes stared up at the firmament, but he knew that she agreed with him.

44

When Vida and Dyce were shown to the entrance of the mine, Julia was already there, waiting for them, though the risen sun still lay hidden behind the easternmost hill. She'd been given new clothes too, trousers and a shirt, and for the first time they saw the pouched flesh of her abdomen that spoke of the lost baby.

'Where's Ester?' she asked. She was hard to read, thought Vida. Like her sister. You couldn't tell if she was pleased or weeping that Ester wasn't there to bully her and order her around.

Vida told her the story she'd concocted – about their synchronized attack, and how one of the scouts had got a shot off clean through Ester's skull.

'She didn't suffer,' she added. *Don't make it worse.*

Dyce waited a couple of beats and took over. 'And you?' he asked Julia. 'You were next in line after Ester, right?'

She jutted her chin out. 'The guy in the poncho killed himself. You all said he would do that, remember? Hanged himself from that tree about an hour after you left. So it was me or the other two, and they said they weren't taking pregnant women – 'cause that was two places.' She pulled a face.

Vida saw now that she'd helped them sell the lie. It was true that the rocking man had probably wanted to die, but he surely didn't want to kill himself – otherwise he'd have done it instead of holing up at the church. Maybe that was what Ester had been whispering to them before she left. One last murderous message: *Eliminate the competition.* Vida pictured the three women, floating over to the man where he sat in his sorrow against the wall. They held splintered planks hidden behind their backs, ready to beat the ghost out of him before they strung him up.

Ed arrived, smiling. He was carrying a fat burner that hung on a rope. He made a show of lighting it with a flint and scraper. The flame was uncertain, and the burner dripped. Dyce had to look away: it was too much like the body that was dangling under the tree outside the town walls.

Ed ushered the new recruits busily to the mine entrance, and now that they were close Vida and Dyce saw how wooden railway sleepers held up the roof of the tunnel. Men and women were moving in and out in an orderly fashion, swathed like mummies, toting tools and lanterns. Ed rested a foot on an upturned bucket like Napoleon, and addressed Dyce and Vida and Julia in the voice he used for show.

'Hi ho, hi ho, everybody. It's Show and Tell today – best part of my job. Course, you understand how I hate leaving the others outside, but our town is only so big, copes with only so many folk. A hundred and fifty, to be exact. Doesn't work too good with a hundred and forty-seven; doesn't work at all at a hundred and fifty-one. And, folks, don't ask how we found that out!' Ed chuckled, wet and false, his tiny eyes retreating.

'Most part of that is food production. We're a farming community, as I hope you saw from last night's meal – and wasn't that a feast? Wasn't that just the best thing you've seen in a long while? Am I right or am I right?' Ed rubbed his stomach fondly, the way you were meant to do with a buddha, and Vida found herself shuddering. What else was in there, besides food? There was something terrifyingly clownish about him.

'I guess I should have told you all yesterday, but if you hate mushrooms you're going to be in the deepest bunker of hell in about five minutes, right next to Hitler and that guy who shot John Lennon, and the red-hot seat they're saving for Renard when he crosses over. This is Mushroom City, and this' – he pointed at the mine entrance, extending his whole hand, the same way he'd gestured at the sick boy with his parents – 'is where the magic happens.'

There was something in his voice: the tone, Dyce thought, of an old-time radio advert, or a western medicine man selling nostrums from a wagon – punching the first syllable of every word and pronouncing every letter, building in exuberance, sentence upon sentence, towards some irresistible climax. *Rolluprolluprollup! Buy two bottles of Cod Liver Elixir and I'll throw in the wart powder for free!*

A thin woman in a headscarf came walking out and seemed to recognize Dyce and Vida. She gave them a conspiratorial smile and said, 'The Callahan Killers.' She smelt sweet, like old grass clippings. Only her face and hands were visible from her wrappings, and they were muddy brown, her fingernails caked black, and Vida thought, *Oh, God, please don't let her touch me with those hands. I don't think I could stand it if she did that.*

Ed set the burner down and adjusted the wick until it burnt steady, making thin ribbons of soot.

'Follow me,' he said. 'Keep right; pass left. Remember the old rules of the road and you'll be just fine down here!'

Vida and Dyce waited for Julia to go first. Better to keep her in sight. She kept close to Ed. They all disappeared into the mouth.

The mines were darker than Vida had expected. The glow from Ed's flame seemed to extend only so far, a bauble of light that struggled against the black. It made her wonder whether there were degrees of dark. A candle flame could brighten the whole kitchen back at the old house: the light from it seemed to enliven the space, halo the people sitting at the table, go in search of the undead corners and cracks. This darkness was different, thick and unfriendly, a plague blanket.

Dyce savored the darkness. He did not take his power for granted: each evening when night came on, he was amazed again that he could see better than during the daylight hours. Where the others were stepping blind, he tried to turn his strength to good, noting the obvious maintenance to the original structure, which was about a century old. It would have been here when the last big storm came. Were the mines used for shelter back then too? It made sense. Where sleepers had splintered or rotted, they'd been replaced with thick logs: birch, cottonwood, pine – wedged into place to keep the soil at bay. The old tracks for the trolleys had been dug up and added to the walls and roof for reinforcement. It felt like an underground tree house, and Dyce had a pang of timesickness for Garrett and the old diversions laid out for him by someone else, the forts and dares and puzzles.

They descended as they went, and they expected the air to grow colder and less hospitable. Instead it was warmer and more humid. Then the air pockets merged and the temperature evened out. It was constant for the last few feet, uterine.

They came to a junction. Ed turned left and they saw the yellow-green glow that crept towards them, like a night-light under the door.

He led them into the chamber itself, lit by a couple of

lanterns overhead. In the soft glow the air seemed to move and shimmer, and it shouldn't have – not this far under the earth, where no air currents stirred except those thrown up by the movement of their bodies.

But the motes were there, suspended. They twirled, balletic, in the haloed light.

Vida covered her mouth in the old instinct, and when Dyce saw her he did the same. The rest of the workers were muffled by the cloths they wore like masks.

Whatever it was, it didn't bother Ed. He just stood there and gestured at the floor and the wooden boxes there, made from pallets. They were filled to the rim with black mulch, like portable graves.

From them grew millions of mushrooms, luminous against the space-dark earth, an underground forest. Each box held a different kind, Vida could see: big brownish ones with fronds; red-spotted ones that looked poisonous; small white ones, bright as buttons. Others looked like failed experiments – shrunken into warts or cups or human livers, frilled or gilled or phospho-rescent. They sprouted in groups, jostling desperate as pimples – Dyce thought of Garrett's ravaged face – or singly, proud and offish. And they weren't just horizontal: some were being trained to grow up the poles that reached the cavern's roof, where the lanterns dangled. And tending them all were the linen-wrapped women of The Mouth, their thin fingers busy weeding in the mulch.

Ed stopped. 'You gotta be real careful around some of these ones,' he said softly. 'Like the oysters. Can't even fart too close.'

He stooped to tweezer out a mushroom the size of his hand, making sure he didn't bruise its brothers. He held it up to the light of his burner.

'Here is the real secret of The Mouth.' He paused for effect.

Vida fidgeted. 'You grow mushrooms?'

Ed regarded her. 'These ones are special.'

'You grow magic mushrooms?'

He narrowed his eyes at her. 'All of you. What have you seen here so far, in your time in our beautiful town?'

'You run a tight ship. You were right.'

Dyce nudged Vida and said, 'No one's sick, Ed.'

'Correct! And that, little travelers, is because of these babies. These here 'shrooms are anti-bacterial.'

'Well, that's great,' said Vida. 'But so's the barberry bush. Why aren't you growing a crop of those?'

'I said these were special. They're special because they are anti-bacterial, but they are also *anti-viral*.' Ed sucked in a vast lungful of air, then exhaled, his fat man's titties jiggling and jubilant. 'You smell that, boys and girls? That there is the smell of *life*! Suck it in!'

'What?'

'You heard me, girlie.' He shook the mushroom at her, its frill trailing over his dirty fingers. 'The elixir, right here. Food and medicine, all in one. Chinese been doing it for ten thousand years. Why you think they live so long? Now just think about it, what it means for us down here, for everyone in the South. I'll tell you what it means. *No sickness, ever again*.'

They were quiet. A woman smiled weakly at them. Ed saw her and said, 'Get back to work, Mona. You got quotas.' She put her head down.

'No one in The Mouth has ever caught a virus in all the years we've been a town. And I don't just mean that no one gets the sniffles. I mean *not one virus*. The good citizens here are immune to *all* of them: the whole bang-shoot. Does that impress you folks? It impresses me. And you three, since yesterday's meal, are lucky enough to be part of it.'

Ed leant forward and held the mushroom to Julia's lips. She opened her mouth obediently and took a bite, chewed it and swallowed. 'Anyone else hungry? I know I am.' He ate the rest of the mushroom in his hand, not bothering to brush the dirt off.

'How does it work?' asked Dyce.

Ed licked his lips, chasing the soft flesh of a fragment. 'Can't tell you, buckaroo. We ain't exactly scientists. This was our lucky find. But you know what? We are going to change history. Am I right or am I right?'

'Not one person's caught a virus?'

'Not one.'

Ed let that sink in, then he went on. 'Dyce and Julia: you'll be working down here. Women are the pickers; men look after the soil and the beds. There are two other growth chambers like this, and also some smaller ones – nine, all said. You'll be told where you're working, but don't ever go on straight along the tunnel we came in. There's a point where we've stopped maintaining it and the structure from there is . . . unpredictable. You all will know when you've gone too far. There'll be signs. You don't want to go too far.'

Dyce and Julia nodded.

'Now you've seen the big secret, kids. It's time to exit Eden. Let's go. We can walk and talk. So what do you think? With new folks I always want to leave this bit till last, but how can you? It's fucking amazing. Am I right or am I right? Rest of the town's just a town, but if you don't have to worry about viruses no more, that means something, don't it? It really is a *town*. We stand a chance to make it the way it's supposed to be.'

Ed seemed to want applause, but Vida couldn't shake the feeling that there was more to it. He hurried them along the shaft, back outside, talking all the way, and the watery light changed back to the clearer atmosphere of the daytime earth.

The sunlight was finally creeping over the lip of that eastern hill: the line of day slid down the opposite side where it would warm the whole valley. The miracle mushrooms would keep growing sleepily in their beds in their climate-controlled conditions. Dyce's eyes watered at the brilliance of it all. He struggled to keep up as the others trotted up the main street ahead of him.

Ed showed off the general dealer and the saloon, the barber and the tailor, all made the way people had seen them in the old movies. Vida kept thinking that the shop fronts were facades, and if she went round the back of them she would find only the pine struts keeping them upright. But people seemed to be using them. They seemed to work in shifts in the mines, and the business of life in the upper world had to be taken care of.

Last was the clinic. 'This is where you'll be, Vida.' Ed was grinning at her, out of breath. 'Put that medical knowledge to use.'

'But if there are no viruses . . .'

Ed laughed. 'Oh, we aren't *perfect*! Shit happens, don't it? People still cut themselves and break their legs – or even just have headaches and toothaches. Or heart attacks, God forbid! We just need to know someone cares, don't we, Vida? That someone's looking out for us.'

She smiled, though it seemed wrong when he was listing all the things that compounded suffering.

'That's what my mama always used to say.'

45

Vida had seen enough yawning staplers, torn folders and inkless pens in her time, and in places you'd least expect, too – the remnants of old lives removed and then abandoned to rot and rust. But each time she saw them waiting frozen and patient in their old settings, primed for their original purposes, it almost broke her heart. Now she ran her fingers over a heavy metal holepunch and turned it over in her hands. A year ago she would have sat down and made it rain confetti for an invisible wedding, just because she could. Vida punched a bunch of experimental circles out of the corner of a manila folder, but then she got to thinking that that was what a virus might look like if you magnified it enough times. She was expecting patients, but the knock on the door still came as a surprise, and Vida dropped the holepunch on her foot.

'Ow. Fuck. Come in.' It was a mistake to have replaced the door glass with hardwood, she saw now. Maybe she was losing her fighting instinct, the constant suspicion that could also save your stupid life.

Ed stuck his head around, that ever-loving smile pasted on his cheeks like it had been stapled there. It had to be him, didn't it?

'Thought I'd give you some time to settle in. How's it going? You ready to rock 'n' roll, Nurse Vida?'

He squeezed in, and Vida felt the room get warmer with his presence, as if he robbed the air of oxygen. She moved to block the confetti from him.

'Born ready,' she said, and gave him a tight little smile. She wanted to rub the bridge of her bruised foot but she didn't want him to know she was in pain. *Don't let them see you sweat.* Isn't that what her mama always said?

'Glad to hear it. Cause there are about thirty folks just itching – and I mean that – to get in here and see what you got to offer. I told them to wait in the saloon, and I'd let them know when they could come on up. Play secretary for you.'

Ed took a seat in the chair opposite Vida and began working his shirt out of his belt.

'But I figure I oughtta test-drive the vehicle, right?'

Vida's heart sank. Oh, God. Not a perv. She had had enough of those on the road. Their bad breath and their sad eyes.

'I'll be patient zero,' Ed was saying, bright and desperate, as his hands worked near his crotch to free the shirt's hem. Vida wanted to tell him that patient zero was something else altogether, and he sure as fuck did not want to be *that*, but she left it. *Pick your battles.* She really ought to get that tattooed somewhere.

Ed's shirt was finally untucked in front, but now he was battling to un-wedge it behind. When he'd pulled the material loose, he lifted the shirt like a sail over his head, exposing the waxy skin stretched smooth and bulbous over the rolls. The only fat man in the South. It didn't seem to bother him.

'What's been bugging you, then?'

'Well, nothing much. Just thought I'd get a check-up. See that everything's in working order.' He thumped his fist against his hairless chest. 'Actually, I get a little short of breath sometimes. And I get dizzy if I stand too long.'

Vida looked in the drawer and found a stethoscope. She polished it on her shirt and then came round to inspect him, making sure to stand behind him so he couldn't see her face.

'Just lean forward and breathe in and out, real slow.'

His skin was damp. His middle labored against the constriction of the belt that folded his flesh. It was like examining a worm, Vida thought. She listened to the wheezing breath and the sluggish beating of his heart beneath all those layers. There was nothing, really, wrong with Ed. He was just overweight. *Never tell the fat man he's fat*, she told herself. *'Specially if he's the mayor or the king or whatever Ed is here at The Mouth. They're all fucking terrified of him, and there must be a reason.* She would have to prescribe exercise. For a man who talked up the virtues of hard work, Ed was pretty shy of it himself. He ordered the others around all day, and gorged on their produce by night. He was starting to look like a mushroom himself.

'Well?' said Ed.

Vida didn't know what to say. *Easy does it*, she thought. *If you've ever needed to practise your pussyfooting, now is the time, little sister.*

'Look, it's not something I studied, but this looks like a vascular problem. Blood flow. A quarter aspirin every morning will sort it out, if you still got. Otherwise, the usual. Try yarrow flowers in a tea.'

'That it?'

'Yeah. Nothing to worry about.'

Vida took the frog-cold stethoscope off and laid it on the table, then sat down again. Ed didn't move.

'Anything else you want to tell me?' She tried to make her voice soothing, the way Ruth did when she spoke to her frightened, heavy women – and her little girls: the ones who came to see her with their bellies swollen like beach balls, though they themselves still had to see fifteen candles set on their birthday cakes. They never came to her until it was too late. *Denial*, Vida thought. *One size fits all.*

Ed smiled, lopsided, and for a moment Vida felt the pity of the thin and fit for the awkward and unwieldy.

'Go on. I'm your doctor, right? Lay it out. Warts and all.' *Oh, God, no. Please don't let it be warts. I bet that's what it is. He's been schtupping all the women in The Mouth, and he's caught something nasty off of them. Or a prostate exam! He's going to ask me to stick my finger up his ass! He wants the FULL examination, doesn't he?*

'I do struggle to, ah' – Ed made a fist and pumped the air – 'get an erection. But only sometimes, you know. It happens to all men, right? When you're stressed?'

Vida didn't blink. 'It's all part of the same problem. The blood flow. Take the aspirin or the yarrow and it'll sort that right out. And, Ed?'

'Yes?'

'Don't worry about it. Worrying is about the worst thing you can do.'

'Okay.' He stood and began shrugging the shirt back on, covering the pale mushroom flesh. 'I'm glad you're here.' He said it quickly, his head down, as if he'd never seen a button before in his life.

'No problem. I'm glad to be here.'

And she was. She really was.

46

There was a hat on a hat stand behind the office door, and Vida took it now and tried it on. A game ranger's hat, canvas, with a fake leather band that had cracked and peeled to the meshed fibers underneath. 'You and me both, hat,' Vida told it. It was too big, but she wore it anyway. What she really wanted was to sit back somewhere shady with her head in her mama's lap, feeling the hair being parted and then pulled close against the scalp. It was always too tight at first, but you got used to the ache. It was odd not to feel it, like one of them Victorian ladies loosed from her whalebone stays.

Now, in her oversized hat, she stepped out into the dusty high street and walked slowly down towards the trading store. There were not a lot of people around, but the ones that were all greeted Vida and she felt like tipping the hat in reply, like a new sheriff doing the rounds in a strange town. *Easy, there*, she thought. *You're just the nurse here, and you aren't even on duty right now.* A couple of horses were pulling a makeshift sleigh up the slope, carting splintered wood to the top fence. It made Vida as happy to see them as if they were reindeer. Horses, and mended fences. They were doing something right in The Mouth, and she was pleased to be part of it.

The trading store door was spring-loaded, and when Vida pushed it open, it groaned and pinged like it was the only thing in the world keeping the town from being buried when the loaded shelves surrendered.

A man was looking up at her from behind a counter. He had a watchmaker's loupe screwed into one socket, the eye huge and watery. *Cyborg*, she thought.

'Miss Vida,' the man announced. He waved a pair of tiny pliers at her.

Not cyborg. Butler.

Vida smiled back and took her hat off, distracted by the shelves and their contents: everything you would ever need – and a bunch of things you hoped to high heaven you never would.

'Thomas Pringle, at your service. Ed said you'd come by for stock.'

'Thank you.' She gave herself up to staring at the shelves that ran along the sides of the store, packed to their edges with old-world objects. Anything half useful was collected here, and nothing that needed a power outlet: coffee grinders; trowels; hats; vinyl records; yellow pencils; measuring tapes in inches; duct tape; duck boards; fishing tackle and lures; hosepipes and tobacco pipes; guns too; thick serrated knives and red-painted axes. And a vat that smelt a little like a pickle barrel. *Mushrooms*, thought Vida, and kept it to herself. *I just bet that barrel is full of fucking mushrooms.*

'I wasn't quite sure what you needed, so I collected all the medical things I could find. You just go through it now and take what you can use.'

Pringle pushed a stainless steel bedpan across the counter at her. *Dear Jesus*, thought Vida. *Please don't ever give me cause to use* that. The bedpan held box-cutters and thermometers and plastic syringes – the needles were there too, but they had seen some use already – along with heavy black thread and a rusted pair of scissors. *There*, Vida thought. *Those might come in handy if Ed ever gets a little too frisky. Now let's see what's going on down below in the lower layer.* She was about to put her hand in amongst the metal to turn everything over for a better look when she saw the instrument on the top shelf. It rested, dusty, above Pringle's head, a soft machine. And it looked okay, though she was no judge. No strings and the fret pins were gone, but that wasn't unusual, even for before. Dyce could replace those, no problem.

'How much is that?' Vida pointing to it with her chin.

'Depends on what you got to trade.'

She shrugged. 'That's a hard one. Services, I guess?' She added quickly, '*Nursing* services.'

Pringle was looking at her. He smiled, the incisors yellowed as piano keys. 'You a muso?'

'Yes. Not me, no. Not for me. For my, ah, husband. Can I see it?'

Pringle set his loupe down carefully and set up a metal step-ladder. It clanged with his progress even though his feet were small and steady. Vida could not imagine him falling.

He handed the instrument over to her and she saw that it was a mandolin. Had been, that was. Someone had loved it and used it, and that had meant reconstituting it with bits of other instruments. Maybe this was the cyborg. The machine heads didn't match, but they were all solid brass. Where the body had been damaged, it had been expertly merged with the convex brown of a violin. Vida shook the mandolin and it rattled. She angled it and the plectrum that had been stowed inside it fell into her palm. She held the stub of plastic to the light, hard and light as a toenail. *Harper's Guitars*, it read. There was a faded phone number. *Try calling* that, *baby*, Vida told herself. *See how far it gets you.*

When she was done admiring the mandolin, she gave it back to Pringle. He settled it gently on the high shelf. Once he was down again he slapped the dust out of his dark trousers and said, 'When you got something in hand to trade, come on back and we'll see what we can do. Got to give the town doctor a good deal. Right?'

'Sure,' said Vida. Nurse, doctor. It made no difference out here. It was the belief that counted. The will to live.

She returned her attention to the bedpan and picked out the things she figured she could use. Then she tipped the rest out onto the wood of the counter and kept the bedpan itself.

'Going to need some gardening tools too,' she added. 'For the herbs.'

'Got to ask Ed about that first.'

'I'll be waiting. While you're at it, ask him if music therapy counts as medicine.'

Thomas laughed, hollow, like there was something that prevented the sound from emerging, making it echo inside him. He screwed the eyeglass back into his socket and bent over the counter.

Vida, dismissed, grabbed her bedpan and her tools and left him in his dim store, alone with all the useful things that were left in the world.

47

The first day of work was tough. The news of a new doctor in town brought all the verrucas and rashes and swollen testicles to the clinic. Vida felt as if she'd spent her day looking through a medical journal of weird diseases. She'd hardly had time to check out the cubicle that had been assigned clinic status. It looked clean enough, and she'd keep it that way.

Vida had no idea how to treat most of them, but she backed up and thought about her mother, muttering, 'What would Ruth do?' when it got heavy.

And what Ruth would do was listen real hard to what the person was saying, look at them properly too, so that the things that were going on in the mind and the heart of the person in front of her found their ways into their treatment. Ruth always told Vida that most of what made people hurt on the outside came from the hurt on the inside, which was why she had never laughed at even a teenager with acne.

So Vida did as her mother had taught her, and prescribed yarrow for just about everything – in a poultice, as a bandage, to be eaten a couple of times a day or drunk as a tea. And then, according to the gripe, she'd tailored each prescription by adding sage or mustard seeds or salt. She thought that just looking properly at the plum-purple heel bruise or the buttock boil or the rotten tooth abscess might set a person on the road to recovery. The rest they could do themselves.

And while they were happier when they left the clinic than when they had first set foot in it, the people she saw did not seem as cheerful as Vida thought they should. *If I had been living disease-free for this long, I would be a lot happier than these guys,* she told herself. *Look at them, dragging their sorry asses around! This is the best they've been fed and clothed and sheltered in years!*

She had wanted to talk to Dyce about it when he got back from his first shift at the mine, but she took one look at him when he got back to their little shack and left off. He'd never worked a full day in his life, and the lifting and digging and fetching of water had taken its toll. All he wanted to do was sleep. He divested himself of his wrappings, then managed to eat their dinner of mushrooms and exchange a story with Vida about the day before he collapsed on the mattress. It was stuffed with hay, which Vida thought was a terrible choice: you needed a lot of it; it got ticks and fleas after one season; and it pricked your soft parts like a cactus.

But exhaustion canceled out discomfort. They fell asleep curled into each other, as they had done in Horse Head, the hay sweet as the mulch where the baby mushrooms nestled.

☠

The second day at the clinic was a little quieter. Maybe the novelty had worn off, Vida told herself. It gave her time to sit and process the past few days on her own. Between a lumpy thyroid and whatever minor horror might come walking in through the door, Vida tried to set it straight in her mind.

The mushrooms were keeping everyone well, right? Anti-bacterial *and* anti-viral, as Proud Ed kept pointing out. Technically, the people of The Mouth had nothing to fear from Renard, if that was true.

If it is true, Veedles, said her mama's voice.

But there were suddenly three spaces available at The Mouth – that was how they had got in. The *only* reason they had got in. So there must have been three people dropping dead real quick.

Where had they got to?

Surely no one left this place on purpose. And if they'd died – of old age or a stroke or whatever – then where had they been buried? The graves out near the church were old, and there were no new graves inside the walls, because she had checked. The way people took care of their gone-befores told you a whole lot about their attitudes towards everything else. And Vida would have noticed a big old pyre for a sky burial. She knew what to look for too. She'd seen some in her day, and they'd stained the earth black, a mark that took years to grow over or fade back to the ordinary red of the dirt.

Would there be medical records? She looked around her office. Unlikely. This wasn't that sort of place. She stared out of the window. It was while she was inspecting her new surroundings more closely that she saw the dust rising in the road – small V-shaped tunnels of air that brought only bad news if you were out in the open. This was when the townsfolk would come running, looking for any shelter they could find. She started getting the clinic ready for the temporary invasion, checking for gaps, securing doors and windows. At least she had provisions.

Within minutes the gale blew in, channeled down between the valley walls. Vida watched people battling it, their clothes flapping, their hats tumbling off in cartwheels, their hair blown into their eyes. She saw the familiar dust devils, the swirling leaves and servile grasses, all the signs of ready Death on his cold, scissoring legs. She thought to find some cloth to cover her mouth and nose – but then she resisted the urge. *Immunity, remember? Okay, Ed. Let's test your theory.*

Vida bent and felt the puff of air that crept under the door. And then, giving in, she opened it and stepped out in the road, the hem of her shirt fluttering against her stomach.

She'd forgotten how uncomfortable wind was, how it scoured and stung and pressed against her body, electrifying the hairs in their follicles. She caught a grain of sand in her eye and it started watering like hell. *Fuck it*, she told herself. She stumbled back into the clinic.

While she was rinsing out her eye, a new patient had arrived and was standing at the threshold.

'For God's sake!' Vida snapped. 'Close the damn door!'

The old woman just smiled at her and smoothed down her peppery hair. Her left hand was encased in a black fingerless glove. As she stroked, Vida saw the fingertips set stiff, at right angles to the digits.

'I'm sorry,' Vida told her. 'This wind makes me nervous.'

'You better get used to it, girlie.' The old lady sat herself down with a sigh. Now she was shaking her faded hair out, fluffing and primping, dragging at the strands, and Vida saw the grit that sprinkled the floor of the clinic. Then she eased the glove off as Vida watched, fascinated. She held the twisted hand out, obscene, naked.

'You seen it before.'

'Arthritis. Sure. You know what causes it?'

'Same thing that causes all a woman's troubles. Having kids.' The old lady wheezed at her own joke and massaged the fingers with her good right hand. 'But what are you going to do? Send them back where they came from?'

'You know about honey and cinnamon, right? You also need to make sure that you're eating as well as you can, to slow the demineralization.'

'Sugar, it's too late for me. I done my time. I just came to see if you had anything new to tell me.'

Vida turned away and got busy pulping the yarrow.

'Poultice, every day. Sleep with it on. Then make the tea too.'

'Ah huh.'

She kept her back to the old woman. 'Can I ask you a question?'

'You can ask, but that don't mean I'll answer.'

Vida could hear the endless friction of the twisted hands.

'What happened to the last doctor?'

'The last one?'

'The person I replaced.'

The woman sighed. 'People die. People move along. You get to my age and you know that. My husband, Geraldo—'

'And when they die, where do they go?'

'Heaven or hell, sugar. Di'n't your mama teach you nothing?'

'The bodies, I mean.'

'To the earth. Dust to dust. Where we all going.'

Vida would get nothing out of her, she saw that. She gave up.

'Every evening, yarrow. And in the morning too, fresh. You come back if you need help.'

The old lady ducked her head. 'Thank you. I will surely give that a try. And I think the wind's dropped. You can come out of your burrow now.' She snickered; was still snickering when she made her way out.

Vida sat and felt the itch in her own scalp where the wind had settled the dirt. She reached up and rubbed, then looked at her hand.

The fingertips were brownish and oily.

She reached into her hair and scratched again, harder, and passed her fingertips under her nose.

Her own smell, still there, but something else: something earthy, bridging the living and the dead. From the mushrooms? She had to get hold of Dyce and ask him what really happened down there. He must have seen how it all worked up close.

There were no more patients. Vida closed up the clinic and walked down to the mines. She met Dyce as he came out of the mouth. Like everyone else, he looked as if he'd been spat out: dirt under his nails, hands cracked, shirt sweated through. He pulled his headscarf off and smiled with relief when he saw her – and it was genuine.

'How's work?' she asked.

'Hard.'

He didn't ask about hers, still queasy from the stories she'd told him from the day before as he'd drifted off to sleep.

'Want to go for a walk?'

'Not really.'

'Come on. Just a little one.'

Dyce conceded, and she took his arm. The two of them walked slowly up the main street and beyond, past the clinic, to the ponderosas at the top of the slope.

'Ah, you're going to kill me,' Dyce complained.

'Ah, but you'll enjoy it.'

Vida pulled him down beside her. They sat there and looked at the town and its wall and the grasslands beyond.

'Gale blew through at lunch time.'

'Did you go out?'

'Yeah.'

'And?'

'I learnt today that wind was always terrible, even before Renard. Uncomfortable. Made me itchy in my skin, you know?'

'You feel okay, though?'

'Fine. It was annoying, but it wasn't fatal. You? What's happening down there?'

'Okay, I guess. Good, even. But that fucking Julia. She looks at me funny. Then it's not so good.'

'What *happened* to that family? They all just . . . broken.'

'Beyond help. They should never have let her in.'

'They let us in.'

Dyce smiled. It was true. But their kind of damage was under control, wasn't it? He and Vida weren't exactly whole people: Dyce was still half Garrett and Vida was still half Ruth. Maybe soon there would come a time when they'd have a talk and realize how different they really were, how they'd only come together as a by-product of desperation. Dyce wondered whether Vida remembered the drunken *I love you* and the ever-after it signified.

'What you thinking about?' she asked.

'Nothing. You?'

'Something's been bugging me.'

'What?'

'The three – the ones we replaced.' She was scratching at her head again.

'What about them?'

'What happened to them? Where *are* they? I asked this lady at the clinic and she didn't want to answer, like it was a secret.'

'Maybe they left.'

'Yeah, right. And went where?'

'Maybe they died: an accident or something. Still a lot of building going on here.'

'Seems like a lot of people out of a hundred and fifty to die off real sudden.'

'But it's possible.'

'Okay. Where are they buried, then?'

Dyce was quiet. Then he caught where Vida was going.

'Oh, man.'

'It's the only place.'

'In the mines?'

'Beyond the signs, where you're not allowed to go.' Vida wiggled her fingers, the way Ed did. 'Am I right or am I right?'

48

Vida lay awake beside Dyce. He had dropped off right away: they really were hitting the hay. She lay staring up at the corrugated roof. It was like the township shacks her mother had grown up in back in South Africa – a square box with a bed, no lights, no toilet, just the bare earth beneath and a waterproof sheet between the bed and the sky. Who knew that it would turn out to be the best preparation for the end of the world?

Dyce slept on. They'd found the energy to have sex, but he was tired. He had drifted off straight after, apologizing as he went under. Still, for someone who said he was a virgin, he was doing pretty fucking well. Vida rested her head on her elbow and looked him over again. She still wasn't used to having this much access to another human body, especially one this good.

Vida ran her hand through his hair: it was smooth even though it was dirty. They said hair cleaned itself after six weeks, but that had turned out to be a lie. He smelt peculiar too. It wasn't the dirt of the straw and mulch composite, though. Nice lips – *very* nice lips: curved and full, the kind that would set in a smile by the time he was fifty. His chest was alright. No one was chunky anymore, except a few people like Ed, and that wasn't healthy. Dyce's chest was flat and hard, and that was fine with Vida. She trailed her hand over his stomach, the twin curves of the muscle on very young men that signposted the abdomen becoming the groin. Dyce groaned in his sleep and Vida imagined him waking up as she sat astride him, guiding his penis back inside her.

Poor guy. Let him rest. They had lots more nights ahead, didn't they? Plenty of time.

She dropped her hand and lay back on her own side of the bed, listening for sounds. The wind moved, restless and search-ing among the shacks. She couldn't stop the wheel of thought. *Is it midnight yet?* she wondered. *Am I the only person awake in this place?*

Vida sat upright.

Yes, she thought. *Yes, I am the only person awake in this place. Which is exactly why I ought to get up right now.*

She would sneak into the mine and take a proper look. Why the hell not?

Because it's the only place they said not to go.

Extra quiet then, is all.

Vida slid her feet off the bed and began to dress, feeling in the dark for her underwear, then everything else. The wind outside disguised the sounds of her shuffling, the clink of her belt buckle – and besides, Dyce was dead to the world. It would take an army *and* their band playing 'When the Saints Go Marching In' to wake him.

She found the hurricane lantern on the floor beside the door where they'd left it. She shook it to feel the slosh of oil – still full, thank God. One less thing to do.

'Where you going?'

Vida jumped.

'For a pee.'

'You're not. You are fully dressed.'

She'd forgotten that he could see her, despite the darkness. Obviously she wouldn't have gone to all that effort just to use the toilet.

Dyce sat up. Vida put the lantern down and found a space on the bed to sit.

'I need to see what's in the mines. If this place is going to be our home, I need to get a handle on what's going on. I can't be lying awake, wondering what's down there. They don't get to, to, restrict our movements that way, Dyce. It's weird. There's something going on.'

'But sneaking in there is crazy. You know that.'

'Yeah.'

'And what do you think you're going to find?'

'I don't know. An answer.'

Dyce was quiet.

'I'll go. I know the place better. Plus, I can see in there.'

'And me? What will I be doing?'

'Nothing. Just stay here. I'll be fifteen minutes. Then we can both get some sleep.'

Dyce dressed, yawning. When he was ready he kissed Vida, his mouth pliant, and she found that she didn't want him to go, after all. What if he found an answer she couldn't live with? Then it would all be over, the sleeping tight beside each other and the coming home before it: the kiss, like this; the touching; the fucking.

But when she tried to protest, no sound would come, and she watched Dyce slip out the door and into the gusty night.

She sat for half a minute, making up her mind. She couldn't bear the idea of just sitting on the bed in the dark, waiting for him. What kind of candy-ass woman did that? Not Vida Washington, that was for sure.

Outside the door of the shack the cold blast pushed at her. Vida stood still, waiting for the lenses of her eyes to adapt and reveal her surroundings.

The town was dead: even the saloon was closed, all the lights extinguished. Vida had in mind to get to the main street and keep an eye out. Sentry duty, she figured. It was the least she could do.

She stepped cautiously between the shacks, her eyes misjudging her feet, so that she jarred her spine as she went. As she turned onto the main drag she found herself beside the barber shop, out of the wind. She peered blindly down at the mines.

'Now, what *are* you two doing?'

Vida shrieked and then damped it down into her throat. The voice that came from behind her was high and girlish. Julia was a silhouette, shape-shifting in the dark, her eyes silvery pinpricks set somewhere in the center of her lank hair. Her nightdress shimmered.

'Fuck, Julia!' Vida whispered. 'Why are you awake?'

'I don't sleep so good these days.' Her hands were knotting themselves together in her nightdress. 'Me and Ester used to share a bed. I get lonely. Don't you get lonely? No,' she said to herself. 'No, you don't, because you have Dyce.'

'So you just wander around? Like a, a, fucking *ghost?*'

'I like to look at things. And listen.'

Vida pictured her with her head pressed up against the thin wall of their shack, sharing their most private sounds, their groans and panting, their sighs. She felt herself flushing.

'Where's Dyce gone now?' Julia asked.

'He's got, ah, Restless Legs Syndrome. Sometimes he just needs to get a walk in.'

'I saw him go toward the mines.' Julia shifted and stepped

back, her shape blurred for flight and discovery, and Vida knew the game was up. This would be the revenge for killing Ester: Julia would go straight to Mister Ed. And then there'd be trouble.

'It's not what you think it is,' she said, but Julia had already turned and disappeared. *Fuck!* They were dead meat.

Vida pelted down the road towards the mine. She didn't care who saw her. When she got to the entrance, she chanced a quick look back at the collection of shacks: the lights were flickering on.

They were coming.

'Dyce!' she called into the tunnel, but there was no reply. She hadn't really expected one.

Vida inhaled her last breath of fresh air and stepped into the velvet blackness of the mouth. It swallowed her whole.

She ran her fingers along the wooden walls and walked as fast as she could without falling against a splintered strut or lurching headlong into a chamber with its precious mushrooms. There were too many junctions. Which chambers were the ones Ed had shown them? Where did the known world end? It was a nightmare.

'Dyce!' she tried again.

This time she heard him coming. The caverns amplified his breathing. He was panicked. Oh, Jesus! He had seen something real bad down there, hadn't he? But he was there, oh praise Jesus, he was standing right next to her, unscathed and solid and *there*.

'Vida! Vida! You were right! There are *bodies* down there! Dead people! Like nothing you ever seen!'

'They're coming, Dyce!' Vida interrupted sharply, in the direction she thought his face would be. 'Julia saw you go in and she's gone to tell Ed. They are coming *right now!*'

'Already here,' came a man's voice from the tunnel.

It was Ed, sure enough, all the laugh gone out of him and the rifle raised to his shoulder, his rubbery chin resting on the stock, his tiny eyes squinting down the sight.

49

'First time in a long time that I've found myself in agreement with the Callahans.'

Ed wasn't smiling. There were others congregating behind him back along the tunnels, holding their lanterns and peering at the intruders, waiting for the say-so. It was familiar territory for them, wasn't it? Home. *The light at the end of the tunnel, that's what they say. What they don't say is that it's the train coming for you, head-on*, Vida thought. She looked at Dyce, but he was scanning for Julia's smug face in the throng, the avenging angel, the eyes shiny with lust, the milk turned to poison in her blood. They weren't upon them yet, but they would be soon.

'I'm a big enough man to say when I've made a mistake. And we can all agree that letting you into The Mouth was a mistake. Am I right or am I right?' There were murmurs from the people behind Ed. Vida gripped Dyce. *God! Are they going to drive us out with pitchforks? At least in the books Igor escapes.*

'You know we can't have this sort of . . . civil disobedience. But you won't go to waste. You'll serve this town if it's the last thing you do – dead or alive. We ain't picky. We are going to make sure of that. And the best part is, all you all have to do is keep breathing.' He mimed their panting. 'That's it: in and out.'

Vida tried to slow her breath, but it was no use. She needed the oxygen, especially down here, but the idea of taking the motes into her body was making her feel sick and a mite panicky. Vida felt it in her throat now, in her lungs. She swallowed. She was sure she could taste it. Her corneas begin to itch. Dyce was rubbing at his eyes. Would it be affecting him the same way?

'How's it tasting so far?'

'*What the fuck is in the air here, Ed?* Just tell us.'

'You're dumber than you look, cowboy.'

'Dyce.' Vida pulled on his sleeve. When he looked at her he saw that her eyes were enormous. He could see every tiny capillary mapped on the whites.

'*We're breathing the spores.*'

That's what the murk in her hair was. The word came back to her from an old history book: *miasma.* That's what was making the dark of the mines so thick, making the light work so hard to illuminate the place. It was *alive*, full to saturation with microscopic particles. Whatever end Ed had in mind for them didn't matter. It was already too late: they had fused with the mushrooms.

'Since you were so keen to see what's down in the deep corners, that's where you'll be going. Sound good? Or I can shoot you where you stand.'

'Easy, now,' said Dyce, holding up his hands. They were trembling, and Vida didn't blame him. Her whole body was in some kind of shock. 'How about this? We'll leave The Mouth same way we came in, put this behind us all. We got you all the horses, remember. Doesn't that count for something?'

Ed snorted, and the gun jerked. Weren't his arms getting sore? *Men*, thought Vida. *Always got to parley.*

'No one leaves The Mouth, Allerdyce. I'm giving you two options and there ain't no third. So you can turn round and go back down, and I mean all the way. I'm giving you permission to ignore the signs.' Ed paused, ever the showman. Except that this time it really was one life-or-death chance. 'Or you can try to come on up. But I must warn you: my finger is getting an ache in it. And as you can see, I am not alone.' Julia's laugh tinkled in the dimness, and Dyce thought again of Ester's lamprey jaws.

'Look,' said Dyce, and stepped towards Ed. A shot went off, cracking against the chapped rafters above their heads. A few splinters of wood fell back down, but nobody ducked. The echoes seemed to come back up from the deeps: *a belch*, Vida thought. That's what you get from The Mouth, right? She found herself grinning, a tight grimace that made a rictus of her round face. Dyce wasn't sure Ed had meant to miss. He and Vida were half-hidden in the shadows beyond the reach of the lantern light: not exactly easy targets.

'Come on, little doggies! Come on by! Get walking!' called Ed, and he began striking out down the tunnel to chase them along. Dyce took Vida's arm and pulled her back with him into a watering shaft, out of rifle range.

'That's right,' Ed was calling. 'Keep going.'

They went on, unwilling, past the main mushroom caverns, and then came to the sign, painted funhouse skulls on chipboard, a cupboard handle still attached, KEEP OUT and DANGER smeared below in mud, or worse. And then, ludicrously, a much neater sign, carefully lettered:

ABANDON ALL HOPE, YE WHO ENTER HERE.

'Just in case you were wondering,' Vida whispered.

Why didn't Ed follow them? He was staying back, still shouting, a little hysterical, she thought. She strained to hear him. 'You come back up this tunnel and there'll be someone waiting to shoot you!'

'Julia, probably,' muttered Dyce.

They went on, Dyce in front, his eyes noting each leak in the wall, each rusting nail. They had long ago lost the last of the lantern light shed by their pursuers: The Mouth had swallowed them, and they were meant to be digested.

The shafts went much deeper than Vida had first imagined, and not straight, either. She tensed her shoulders, bracing for some creature to come bounding up from the bowels, a minotaur, some horned man made mad by his imprisonment under the earth.

Dyce whispered, 'I know where we're going. I'll show you. But you better brace yourself.'

They knew by the smell that they were close. The air had changed again – thicker, more moist, as if it were licking their faces – and the sweet butchery smell of death hung over all like a gas.

They had reached the final chamber.

Vida moved blindly over the threshold. Her boots were sucked into the myriad mushroom bodies on the floor of the cavern, like walking on the moon. She could almost touch the air now. Her lungs felt as if they were turning inside out. Her hand came up against a sudden wall. It was slick with the effluent of hundreds of creatures. The cavern was a crypt, and the stink was unbearable.

She wiped her hands on her clothes and tried to breathe through her mouth.

'What's here, Dyce?' she asked, though she already knew. 'Tell me what you see. And stay close while you do it. If I let you go I'll never find you again.'

He was breathing heavily against the wet. 'Bodies. Just . . . *bodies*. Men, women, little kids. *Kids!* Fucking everywhere. And, Vida: there are mushrooms. Mushrooms just growing *out* of them.' He sounded as if he was going to cry, though with wonder or disgust she couldn't tell. 'Out of their *mouths*. Out of their ears and their *eyes*. Their *chests!* Like *flowers!*'

And then he was crying for real, she could hear.

'Dyce,' she said gently. 'Can you tell how, uh, fresh they are? How recently they died?'

'There's new bodies. I'd say a week old, maybe. And there are older ones too, skeletons, all bunched in groups.' Arranged, he wanted to say. Like a family photo.

'How many altogether?'

'A hundred, easy. Always groups of three. Like the three little pigs. Or the three bears.' He choked, then spat.

'Do you want to go back out?'

'Yes. No. I don't know.' She felt him wiping his face on his sleeve. 'But that's not everything.'

She waited. Let him get to it in his own time.

'They all have their necks broken. Or, or, stabbed. At the back, right there.' He chopped at her neck in the dark, forensic, and Vida shuddered.

'Jesus! Don't do that!'

'Between the axis and the atlas.'

'You mean, like a sacrifice?' She was going to vomit. Only the idea that it would deliquesce here with the remains of the dead and go on to feed the pink-cheeked residents of The Mouth kept the gorge down.

'It sure looks like that.'

'Dyce.' She breathed in, unwilling. 'I think the reason these mushrooms are special is because they're grown in human bodies – people who've survived some sickness. Maybe they take on the properties of the disease. You know, like homoeopathy: the hair of the dog and all that. Then, once you eat them, you're immune to whatever it is. Or maybe everything, if they're anti-viral *and* anti-bacterial, both. I'm not sure, exactly. Mama would know. But maybe Ed isn't exaggerating. Maybe the mushrooms really are the elixir.'

'And maybe sometimes there aren't enough sick people to be vectors.'

'Oh, Jesus.'

'Sometimes they need to sacrifice the healthy ones too.'

'Oh, *Christ!*' She pictured Ed with a cleaver, up to his elbows in gore. And then she did vomit: she couldn't help it.

Dyce let her finish. Then he grabbed her and held her.

'I'm going to get us out of here, I promise.'

Vida scrubbed at her face. 'How, exactly?'

'These old mines always had another exit. Disaster management, you know?'

She nodded. It made sense.

'You ready?'

He led Vida out of the chamber and back into the tunnel. The air was cleaner – she felt it – but the stink would never go away. It was lodged in her sinuses, osmosed into her clothes, a new and permanent part of her.

'Wait here,' Dyce said, and he helped her to sit.

He started taking off his shirt. Then he buttoned it up like a knapsack and tied the flapping armholes closed.

'What are you doing?'

'When we get back to Horse Head, we're going to take a picnic with us.'

Vida smiled. And then she pictured Dyce going back alone into the dark, seeing what she'd been spared, so that he could harvest the bright white eyes of the newly dead.

She retched again, but her stomach was empty.

50

Dyce led them down and down into the guts of the mines. He had made Vida tuck two fingers into his belt at the hip and wedge them there between the cloth and skin, the good human contact her anchor. He let her know when there was a step up or down, or a stony stream to cross. Her boots would never be clean, Vida thought, no matter how much she washed them afterwards.

The deep structure was not in good shape, but Dyce didn't tell her that. From the look of it, the walls had calcified: nowhere did the roof seem as if it would come crashing around their heads. The warmth of the mushroom farms was long gone, and they shivered in the cool and neutral air meant for creatures other than them. They went on, it seemed, forever, stumbling in a terrible limbo that was neither torture nor comfort.

'You feel that?'

Vida hadn't.

'Underneath. It's getting damp again.'

It was true: the dry earth beneath their boots was surrendering to mud. It was deepening as they went, until they were sloshing through winter melt, ankle-high.

Dyce tried not to think about quicksand – all the stories Garrett had told to scare the bejesus out of him when they were kids. *Don't panic*, he told himself. *The ones who panic are the ones who go under.*

Vida pulled on his belt. 'Wait. I want to tie my laces. I won't be able to take it if I leave my boots behind.' He stopped, and she bent down and reassured herself. She had her doubts about another exit. Dyce had seemed so confident, and it was something to do. But – really – what did he know about a hundred-year-old copper mine? He was a kid.

They got going again.

'You ever have to hide in a mine when the wind came?' she asked, testing.

'Yeah, sure. Three days, once, with Garrett and this other guy we were travelling with. Old Jay Loram – you know, The Man Who Lost His Nerve.'

'How long back?'

'Long time. There were still horses. Not ours. Ours were dead, but Jay still had his, an old gray mare, like the song.'

Vida knew what he was doing, talking just to take her mind off the dark and the water at their calves, now, and the way the air seemed to be changing too. It was definitely harder to breathe, and she could hear the inhalation of his lungs as he spoke and splashed through the muddy water, could hear what it was costing him to sound normal.

'Called her Half Price, cause she definitely wasn't what she used to be. Had a limp. Not a horse for riding. Then again, towards the end, not many were. So she took the packs, Garrett's and mine too – which was why Garrett could stand to travel with Talky Jay in the first place.'

Vida made a noise to show she was listening. Dyce stopped to choose between two tunnels. Left.

'Ever tried to get a horse into a cave? Jeez. Turned from a donkey into a mustang, then into a fucking mountain lion. Like we were trying to make her eat a hot coal. Not a way we'd ever get her in, and the wind was coming. Garrett and me, we quit trying, and Jay saw he had to leave her outside. Ended up that he had to tie her there and hope she was still there when we got back, however long it took. He was crying like a baby while he did it.'

'And was she still there?'

'Some of her was. Looked like all sorts of somethings got her.'

'God. Don't you have a happy story?'

Dyce was quiet, but at least it had worked – kept Vida from noticing how tight her throat was, like sucking through a straw.

The water reached to their knees now, and it was Dyce's turn to feel a flush of panic. How much further until they were swimming? What would he do then? Turn to Vida and confess his worst fear? *I know I'm your only chance, baby, but the thing is – I'm a scaredy-cat!* He knew how to swim, but that wasn't the problem. He pictured Garrett laughing at him. The thrashing, the desperation, the flashbacks would sink him. Dyce searched for the words to prepare Vida for the worst case. It wasn't fair to her. But fair wasn't getting a lot of action these days, was it?

'Vida. I have to tell you something, just so you know.'

'What?'

'I'm fucking terrified of deep water. Soon as I can't touch the bottom, I'm useless.'

She yanked him back by his belt. 'Are you serious?'

'Paralyzing phobia is what it is. It's not that uncommon. And stop yanking. You nearly cut me in half.'

'Is *that* why you let me cross the lake, that day with Ester?'

'Hey, you offered. I wasn't going to argue.'

He could hear her head shaking in disbelief, even in the dark.

'So I'm a coward. Can we get going?'

They went on.

'Dyce.' This time Vida grabbed at the back of his shirt. 'Is it changing? Going uphill, maybe? Is that possible?'

It was.

Praise Jesus. It was! The water level was beginning to drop as the tunnel curved up. Vida could feel her panting ease a little as the oxygen circulated slowly around their thirsty faces. And it was getting lighter! Vida felt her irises adapting.

But as it went up, the shaft also narrowed. They went from being able to walk upright single file to having to crouch pretty quick, unless they wanted to brain themselves. Dyce could see that they'd have to crawl the last bit. But he could also smell the exit ahead. That was what counted – the sweet night air and the promise of the vault of sky. You could endure anything if you knew the end was in sight.

Vida saw it first, crouched low against the merciful dry dirt – the glimmer of light that her eyes had been craving.

Except it wasn't moonlight.

It was moving, flickering orange, crackling and fork-tongued – a camp fire, for sure.

And there were voices, two men talking. Dyce shushed Vida, though there was no need. He lay on his stomach and wriggled forward to get a better look.

The escape tunnel looked unprofessional, as if it had been dug by thieves, a channel through which they could access the main network, pillage copper from the rich green seams during the midnight hours or, better yet, he thought, hold up unsuspecting miners for whatever they'd found. *That's what I would have done*. That was a century ago, though, and the exit had been covered over partway by the dead and leafless bush at the head of a talus. Below it, rock debris sloped down a couple of feet and then evened out into grassland, mostly flat, birches here and there.

They'd crawled through the mountain that protected The Mouth and come out less than a mile away on the other side.

The men sat directly below Dyce. If he squirmed just a little way out, his legs still in the opening like a rat in the jaws of a python, he could see them properly.

For a second, Dyce thought that the scouts they'd killed had risen from their graves. These two were dressed identically – the gray-blue bull denim shirts, the pleated pants with the double stripe of black, the shiny brown boots that had never felt a mile of real walking.

But these were different men – one tall and lazy, the other short and dark and mustached, his clothes a size too small. Dyce marked him as the one to avoid. Men who paid that much attention to the way they looked usually had something to hide.

'You don't need to stay up. It's my shift.'

'Couple of hours till morning. No use going to lie down now. Can't ever sleep the night before. Don't know how he does it.' He jerked a chin over at their leader's tent, where Malison's gentle snores told his men all they needed to know.

'Know what you mean. Only so much staring at the roof of a tent a man can do.'

'The first three minutes are riveting.'

He snorted. 'Where you from, anyways?'

'Bozeman, in what used to be Montana. You?'

'The capital. Never heard of Bozeman.'

'Lucky you.'

The tall man stood and stretched, then sat down again.

'What's the deal with this place tomorrow?'

'The Mouth. Heard they found themselves a vaccine or something. And it don't seem right the scouts never came back, does it?'

'Those weren't field men. Christ. Send a couple of cartographers off into wild country like this and it was bound to happen.'

'Still, can't have Northerners killed out here. Sends the wrong message.'

'Yeah.'

The chubby tanned man leant over to his pack and found a sachet. He bit the corner off and spat it out on the ground.

'Jello. You want some?'

The tall one shook his head and raised his hand. They were quiet, staring vacant into the flames, the way you were meant to.

'It's not tomorrow – it's the day after that's giving me the heebies. The next stop after The Mouth.'

'We doing two towns?'

'Next one's not a town. What they call a ghost colony down here – just sick folks, like a hospice. You know, where they go to die. Nasty.'

'So why the fuck send us?'

'Speed things up, I guess, since we're all the way down here anyways and it's just around the corner. Supposed to be hiding someone who's been fucking with Renard. Local law can't get in there.'

'He killing the sick now? What are we – Nazis?'

'Don't say that.'

'Yeah. Okay. Still, though.'

Dyce watched, keeping low. How the hell were two men going to take on the entire settlement of The Mouth?

Unless there were more than two.

Dyce held a hand up in front of his eyes to block the glare of the firelight that flared out, bleaching his night vision.

And there beyond the men, he saw the army, bedded down silently for the night in the pale tents under the birch trees. Now that he knew to search for them Dyce saw the horses, drowsing on their feet. He did a quick calculation. At least fifty tents by the stream that he could see. But there would be others hidden behind those or obscured by bushes. So, a hundred soldiers, with a hundred mounts – and Horse Head in their sights.

Fuck.

51

Back in the tunnel, Dyce gave her the bad news.

'Out of the fucking frying pan,' Vida whispered. 'Shit! We got to get back to warn Mama.'

'We got one full day, I reckon. But even if we make it back there before the horses, it'll only be by minutes at best. It's not enough time.'

'We could steal one.'

'No.'

'Why not?'

'I have a better idea, and it'll save us trying to wriggle out of this hole in full view of a hundred men with guns.'

'Okay, Hannibal. Lay it out.'

'You think these soldiers are going to ride into battle tomorrow carrying their tents and their mess kits and their canteens? No way. Just rifles and ammunition, that kind of stuff.'

'I'm with you.'

'So if we lie low here till morning – till after they charge off to The Mouth – we'll have that whole camp mostly to ourselves. Couple of camp followers, maybe, but we can probably take them. It'll be like stopping time. We'll just walk right into every single tent.'

'And what?'

'And poison everything.'

'Jesus! *Kill* them all? Who are you? Renard?'

'Those plants you suggested to the poncho guy at the church, we can find them around here, right?'

'In my sleep. But that's not the point. You can't just go around wiping people out like that.'

In the thin light of the tunnel Dyce's eyes were flat and hard. *Ears McCreedy*, she thought. *That's who he looks like. Fuck. I always thought I was the hardcore one.*

'Don't think of them as people. Think of them as the hands and feet of Renard.'

'That's a slippery fucking slope.'

He squeezed her shoulders. 'They're soldiers, Vida. Soldiers come to murder innocent people. *Sick* people. They don't care! God, they aren't *even* soldiers. They're, they're, executioners!'

'Look. I got the same anger you do. I do. But it's a big decision. Feel like we ought to take a minute. Think about the consequences.' *For our immortal souls*, she wanted to add.

He let go of her and they turned around like dogs, trying to sit down somewhere comfortable. They quietened down, each hunched over their separate struggle. Vida felt her heart hammering. Sometimes life gave you a clear and predictable set of choices, and this was one of those times, wasn't it? Her stepfather Evert had once told her that everyone makes their decision – what to have for breakfast, who to marry, whether to blast someone's head off – in ten seconds, straight off. Less. Everything after that is time spent justifying the action to yourself.

'Minute's up, Washington. What do you say?'

'Fuck Renard. And the horse he came in on.'

'That's my girl. You know it's the right thing. Now let's see if we can hunker down here; try and get some sleep before the whole fucking circus comes to town again. There isn't long to go.'

Vida and Dyce curled up in the tunnel, warm and familiar, and tried to doze.

☠

Sunrise came with the sounds of industry, of camping breakfasts and nervous jibes and smoking. Always the smoking. When it was Vida's turn to look, she spied a giant pot of porridge from which each man, tottering stiff from his night on the hard ground, scooped a bowl. They sat in clusters, eating and talking. A blond man stood apart, haloed by authority. He was holding his head in the breeze like a dog sniffing for clues. As Vida watched, he put a hand to his face and stroked his neat beard. *God, that's dedication*, she thought. What must it take to keep a goatee clipped like topiary during a war?

With breakfast done, the blond man started harrying his men to get going. Obedient, they turned their full attention to the horses, laying the blankets on the withers, overlaying them with the saddle. Maybe it made you less nervous, Vida thought, if you had to do the same number of things each time: adjusting the cinch, folding the loose straps away, tying them off. When they were done, the men led them each to a space at the river to drink, like a baptism. If the horses drank before they were saddled, you fell off: their stomachs bloated.

The preparation of Renard's men was no less complicated: underwear, long white socks, pants, and boots that swallowed up the pants cuffs. Then their shirts, tucked in and belted, weighed down with leather pouches. Extra ammunition, Vida bet. She was pleased to note that no man took a flask with him – another unnecessary attachment for a battle so close. They would drink their fill before they left and be back to celebrate before lunch.

After the belt came the jackets – some plain, some decorated with pins and flashing with gold – and then the rifles hung over shoulders. The morning prep summed up the difference between North and South, the same way there was in the South African War a century back, or the Civil War before then. There was still ritual among Renard's men, even in battle. Especially in battle.

The old rituals had never served the South, and now they were gone, outmoded and unmourned. There was no pretence that there was a difference between the living and the dead.

When the men began to hook their boots into their stirrups, Vida crawled back into the tunnel. The soldiers made no show of trying to be quiet: their approach was supposed to terrify the people who heard them coming. She and Dyce felt them thunder off, the tunnel shaking some, like there was a minor quake. The roof showered them with grit.

When the sound died, Dyce led the way up and out of the tunnel, watching carefully for the camp guards, a couple of men left to keep an eye on things. They saw no one.

The two of them kept low, anyway, out of habit and because it was smart. They made their way through the bush and slid down the talus. In the camp itself, fires still smoked inside their rings of stones; dirty dishes leant in towers; clothes were heaped in small piles outside the tents of their owners. Vida sniffed. Bizarre. Over all there was a miasma of aerosol deodorant, like a locker room. Beneath that the place smelt like porridge oats and horseshit and woodfire smoke, with the occasional waft of human excrement: the morning ablutions had happened somewhere upwind, in a rocky dip. Vida could see the strips of white toilet paper littering the ground there, stuck to the stems of low grasses.

Jeez, toilet paper. I remember that stuff.

'They could have just burnt it.' Dyce was next to her.

'Bet it's two-ply too.'

'Three-ply. Nothing's too good for the holy asses of the North.'

'Come. I want to show you something. And I need another pair of eyes.'

Vida led Dyce to the river where the ground had been churned up into mud by the horses. It wasn't deep: she crossed over on shallow stones. A little way up the river she bent to peer at the water hemlock there.

'Leaves are a little like a tomato plant. But look for the flower.'

At the top of the stem radiated about a dozen smaller stalks. Tipping each was a white compound flower, a frothy nosegay.

'Careful when you touch these. Whole plant is poisonous, roots especially. It'll give you seizures until your heart can't take it, or your lungs give out. Use a cloth when you pull it out.'

Vida demonstrated, untying her mask from around her neck and covering her hand with it.

'As many of these as possible. We're not going to find death camas or locoweed around here, but we might find larkspur. Those two together ought to do the job.'

She carried on up the river and Dyce followed. Things were different when you were looking at them up close: the detail could make you crazy.

Vida was bending down next to a scrawny shrub. 'Not the best example, but this is larkspur. They can get tall pillars of real pretty purple flowers, but this one's young. But that's good for us, I think: more toxic. Get a good look at those leaves.'

'Sure, I got it. Kind of maple-leafy.'

'I suppose. Same as before. Pull them up, roots and all. I'm going to get these back to camp. Bring what you find. And be careful. 'Cause I'm not carrying you again.'

'Ah, you loved it. Fell right into my trap.' Dyce winked.

Vida put her arms around his neck and kissed him full on the mouth. 'You got me. I'm a sucker for the pathetic ones.'

She turned and made her way back to the camp, and knew that he was watching her as she went.

She hunted down a cleanish pot and went to fill it from the river. The water was clear and fast-moving: it looked okay, and she was going to boil it, anyway. 'Just like old times,' she muttered. She rinsed the plants, loosening the last clods from the roots. At the stone circle she got the fire going again and set the pot over it. They hadn't even put the knives away properly. She set herself to slicing the plants on a flat log.

Dyce returned: two more water hemlock, but no larkspur.

'I can go look some more.'

'It's fine. I think we have enough.'

The poison was a pale-green soup that smelt like nothing at all. Dyce had expected something out of *Macbeth*, but it just looked like that disgusting tea his dad had tried to get them to drink, said it was good for longevity: antioxidant. Look how that had turned out.

He found a couple of metal cups lying beside an empty pack and they scooped the infusion into each one, like dippers in medieval wells. Then they went from tent to tent, methodical and matter-of-fact, starting at one end of the camp and making a clean sweep. They untwisted every canteen and flask lid they could find and poured a teaspoon's worth into every one. They made sure to wipe the rims of the chlorophyll residue.

Dyce found cigarettes too and dropped the concentrate into the tobacco. The cutlery they tainted, handle to tip, as well as all the rations they found – then combs too, toothbrushes and dental floss and mouthwash. And other things, that Vida and Dyce didn't recognize, even.

By the time they were done, they'd gone over the entire camp, item by item, as if it were a murder scene in reverse. They emptied the pot at the foot of a birch tree. Dyce covered the green dregs with dirt, and then regretted it. What if the horses got to it? It was too late now. Vida replaced the pot and the knife, same as she'd found them.

After almost two hours of work, they washed themselves in the river, head to toe. It was the cleanest they had been in weeks.

'Careful where you hang your clothes,' said Dyce, and Vida smiled.

They retreated to their burrow, and there they waited in the dark.

52

When the first volleys of gunfire came, like the breaking of boughs, Tye Callahan was gutting a walleye, throwing the strings of red and purple innards to his bird. He hadn't expected Renard's army to be there so fast.

But fast was good.

Tye washed up and wrapped the fish in its basket of rough-woven cattail. He made sure to stamp out his fire properly. The scouts' scope, retrieved from the hidey-hole, was a neat rubber-ized tube, with measurements and markings all along its flank that Tye didn't understand well enough to parse. It belonged to one of the rifles that had been taken, with a small mount on its side that would clip into the stock. Tye had used it to start a fire, just to test whether he could, aiming the wider end at the sun and letting the lenses concentrate the light onto dry leaves like a kid frying ants. It had worked. Now he made sure it was to hand.

He set off towards The Mouth. He was wary of the Northern soldiers who might mistake him for a returning resident, and he took a wide berth, aiming for a spot some way off along the ridge, a spot from which he would have a good view and put the scope to use. He hurried through the brush, his bird above, fluttering from branch to branch, leading him along the clearest paths. Usually he'd have stopped to rest – his shins ached and his callused toes were rubbing themselves raw and new again in his boots – but the excitement of seeing the town leveled spurred him on, and he only slowed when he crested the rise and caught the distant blossoms of blue gunsmoke lingering in the still air.

He cleared the rocks from a patch of dirt with his foot and then laid his old body down, groaning. He pulled his pack round in front of him and rested the scope on it, settling his chin on the rest. His bird sat beside him on the bone-white remains of a tree, ignoring the battle, eyeing the fresh stain of fish blood that darkened Tye's pack.

Renard's men had followed his suggestion and positioned riflemen along the valley walls. When the residents had taken cover in the shops and shacks and in the mine, the riders in the cavalry with their flaming torches had broken through the top fence and come galloping through the ponderosas, down the main street, setting fire to the brittle wood structures as they went. Blackened bodies lay in the street, motionless except for the hair or clothes that waved and billowed in the dusty wake of the horses.

Tye saw three men run from the saloon and try to mount the dead scouts' horses, but the animals were panicked. The men – one mustached and wheezy, Tye marked, and the other younger, maybe his son – tried to calm the horses and throw a leg over anyway. The creatures shunted and bucked. At the next volley of shots from the hills the two men fell beneath the thrashing hooves and were trampled. Tye watched the hairy one squealing and trying to cover his face.

The fires were driving the rest of the townsfolk crazy. Most of them looked as if they were trying to get to the mines, but the street was too exposed. They were cut down as they ran, some dead even before they hit the gravel, sliding face-down to twitch and grovel along the main road they had been so proud to stroll along. A couple of riders who felt kindly were passing by each person who had their hands up in surrender and putting bullets into their heads. The mercy shot.

It took them about half an hour to work their deadly way to the mouth of the mines. The riders saw that there was no logic in wandering into the darkness in search of the few who'd scuttled away. One dismounted and walked to the threshold. Tye saw his hand go to his belt, stacked with grenades like pinecones. The man selected three and pulled the pins as quick as he could before he lobbed them into the tunnel. The rest of the cavalry was already in retreat.

The blast exploded the wooden struts along with the rock. Debris spewed out from the mouth and the whole structure collapsed in tornadoes of dust, the last breath of the beast.

With the town burning and the residents dead, the soldiers rode up the main street. They stopped to take the scouts' horses with them, and Tye cursed them when he saw that. In minutes they were gone over the hill, whooping like frat boys. The snipers, too, were pulling back. They found their own horses and fell back with the rest of the troop. The Mouth lay devoid of life, as though the Lord had struck it down with white-hot bolts from the sky.

Tye stood up and brushed himself down. He took his pack and then called his bird to settle on his shoulder. She dipped her head towards the fish and Tye said, 'Later. Later. Work first. You know that.' He scratched her on the side of her soft head, the way she liked it.

He followed the ridge along the town, and then past. It wasn't hard. The hoof prints in the dirt led down and around the westerly ridge of The Mouth, directly to the white triangles of the tented camp. They hadn't even tried to hide it. Cocky. But why wouldn't they be? They'd just wiped out an entire settlement.

None of the dismounted soldiers paid him much attention as he strode down the slope. They were unsaddling their mounts, dipping their own sweaty heads in the river, pulling off their boots and throwing them every which way. And then came the drinking – that shitty homebrew that everyone was sucking up nowadays. He could smell it from here. Tye shook his head and spat to one side, and his bird flapped up and away from him. 'Sorry,' he told her. He didn't know how they could drink that rotgut: like mixing piss and gasoline. Everywhere the cups were being raised and clinked so hard he thought the metal would buckle and split. The men, sitting in their underwear, were saluting a job well done. At first they just shouted the lines to one another, but it turned into a chant soon enough:

Here's to the girl with the bright red SHOES!
She smokes your cigarettes and drinks your BOOZE!
She hasn't got a cherry but that's no SIN,
'Cause she's still got the BOX that the CHERRY came IN!

Tye made his way across the camp. He thought he would get there untested, but one man was still sober enough to raise a rifle to him.

'Get lost, old man.' From his breath, the guy smelt like he was dead already. Little green flecks were caught between his incisors.

'I'm Tye Callahan. Renard's man. Come to help.'

'Tye fucking Callahan! Why didn't you say so? Malison! Sir!'

A blond man, still booted and suited, appeared at the guard's elbow. He had hangdog eyes, Tye thought, the kind that marked an ex-drinker: a man who had fought the hardest battle of his life with himself. That was the kind you wanted on your side. That type knew what it was to suffer.

'Malison! This here's Tye Callahan!'

Tye tried to stand a little taller, wishing for the harrier on his shoulder, but she had made herself scarce.

'Well, now. I am pleased to make your acquaintance,' said the man slowly. The gold goatee made his lips look wet. 'We got something for you, brother. A thank-you present from the man himself.' He turned to the man with the rifle. 'Go get it.'

'Hope it's not a fucking toaster oven,' growled Tye. But the truth was, under the liver spots and the sunburn, his old heart was swelling with a young man's pride.

Malison nodded. 'Sit down. Have a drink.'

'You got anything 'cept that horse piss?'

The man laughed, hollow. 'Didn't have you pegged as a teetotal.'

Tye smiled. 'Temperance is my middle name.'

53

Unbelievable. The returning soldiers were unscathed, sweaty and dusty, but none bleeding or even holding a bruise or a pulled muscle. Vida saw the two spare horses and thought for a moment that The Mouth had managed to kill two of Renard's men – but as she watched the animals draw closer, she recognized them. The scouts' horses, reclaimed! Dyce tugged on Vida's leg, and she retreated, happy to let him watch the awful consequences of the thing they'd done.

Predictably, the men were tying their horses at the river's edge and then kicking back. From the myriad tents they brought out booze and food and cigarettes. Vida watched as they stood around, laughing and swigging like Vikings from the poisoned canteens, their free hands on hips. Dyce knew the stance, the invisible guns, the revelations of victory that were being lodged in song – first to one another, and then they would go back to Renard, along with the spoils of victory. Some of the men were pulling off their boots; others were stoking the fires, readying themselves for lunch. There was no sign of the ill effects of the poison. *Fuck.* Dyce retreated.

'Any idea how long this is going to take?'

Vida fiddled with a braid. 'I thought it'd be working by now.'

'But you know the plants, right?'

'I've never tried *killing people*, Allerdyce, so this is new.' She gave an unhappy shrug. 'I know them to avoid them; never worked with them directly.'

'Kind of wish you'd said that before.'

Vida gave him the side-eye, but he wasn't smart enough to stop.

'What if all that boiling broke down the poison or something?'

Vida relented. 'Give it time. It'll work.'

'It better, or we've just given them a nourishing supplement to help them exterminate Horse Head.'

She glared at Dyce. 'I *said* we ought to think more carefully about it. This was *your* idea.'

'Yes. But the execution sucked.'

He turned, shoulders stiff with anger, to devote himself to crawling back up to the lookout like a giant baby. Vida wanted to put her boot in his ass. Was this the real Dyce? Pissy, childish, looking for a locked door to sulk behind. Vida felt her mama's voice rising like a sinus headache.

What were you expecting? I told you he's too young. Green, I said. And what did you say? 'Mama, I love him!' Agh.

Vida breathed deep and damped it down. There must be some other way of letting Horse Head know about the attack before it happened.

When he first heard the man moving through the bushes, Dyce had his whole head out in the sun, the light blinding him. He ducked back into the dark so that he could see better – and saw Tye Callahan start making his slow descent to the camp, where the celebrations would be going on for some time. Even if he hadn't been able to see him, Dyce would have caught the whiff of fish and blood and burnt leaves.

He watched as Tye was confronted by a man with a rifle, who clapped him on the shoulder soon enough. He was duly welcomed in, and all of Dyce's suspicions about the old man were confirmed: Tye Callahan was a traitor.

A goateed soldier was presenting Tye with a box. The old guy opened it. From where Dyce had worked his way out of the tunnel a little way, it looked like a pen – the fancy kind, for signing certificates. But then the soldier took it out of its case and held it up to the sun. Dyce saw what it really was: a syringe.

'Motherfucker,' he said in wonder.

'What now?'

'Have a look. See that syringe?'

'Sure.'

'That there is the fabled vaccine, I'll warrant.' The antidote to the winds and whatever they brought with them: Renard's secret weapon. Tye's betrayal was being rewarded with immunity. Dyce could see that he'd live another forty years – and not only because of what was in that needle, but because of the honor they were showing him. He'd roam the land with his chest puffed out, and his aching back and arthritic fingers wouldn't bother him a whit. The soldier flicked the plastic and then approached Tye. The old man rolled his sleeve up, the way he might have done for a shot of penicillin after a night in a cathouse.

The bearded man held Tye's arm and found a vein. He pushed the plunger.

Tye was still grinning, showing off the cotton wool taped in the crook of his elbow, when a soldier collapsed some way off. Dyce saw the man drop beside his tent, his body convulsing, his heels drumming the ground like a tantrum.

The others rushed to help him. All they could do was hold him down, keep his head back and his airway clear, and stop him from wriggling his way into the campfire.

'That boy okay?' asked Tye. 'Looks like he's frothing at the mouth.'

And he was. The foamy green spittle plopped beside him in the dirt, like a cat who'd been eating grass – or a rabid dog. After that it was over pretty quick.

The men stepped back and looked at each another. Then the ones who had touched the dead man began running to the river to wash their hands, shoving at each other. It would have been funny in another time: in a silent movie, maybe, when Stan and Ollie stood a chance against the odds.

Near the river another man dropped as if he'd been pole-axed. The bucket of water he'd been carrying fell with him and sloshed into the dirt. The man lay in the mud of his clumsiness and squirmed in it. *Jesus*, thought Dyce. *Looks like he shat himself.* The sense memory of his own sickness washed over him, and he shivered but couldn't look away.

Next to fall was Malison, right there beside Tye – the regal composure turned to thrashing face-down in the dirt until he had grazed his face and mussed the manicured goatee with blood and foam. The old man hunkered down beside him. Malison's chest was rising and falling so hard that Tye expected to hear his ribs popping in their joints. Sounded as if his throat was closing; some of the Callahans got that way near nuts. His eyes rolled back until the whites were showing. His back arched and then he lay still. Around him his subordinates mimicked him to the last, curled like unborn babies, vomiting as their hands turned to claws.

Tye got up from his haunches and made his way over to the first row of tents. He put his gloves on and found a canteen. He opened it and sniffed the brew inside. He scrunched his face and pulled away. Then he smelt again.

He knew that odor – indistinct, hiding beneath the pungency of the hooch: winter grass. Water hemlock. He'd used it before, so he ought to have recognized the effects. Tye shook his head at himself. Getting old.

He looked up into the hills around the camp, and Dyce thought for a second that he'd seen his head poking out from the hole, but the eyes moved on, squinting and suspicious.

Tye turned to a box crate that had once held cutlery, and set it upside down. Then he stood on it like a street preacher. He cleared his throat and began – and he left his gloves on.

'Boys! You've been poisoned. Can't say how many of you, but it got into your canteens. It's water hemlock. That's bad news. You should be able to tell that by now.' He swept his arm out over the plain. The white cotton wool ball taped there was ludicrous.

The leaderless soldiers began to congregate, looking for instruction.

'And mark me: every man here has been exposed. Now, I can help you folks. I know who did this – trouble-makers from the ghost colony they call Horse Head.'

More men were moving in, and even in his horror Dyce reveled in the looks on their faces. They had been forced to look to this charismatic Southern snake for guidance. *Jeez, Garrett. If only you'd hung around long enough to see this.*

'If you got some of that poison, you saw for yourselves how that ends. But perhaps, before you die, you'd like to make sure the people who did this pay for it. I have no remedy to save you from what might already be inside you, but while you live, let's fight. What do you say?'

There was a murmur from the soldiers. Dyce had to admit: Tye's speech made sense, as much as any call to arms ever did.

Now even the sick soldiers were rallying. This was what they knew – taking orders from a man who looked as if he knew what he was doing.

Tye stepped down from the box and walked through the men, hoping that these soft-bellied Northerners had more fight than his own Callahan men. They donned their battle dress for the second time that day, but this time it was quicker. They grabbed their guns and mounted their horses. Tye looked back.

Even as they rode, some men were falling from their saddles, shaking themselves to death beneath the birches.

54

There was only one man in Horse Head who was watching the horizon when the high-flying harrier came into view. From his bed he saw the bird swooping low with rage, shrilling its *skree-skree-skree*. In the two days since Felix Callahan had joined the ghost colony, it was the first time he'd felt under threat.

When he'd stumbled over the ridge, they had taken him in, ignoring his pleas for a gun and a bullet. Suicide was bad for morale, a bald man told him. Felix realized his mistake in coming, and kicked up a stink as they led him into the camp till they found him a place to sit and rest, when he went down and could not get back up. His skin was still coming up in the purple-red welts that itched more than bed fleas and hurt worse than bee stings. The stitches on his head felt as if they would split open with the force of the headache that descended, washed in red.

A woman brought him food and some mashed herb he thought might be yarrow. When she came back she brought another, older, woman with her and then left them alone to parley. The gray-haired woman didn't flinch even when the sputum sprayed out of his mouth. He coughed and apologized in turns. She sat there with a battered blue notebook and asked him what he thought was wrong with him, and how long he had had those stitches in his scalp. She looked a little familiar, but

Felix had other things to worry about: keeping his lungs from jumping out of his chest like bullfrogs, for one.

When she left he tried to set his hot head back to what he did best. From the makeshift bed he had a view of the horizon. He forced his eyes open though the light pierced his thin skull like a machete. Watching for clouds helped some to take the edge off the urge to scratch his skin raw. And off the fact that he had lost the name of his old cat. Was it Dancer or Danny or Danger? None of those seemed right. Felix gave himself over, and waited.

Over the next days he watched the predictable weather systems changing, the clouds outside a mirror of the confusion in his skull. *We're not talking just a change of underwear, either*, Felix realized. If his old theory was right, right about now there would be a great wall of warm air rising from the Atlantic like the Kraken. When it swirled inland, they would be fucked – and there'd be no need for a gun in his hand after all. He squinted. The clouds looked like distant sheep. Then, as Felix watched, they billowed up in puffy pillars with heads that flattened as they met the thin air of the higher currents.

The hundred-year storm was here.

'You'd better believe it,' he whispered with a grin. There was some comfort in knowing that he had been right. The skyscrapers rose like an angel city, crossed over from another realm, and for the first time Felix gave some serious thought to all that jazz about the home of the ancestors. He shivered in the bed: the fevers and the chills and something else too, that was deeper than weather. *Brother, have you heard the Good News?*

The bird was a speck of black against the cumulonimbus. It was not behaving the way other birds did. Before a storm they all hunkered down somewhere sensible, and one way to tell how bad it was going to be was how quiet the air was. If there was complete silence, the way there was now, you might as well lay down and die.

The harrier was upset. It wasn't flying from tree to tree or circling a patch of earth for an ordinary blood sacrifice. This bird flew fast and straight and purposeful.

Felix watched it grow bigger, aiming directly for Horse Head. At this rate it would fly right over his head and he'd have a good chance to see the pattern on the underside of its wings. The females were tawny brown, mostly, and she might be nesting somewhere close by.

But as the bird approached, Felix saw the pall of dust beneath her – and then he felt the ground vibrate. A herd of something, he reckoned, bison and bears and deer all spooked by the coming weather. Animals were smarter than humans a lot of the time. Felix had kept a red-spotted toad in a box in his shack for some months, correlating its behavior with the changes in weather outside. A day before the rains came, Hopkins would get excited and try to escape the box. But she had been no good at predicting wind. When she died in the winter, Felix sat a while, looking at her. He had ended up cutting out the parotid glands, and boiling the body up. The French did it, right?

What he saw now as the stampede grew nearer made him choke on his own spit. A herd of horses!

Felix called out for the people in the shelters nearest him to look, and the camp came to a standstill.

At the head of the stampede, crouched low on the back of the lead horse, was Tye Callahan, kicking his heels into the beast's ribs as he came.

'Mother *fuck*,' said Felix. 'Cain't even let me die in peace.'

The other horses followed. They were all saddled, but there were only a handful of riders amongst them, and those few that remained were toppling off as though shot down by distant snipers.

Felix checked the hills for gunsmoke, but there was none. Still the stampede came on, and Felix saw that Tye did not need soldiers to eradicate Horse Head: four hundred panicked hooves would do the trick.

Felix heaved himself up. He began to hobble down the slope. 'Anyone got a rifle?' He called out.

'Pete. Pete's got one.'

'Where's he? He the one that looks like an Indian?'

He found Pete outside his tent, watching, shocked.

'Shut your mouth, son. No time for gawping.' He leant over and coughed a blob of bloody phlegm into the dirt at Pete's feet. Felix straightened up again. Damn! He hadn't felt this good in days! 'You got a gun? Got to take that lead rider down. Maybe them horses will disperse. Otherwise he's going to run this place flat.'

Pete dodged inside his tent. When he came back he was holding an ancient musket, like something from a museum display.

'Fuck me! Who was the last owner? Blackbeard? Does it even work?'

'On and off. It's loaded, but I don't have the aim for that shot.'

Felix took the gun and knelt beside a rock and rested the muzzle in a cleft. The warmth of the sun-baked stone made his forearms burn and itch. When this was over he was going to dunk himself in a river, like a bear with fleas.

Felix lined up the sights, factored in the very slight crosswind, aimed a little high to compensate for the humidity, and a little higher still for the age of the gun. There'd be no leading necessary. Tye was coming straight on.

'Well, let's hope the last ten years spent measuring my dick have paid off.'

Felix breathed in nice and slow. He pushed the air back out from his lungs, willing himself not to cough, and pulled the trigger.

55

Dyce and Vida scrambled out of the tunnel and rolled down the talus, all call for quiet unnecessary now that the riders of the apocalypse were upon them. They got back up, intending to merge with the main body of the stampede and head off a couple of the horses driven mad with the smell of blood.

Dyce made Vida get over into the birches after the group of escaped horses, who were still trying to force their way through the foliage, white-eyed and frothing with fear. The hair of their dead riders caught on the bushes as they went, the twigs snagging at their flesh like crowns of thorns. Vida caught the bridle of a little painted pony whose rider's ankles were bent like ballet shoes. The man swung in his sorry pendulum. She found herself shuddering in pity, but it didn't stop her from lifting the rifle and bandolier from his twitching torso. They struggled to release the dead men from the horses, but the corpses fell at last to their resting places on the ground under the birches. Their horses tossed their heads but otherwise let their replacements remain.

Vida looked over at Dyce, who had managed to catch and hold his own mount, a bay with a white star on her forehead who in another time would have had a kindly face. He was tying the shirt with the mushrooms in it over the saddle.

They raced behind the stampede, past the blurred buildings of the abandoned town, covering two days of hiking in minutes.

Vida said it into the air as it whipped past, cold, the harmless wind of high-speed travel: *Fuck Renard!*

Dyce and Vida tried to stay on, clenching with their knees, but it was impossible to do that and shoot at the same time. Their bullets aimed at Tye flew high and wide.

They heard another gunshot ring out from the slopes of Horse Head, and saw the puff of smoke that was swept aside by the hand of the rising wind. More horses in their terror scattered from the sides of the stampede, heading for the trees.

The bullet had hit Tye Callahan in the right shoulder. He jolted sideways and fell out of the saddle, but his good arm thought for him and he managed to wrap his limp hand in the reins and hang on. Others were not so lucky, and those men were dragged after their mounts, the skin being scraped from their senseless faces.

On the ground, Felix was shoving the ancient gun back at Pete. 'Reload. Reload!'

Pete took the gun and found another bullet as fast as his shaking fingers allowed. He pulled the bolt and ejected the spent cartridge. Felix checked the progress of the stampede. The horses were charging up the slope, past the muck-green pond, and over the boundary markers.

Pete handed back the loaded gun and Felix lined the shot up again. This time Tye was hidden behind the flank of the horse as it turned, adjusting its balance to compensate for the man hanging from its side. Felix didn't need to consider the wind or the humidity: it was a straight shot at a growing target, not more than forty yards away. But there was no good shot to take – leastways, none that would spare the horse.

'Sorry,' he said, and he pulled the trigger, but at the last his eye flickered. Something metallic glinted up from beyond the graves and his aim was off.

There was no time to reload: the horses would be upon them.

Felix jabbed the gun at Pete again, though he knew it was no use. He had to be doing something other than just watching his death come towards him.

The metal creature seemed to leap up from the dirt and grab hold of Tye's horse by its foreleg. As Felix watched, with his lungs burning and his heart on fire, the horse tripped and then fell to its knees. And as it was felled it rolled on Tye, the weight of its giant ribcage crushing him into the dirt, horse and rider fused into a satyr.

They slid to a stop. The horses that followed had seen their leader fall, and it set off some kind of slackness in them. The creatures at the front reared up, and the ones behind them fell back or skipped sideways to avoid being sent under the killing hooves of their companions. They had lost their momentum.

Now they came to a stop in a swirl of dust, and stood and stamped, whinnying in outrage and fright, about seventy all told. Some still had the cargo of their dead owners caught in their stirrups or dragging at their reins. The missing horses would lose themselves in the hills, trailing their terrible treasure.

Tye's horse lay on the ground, panting and groaning and trying to get up. Each time the animal moved, the man trapped beneath it screamed. The shrieks had a whistle to them, and Vida knew that Tye's lungs had been shredded by his own splintered ribs – the syringe and its immunity gone to waste. He had meant to go with a brave face, but now that his death was imminent, the Callahan pride was revealed as the artifice it was.

Felix made his slow way over to his kinsman. He had to hobble to do it, but he was determined to finish the job.

He fired a round into the horse's head to end its suffering, and it was still.

Then he knelt beside Tye, resting a hand on the battle-warm body of the dead horse for the support it gave him.

'Hey there, cuz.'

Tye wheezed. The blood ran from his mouth. It kept coming, thick and bright as venom, as he spoke. 'Fuck. You.'

'We say "Fuck Renard" around here.'

'Fuck. *You*.' Tye managed to gather the bloody clots in his mouth. Then he spat them up into the lined face of his cousin.

'You always had a way with words,' said Felix. He wiped the blood and spittle away. 'I was going to put you out of your misery, but I see that you won't be needing me much longer.'

He got up, groaning himself at the ache in his legs. He rubbed the muscle there. 'That scar ain't never going to let me in peace,' he told Tye. 'Something else I got to thank you for.'

The man didn't respond. Blood was pooling slowly in Tye's eyes, a tide of red rising in a ring around the ice of his irises. Killer's eyes, Felix had always thought. He noted the change and then he turned his back on the dying man. He went to where Dyce and Vida were standing by their new horses, unsure of what to do next.

'Looks pretty bad,' said Dyce. He was fiddling with the make-shift sack of mushrooms. Their smell rose, dank and earthy, as he handled them.

Felix shot him a look. 'Not long now,' he said.

'Pity you had to shoot the horse, but I guess you had no choice.'

'Only got the one shot in. Other one went a mile wide.'

'Then what brought the horse down?'

They all limped back to the body of the animal. Tye grimaced and set his face against them. Vida could no longer tell what color his eyes had been for the vessels burst there. She pictured the ragged lungs inside his chest, a pirate's flag that would never be lowered.

Vida stepped around the horse and leant her shoulder against it, so that the sweaty carcass shifted and the savaged foreleg came into view.

Clamped around it were two rows of rusted iron teeth: Tye's bear trap – set for the black bear that had been sniffing nightly around the graves.

She sat back on her heels. She wanted to tell him what it was, but she realized that the whistling sound had stopped.

The harrier dropped from the sky as though it too had been shot, wings folded to its side. She reached the patriarch, but instead of cooing and rubbing her head against him, the bird began to peck at Tye's slack face. Dyce and Vida watched, stunned. There was an audible *pop* and the bird wheeled away with an eyeball in her beak, the string of its nerve dangling like the reins on a bolting horse.

The bird wasn't done with her master. She gulped the eyeball down, remorseless, and came back. When they could move, they managed to shoo her away. But she had been tenacious, making directly for the rest of the soft parts, pecking deep V-shaped gashes in his lips and lacerating the thin flesh of his nostrils.

The bird, soundless, disappeared into the sky, trailing skin from her beak.

Vida looked at the slippery death's head that had been Tye Callahan. His eyelids were gone too, torn right away by the harrier.

'I guess *no one* liked you,' she told him. She shaded her eyes, mercilessly intact despite the things they had witnessed that afternoon, and looked at the clouds forming overhead.

56

Vida's relief that Tye would not get up again lasted a couple of seconds. She couldn't believe that the Weatherman had made it through, and yet here he was – saving their asses again. It was getting to be a habit. He even looked the same, though they weren't used to seeing him fully clothed: the scraggy skin, now purpled in splotches with edges like doilies, the stitches, healing nicely. Mercifully, there was no dangling scrotum. He must have been a sight three days ago, when whatever was eating him had just taken its first bite.

Felix was looking at them with a mixture of sadness and respect.

Ah, fuck.

Here it came. Vida swallowed, helpless.

He's going to say something about Garrett being gunned down by Walden in the shack. Shit, shit, shit!

The Weatherman nodded at Dyce. 'Thought I recognized you folks. You Garrett's brother, aintcha?'

Vida shifted from foot to foot, unsure of what to do with herself. The hard truth was coming back to get her like a fucking train – *narrow gauge*, she thought. Meaner than Tye, or Ed, or Ester with her cushion-baby and her milk fever.

'Yeah. Allerdyce.'

'Dyce, yes. I'm real sorry about your brother. Didn't like him at the outset, but I reckon he was a good guy deep down. Definitely didn't deserve to get himself killed the way he did.'

Vida felt her spine stiffening with dread. There it was, out in the open at last, like the trampled corpse at their feet.

Dyce frowned. 'We talking about the same guy?'

'Blond ponytail. Bad skin. That guy who got little Bethie Callahan up the pole, pardon my French.'

Felix saw that something was wrong with the picture: Dyce was confused and Vida had gone a terrible ashy color. She looked as if she was going to cry.

He kept talking. 'Buried him best I could. I'm too old to be digging, but I'm a believer in the old ways. Walden I just covered over with rocks. He didn't even deserve that, but he was kin and I try to do right. But I want you all to know that I put some dirt between your brother and the open sky. Hammered a cross in there too, even though I figured he wasn't the type to go in for religion. I didn't put no flowers on, now. I'm not a sissy.'

Dyce turned to Vida, a half-smile on his lips, as if to say, *Are you listening to this crazy old man?*

But he was met only with Vida's horrified face. She couldn't look away. Her eyes started watering.

'Garrett's dead?'

'Dyce . . .'

'He's *dead* and you *knew*?'

Dyce stepped backward, as if an earth tremor had shaken the ground open between them.

'Oh, *God*. Oh, Jesus *Christ*!' His voice was hoarse with grief. Vida's arms were dead at her sides, as if someone had punched her on the shoulder. *What do I do? How do I take it back? How can I make this right?*

He turned and stumbled back towards the bay, who turned her face and nuzzled at him. Vida wanted to call out, but her throat was too dry and swollen. She struggled for air as she watched Dyce throw himself onto the horse without checking the cinching, and then jab at its sides with his heels. Vida felt every one of the blows.

'You really didn't tell him?' Felix asked. He shook his head.

Vida ignored him. She was weeping without sobbing, standing straight in the wind that was catching now at the leaves around them, at the fabrics that made up the shelters of Horse Head and the clothes of its inhabitants, at the fibers that made up her dumb, regretful body.

The storm was coming.

It didn't matter.

She forced herself to watch as Dyce galloped away, the thin silver cord she had always thought was between them stretching thinner and thinner until she knew it would snap.

Vida bent over and hugged herself as if that would neutralize the slicing pain in her abdomen, but it only got worse. She doubled over and howled, and Felix winced. He wanted to cover his ears. That sound was more wolf than human, like one of the tame dogs turned wild who had seen its mate torn to pieces. She lowered herself by degrees until she was curled up in the dust of the road like one of the dead.

Nothing would have made a difference to Vida except perhaps her mother. Ruth must have known that. Now she separated herself from the curious throng that had gathered at the edge of Horse Head and made her way to her daughter as quickly as she could.

When she got to Vida she tried to put her arms around the younger woman, but she was defeated by the constellation of knees and elbows.

'Vida,' she said. 'Vida, Mama's here. Come on now, baby girl. I just want to hold you in my arms.'

Vida kept sobbing until the air in her chest was gone. After that the whole process began again, and Ruth saw that she would have to find some other way to get through to her. She sat down on the road beside her daughter as Felix tried to intervene.

'Hate to interrupt, ma'am, but the wind's picking up fierce. You know we got to get to shelter.' He gestured. The clouds on the horizon were much darker. There were sheets of rain coming down in the distance like stone pillars: they promised the ruin of civilization.

Vida and Ruth both ignored his directive. The sobs had stopped but the ratcheting of her breathing would have set off the alarm in a hospital room. Ruth put her arms around her daughter, and this time Vida let her.

'Veedles. You remember that magazine I gave you?'

Vida nodded and wiped her face with both hands, smearing snot and tears over her cheeks. 'Mami Wata,' she said miserably.

'Now,' said Ruth, stern. 'What would Mami Wata do? You think she would lie down in the dust and play possum when there were important things left to do? Things that *lives* depended on? I know it hurts, angel girl, but you got to do your crying later. Right now we got to *move*.'

Vida struggled to sit up, the shame flooding through her as if she had wet her pants. Her mother was right. Of course she was. Vida rubbed her eyes and strained to get her last glimpse of Dyce, the shadow of his shadow, a molecule, a mote.

And what she saw was that there was something different about the way he rode. He didn't look lopsided anymore. It took Vida a while to work out what it was, but she got there.

Dyce didn't have the mushrooms strapped to his saddle.

She looked around her in the road and there it was – the shirt-sack with its redeeming burden, lying abandoned beside her patient horse, who had somehow avoided trampling it.

Vida got up and went around Ruth. Her mother watched her carefully but said nothing.

When Vida picked up the sack she felt the terrible mixture of hope and unhappiness mingle in her chest. The shirt's fabric was soft between her fingers, Dyce's smell of biscuits still clinging to its folds. Its medicine burnt; he was here, he wasn't here.

She brought the precious sack back to Ruth and Felix, and said in her new voice, thick with sorrow, 'Come on. Let's get out of the wind. I have something to show you that will make this all worthwhile, I swear.'

57

There was only one thing on Dyce's mind as he spurred the horse on, and it wasn't what he had expected, considering the bomb Felix and Vida had dropped on him.

Ears McCreedy.

The horse had circled back to the familiar decaying road, and she wanted to stop there. Dyce made her follow the rough line of clear ground that the asphalt made, all the way to the abandoned town where he and Vida had spent a night. They raced down the main street. He didn't even turn his head to look toward the cinema, though he felt its emptiness yawning towards him. *Goddamn it!* He'd opened up to her! Told her things he hadn't thought he knew about himself, and for sure had never told anyone else. And all the while she was sitting on the only secret between them that mattered: a leash to keep him close.

Dyce kicked at the horse, angry, making her pay in Vida's place, and they sped up as she tried to rid herself of the Devil on her back. They rode on, Dyce didn't know for how long. Time had gone soft, saline and saturated with tears. The horse knew her way, unerring, and followed the trampled grass that led up and up to the cracked fence at the top of The Mouth.

The town had already done all the burning it ever would, but it still smoked, and Dyce coughed at the acrid smell. It was a time for masks if ever there was one. There were already creatures come to investigate, called down from the hills by the smell of carrion: cats and dogs. And coyotes and bears and wolverines. The darkening sky overhead promised a lean time ahead, and they had to make the most of it while they could. He thought again of the disastrous all-you-can-eat buffet – and then of his dad, and then of Garrett, dead and gone too, and his stomach twisted. The waste of it. Dyce checked the clouds again and his heart shrank. Their bottoms were weirdly teat-like, lobed like bubble wrap, the sick yellowish-gray that came before tornadoes. The low pressure was making his head feel stuffed with cotton wool. He had to be quick.

It was like walking through a graveyard after an earthquake, but Dyce thought he was fine until he saw Julia's wasted body lying among the others. He recognized her by her dress that was tugged at by the wind, a snake skin, brittle with age and yellowed with useless milk. Of all the corpses pecked at by birds, or tugged at by dogs or coyotes, hers was the only one left untouched. As he rode past he could see the pattern of footprints around her, a circle demarcating the unclean, and he did the same.

When he came to the remains of the saloon Dyce dismounted, but he found that there was nowhere left to tether the horse. He wrapped the reins around a dead man's boot. He looked a little like Ed, but between the head wound and the scavengers, it was hard to tell for sure. The horse whinnied in protest, but Dyce ignored her.

He stepped into the hot black debris, careful, trying to work fast, testing the ground for its heat. It was not easy to find their shack. They'd all collapsed, fused and disintegrated, a mess of metal and molten plastic and blackened wood.

He judged the place where he thought it ought to have been and began hunting through the debris. He covered his bare hand with his shirtsleeve and lifted the fallen sheet of corrugated iron that had protected their possessions from the flames. There was something atomic about the way their things had stayed where they had been left. Everything was a zombie relic: blackened, carbonized, gone to hell and come back again, the same and not the same.

Dyce lifted a small furry body with his boot. It was too hot to touch with the bare skin. He flipped it over. Ears's fur was singed into beads, and his eyes were gone. Dyce picked him up gently and held him like a baby in his arms.

Vida's things were here too, also burned and brittle: her canteen, her jacket, and the fucking remedy book. She thought she knew everything. Dyce didn't want to take it, but he couldn't bring himself to leave it there; the years of being bookless had turned paper into gold.

He picked the book up from the dirt. Pages were missing, cracked and crumbled, and those that remained were halfway to charcoal. The burnt inks stank: the smell would never go away.

That was that. Dyce looked around. There was nothing else he cared about.

When he got back to the place where he had left his horse, she wasn't there. Dyce turned in a circle. She had managed to drag Ed down the main street. Now she was standing wide-eyed at the mouth of the collapsed mine, stamping her feet and snorting in disgust.

Dyce trotted down between the feeding carnivores and freed her reins from the corpse. 'Sorry, old girl,' he said. 'Things got a little hinky back there for a second.'

The camp's lower perimeter fence had burnt too. Dyce could see the ebonized earth where the fire had ventured into the grasslands and then been blown out. The church was gone, vaporized, as if it had never existed. It had long since passed from being holy to the refuge of the hopeless. He kept looking. The lonely man in his poncho was still swinging from his tree, as if his purple face and popping eyes had been set on purpose to witness the entire spectacle. Dyce couldn't look away. The body kept turning in the wind, like one of the Weatherman's instruments.

Then he led the horse away, up toward the ponderosas. He packed the remedy book and Ears McCreedy in the horse's saddlebag and then hoisted himself back up. He rode on. The passing terrain blurred under his horse. He and Vida had walked this way, but keeping watch for viruses made everything deathly slow. They'd had to stick to the ridge line for protection instead of blazing a straight line across open ground, and they'd had to stop often and be quiet and watch the hills and the tall trees, instead of just walking. Dyce wondered now how they'd ever got anywhere without horses. He imagined himself riding for the coast, Garrett mounted beside him – a couple of real cowboys, suave and invincible – and then the horses pulling up at the foamy breakers, leaving deep gouges in the sand. Dyce had never seen the ocean. No one he knew had. But there were pictures of beaches: the sand always looked clean, washed over and over by the relentless waves. The rocks there had no sharp edges.

'You float better in salt water,' Garrett had said when Dyce first complained about the plan to get to the coast and across to the other side. 'Buoyancy changes 'cause the water's denser with the salt dissolved in it. It'll hold you up, like Jesus walking on the water.'

He looked at Dyce, pretended to eye him up and down, and delivered the punch line: 'You look pretty dense yourself. Not a hundred per cent sure it'll hold *you*, little brother.'

Garrett had had a good laugh and while he did, Dyce made a note to put a spider in his brother's bed. He hadn't got round to it. Never would, now. All the lists, the IOUs, the concessions, the victories, they were all wiped clean.

Finding the Weatherman's shack wasn't difficult. There was something in Dyce that brought him back to the place, a magnetism that relied on smell and sound and touch as well as elevation. He'd had an image of the place in his mind, grown from the seed of his blind and fragile recollection – but when he came to it, it was entirely different. Dirtier, that was for sure. The shack itself was ramshackle, stained brown with rust, meant to go under the radar. But the surroundings were something else – the glade of sweet almonds and the stream and the way it was all set at the foot of a decaying dam wall that was, in turn, set at the foot of a mountain, as if they were backdrops stored in the wings of a stage production.

But there were no footlights here. This was illuminated by real sunlight – filtered through the storm clouds of the apocalypse.

He tethered his mount to the old hitching post and said, 'Now, I hope you'll consent to stay a while. I got business to attend to.' She twitched her ears.

Dyce walked around the back of the shack. The graves were there as the Weatherman had said, side by side. Walden's cairn had been pillaged, the rocks pulled away by some scavenger. They had eaten their fill of what they could reach before the meat turned bad.

Beside that was Garrett's grave, a shoddy job. The cross had lost its horizontal beam, and the rocks laid over the top of it were mismatched and thrown together – no respectful cairn here, nosir.

Dyce took a breath and began to pull the rocks away. When they were cleared, he dug down into the earth with his hands, the grime pushing deep under his fingernails until they bled. He needed to see Garrett's face, no matter what he was now. He needed one last look to make sure he was no revenant, no mistake.

The stink rose to meet him as he kept digging. The earth began to turn slick and slimy, and he knew he was close. *It's no worse than the mushrooms*, he told himself. *You just man the fuck up, now.*

The face Dyce saw at the bottom of the grave was certainly Garrett's. His dumbass ponytail had wrapped around his neck, though the cheek skin tags that clung to the skull were too far gone to tell if they were scarred with acne. Dyce sat back on his boot heels and wept.

'We nearly made it, you asshole. We almost made it right to the end. But we shouldn't have taken up with the girl in the cave. Should have left then and gone on. Reckon we could've outrun those Callahans. Can't say for sure whether we'd have made it to the coast, or whether we'd be out at sea right now with this storm coming in hot – but we'd have gotten as far as we could. Dad would have been proud, huh? Here you are in a hole and I didn't even know. Couldn't bury you myself and I'm sorry, bro. I am so *sorry*.'

He wiped his face on his filthy sleeve. 'Can't say I'd have managed to take your fat-ass corpse all the way to the coast, but I like to think I'd have given it a go. And if that hadn't worked out I'd have buried you on a hill with a view. That would've been nice. It would've been *something* at least.'

Dyce groped in his bag. 'I brought you a visitor.' He held up the blackened squirrel and laughed. 'Only thing around here that's dirtier than you. Say howdy-do, Mister McCreedy. I was going to bury him with you, but now that I think about it, Ears is all the family I got. So I'm going to hang onto him, if that's okay.'

Dyce was settling the squirrel beside him when he understood that the drumming he heard was not the sound of his own forlorn and struggling heart.

58

Her horse's hoofbeats sounded loud even to Vida's ears. She had come up along the river and through the glade of almond trees, guessing at Dyce's route as if he had left a scent trail for her to follow like an ant. The star-faced horse was tethered out front, grazing a fresh circle around her post.

The shack. Where else? She thought of Garrett dying there in the dirt where the bay now stood; how she'd shown her naked body to him. She blushed, but she was not sorry. Dyce was kneeling there beside the grave that the old man had dug, brown to the elbows, as if he was wearing gloves. Even from here she could tell that his eyes were zombie-red. He kept wiping them on those filthy sleeves, rubbing the grave dirt in, striping his cheeks. He seemed immune to the stink.

'Fuck off,' he said, without turning around.

'Dyce. I'm sorry I didn't tell you.'

'I don't want to hear it, okay. Just go.'

'In a minute. But I came to tell you something.'

'Who else died?'

Vida flinched. At least he didn't see that. *He didn't see that because he won't fucking LOOK at you.* She sat taller in the saddle. Her back and torso ached.

'I just want you to know we're riding north. Felix says the storm will be at its worst this far south. If we head north we might be able to avoid it. Dyce, he reckons this whole place will be *flooded*. Like something out of the Bible. This weather we're having? It's just the leading arm of the system. The next front is going to blow these mountains flat.'

He shrugged.

'Don't you want to at least *try*? The horses, they've given us a chance to survive. And the mushrooms too. I mean, imagine what must be in this air already, and we're still walking and talking – which is more than most.' She gestured at the grave. 'But we have to get going now.'

'Go then.' His lips were pressed tightly together. 'Go *on*.' He was talking to her as if she was a stray dog he was trying to discourage. What would her mama do?

Vida tried to set her anger aside, hearing the strain in her voice, hating it. 'You have to come.'

'I don't *have* to do anything.'

'And what are you going to do then? Just sit there until your phobia turns real and you drown, like the fucking unicorns who missed Noah's last call?'

Dyce didn't have a good answer. He didn't really know.

'Well?'

'I was thinking I might, uh, relocate Garrett. Somewhere better. The proper kind of funeral that I never got a chance to do.'

'Jesus Christ, Dyce! Can't you *smell* him? I don't want to be funny, but he's ninety per cent worms now. You're going to need a bucket.'

'Then I'll find a fucking bucket.'

'That's not a solution.'

'Your *solutions* haven't been real helpful so far.'

'Dyce, you can hate me all you like, but if you stay here you'll die. Ride with us and you can hate me a bit longer.'

'Only so far north you can go anyway before you hit the border. Then what? I'd rather die with Garrett. A family plot.' He snorted.

'Mama reckons she knows a way through. Same way she escaped down South – if they haven't closed it up.'

'What happened to "Fuck Renard"? Now you're running to him for protection?'

'Survival first. Fuck Renard later.'

Vida got distracted. There was something sitting beside Dyce in the sand, a charred animal, it looked like.

'Where'd you find Ears?'

'Went back to The Mouth. Some stuff survived. I got your remedy book, actually. It's in my saddlebag. You should take it. I don't want none of your things. Didn't find your precious photocomic though, if you're wondering.'

'I wasn't wondering. I traded it.'

'What?'

'I traded it, back at The Mouth before everything was shot to shit.'

For the first time since they had started talking, he flickered. 'For what? That was your whole fucking *heritage*, isn't that what you said?' He held up a hand, mock-psychic. 'Wait. Wait. Let me guess – you traded it for another knife to stab me in the back.'

'Okay, that's it. You know what? I actually thought I *loved* you. You believe that?' She shook her head, defeated. 'Now it's just bullshit self-pity and drama-rama. I don't know you at all.'

'Ditto, sister. Sing me that sad song.'

They were quiet, regarding one another in the bitter, honest daylight until the wind did their work for them and swept a gust of grit into their faces. They both ducked their heads into the crooks of their arms. It subsided, a mean little taster of what was ahead.

'If you change your mind, follow the hoof prints. But the rain's going to wash them away soon enough, and then it'll just be you and your bucket of Garrett and the end of the world. Hope that works out for you.'

Vida turned her horse round. She stopped beside Dyce's bay and took the charred remedy book from the saddlebag. Then she disappeared, back along the stream, through the nut trees and back to Horse Head, as if she was a ghost rider passing through on the wind.

Dyce stood up stiffly and looked at the sky. The dense clouds seemed to be rising higher than they had before; he was smaller and lonelier beneath their mindless weight.

He made up his mind. Garrett was all he had left. 'No offence, Ears,' he told the eyeless squirrel.

Inside the Weatherman's shack, he found a spade and a zinc tub, two stained bed sheets and a coil of rope. Felix wouldn't mind. Dyce brought them back and laid them beside Garrett's grave. He half hoped that Vida would change her mind and come back to ask him again. She'd see the implements – see that he really meant what he'd said about moving his brother – and maybe he'd go with her this time.

But she was taking her time about it. Dyce kept digging in the grave dirt. Where the fuck was he going to take Garrett? He laid one sheet out flat in the dirt and weighed its corners down with rocks. He moved the body piece by piece, like a puzzle or an anatomy lesson, the kind of thing Garrett would've loved. Had it only been a week and some days? This was probably the worst stage. No one ought to see someone they loved that way.

Dyce began to retch. When it was over he tied his shirt around his face.

By the end of it Garrett was missing some fingers, but Dyce left them. He couldn't be on his knees any longer, this close to the green rot and the white squirm. He wrapped the body up. He wound the second sheet over the first. There would be leakage, but that was too bad. He bent the body and, with a terrible squelching, it was squashed into the tub. Dyce set the spade on top and said, 'Make yourself useful, bro. You look after that for me.'

He tied one end of the rope to the tub's handle and the other to the saddle of his horse. Then he set Ears on the saddle before him, mounted and began the ride south into the teeth of the storm, his brother scraping on the dirt behind him like a go-kart.

59

It was manageable as long as he imagined the tables turned and Garrett riding into a storm, dragging Dyce behind. It seemed cool when Dyce thought of it that way round, like the dramatic ending to a Technicolor western. He could hear the gravelly voiceover for the trailer: *A brother gives his life to bury his kin.*

But there was no thrumming soundtrack – just the low growl of the wind and the scrape of the metal following him. He thought that it was only the steady gait of the horse that was keeping him sane. You needed that distraction, when the rest was darkness – some small thing to cling to. Dyce had had enough practice in shutting things out: he'd done it when his mom died and his dad went after her. *Think about something else. Count the trees. Sing all the lines of a song. There must be something happy you remember.*

But he kept coming back to the same question. It ran underneath the sorrow and the fear, a curious water table.

What would Vida have traded for her magazine?

Not a gun; not food; not clothes; not medicine. 'It makes no sense, Ears,' Dyce said softly. Vida had held onto that photocomic her entire life, and then all of a sudden she had let it go, as if it was a pair of jeans she had outgrown. 'It would be like Garrett trading you, Ears. Not that anyone wants a stuffed squirrel – no offence – but you know what I mean.' Garrett would've died of starvation rather than trade the squirrel. Same went for Vida and her magazine.

When Dyce finally looked up, snapped out of his dull-eyed contemplation, he was in amongst the ponderosas again, at the top slope of The Mouth. Their smell was so sweet and kind that for a moment it took the edge right off the doubled-up corpse behind him. His horse had walked there on her own, without prompting, the only path she knew.

When the rain began to fall, the drops were as big as marbles. They exploded in the dirt. He had a couple of minutes before it all went to hell.

Dyce climbed off the horse, slow and stiff – he probably wouldn't be able to lift his arms in the morning – and wrapped her reins around a pine. He made his way down into the scorched town again. The fire-warm debris was sizzling lazily as the rain fell, the festive rankness resisting being dampened. Dyce pulled his mask up and tried to ignore the fallen dead around him, the creatures tearing into their bodies without hindrance. The high stink of barbecued flesh made it feel like the day after the world's biggest Labor Day picnic.

He would find the spot where he'd discovered Ears and the remedy book and just keep looking, Dyce reckoned. He and Vida had not planned to leave The Mouth, and neither of them had been able to take their belongings, so whatever Vida had traded her magazine for would still be there.

He lifted the fallen sheets of tin and began sifting through the dampening ash and soot with his fingers. The rain was coming harder now, and it would turn the ground to paste. It was soaking right through Dyce's shirt and he shivered as he scratched around, more desperate as the minutes ticked on.

True night was coming: there would be more critters come to the buffet. The lean ones might even take Julia.

But then, there in the dirt, being washed clean by the rain, he saw something unfamiliar – the flat brass nub of a machine head.

As the rain began to gush in earnest down his collar, Dyce picked up the cog. He fingered the tiny teeth and the perfect hole through which the string had slotted. He kept feeling. He eventually found three more, the remnant metal and wood fragments of an instrument. It looked like a kind of mandolin. Vida had traded her photocomic for the one thing Dyce had always wanted – music.

He took all the treasures. He could carve the neck and body someday, but the machine heads themselves were rare things.

'Going to just squirrel those away,' he told Ears, smiling. 'Get it? Squirrel?' Dyce made a face and straightened up. 'No time for small talk. Isn't that what Garrett would say? You got to move. So *move*.'

Dyce fought his way up the slope of the main street, back to the bay. The rain had begun in earnest. Somewhere up there the Lord God was mopping the floors of his holy house, and the water bucketed down. The town had not been made for times of deluge, and the road itself began to crumble and dissolve as he went, frighteningly fast. Dyce had thought he would have time to get away safely to higher ground – but any longer and it would be like being back underground. He felt icy as he pictured what the mushroom mines would look like as they flooded – and they would, soon enough, as the water table rose to meet the waves coming down, the earth already saturated. All those shallow graves coughing out their wet insides!

As Dyce reached his stamping horse the first corpse rushed by them, as if the dead woman was on her way to somewhere else and had to keep the appointment. Dyce guessed she was, wasn't she? Going to meet her maker, same as he would if they didn't make a move out of the water's stream.

The thunder cracked above them and the star-faced horse reared against the fright. He took hold of the reins and tried to speak gently.

Then Dyce just stood. There was no point in trying to get out of the rain. He was as wet in his clothes as he had been the day he was born.

And so was Garrett.

He knelt beside the tub. Inside it the skinned corpse of his brother seemed to be hugging its knees.

'Bro,' Dyce told him. 'What should we do? This ain't exactly what I had planned.'

Garrett was even less help than Ears McCreedy.

Dyce wiped his face but it was useless. He couldn't think.

'I can't drag you through this. You know that, right? It just ain't going to happen.' The rain poured over them, living and dead, in impersonal sheets – a strange and silent flood, determined to wipe the human plague from the face of the earth.

'So I'm sorry. I really am.' He lifted the spade out of the tub and set it down: he wouldn't be needing it.

'I'm going to have to leave you now. If you love something, set it free, right?' Dyce wanted to stroke his brother's hair, something like that, but he could think of nothing that didn't fill him with nausea.

'You know, I'm always going to be asking, what would Garrett do?' Dyce laughed, and his chest hitched. 'Maybe I ought to make myself a bracelet or something.' He wondered what had happened to the swan pendant that had gone to poor Bethie Callahan, and then checked himself.

'So. Goodbye. I'll see you on the other side, okay?'

He touched the collar of Garrett's old shirt – the only place on his brother's body that wasn't covered in gore – and then he untied the rope from the handle of the tub. Dyce coiled it again and sloshed back to the horse. The water was up to his calves. It was about all he could take before full panic set in. He slotted the rope into the saddle bag and then he climbed up on his horse again, thinking that his coccyx was never going to be the same. He turned the bay. She set her ears back against the solid rain, and they began the ride north, her forelegs cleaving the waters without the tub to drag her backwards. At the fence line, he looked back.

The tub looked as if it had grown claws. It was moving like a palanquin as the water rose above the gravel and dirt and gradually launched it on the ripples. Garrett would be carried down through the new river in the trees, a Viking buried at sea.

60

Without the sun to judge, Dyce felt night come on fast. He was glad to be able to see in the rumbling dark. 'My special super-power,' he told the bay and patted her sodden neck. She seemed eager to run too, even after the torturous exertion of the day.

When they got into Horse Head, it was empty. Here too the rain had washed some of the graves open. A couple of bodies sloshed around in the thin, churning mud. Dyce knew none of them. Still, it was hard to watch as the torrents tugged at the corpses. You never got used to it. They looked to be clawing at their throats for breath, as if they were suffocating.

Higher up, Dyce found the tracks of the other horses, long gone, a deep muddy groove that would harden into a new canyon. He set the bay's feet into the trench and held tight. When they galloped down into the valleys they would lose the tracks under the rising water, and Dyce had to keep his bearings and search the upslope for the trail. *Like connecting the dots*, he thought, *or those construction kits Garrett had when we were little*.

Horse and man rode through the night, Dyce half asleep in the saddle, following the path that Sam was probably leading the others along, his sick eyes their compass in the dark. The horse ran when she could, but she had been tired at the outset. Even the flashes of lightning at their backs could not stop her from slowing to a drunken walk. The changes of pace would wake Dyce each time: he would see the storm catching them and jab his heels into the horse's ribs. Each time she whinnied in protest – *I'm trying! I'm trying!* – and picked up her pace. It seemed to Dyce as if he spent his days apologizing.

There was no rising sun in the east. The dark lifted by degrees. There was still no sign of Vida and the others out front.

The storm seemed to hover at his back. Dyce must have ridden for days, hoping that he'd crest the next rise and see the others. His tired horse gained no ground on them that he could see.

Near noon on the eighth day, Dyce stopped again on a grassy hilltop, which he had done as often as he could afford to let his horse crop. This time she wouldn't, turning her elegant nose away. She drank from a puddle, her eyes cloudy, and Dyce let her stand where she was, frightened and exhausted.

When Dyce got back up into the saddle, the bay wouldn't move. She seemed ready to lie down and die where she stood. Dyce kicked his heels into her sides, and she flinched and twisted her neck to curl her lips back at him, but she wouldn't walk.

Dyce dismounted. He went over to a birch tree and snapped off a thin branch midway up, stripping the leaves with his hand as if he was about to weave a basket.

He got back on the bay and whipped her with the crop. This time she moved on down the slope, wading slow through the water. Dyce's throat was thick with self-loathing.

When she stopped responding to the whips on her flanks, he began whipping her around the ears. That seemed to fill her with a flash of new energy, some final rage. The mare pushed on for an hour before that stopped working. Dyce couldn't bring himself to try anything else.

He got off and sloshed round to stroke her muzzle and to apologize once more, but she hung her head and would not look at him. He had to leave her where she'd stopped, standing fetlock-deep in the water. Dyce thought about dragging her out of harm's way, but she might nip him if he tried to interfere with her again. He hoped that she would have the sense to move out of the rising stream.

He took his meager belongings from the saddle bags, and made sure of Ears. He waded on out of the water and up the steep, slippery incline. It was hard going: little waterfalls were gushing over the ridge above him, and the climb was almost vertical – a ladder leading to some unknown heaven. How had the other horses managed the ascent? He set his feet into the shallow ledges, and prayed as he climbed. Whether it was to God or Garrett he couldn't tell.

At the top he heaved himself over and lay there, panting. It was rocky, lichen had turned to grease in the wet. He looked back down into the valley, and saw that it was an angry mess of foam and water. His horse was gone.

Dyce went around to what he judged to be the north side of the hill. He looked out, following the trail of the horses with his eyes as far as he could.

And there, the specks of gray through the sheets of rain, he saw them, milling about.

And running east to west beside them, all the way to the horizon, was the tall concrete wall that was causing their hesitation.

The border.

It was real.

Dyce had never thought to see it in person and up close. He had thought it would be more impressive, like a space station.

He supposed it was, the sheer size. But even he could see that where the horses stood, there was a gap – a break in the continuous slab. An artery of water ran through the border wall there. The North Platte, Dyce knew. Once a steady tributary, it was now a muscling river of white and brown. Great coils of razor wire spanned the gap like knotted hair, but the water had risen high enough so that it was submerged in the very middle. Now and again the debris rushed past and through, or caught and lodged there, immovable.

Dyce watched as people began, one by one, to lead their horses into the water, pulling them until they swam, and then both rider and horse were swept north toward the submerged wire fangs. He strained to see further, scanning the distant river banks for survivors, but he could see none. Fuck!

He had to get there before they all went through without him, like the crippled boy in the Pied Piper story.

Dyce set off at a jog that turned instantly into sliding down the hill, bruising and cutting himself on the rocks as he went. He tried to stick to the series of poles that still stuck out of the swelling waters, markers for a road once upon a time. Sometimes the water gave way to the relative smooth of the crumbling asphalt, otherwise he waded when the water level rose.

When he reached the spot where he'd seen the group, they had disappeared from the banks.

But they were not gone.

Swirling in the middle of the river were the dark bodies of the horses, writhing, almost all of them. They had been caught by their flailing hooves on the blades of the wire, as they were meant to be, and they twisted and shrieked, sucked under by the flow of water and then released to catch their breath. Dyce had to put his hands over his ears.

There were people caught there with them, caught up in the branches of broken trees, or submerged with panic. From what Dyce could make out, some were dead, though most had made it across. He couldn't look away. His horror was mitigated when he saw an arm in a familiar shirt, waving helplessly.

When she came up for air, Dyce knew that Vida – his mermaid, his Amazon – was trapped. She had stood the best chance of anyone of getting across the river. He tucked Ears into his belt and the brass machine heads into his pocket where they clinked like coins, and then he pushed himself into the chilly brown water. It swept him off his feet.

A ponderosa trunk came barreling past and he shook the water out of his eyes to see more branches racing along the surface like alligators. Dyce ducked under – and found himself in the dark, muffled wet of his nightmares.

He felt the panic squeezing his chest, the needles and pins that always began in his feet and hands and would turn him immobile. He fought the urge to take a breath. On the river bank he had forgotten: it was only Vida he'd considered – Vida dying, Vida sucking in the dark water around her while he watched. But now the horror was here. He was in its watery, suffocating heart.

He felt debris sharp around his legs, tentacles or hands – Garrett's hands! – pulling him deeper underwater. He would die in the cold black depths and be with his brother for ever, bullied into the afterlife.

Dyce thought of Vida, and struggled towards her: the night in The Mouth when they had danced. The way he had twirled her, she with her loving, drunken arms around his neck.

But Garrett's hands were there instead, holding him down in the past, under the tea-stained memorial waters of Tumbelsom

Lake. Dyce tried to pry the tentacle-fingers off his body, thrashing at the water, trying to think of Vida, Vida, here and now, the way that the drops of water had glistened as they slid off her, like scales.

The ghostly fingers gave up at last and floated loose, dissolving in the water to reconstitute themselves with the rest of poor Garrett where he lay fingerless in his Viking tub-ship.

Dyce surged to the surface and gasped for precious air as the current swept him into one of the dead horses caught on the wire. He grappled with it – *VidaVidaVida* – and then caught hold of the strands of its tail.

She was so close!

She floated on her back next to him, her head under the water, her arms limp.

Dyce steadied himself against the flow and kept hold of the horse's tail. He dived down as far as he could, his eyes wide against the water.

The razor wire was wrapped around Vida's boot. He grabbed it like a stinging nettle and it slashed his hand. Dyce let go of the horse to pull with both hands at her leg.

The razor wire tore loose from the bottom of the river and they were free, sent tumbling in slow motion further and further from The Wall.

Then they were caught in an eddy and the water seemed to flatten, forgiving. Vida surfaced, coughing and coughing, her eyes closed so she didn't have to face the burning. Dyce kicked against the current, trying to haul her weight to the bank.

He stumbled in the sudden shallows and dragged her up onto the ground that sucked at their streaming boots. They lay there, whipped by the wind, bleeding and frozen, on Northern soil.

61

They lay dazzled, and Dyce thought: *this is like the night at the locomotive museum. All I want to do now is go to sleep.*

And then he thought: *we have to find shelter.*

If the Weatherman's predictions were right, the worst of the storm was still coming – the mighty fist at the end of the arm that was swinging up across the southern lands, tearing trees up by their roots: the opposite of Creation. Renard himself could not have ordered a better way to clear the countryside of the last few pockets of stubborn resistance.

Dyce lifted his head and looked through the rain to see if he could see any of the other survivors, but there was no one on their side of the river. He scanned the opposite bank and made out a group, maybe half of the hundred or so folk that had started out. He strained to see if Ruth was among them, but they were just shapes muddled together, indistinguishable.

Dyce pulled Vida up beside him and she opened her eyes.

He was real.

He'd come back for her.

She smiled and tried to snuggle into him and fall back under.

He shook her. 'No sleeping, princess. We're not safe yet. We've got to get further north.'

She was still grinning. 'You came.'

'I changed my mind. I went back to The Mouth. Found what you'd traded your magazine for.'

Dyce took the machine heads from his pocket and held them out for her to see – the remnants of the mandolin.

'I was going to give it to you after work that day, but you were so tired.'

He wanted to take her face between his hands but he was too tired.

'Best gift I ever got – if you don't count the stuffed skunk's butt that Garrett got me for my birthday.'

Vida laughed and winced. She looked down. Her boot was gone. It had protected her leg from the worst of the lacerations, but still the skin hung in red and white ribbons.

'That's going to be your first set of scars,' Dyce pointed out.

'You think?'

They took a moment to think back on the last week, with all its hurts and tribulations.

'If we're going, you'll have to help me,' she told Dyce, and held out her arms.

'Payback.'

He lifted her in fits and starts, and they began to hobble up the slope through the last of the shrubs that hung onto the muddy dirt by their root tips. The rain was so hard they could barely see in front of them. They were in the North and they couldn't tell to look at it.

'Strangers in a strange land,' muttered Vida.

Still the filthy water came rising. They walked as best they could, a three-legged race to higher ground.

When they reached a tar road, Vida wanted to get down on her bleeding knees and kiss it. They kept walking, trying to keep to the midline, barely visible. At least they didn't have to wade. Dyce knew when he took his boots off that there would be fungus growing there, like the trench-foot soldiers got a century ago.

And then there came a sound through the static of the rain and the wind: a sound neither of them had heard in years and had not thought ever to hear again – the loud, sharp honk of a driver behind the wheel.

They turned to see a pair of glowing headlights. The Jeep pulled up alongside them, displacing the waves of water with its huge tires as it came. A door was flung open. They peered into the warm, dry cabin, lit by actual electricity, and it took them a full minute to understand what the driver was yelling at them: 'Get in! Get in!'

Dyce lunged forward and dragged Vida with him, up onto the polyester seats in the back. He leant across her limp body and closed the door, tugging hard against the wind. The car smelt of French fries, and his mouth began to water.

'You folks not get the evacuation notice?' asked the man from the driver's seat. He was someone's dad, wearing a red baseball cap with HASH HOUSE HARRIERS stenciled on it.

Dyce and Vida, dripping and dumbstruck, could only look at him as the Jeep ploughed on like a tractor through the flood.

'Good thing I found you, unless it was suicide you were aiming at. Reckon I'm the last one crazy enough to be driving in this. Where you folks from, anyway?'

Dyce wavered, grappling for an answer. The dashboard of lights and gauges was mesmerizing; the wipers were making him dizzy.

'Bozeman, in what used to be Montana.'

The driver slapped his knee. 'Shoot! Terrible time to take a vacation, kids.'

He leant forward and pulled a flask up from the passenger footwell. He handed it back over his shoulder.

'Hot chocolate. The lid's a cup.'

Dyce took the flask. He unscrewed the top and poured some out for Vida, trying not to spill.

She coughed at the sweetness of it on her first sip, and then drank it down in one go.

Dyce tried it next – thick and sweet as childhood. He wanted to cry.

And over the hiss of rain and the sloshing of water around the tires, Dyce heard something else, like the harps of heaven: country music on the radio. He leant forward. He didn't want to miss a note.

Vida watched him for a while in the darkness, but the passing phantom lights of the water-logged homesteads kept catching the corner of her eye. She reached for the cup again and emptied it. Then she took Dyce's hand to hold him in the present, make sure they were in the here and now, together.

The North!

She had always thought that the old rage would swallow her if she ever set foot over the border, but now that they were here, it was a deep weariness that had settled in its place.

The North.

She was ready – for whatever territory emerged once the waters had fled, peeled back like the skin from an apple, the landscape nude and new, stretched out before them.